Praise for

T.M. LOGAN

'Smart, intense and with a humdinger of a mid-point twist. I loved it'
GILLIAN MCALLISTER

'Taut, tense and compelling. Thriller writing at its finest'
SIMON LELIC

'T.M. Logan's best yet. Unsettling and so, so entertaining.
The perfect thriller'
CAZ FREAR

'A tense and gripping thriller'
B.A. PARIS

'Assured, compelling, and hypnotically readable – with a twist at
the end I guarantee you won't see coming'
LEE CHILD

'A compelling, twisty page-turner, and that's the truth'
JAMES SWALLOW

'Outstanding and very well-written . . . so gripping
I genuinely found it hard to put down'
K.L. SLATER

'A terrific page-turner, didn't see that twist!
A thoroughly enjoyable thriller'
MEL SHERRATT

'Another blistering page-turner from psych-thriller god
T.M. Logan'
CHRIS WHITAKER

'Even the cleverest second-guesser is unlikely to arrive at
the truth until it's much, much too late'
THE TIMES

THE
MOTHER

T.M. Logan's thrillers have sold over two million copies in the UK and are published in 22 countries around the world. His novel *The Holiday* was a Richard and Judy Book Club pick and became a *Sunday Times* bestseller in paperback. *Trust Me* and *The Curfew* were also *Sunday Times* bestsellers in hardback. Formerly a national newspaper journalist, he now writes full time and lives in Nottinghamshire with his wife and two children.

Also by T.M. Logan:
Lies
29 Seconds
The Holiday
The Catch
Trust Me
The Curfew

THE
MOTHER
T.M. LOGAN

ZAFFRE

First published in the UK in 2023 by
ZAFFRE
An imprint of Bonnier Books UK
4th Floor, Victoria House, Bloomsbury Square, London, WC1B 4DA
Owned by Bonnier Books
Sveavägen 56, Stockholm, Sweden
Copyright © T.M. Logan, 2023

A CIP catalogue record for this book is
available from the British Library.

Hardback ISBN: 978–1–80418–083–9
Trade paperback: 978–1–80418–084–6

Also available as an ebook and an audiobook

1 3 5 7 9 10 8 6 4 2

Typeset by IDSUK (Data Connection) Ltd
Printed and bound in Great Britain by Clays Ltd, Elcograf S.p.A.

Zaffre is an imprint of Bonnier Books UK
www.bonnierbooks.co.uk

For my mother, Vera, with love

I have longed for death in the darkness and risen alive out of hell.
Amelia Josephine Burr, 'A Song of Living'

Children are the anchors that hold a mother to life.
Sophocles

Friday, 22 September, 2023

I watch from the shadows at the back of the church.

Here on the balcony, where I can observe without being seen.

Beneath a dark woollen cap my hair is cut barber-short, shaved close at the sides and dyed almost black. A heavy jacket broadens my shoulders, collar pulled up against the unseasonable chill that seems to seep from the thick stone walls. The dark-framed glasses have no lenses, only clear plastic. I hold myself still and quiet, all but invisible in the shadows where I have hidden since last night.

I can see the two boys on the front row, handsome in their dark suits and white shirts, soft cheeks and smartly combed hair.

I make my heart into a stone.

I have become good at this: I imagine it not as flesh and blood but instead a solid mass of granite or marble, a fist-sized piece of stone in my chest that nothing can touch. It is the only way I have been able to survive.

I tear my eyes away from the boys and study my surroundings instead. Dark-varnished pews worn smooth with time, the oak as hard and unyielding as a prison bed. Black-bound hymn books and dusty kneeling cushions hanging from hooks. Wooden signs on each of the pillars carry hymn numbers for the last Sunday service.

A plain coffin on a stand in the nave, undecorated with flowers.

There are media here, of course. Not as many as for my husband's funeral – that had been standing room only, from what I'd heard – but still a handful set back from the small scattering of friends and family. Typing on their phones, making notes, recording, taking surreptitious pictures. I don't recognise many of the faces; I'm confident none of them would recognise me. Not now. And especially not here.

The vicar begins a short eulogy, such as it is. His quavering voice echoes against the vaulted stone ceiling of the church, rolling away from the chancel, his words filling the silence.

'We are gathered here to mark the life of Heather Elizabeth Vernon.' He glances down at his notes. 'We seek to remember Heather not for what she did, not for a single act, but for the person she was. We ask the Lord to forgive whatever sins she committed through human weakness and to remember her as a mother, a daughter, a friend and colleague. We offer her sons, Theo and Finn, our deepest condolences and we ask the Lord to give them the strength to honour the best of her memory.'

He seems regretful, almost tentative, as if braced for an angry rebuke from a member of the congregation.

I tune him out.

With small movements of my head, I study the other mourners for anyone I recognise, anyone from the time before. Any of my friends, former neighbours, what little of my family remains. There are a few familiar faces, but most are strangers.

The brief eulogy is already winding its way towards a conclusion. I return my gaze to the two boys in the front row. Surrounded by people and yet seeming – to me – to be totally alone. The younger boy, Finn, sits with his head down, shoulders shaking with sobs, and I feel that old familiar ache in my chest. The stone softening, thawing. The urge to go to him, comfort him, sit next to him and hold his hand in mine. He has just had his thirteenth birthday: he was a late summer baby, born a week after his due date with a full head of dark hair and the bluest eyes I had ever seen. Theo is a head taller, the resemblance to his father already so striking it almost takes my breath away. He sits like a statue, eyes front, unmoving, as if staring at a fixed point above the altar. Determined not to crack, not to cry, right arm resting across his younger brother's shoulders.

I wonder if they ever talk about their mother, already lost to them for so many years before today. If there are pictures anywhere of the four of us together, or if they have all been taken down and put away in a box, sealed with tape and consigned forever to a dusty attic or perhaps burned in the fireplace of the big house in Bath. I wonder if they believe what they have been told; if they believed it from the start or if there has always been a whisper of doubt, a glimmer of hope that I can't have done the thing of which I was accused.

I wonder if they will ever forgive me.

In the shadows at the back of the church, I repeat my silent mantra, my prayer, my promise. Six words that have pulled me back from the brink more times than I can remember.

I am coming back for you.

I am coming back for you.

Even if the ceremony, the church, the coffin, all conspire to tell a different story.

It is not a large church; I am perhaps twenty-five metres from where they sit, but they may as well be on the other side of the world. Even so, the urge is almost overwhelming. I imagine standing up, descending the narrow stone staircase and walking up the aisle, taking off the cap and the glasses and the coat to show them my face. I imagine sweeping them both into my arms and pulling them close. Telling them that they are not alone in the world, not orphans, and that their mother will never, ever, leave them again.

But that is not possible. Not yet.

Not while they're attending my funeral.

PART I

THEN

Friday, 12 July, 2013

1

Theo didn't want to go to sleep.

He was going through a phase of wanting to stay awake as long as he possibly could, of inventing one reason after another for why he couldn't drift off: too hot or too cold, hungry or thirsty or scared or insisting he needed the toilet again. When he finally gave in, he would be fast off for the night – but until then he was determined to play the game.

I had read him a second story, and kissed him for a second time, and turned his light out for a second time, checked his pillow was turned over and his duvet was tucked in and his nightlight was working. It was a game we had been playing since well before his fourth birthday; a game my eldest son seemed to evolve new strategies for every night.

I was trying to draw a line at two stories because I knew the theory well enough from the books: when a child does this it's best not to engage directly, not to talk, not to turn on lights or start the bedtime routine all over again.

But the parenting books were one thing. Reality was another. And if Theo kept shouting the way he was, he would wake his little brother and then both of them would be crying out and awake for the next few hours and then all three of us – me included – would be cranky and grouchy and even more exhausted in the morning. Because no matter how late either of the boys stayed up, it didn't make any difference to morning wake-up time: two-year-old Finn would bounce out of bed before 7 a.m. and he would go to wake his big brother. I was so tired already, but it was that wired, anxious exhaustion that meant I wouldn't be able to actually drop off to sleep without one of my pills. And I just really needed to make a start on dinner for me and Liam, and get another load of washing on and make some headway with that work report I had to get done this weekend.

There was never enough time.

And there would be barely any time tomorrow because I would have the boys from late morning onwards, they both had swimming then Theo had his football and Finn was invited to a birthday party of one of his little friends from nursery, I'd promised I would take them both to the playground and we would need to take the puppy for his walk too. Liam had his constituency surgery from midday and then a media thing at the local food bank and—

Where the hell *was* my husband, anyway?

I checked my watch again. Ten to eight. I had never wanted to be one of those wives who harried their husbands and tracked their every move. But Liam had promised to be back an hour ago. Then again, he'd been working late a lot recently. Almost constantly. I got that, I understood it was a part of the job, of what he'd signed up for. But all the time? A Friday night?

My phone was charging on the kitchen island. I unlocked it and checked for any new messages from Liam. There were some on a few of the email groups I was a member of – the babysitting circle that had grown out of my NCT group, my Monday choir, and a neighbourhood group made up of a few of the local streets in our corner of Bath – but I would read them later. There was nothing new from Liam, not since this afternoon. I read his last messages again, sent at 2.59 p.m.

Probably going to be late again, sorry. Committee overrunning and then got drinks thing on the terrace pavilion at 4, back 7ish?

I had replied as I hurried from one meeting to the next earlier that afternoon.

OK see you later.

A single thumbs-up emoji from my husband in response.

He'd sent nothing since then. There was no kiss at the end of his message either. When had he stopped doing that? When had I stopped doing it, come to think of it? Months ago? Years? When we were first married we'd done it all the time. Now it just seemed to be one of those things that had fallen by the wayside in the daily battle to keep a handle on family life with small children. To keep all the plates spinning and catch any that dropped before they hit the floor.

I put the phone down and took a bottle of wine from the kitchen counter. I'd had a couple of glasses with a (very) late dinner last night but it was still two-thirds full. I uncorked it and poured a generous glass, sipping it as I leaned against the counter, savouring the dark heavy fruit of the French red and the tiny release of tension I felt with the first mouthful. I stood very still in the kitchen, listening for any sound from upstairs.

Please go to sleep, lovely boy. Please go to sleep. Please don't wake your brother up. Just this once, just for me. Just tonight.

A silence, blissful silence, the only sound the soft ticking of the clock on the kitchen wall. The uplighters were on low, the black granite island finally cleared of the boys' toys and colouring books and dirty dishes from their tea, my laptop open in their place. The kitchen was the thing that had sold me on the house – that and the school catchment area, of course – and I still liked the space, the feel of it, clean lines and Italian marble.

The wall-mounted TV was muted into silence, switched over to a rolling news channel now the boys were finally in bed. I watched the images on the screen for a moment, sipping my wine, bathing in this first moment of peace in the day. The story was a round-up on the day's events in Brussels, David Cameron grinning and shaking hands with various other suited EU leaders. I stood like that for a quiet moment, basking in the silence as the prime minister was replaced by a shot of Andy Murray with his first Wimbledon trophy, surrounded by a crowd of fans. I turned away from the TV and began to gather ingredients from the fridge for carbonara.

Our puppy, Jet, snuffled contentedly in his sleep, curled up in his basket next to the radiator. A smart sixth-month-old collie presented to us by Liam a few months ago after much pleading from the boys: a gift for our sons and a little extra peace of mind for him, he'd said, now he had a job in the public eye and spent so much time away from home. *An extra pair of eyes to look after my family*, he'd said – Jet was already fiercely protective of the boys and amazingly tolerant of their enthusiastic affection. I loved the black-and-white puppy too but Liam's frequent absences meant Jet had become another responsibility for me. His paws twitched as he slept, in pursuit of some dreamed-of flock.

The cry came again from upstairs.

Two syllables, always the same high note, always the same Pavlovian reaction that made my head turn towards the sound like a terrier catching a scent.

'Mummy?'

I sighed, setting the heavy crystal wine glass down and walking slowly out to the entrance hall, past twin ranks of the boys' little shoes lined up beneath the coat hooks by the front door. My legs felt heavy, almost leaden, as I climbed the stairs again. I pushed the door of my older son's room open, the frame *shushing* against the thick, soft carpet. Theo was sitting up in bed, duvet bunched around his waist, his outline reflected in the dim glow of a night-light on the floor.

'Can't sleep,' he said in a small, sad voice. 'Can I have an Auntie Amy story?'

'She's gone back to her house, Theo. She always goes home before your bedtime, you know that.'

We had established a routine where my sister-in-law would do an early pickup from nursery on Mondays and Fridays, bringing the boys home and making their tea, holding the fort until I got in from work. It was one part of a complicated patchwork of child-care that made up the working week. Amy would stay longer if she was asked – she took great pride in her status of favourite auntie – but I didn't want to ask too much of her.

'I drew you a picture at nursery, Mummy.' From under his pillow he produced a folded sheet of paper, a large crayon butterfly carefully coloured in yellow and purple. 'Do you like it?'

'It's lovely, Theo.' I smiled, took the paper from him and put it on his little bedside table. 'Now it's time to go to sleep.'

'I want to see Jet.'

'Jet's asleep, Theo. Just like you should be asleep.'

'Can't sleep. Want a Daddy story.'

I sighed. This was turning into one of the endless circular conversations in which my son was becoming an expert.

'Daddy's at work, Theo.'

'FaceTime?' he whispered hopefully.

'He'll be home soon and he'll come up to see you then. But he'll only come up to see you if you're really quiet, as quiet as a mouse, and you try really hard to get to sleep now. OK?' I kissed him on the forehead and settled him back against his pillow, pulling the duvet up around his shoulders. 'Now close your eyes.'

Out on the landing, I pulled his door almost closed and dimmed the light. I paused for a moment outside the next bedroom, which bore a wooden doorplate of a steam train, my younger son's name spelled out in colourful letters beneath it. I listened for any sound, any hint that Finn had been woken by his brother's voice.

Back in the kitchen, I began preparing dinner, grating parmesan and boiling a pan of water, one ear tuned to the sound of Theo's voice in case he still refused to go to sleep.

I checked my phone again. Nothing from Liam. I called him but his phone rang out, before going to voicemail.

There had been a certain novelty to his new job at first, an excitement about the boys seeing their dad on TV and in the news, the snippets of Westminster gossip that he would bring home. But it hadn't been long before the buzz had worn off. In theory we shared everything – childcare, housework, bills, responsibilities – and in theory my career was just as important as his. But in practice, I was the one who worked a couple of miles from the nursery, I was the one who did most of the drop-offs and pickups, the one who had to drop everything when something happened. There were so many people who wanted a piece of my husband now, and less and less of him available to me and the boys. Which meant I had to pick up all the slack at home.

I reached for the bottle of red wine and topped up my glass.

2

I didn't want to have an argument with Liam. I had no energy for an argument with him and yet more and more on days like this, on evenings like this, sliding into an argument was all too *easy* and I found our conversations devolving into low-level snipping and sniping about who was the most tired, who'd had the least sleep, who had done the most with the boys and the most around the house. The little time we spent together – just the two of us – often wasted in pointless friction that I would almost always regret afterwards. I didn't even know how those little skirmishes started most of the time, but it was where we seemed to end up more and more, these last few months.

I told myself this as I finally heard his key in the lock. I was slumped on the sofa, laptop balanced on my thighs, Liam's spaghetti carbonara congealing in the pan. A comedy panel show was on the TV.

I glanced up at the clock on the mantelpiece as I heard the metallic *snick* of the front door opening: 9.31 p.m.

Liam appeared in the lounge, dumping his briefcase on the floor and his suit jacket over the back of a chair. His white shirt was creased, his tie at half-mast and five o'clock shadow darkening his strong jaw. But, even tired, he still retained a rumpled charm, the kind of easy good looks that had made him a tabloid favourite.

'Hey,' he said. 'Sorry I'm so late. *God*, what a day. Committee was a nightmare and I didn't get to the reception until gone six, then I was stuck with old Strachan and his lot. That bloke can talk for England. I couldn't get away.'

He leaned down to give me a peck on the cheek, warm stubble rough against my skin. An acidic tang of cheap white wine on his breath. Something else too . . . something sweet?

'Who else was there?' I said.

He waved a hand dismissively.

'Oh, you know, the usual crowd and some extras that Strachan was trying to impress. He wanted me to meet people from some American delegation and it turned into a bit of a marathon session, they were his guests at the reception and they'd brought in all the big guns, the vice-president from their European division and—'

His phone rang somewhere in his jacket, the generic ringtone he used for his work mobile. He retrieved it from his pocket, looked at it briefly and stabbed the screen to reject the call.

I closed my laptop and set it down on the floor beside me. 'Your dinner's in the kitchen. Carbonara. I thought we could watch a film.'

His face pinched with awkwardness. 'Already eaten. Sorry.'

'Oh.' I felt myself bristling, biting back a response that was on the tip of my tongue. 'Right.'

'Sorry, love, there was a big sit-down buffet and I couldn't really . . .' He tailed off, seeing my expression. 'Are the boys all right? How have they been today?'

'Fine,' I said. 'They both had a good day and your sister made them pancakes for tea, helped with bath-time and read Finn his story.'

He must have sensed the implication in my tone – *your sister who sees more of your sons than you do, who is doing more day-to-day than you are* – something passing across his face that I couldn't place. Just for a moment; then it was gone.

'How is my little sister?' He pulled his dark patterned tie off and laid it on top of his jacket. 'She OK?'

'She was brilliant, as always. I think the boys want her to move in.'

'I'm sure they do.' He turned to leave the room. 'I'll just give them a quick kiss goodnight.'

'Liam?'

He turned back. 'Yup?'

'Do you have to? You might wake Theo again and it was an absolute nightmare getting him down tonight. He had me up and down those stairs like a yo-yo.'

'Oh.' He gave a disappointed nod. 'OK.'

I indicated my half-empty wine glass. 'There's a bottle open in the kitchen.'

'Think I'll call it quits for tonight.' He rubbed his hands over his face. 'The parly plonk is going to put me off wine for life, I reckon.'

I took a closer look at him. 'You look shattered, Liam. Do you want me to get up with the boys tomorrow, so you can have a lie-in?'

'No it's fine, I'll get up.' He gave me an awkward smile. 'Barely seen them all week.'

'So: a film.' I patted the sofa next to me, summoning a smile. 'Your turn to choose. Whatever you want, as long as it doesn't have Jason Statham in it.'

His smile froze. 'I've actually ... just got a few things to go through before tomorrow.'

I felt my own smile fading. The familiar prickle of annoyance taking its place, the frustration that his work was so all-consuming that we couldn't even find an hour to spend together on a Friday night. That this third person in our marriage – his job – seemed to be more important than everything else.

'Right,' I said, picking up my wine glass again and turning back to the TV.

'Sorry, love.' He put his palms together in a gesture of contrition. 'It's just some briefings I have to read before tomorrow so I'm up to speed.'

I ignored him. I had tried, and failed. That was all there was to it. I wasn't going to get into a long discussion with him about it on Friday night.

He retreated into the study off the lounge.

I spent an irritated ten minutes flicking angrily through all the channels trying to find something to watch. In the end I switched off the TV in disgust and threw the remote down on the sofa.

Liam was on the phone, his voice inaudible through the study door.

It wasn't his fault, I knew. He was just trying to please everyone, that was all. He didn't know how to say no.

I stood up stiffly and took his suit jacket off the back of the chair, shaking out the creases and straightening it to hang it up in the hall. As I looped the shoulders onto a plastic hanger, the smell rose up to me again. I held the navy jacket a little closer to my face. *There.* Did he have a new aftershave? It wasn't familiar. I threw a quick glance towards the lounge, the closed door to the study, thought about checking the pockets. I was about to dip a hand towards the left inside pocket when I stopped myself. *No.* I was not that kind of wife. And he was not that kind of husband. He *had* been late coming home a lot recently, and we hadn't spent a lot of time together, and he did always seem to be preoccupied with one of his phones. But that came with his job.

He was just busy, that was all.

I hung the jacket on a hanger in between the boys' red and yellow anoraks and went back into the kitchen to finish the washing-up.

It wasn't *him* I was angry at, it was his work. I knew that, on some level. And in any case, my frustration had already burned itself low, a fifteen minute time-out for the irritation to fade. Tomorrow night we would get the boys to bed early and I would have some proper time with Liam. Sunday was a free day and we would spend it together, the four of us, maybe take a picnic to Royal Victoria Park and play some football. Liam and Finn versus me and Theo, those were our normal teams – biggest and smallest against the two in the middle.

I had my hands deep into the warm sudsy water in the sink as a tinny song started blaring behind me in the hallway. The opening chords of '*Cigarettes & Alcohol*', on full volume by the sound of it.

I grabbed a towel and hurried back into the hall. The ringing might wake the boys up. I went to his jacket, slipped a hand into the breast pocket and found his iPhone – his personal mobile – blaring his favourite Oasis song. I pulled it out and saw the display on the screen, a familiar name. Liam tried to be strict with his personal and work phones, to keep some separation between working life and family life, but it wasn't always possible.

I knew the caller and was about to answer when the ringtone abruptly stopped.

I sighed, returning it to Liam's jacket and listening for any sound from the boys' bedrooms, any indication that the noise had woken them up.

All was quiet. I returned to the kitchen, to the mountain of washing-up, my mind wandering to the divisional report I had to finish for Monday and whether it was too late to do some work on it now. I would be busy with the boys most of tomorrow, Sunday would be better but I never liked to leave things until the last—

Liam's mobile started ringing again.

Bloody thing.

I retraced my steps, swiping at my hands with the towel and wrestling the iPhone from his jacket pocket for a second time. Same caller. Clearly she was keen to get hold of Liam at almost ten o'clock on a Friday evening. I was about to answer the call when it stopped again, the screen going dark once more.

Whatever it was, apparently it couldn't wait. I took the phone through the lounge and into the snug that Liam had converted into a home office. The door was pulled to but not quite shut; I could hear my husband's voice on the other side, his words soft and indistinct.

The iPhone began to ring for a third time, vibrating against the palm of my hand.

I pushed the door to Liam's study. He was half turned away from me, sitting forward in the desk chair, elbows on his knees, head down. He had his work phone, a Samsung, pressed to his ear, his voice low and conspiratorial. Fragments of the conversation reached me as the door swung silently open – *no I have to do it and you know why, I can't carry on like this, I need to be honest about it and I need to tell her* – before he stopped abruptly at the sight of me standing in the doorway.

'Listen,' he said hurriedly. 'I've got to go.'

He ended the call, a woman's voice still talking on the other end as he cut her off.

3

'Hey,' he said, sitting back in the black leather swivel chair. His face was flushed. 'Sorry. Work stuff. Are the boys OK?'

'They're sleeping. Who was that on the phone?'

'Christine.' His constituency office manager felt like a constant presence in our lives now, almost another member of the family. 'Just sorting out a few bits for the media thing tomorrow lunchtime.'

I felt a prickle of alarm at the back of my neck. I could put up with a lot – with all the running around and juggling the childcare and the housework and my own job, not having a minute to myself never mind any time with my husband – but I couldn't put up with this. If *this* was what I feared it might be.

'Really?'

'A few last-minute wrinkles.' He gave me a rueful smile, all dimples and dark rising eyebrows. The smile he had given me the very first time we met; the smile I had fallen for. 'Sorry.'

He seemed to be apologising to me a lot this evening. Virtually every time he opened his mouth.

'You were just talking to Christine?' I said. 'As in Christine Lai?'

A split second of hesitation. 'Yeah, you know that new arts centre on Station Street, I'm doing the official opening—'

'Because she was just calling on your other phone.' I held up the iPhone, heat gathering in my throat. 'Three times in the last three minutes.'

Liam's smile faded. He raised a hand to his chin, rubbed the stubble along his jawline. He couldn't meet my gaze. *Busted.* He had the good grace, at least, to look a little bit sheepish. Finally, he gestured vaguely at the phone in my hand.

'Maybe it was her assistant calling through using her—'

'Really? You just flat-out lied to me and that's the best you can do? *Really?*'

His eyes flicked up to mine for a second before dropping again. 'Yeah.'

'Give me *some* credit, Liam.' The angry heat was spreading into my chest, up my neck, I could feel it flaring into my cheeks, the tingle of a fight-or-flight response that had come out of nowhere. I had wanted to give him the benefit of the doubt, had wanted to be calm, but the frustration was rising too fast, the hurt and confusion that he had lied so easily, so fluently, the anger that he was trying to take me for a fool, and the phone – the *bloody phone* – was ringing in my hand again. 'Here's an idea – how about we ask Christine? See if *she* knows?'

I stabbed a finger at the screen to answer it.

'Christine? Hi. Yes, he's here.' I listened for a moment. 'No, no, you were just speaking to him, apparently? Sounds like he should give you a pay rise if he's got you working this hard on a Friday night, calling him on both phones at once.'

Without hanging up, I tossed the phone across the desk towards him.

'So who was it? Who was that on your other phone?' I raised my fingers in air quotes around his words. 'Why is it that you *can't carry on like this?*'

'Keep your voice down, you'll wake the boys if you—'

'Don't you dare talk to me about the boys!' I jabbed an angry finger at him. 'You're never here to spend any time with them! And when you are, you're skulking about in here talking to random women and lying about it to my face! As if I don't see enough crap on social media already about your bloody Westminster groupies!'

Liam picked up the iPhone.

'Hi, Christine,' he said quietly. 'Can I call you back in a few minutes?'

I stayed where I was, the heavy oak desk a barrier between us. I tried to stem the flow of my anger, my upset, but it was as if someone had opened a floodgate and it was all pouring out of me, all the frustrations of the week. Our life, our marriage, our family, were built on the idea that we were a team, we were both in it together, pulling in the same direction. If there *was* no team, if it was just me doing all the heavy lifting while he played by his own rules, then the whole idea fell apart.

I felt as if I'd been knocked to the ground, winded, my legs kicked from under me.

'So come on, tell me,' I said. 'Why are you lying to me?'

Liam laid the mobile face down on top of a pile of paperwork.

'It's complicated. It's not like . . . what you're thinking.'

'You didn't answer my question.'

'I'm trying.'

'So what is it then?'

He blew out a heavy breath, shoulders slumped, before raising his eyes to mine.

'A situation that's developed,' he said finally. 'A difficult situation. Sensitive.'

'So sensitive you can't even tell your own wife?'

'No, it's not that. I . . . I don't want to put it on you. It's for me to deal with, to sort out.' He gestured towards me, palms up. 'Look, you have more than enough on your plate already, without me going on about my job all the time, the ins and outs of every single thing that comes across my desk.'

I thought about this for a moment, weighing his words, the way he delivered them in his interview voice – as if he was giving a sound bite for local TV.

'You still didn't answer my question.'

'It's the truth. I thought you'd be pissed off that I was taking calls this late and I'm still figuring out how to keep all of that *stuff* – especially the bad stuff – separate from you and the boys. I've got to box it off from our home life, compartmentalise it, but it doesn't always work.'

'What's it about?'

'You know I can't tell you that.'

I thought again of the sharp-sweet smell that clung to his jacket. Expensive. Unsubtle. Unfamiliar. The nagging doubt that I had suppressed and silenced for the last few weeks, but was now back with a vengeance.

'Or is it that new intern in your office, the one barely out of bloody university?' I had met her just once, at a Chamber of Commerce event earlier in the year. A glossy blonde with flawless skin and a double-barrelled surname. 'What's her name? Francesca? Is she why you're constantly late?'

Liam shook his head again.

'Fran wasn't there tonight.'

'Why are you being so secretive about this? You don't trust me?'

'Look, can we talk about something else? I'm sorry, OK? I didn't want to create a bad atmosphere, I don't want to bring my problems into our house.'

'Not much chance of that. You're never at home.'

'I know, I'm sorry. It will get better, I promise.'

'What's going on, Liam?' I crossed my arms tightly over my chest. 'I mean, you're hardly ever here anymore. Even when you are, you're so preoccupied, so wrapped up with whatever you've got going on, it's like living with a stranger.'

He sat back in the swivel chair, letting his eyes close for a moment, before dragging them open again to fix on me. Seeming to come to a decision.

'So . . . a colleague confided in me.' He paused, as if searching for the right words. 'About potential breaches of the MPs' code of conduct, law-breaking at Westminster – really serious stuff. She was extremely worried and upset about it all, didn't know what to do for the best. I was . . . comforting her.'

He still sounded as if he was making it up off the top of his head.

'*Comforting* her?'

'Yes.'

'In the middle of a reception in the terrace pavilion, surrounded by dozens of other MPs?'

He swallowed, Adam's apple bobbing. 'There was . . . a sideroom.'

I looked at my husband then, my tall, good-looking husband, with his strong jaw and his five o'clock shadow, his deep brown eyes and his easy charm and his vote-winning smile, and I was struck by an unassailable certainty: that he still wasn't telling me the whole truth.

'Do you think I'm an idiot?' I said finally.

'Heather—'

'You know what?' I held a hand up. 'Don't answer that.'

I slammed the door on my way out.

4

The pain was there first, before anything else. Pain that seemed to be at the centre of everything, pushing all else to the edges, a heavy bass throb that thrummed against the inside of my skull. A sour, metallic taste in my mouth. Maybe it would ease if I lay still, I thought. Maybe I could slide back into sleep, back into oblivion, if I could just—

'Mummy?' A small, familiar voice. Very close.

I opened one eye, just a crack. The light from the window was dazzlingly, eye-blisteringly bright where it streamed through a gap in the curtains. Slowly, two small figures came into focus next to my bed, silhouetted by the early morning sunlight: Theo and Finn in their dinosaur pyjamas. Theo's darkening hair sticking up in every direction; his brother clutching onto his muslin cloth, thumb planted firmly in his mouth. They were holding hands the way they had started to do, Theo leading his little brother around the house as if they were playing one of their games of *Peppa Pig* or Soldiers or Follow the Leader.

'Hmmm?' Words were out of my reach, too much, too hard, with my head throbbing like this.

Theo gave my shoulder a gentle poke with one small, warm finger. 'Mummy, are you awake?'

'Hmm.'

'Can we watch CBeebies?'

It was no good. I tried to speak but my lips were gummed together. I rolled onto my back, felt with my left arm on Liam's side of the bed. Patting the duvet that was flat and unslept in. Unwelcome memories returned of our argument last night. With an effort I opened my mouth and hunted for the words, dragging each one up from the deep, every syllable feeling like a fresh hammer blow to my skull.

'Daddy can make you breakfast, Theo.' I tried to summon the one crucial piece of information I needed more than any other at this moment: was it a weekday today or not? Did I need to get them ready and dressed, fed and teeth cleaned, get myself ready and dressed, out of the door in time? *No.* It was a . . . Saturday. I was pretty sure. Yes. I was sure. *Thank God for small mercies.* 'It's a Daddy breakfast day today.'

I closed my eyes again, familiar guilt mixing in with a wash of relief. I loved my boys more than anything else on earth but sometimes I could have been persuaded to sell my soul for just twenty more minutes of oblivious, uninterrupted sleep.

I waited for the sound of their feet padding away into the hall, but it didn't come.

'Mummy?' My son's small voice came again.

'Daddy can . . . put the telly on for you.' My throat was scratchy and raw. 'He's on the big sofa. Then he'll make you breakfast.'

A pause.

'He's sleeping,' Theo persisted.

With an effort, I opened my eyes again. The digital display on my alarm clock read 7.02 a.m.

I tried to remember what time I'd turned in last night. I'd had an early one . . . or was that the previous night? My brain felt deep-frozen, a solid block of ice that would not thaw out. I shifted position. My neck was stiff, cricked in that way it sometimes got when I was so tired I fell asleep and didn't move on the pillow all night; when I was so wiped out with exhaustion that I didn't even turn over in my sleep. And there was a tackiness on the sheets too, a grubby residue of something that had dried. Must have nodded off with a drink in my hand; but it was change day anyway for the bedsheets, ours and the boys.

I sat up with a groan and swung my legs out of bed, waiting for the swish of nausea to pass. This was not like a normal hangover. This was something different; something else. Something worse. Through my fog-addled brain I squinted at the bedside table, where an empty whisky tumbler sat next to my Zopiclone pills, the blue-and-white box open and one of the blister packs half-empty. I *never* left them there normally, always kept them on the top shelf of my wardrobe where my sons couldn't reach. Why were my pills there? A wine glass lay on its side on the floor, a dark stain soaked into the thick, honey-coloured carpet by my feet. *Oh, God.* That was never going to come out.

Even though I knew my husband's side of the bed was empty, I glanced over at it anyway, the sheets still tucked in on the far side, the pillow untouched. Fragments of memory from last night, of Liam coming home late, of our argument. A pinch of regret: it wasn't the first time he had slept downstairs, these last few months.

Gingerly, I got to my feet with a groan and gave each of the boys a groggy kiss on the crown of his head. Their hair still had that sleepy-sweet shampoo smell from last night's bath. The air in the bedroom was cool, the pipes only just starting to clank and groan as the central heating clicked on. I pulled on my dressing gown and went out onto the landing, the boys trotting dutifully after me, still hand in hand. Every step felt as if I was wading through water, pushing against the current, and I braced myself with both hands on the varnished wooden banister. I felt like an invalid who had just learned to walk again.

'Liam?' I winced at the sound of my own voice, the single word sending a fresh thud of pain straight through my forehead like a steel bolt. There was no answer from downstairs. I called again. But there was no response at all except for a soft clicking and tapping from somewhere beneath me.

I started slowly down the stairs, gripping the banister tightly in my left hand, wary in case the swoop of dizziness returned. I was three steps down before I realised something was not quite right.

'Theo, when you went down to see Daddy, did you open the stairgate?' I indicated the white metal barrier, standing open at the top of the stairs. 'Remember, you need to be careful with your brother.'

My eldest son shook his head. 'Already *was* open.'

I frowned and continued down the stairs. Talking was still too painful and I didn't have the energy to pursue it with him. The boys continued to hold hands as they came down the stairs behind me, little Finn sliding down each step on his bottom as his brother led the way.

The parquet flooring in the hallway was smooth against my feet, watery rays of early morning sun filtering through the blue-tinted glass of our front door. The door of the lounge was ajar. I pushed it open further, peering through the gap. The room was still dark and heavy with shadows, curtains drawn as if to hold back the day.

'Liam?' I rotated my head, trying to ease some movement back into my stiff neck. 'The boys are up.'

I pushed the door open wider and peered around. Liam was beneath a mounded duvet on the long sofa, his hair dark against a pale cushion being used as a pillow, the rounded heft of his shoulder just visible in a white T-shirt.

The clicking and tapping from behind the kitchen door had become more urgent.

Theo's excited voice came from behind me. 'Shall I let Jet out, Mummy?'

I couldn't face the puppy's exuberance; not yet.

'Just give me a minute, Theo,' I said. 'Let's get Daddy up first.'

Slowly, my eyes began to adjust to the darkness of the lounge. Shadows coalesced into solid shapes: the armchair, bookcase, low table, the long sofa facing the TV. I felt another bloom of regret at our argument, the way it had blown up so fast – I'd had too much wine, I was so tired, I must have overreacted. What had the argument even been about? That phone call? There was probably a reasonable explanation for it. A misunderstanding. He had been working too much, pushing himself too hard.

I would ask him about it later, when my head had stopped pounding.

'Liam?' I said softly. 'I'm putting the kettle on; do you want one?'

I moved further into the room, my feet sinking into the soft rug in front of the fireplace. The floor next to the sofa was a mess of Liam's papers, files, notes and folders from his briefcase, gaping empty like an open jaw. I dredged up a memory of what he was doing this morning.

'You've got your constituency surgery at nine, love.' I bent down to move a few of the papers out of the way. 'I can do you some toast if you want to jump in the shower.'

My husband seemed determined to ignore me. He was turned away from me, away from the ghost of daylight trying to force its way through the curtains. I leaned over him and touched his broad shoulder, gave him a gentle shake. He had rowed for the university as a student and still had a rower's physique, lean and powerful. I had always loved his shoulders, the way I could rest against them, drowse into sleep when we sat together on the sofa on a Sunday evening.

My husband didn't respond.

I gave him a little pat, letting my fingers rest on the curve of his shoulder for a moment. There was something strange about the feel of the muscle beneath his T-shirt, something not quite right.

'Liam?' My voice sounded rough and far away to my own ears.

I eased the duvet down, tugging it gently away from his arm. He offered no sound, no resistance, no movement at all. I touched him gently on his forearm, his skin cool to the touch.

A low, liquid fear loosened my knees and sent a fresh wave of dizzy nausea rising higher.

I perched on the edge of the sofa and was easing the duvet down further as a sharp, coppery smell caught at the back of my throat.

I stopped, a hand going to my mouth to stifle a scream.

Liam's white T-shirt was stained a deep crimson, the sheet, the sofa, the cushions darkly sticky and saturated beneath him.

There was a single jagged tear in the centre of his T-shirt, over the ribcage, congealed gore almost black around the wound.

Blood. So much blood.

PART II

TEN YEARS LATER

NOW

Friday, 1 September, 2023

5

The day is impossibly bright.

After the institutional stink of the jail – of dirt and disinfectant, of drains and overcooked food and the body odour of too many women living too close together – the outside air is so fresh it is almost intoxicating. I stand for a moment, filling my lungs, shielding my eyes against the glare of the day. On my left is a familiar five-metre mesh fence topped with coils of razor wire, blades glinting in the sunshine. But on my right, for the first time in more than three thousand days, there is nothing between me and open green fields rising gently to a low ridge lined with tall oaks. Away in the distance is the incongruous sight of a Victorian country house, chimneys and grey walls just visible behind a screen of trees.

Somewhere nearby, a bird is singing.

A guard had ushered me out through the entryway without saying a word. Freedom, in the end, achieved with a single step over an invisible threshold, out onto the smooth tarmac of the prison access road. Clutching a clear plastic bag with my belongings: the clothes I had worn when I came here from court, and the meagre collection of toiletries and other small items I didn't want to leave behind. And then for the first time since I'd arrived, the heavy green steel gate was at my back. The mesh fence was at my back. The signs

surrounding the door were at my back: WELCOME TO HMP EAST-
WOOD PARK. THESE PREMISES ARE UNDER CCTV SURVEILLANCE. NO
UNAUTHORISED PERSONS ALLOWED BEYOND THIS POINT.

I take one last look at the gate behind me. I am never coming back.

My watch is in the clear plastic bag of my belongings but the
battery has long since died, the hands frozen, pointing at the time
on some long-ago day. I snap it onto my wrist anyway. According
to the clock in the prisoner reception block it is just after 8.30 in the
morning. Today is the first day of September: a date that had been
inching towards me with ever-decreasing speed for longer than I
can remember. I've dreamed of this day for so long, but now it's
here I am momentarily frozen just like my watch – paralysed by the
knowledge of what lies ahead.

As today's only *time expired inmate* – according to the official
prison terminology – I had been unlocked fifteen minutes earlier
than everyone else to get me down to the reception centre. Once
there, I was searched, patted down and had my licence conditions
read to me by a senior officer. Then I had to sign a four-page release
document that detailed what I had been sentenced for, how long
I would be on probation, what kind of breaches could get me sent
right back here to serve out the rest of my sentence and a dozen
other things. My belongings were checked against the property
card that had been filled in when I arrived. Then it was into a holding cell where I was given a travel warrant for the bus, a £76 prison
discharge grant and a printed-out sheet detailing my appointments
to arrange benefits and meet with my probation officer.

The escorting officer had walked me wordlessly through the
courtyard and up to the front gate, unlocked it and heaved it open
with a squeal of rusting hinges.

That was it.

It was over.

And so barely an hour after waking up in my window-barred,
triple-locked cell – D-26 on B-wing – I find myself standing outside in
the open air. Back in the real world. Free. And completely alone.

The narrow access road into HMP Eastwood Park is a dead-end, no through traffic, just a car park for staff and a smaller area for visitors here by the entrance. There is no one to meet me today, no car to pick me up, but that is not a surprise. I hoist the plastic bag of clothes over my shoulder and begin walking in the way that has become second nature in this place: aware of everything while making eye contact with no one. The road takes me past the squat staff training centre and the olive-drab Portakabin that doubles as the family visitors' centre, past the rows of little houses, past the little stone church at the end of Sundayshill Lane and out onto the main road.

It is a four-mile walk to Thornbury, the nearest town of any size.

At one point the route takes me near the M5 and I take a short detour to walk up and out onto a footbridge over the motorway, mesmerised by the rush of traffic flashing south and north. The sensory overload of so many cars, so much movement and speed and freedom, has me gripping the railing tight with white-knuckled hands. So many lives, busy with purpose and direction, working and living, travelling, raising families and building something real for themselves.

I feel unmoored from everything, untethered, as if I might float away up into the diesel-heavy clouds. My own life was a blank. My husband was gone, my mother too, my sons strangers to me. My house, my job, my career, my reputation, all gone. All of it burned to the finest ash and blown away in the wind.

Life as I knew it was gone forever.

Another journey was about to begin.

But first, there was somewhere I had to go.

6

I find an Oxfam charity shop in Thornbury and hand over the bag of clothes. It was the smart work outfit I wore in court nine years ago and doesn't fit me anymore. Even if it did, I no longer have any use for it – I'd quite happily put a match to the grey material if I didn't think someone else could get some wear out of it. All I have left are the faded joggers and sweatshirt from prison, the slender wristwatch that doesn't work and a few toiletries stuffed into the pockets of my tattered denim jacket. That, and the scars on my skin that will be a permanent reminder of HMP Eastwood Park.

The shop assistant asks me something about gift aid, but I just shake my head and pay in cash for a few items I've found on the shelf – large sunglasses, a small backpack and a grey bucket hat that I hope gives me the look of a rambler out for a country walk. I buy water and a sandwich from a garage across the road and wait an hour for a bus to Tytherington, sitting on the back row of seats so that I can see everyone who gets on and off, and no one can come up behind me. It's another hour's wait in a tiny pebble-dashed bus shelter for a single decker to take me further into the Gloucester-shire countryside, past endless hedgerows and farms and neat fields thick with crops, everywhere green and lush and bursting with life.

There had been no colours in my life for so long, nothing beyond filthy grey and muddy, washed-out blue that I had forgotten what it was to be outside, *really* outside, without walls, without doors and barred windows and queues and people everywhere I turned, with all this variety of light and space. I get off in Kingswood next to the village hall, scanning my surroundings as the bus rumbles off empty down a well-kept street.

For the last mile of my journey there's no bus, no public transport, and I can't risk hitching a lift if there's even the slightest chance of being recognised by one of the locals. I will walk instead, tracing a familiar route down country lanes thick with hedges on both sides. There is little traffic, just the occasional tractor or four-by-four, and none of the drivers pay me any attention as I tramp along the grass verge, my heart lifting a little with every step as I imagine the distance between us closing, yard by yard.

I know it will be a long road back.

But I need to *see* them.

Not in a creased photo stuck to a cell wall, or a blurry image in my head after lights out. To see them *properly*, with my own eyes.

To stand under the same patch of sky as them, to breathe the same air and be warmed by the same sun.

After twenty minutes of walking, sweat gathering at the back of my neck, the roof of the big country house looms into view through a screen of horse chestnut trees. The familiar mortared stone perimeter wall encircling the grounds. Dormers had been built at the turn of the century by some Victorian banker as a wedding present for his daughter. Liam's grandfather had bought it decades later and it had been in the family ever since, a 15,000 square foot weekend bolthole set in its own twelve acres. Named for the rows of four large dormer windows that lined the roof on each side and flooded the second-floor bedrooms with light, it had enough modern security measures to make it hard to approach undetected from the front.

I slow my pace. It looks as if extra security has been added in the decade since my last visit. The front gate is taller and new cameras cover it from several angles. It made sense, I suppose. When tragedy strikes at the heart of your family, it's only natural to raise your defences higher, to work harder than ever to protect what you have left. Even if the wrong person is locked up for the crime.

But I knew this place, had spent dozens of weekends here before and after we were married. I knew the paths and back ways through, the tracks used by the locals – the tracks I had used myself when taking the boys for walks around the edge of the grounds, looking for conkers in the autumn and new lambs in the spring. I skirt around the north side of the wall, avoiding the front drive, following in the shadow of the stone structure all the way around to the back of the house. When I reach the small rear gate, I walk away from the wall and up towards a copse, the ground rising gently beneath my feet.

The copse is small but thick with trees, an oasis of shade and greenery standing a little higher than the grazing land around it, a place the boys had loved for picnics and hide-and-seek when they were little. I find an old beech tree at the edge and scramble up onto the lowest branch, wedging myself in against the trunk as I get my breath back.

I can see the back of the house from here, the immaculate lawn spread out behind the wall, the patio, the courtyard and stables off to one side, the walled garden on the other. Perhaps a hundred metres from my perch in the old beech tree, the maid is laying the long table for lunch, wheeling out plates and dishes across the patio and arranging them at five place settings on the pristine white tablecloth. All of it shaded beneath a pair of large white sun umbrellas.

Today is Friday. The Vernons always spent the first weekend of the month at Dormers, all together as a family – come rain or shine – according to a family tradition dating back to when Liam's dad had been a boy and the big country house first came into the family. I also knew they would have been informed of my release date and would probably not want to risk bumping into me in Bath when I was fresh off the bus from prison.

I knew my in-laws. If *I* was them, I would have brought the boys here today, before the weekend. Put a few days and a little distance between me and them, in a safe place. Perhaps they might even tell Theo and Finn about my release. I settle back, taking small bites of my garage-bought cheese sandwich, listening to the bright chirping of birds in the trees around me and the far-off drone of a tractor. Waiting to find out if I have guessed right.

I don't have to wait long.

My mother-in-law comes out first, emerging from the kitchen in a long floral dress, the gold at her wrists and throat glinting in the sunlight. She says something to the maid, who hurries back inside.

A moment later, another figure emerges from the French windows off the drawing room.

The breath catches in my throat.

For a second my brain scrambles, trying to catch up, because what I'm seeing is impossible. It cannot *be* – and yet, here he is. This figure in shorts and a red football shirt, tall and lean and dark-haired, looks for all the world like my husband. Like Liam.

It's only as he walks slowly towards the table shading his eyes that I realise my mistake.

Theo.

My eldest son is fourteen now and *so* like his father already, the way he walks, his mannerisms, the set of his shoulders. He is all Liam: his jaw, his hairline, his height.

I cover my mouth with a hand, tears pricking at the corners of my eyes.

Finn follows him out, small and slight and dressed in cut-off jeans and a black T-shirt. A full head shorter than Theo, skipping past his brother to be the first to sit down at the table, saying something in a high voice, his words too far away for me to hear.

My baby. My youngest.

A warmth expands in my chest, my heart filling and growing and pushing on my lungs until it feels as if I can't breathe. Sitting completely still, I drink it all in, absorbing every detail – everything about my boys utterly familiar and yet brand new at the same time.

It is the first time that I have seen my children in ten years.

The first time I have laid eyes on them moving, talking, laughing, rather than staring at a couple of pre-schoolers in an old photograph creased and faded with age. They were never brought to visit me in prison, no matter how hard my mother tried to persuade the Vernons. Not even once. As far as my in-laws were concerned, it was as if I had ceased to exist and had no part whatsoever to play in their future.

I try to recall the last time I had come to Dormers. A decade ago, only two weeks before Liam's murder.

Wiping away tears, I try to remember.

Sunday, 30 June, 2013

Dormers Hall, near Hale's End, Gloucestershire

Finn wanted to be picked up. He had stopped walking, his little san-dals rooted in the thick grass, head lolling forward as if he couldn't possibly take another step.

'Not far now, Finn,' I said to my younger son. 'What's the matter?'

'I've got bendy legs,' he said, arms held up to me. 'Can't walk any more. Mummy carry?'

To be fair, the four of us had already walked to the stables, fed an apple to each of Colleen's two horses, Bronte and Star, out through the walled garden and played Pooh sticks in the stream below the old mill race. Theo ran ahead now with Jet trotting by his side, Amy throwing a tennis ball for the dog to fetch.

'Bendy legs,' Finn said again, in his smallest, saddest voice. 'Can't walk.'

I smiled, scooping him up and slotting him onto my hip, his skinny legs warm against my arm, that little boy smell – clean skin and soft cotton and baby shampoo – that made me want to breathe him in and never let him go. He was still light enough to carry, a beautiful compact weight who fitted just-so against my hip. One day he would be too big to pick up. But not yet.

My younger son gave me a chubby-cheeked grin, suddenly perky again, one small hand gripping the strap of my maxi dress.

With his other hand, he traced a soft finger down the line of my jaw. 'Mummy carry.'

I smiled back. 'Are you hungry, little man?'

He nodded, giving a happy jig against my side. 'Cake?'

'If you eat up all your sandwiches.'

I lifted him a little higher and we set off again through the thick grass, dappled with sunlight between the shadows of the beech trees. The air was warm and clear, the only sound the soft rustle of leaves above us and the faint clink of Jet's collar as he wandered happily off the lead. This. This was all I needed. These two boys and their dad, our little unit, and it didn't matter about anything else, about all the rush and craziness of everyday life, non-stop days and sleepless nights, the worries that had been nagging at me, because I was lucky. I was blessed. I had these two and I had Liam and sometimes I just had to remind myself that we could get through anything together. That being part of our little team of four was like holding the whole world in my hands.

Theo saw his brother being carried and turned to my sister-in-law, holding his arms up. Amy turned and knelt down, letting my eldest climb up onto her back and shifting him securely into position, before spinning in three quick circles to his peals of delighted laughter.

Together, we crossed back over the stream at the old oak foot-bridge and turned towards the house and the acre of neatly mowed lawn spread out in front of it. As we drew closer, my sister-in-law threw a stick for Jet, our puppy bounding off in pursuit as Theo climbed down from her back to give chase. Finn squirmed down off my shoulder to follow, both boys running after the collie with high-pitched squeals of excitement.

Amy tucked a strand of chestnut-brown hair behind her ear. 'They've really taken to Jet, haven't they?'

'He's an absolute sweetheart,' I said. 'They love him to bits.'

We watched for a moment as Theo threw the stick for Jet, the puppy haring off again with seemingly limitless energy.

'So,' Amy said, 'how's that clever big brother of mine doing? Got his eyes on Ten Downing Street yet?'

'He's . . .' I hesitated. 'Busy.'

'What's up, Heather?' She lowered her voice. 'You've been on edge since you got here.'

'To be honest? I don't know how Liam is. Your guess is as good as mine.'

'Work stuff?'

'He's so wrapped up in it all. We hardly get any time together, and when we do he's so distant. So . . . hard to reach.'

She put a hand on my arm, her voice softening with concern.

'Is everything OK between you two?'

I blew out a breath.

'Hard to say. I've tried talking to him about it but he won't open up. Sometimes I wish he'd just done what your dad always wanted him to do.'

'Working for Dad is not all it's cracked up to be,' Amy said with a wry smile. 'Trust me.'

'You must be doing something right. Congratulations on the pro-motion, by the way – sounds like the company's really going places.'

She shrugged off my thanks. 'Talk to me, Heather. I want to help.'

We walked on side by side, while I tried to find the right words.

'Liam just seems really . . . preoccupied recently. Like he's not really there. Half the time I'm talking to him and I can tell he's not really listening, that his mind is somewhere else. How does he seem to you?'

She looked towards the house. 'I know he's been full-on with the select committee, the extra responsibilities he's taken on and all the constituency stuff on top of that. You know what he's like – never been able to say no to extra work.'

I hesitated again, trying to think how to broach the next question. How to put into words a worry I had not shared with anyone else, not even my mother.

'But what if it's not?' I said quietly.

'How do you mean?'

'What if it's not work. What if it's something else?'

'Like what?'

'I don't know. Just wondered if he might have talked to you.'

My sister-in-law frowned slightly. 'You mean, another woman?'

I shrugged, but said nothing.

Amy gave me a sympathetic smile. 'To be honest, Heather, I don't think he's got time for that, or anything else.'

She looked towards the patio, where my parents-in-law sat beneath a large sun umbrella, Colleen directing the maid where to lay out a selection of sandwiches and iced drinks from a trolley. She saw us looking and beckoned us over with an impatient wave of her hand.

'Come on,' Amy said. 'We'd better sit up before my mother loses her temper. Talk to you later, OK?'

We pulled up chairs at the exquisitely laid out table and I fought down the familiar feeling that I had to be on my best behaviour. It was ridiculous to still feel this way, six years after we'd got married, after we'd celebrated in a grand marquee on this lawn and I'd been officially welcomed into the family. But ridiculous or not, I could never quite shake the feeling of being judged every time I visited, judged for myself, for the boys' behaviour, for how good a wife I was making for their golden firstborn son.

'Lunch looks lovely,' I said to Colleen.

She gave a tiny nod of acknowledgement. 'Now we just need the men to join us before it all spoils.'

Liam stood off to the side, by the gate to the cobbled courtyard, typing on his phone. He had his sunglasses on and didn't acknowledge me or the boys. Peter – as ever – had his own phone clamped to his ear, striding towards us from the house and talking loud enough for us all to hear.

'No,' he was saying repeatedly, his voice sharp. 'No. No. NO. Listen, it's not happening, I told that idiot Sorensen but he obviously didn't relay the message. Why are they not listening? It's over.'

A woman's voice was audible at the other end of the call, but Peter was already talking over her.

'Listen to me: just tell him it would be a mistake to go down the legal route at this stage. Our decision is final. And get Mike Hammond to call me. Urgently.'

He ended the call and tossed the phone onto the table, where it landed with a clatter between white china plates piled with sliced watermelon and grapefruit. Immediately, his face changed, the dark scowl replaced with a wolfish grin as he took in his grandsons.

'So,' he said, towering over them. 'What have my two little rascals been up to this morning?'

My boys stared up at their grandfather with wide eyes and closed mouths.

I put a hand on Theo's shoulder. 'We fed the horses, didn't we, boys? And these two were both very brave holding the—'

'I tell you what we need to do.' Peter knelt down to their level, talking as if I wasn't there. 'We need to get you up on those horses, the two of you, get you some riding lessons now you're getting so big and turning into such fine young men. What do you think? Would you like that?'

Theo and Finn blinked at him, wordlessly.

'Mm-hmm,' Theo said finally, with a small nod.

'That's the spirit!' Peter ruffled his grandson's fine brown hair. 'Now, where's your father got to?'

Liam still stood off to the side, by the courtyard gate, thumbs flying over his phone. Even from a distance I could see the tension in his body language, his shoulders stiff, a muscle working in his jaw.

Finn was reaching for a perfectly cut triangular sandwich but froze when Colleen tapped her fingertips smartly across the back of his hand.

'Not,' she said, holding up a manicured finger, 'until you've gone indoors and washed your hands, young man.'

Finn stared up at her with wide eyes and for a second I thought he might burst into tears, before Amy stepped in to break the tension.

'I'll take them,' she said. 'Come on, you two.'

She took both their hands and headed for the house.

Peter's phone rang on the table and he silenced it with a jab of his long index finger.

Liam sat down next to me, eyes still hidden behind his sunglasses. Colleen handed him a plate neatly arranged with sandwiches, olives and fresh fruit.

'Thanks,' he said absently. He set the plate down on the table but didn't touch it. Instead, his eyes were drawn back to his phone again and he began scrolling, tapping, frowning.

'Everything OK?' I said quietly, touching him lightly on the arm.

'Yeah,' he said without looking at me. 'Fine.'

'Work?'

'Whips Office wanted to check something,' he said, turning his phone face down on the table and finally looking around, as if for the first time. 'Where have the boys got to?'

7

By late afternoon I'm on a local bus to Bristol, finding a seat on the empty back row and keeping a wary eye on my fellow passengers, my sense of dislocation growing with every mile.

There were so many parts of modern life to which I had never given a second thought. I had known they were there, humming away in the background, but I hadn't worried about them causing any kind of issue in my life – my old life, at least. Because back then I had been a middle-class, white professional, which meant I'd always had the benefit of the doubt. Until Liam's murder, I had never really appreciated how privileged I was – and what it might be like to lose that privilege overnight. Because from the moment Liam died, all of it – the police, the press, the courts, the *system* – had turned against me. And from the moment the guilty verdict was read out, I became the enemy, the outsider, the *other*, to be feared and reviled and never to be trusted again.

The world had moved on. Brexit. Trump. Covid. Ukraine. A royal funeral and a new king. But I was the same. For me, time had stood still. I had only been a bystander to the last decade, nine months on remand and nine years of my eighteen-year term served. I was a traveller from another time, a different decade, newly arrived in 2023.

At Bristol bus station, I find another bus that will take me into the centre of Bath. There are *so many* people. More than I ever remembered. I imagine them all seeing me in my prison-drab clothes, faded jeans and sweatshirt, my no-brand trainers, my washed-out face and dark eyes, and imagine them judging me. *She doesn't fit. She's not one of us.* They think they're safe, superior, insulated from the cruelty of fate by money, status, property, by marriage and family and friends. But I look at them and all I see is naivety. These people are so *unaware.* The reality is, you can lose everything. At any time. One night, one moment, can blow your life to pieces so completely that it can never be put back together again.

I'm living proof of that uncomfortable truth.

I get off the bus and walk with my head down, hands in pockets and the collar of my jacket turned up, not making eye contact with anyone. Sticking to the main roads, busy roads, relying on memories of this place. Feeling like a child as I relearn old skills at the same time, judging the traffic and crossing roads, navigating crowds and sidestepping teenagers zipping along the pavement on motorised scooters which seem to be a new thing. My destination is in the suburbs, south-west of the city centre, and I'm glad to get away from the tourist-clogged streets around the abbey and the Roman baths. An indirect route takes me through Oldfield Park and Twerton, tree-lined streets busy with traffic.

By the time I get to Haycombe Cemetery my feet are aching, but I don't care. It is good to walk without stopping, without thinking. I head in through the black iron gates and follow the road up to the left, up a gentle rise that leads to the far corner of the site, past ranks of white and grey headstones. Hundreds of them. Thousands.

My mother's grave is at the end of a row. A simple stone, unadorned with flowers, her name and her dates and nothing else. The bare minimum. I crouch and pull away the weeds sprouting around the base, uprooting a curl of ivy from the side.

When I've tidied it up as best I can, I kneel on the damp grass and lay my hand on the top of the stone as if to tell her I'm here, to feel her somehow. As if it might ease the guilt of my absence. Not for the first time, I wonder if this is the dark truth I carry inside myself: that I am cursed to lose those I love. More than that: I am in some way the *cause* of it. My father had died when I was barely into my teens; Liam before we'd even reached our seventh anniversary; and a few years later my mother, the only one who had never stopped believing in my innocence, fading away into Alzheimer's in her seventies while I languished in prison. Alone in the care home as the dementia took hold, unable to remember from one day to the next, no regular visitors to whom she could anchor her remaining self. No visits from her only child. As a prisoner in a closed category secure facility, I had not even been permitted temporary release for her funeral.

I am the common denominator. The dark link to all these people, gone from my life forever.

Perhaps it was true, the terrible thought that always waited for me in the dark like a malevolent spirit: that my sons would be better off without me.

No.

Not that.

I wasn't going to lose my boys. They were all I had now, the only stake I had left in this world. I touch my fingertips to my lips and rest them on the top of the cold, rough headstone, swallowing down a lump in my throat.

'I'm sorry, Mum.' I study the carved words one last time. 'Love you.'

I stand and walk back out onto the path, angling across the hill, searching up and down the rows for another grave that I have never been able to visit until today. Another funeral I had not been allowed to attend. But it doesn't take me long to find: a white marble headstone on the far side of the site, the plot neat and well tended. At the foot of the stone, fresh white lilies that look as if they are only a few days old.

Liam Fitzpatrick Vernon
1977–2013

This time I can't stop the tears. My funny, loving, smart, handsome husband, who had known me better than anyone had ever known me, who loved his family so fiercely, who always looked for the bright side, who was a great cook and a terrible dancer and who told the lamest jokes but still somehow made us all laugh, who sometimes used to stare at me with this little smile, as if I was the most amazing person in the whole world and he still couldn't quite believe his luck.

It has been so long, so many years, and I still don't know why he had died or who had wielded the knife that night. Perhaps it had been an act of passion or desperation or extremism. Perhaps punishment, revenge, a warning to others.

All I know is that I'm innocent.

But my conviction has hardened into an unchallenged fact over the last decade, it has become a given, a concrete reality. The fingerprints, the photos, the burner phone, the guilt-ridden message my husband had not lived long enough to send – they made for a damning combination. My culpability for his murder has become the received wisdom, the court-sanctioned narrative of what had actually happened. Each repetition building on the last, like layers of sediment settling on each other over the years to form a new reality.

From that fertile sediment, lies had sprouted like weeds.

An entire forest of lies had grown up since Liam's death – lies that stood between me and my sons, that threatened to keep them away from me forever.

A forest of lies so thick, so tangled, so dark, that no one could see through it anymore. I knew why the first lies had been planted – to frame me, silence me, to bury the truth so deep it would never see the light again – and I knew what I was going to do.

I was going into the forest.

And I was going to burn it to the ground.

8

SATURDAY

I dream of Liam for the first time in a long time.

Snatches of sleep in which I'm talking to him, arguing with him but I can't hear what he's saying, his words muffled and distorted as if he is underwater. In my dreams, he is standing white-faced in front of me, first in his suit then suddenly he is in his dressing gown, then a football shirt, a white T-shirt, then his wedding-day suit, and every time I look down, there is the same bloody, murderous gash over his ribcage, dark with congealed blood.

In my dreams, there is a long knife in my own hand.

The same knife held by a killer who had been in my house, who had come upstairs, who had been in the bedroom with me, had stood over me with nothing to stop him from plunging the knife into my chest too. How long had he been there? Would he have killed me if I'd woken up? Had he stood over the boys' beds as well, deciding whether they should live or die as I slept on, oblivious across the landing? Holding the power of life and death in his hands, deciding finally – like some munificent god – to grant them their young lives?

I wake with a flinch of alarm that I'm not where I'm supposed to be. Something is wrong. I'm not in my usual bed, not in D-26 on the wing at Eastwood Park. My heart is thudding in my chest, fast and shallow, and it takes a few seconds to remember where I am.

Southmead House, a probation hostel for recently released offenders.

There are four of us to a room, narrow single beds crammed into the space so tightly they are almost side by side. The air is thick with the smells of sleep and feet and exhaled breath. Details return in a rush: I had been placed at an 'approved premises', a squat two-storey concrete building tucked away at the end of a row of terraced houses near the train station. A couple of dozen women and the same number of men on the floor below. Two of the other beds in this little dormitory room are occupied, sleeping figures heaped beneath the blankets.

The fourth woman is standing next to my bed. Close enough to touch.

She is about my age, perhaps a few years younger, with fingernails bitten to the quick and a yellowing bruise under her left eye. Her dark hair is pulled back into a messy ponytail and there is a line of small tattooed stars inked haphazardly behind her ear. She is trying on a jacket, admiring herself in the small mirror on the back of the door. I squint up at her. She's trying on *my* jacket. She turns this way and that, putting her hands in the pockets, posing as if she is in the changing rooms at Zara. The old me would have waited for her to take it off, or asked politely if she could give it back. But that part of me was long gone, like a distant second cousin I could barely remember. In prison, showing weakness was the quickest way to losing what little you had.

'What are you doing?' I say to her, my voice still scratchy with sleep. 'With my stuff?'

'Reckon it fits me pretty well.'

'Take it off.'

'I could give you a fiver for it?' Her soft Bristol accent curls around the words.

'Take it off,' I tell her again. 'Now.'

Her eyes have the excited glaze of something synthetic buzzing through her bloodstream. 'Can I just borrow it, for like, one day?'

'Now.'

She pouts and shrugs the jacket off, dropping it back on the end of my bed. She's wearing tracksuit bottoms and a grubby purple T-shirt underneath, track marks clustering around the pale blue veins of her forearms like dark freckles smudging the skin. She sees me notice them and crosses her arms with a shrug.

I gesture at her feet. 'And the trainers too.'

She looks down at my shoes on her feet, makes a face. 'Really? Do you wanna swap? These are a *perfect* size for me. You know, I have so much trouble finding the right size 'cause my feet are in-between the regular sizes, you know, in one shop I'll be a six and then in another I'll be a six and a half but I—'

'I don't want to swap.' Her own shoes are a tatty pair of flats kicked under her bed that look as if they are about to fall apart.

I sit up, bedsprings creaking beneath me, and rub a hand across my face. Unlock time in prison had been 7.45 a.m. on the dot, every morning, weekdays and weekends, Christmas and bank holidays and every other day of the year. But there's no clock in this room, I have no phone and my watch doesn't work.

'What time is it?'

My room-mate shrugs. 'I know you, don't I?'

I swing my legs out of the bed, pulling my sweatshirt on over my head and looking around for my joggers. Inside, I'd had this on a regular basis, especially in the first few years – *that posh bitch who killed her husband in cold blood* or sometimes *that stone-cold bitch who let her kids find their dad's body* or simply *that stuck-up bitch who thinks she's better than everyone else.* I learned to deflect and ignore as much as possible, to flatten my accent and keep my head down, to fit in as best I could.

'Don't think so.'

'Yeah, I do. You were at Eastwood Park, weren't you? Me too. D Wing, got out a couple of months ago. I'm Jodie, by the way.'

'Heather.'

'First day out?' Before I can answer, she carries on at machine-gun pace. 'God, I remember my first time coming out, totally lost it, went on this massive bender and ended up back in the police cells on Monday morning, no memory *at all* of the weekend. I'm not staying here for long though, my mate in Swindon's got a spare room and as soon as I can get some cash together I'm off up there to stay with her. And then I'll get my own place sorted so I can have my daughter come to live with me again.' She sits on the end of my bed. 'So, Heather, who have you got?'

'What?'

'Your PO,' she says with a shrug. 'Who's your probation officer?'

I take out the folded sheet of paper I'd been given when I left Eastwood Park, and look for the name.

'Trevor Boyle.'

'God,' she snorts. 'Good luck. He's a right wanker.'

'There's no shortage of them.'

She laughs. 'I tell you what, d'you want me to go for you? Pretend to be you, if you want. For the trainers.'

'What?' I shake my head. 'No. I don't want to get into trouble.'

'It's no bother, I've done it before. Just say you've lost your ID. If I wear my hair down I could pass for you, no problem.'

'I'll be OK,' I say. 'But thanks for the offer.'

'No problemo.' She flashes me the smile again. 'If you change your mind about that jacket though, let me know.'

9

'Do you understand what I'm saying to you, Heather?'

I nod at the man behind the paper-piled desk. Trevor Boyle is in his mid-fifties, a small man with a grey goatee and a paunch rolling over the belt buckle of stonewashed blue jeans. His paisley waistcoat is unbuttoned, a T-shirt beneath it that may have been white a few years ago.

'Yes,' I say. 'I understand.'

'This is important, Heather. For you, for your life going forward. If you want to stay out of prison, that is.'

'I know.'

The probation office is in an unloved red-brick building on the edge of an industrial estate, windows fogged with condensation and sagging stone steps that lead up to a row of buzzers beside a dented front door. The reception area reminds me of a GP's waiting room, except for the clear plastic barrier completely enclosing the front desk and the selection of leaflets on the low table. 'Finding Work with a Criminal Record'. 'Integrating Back Into the Community'. 'Life After Prison'.

Trevor Boyle studies me for a moment over the top of his small round glasses.

'So do you?'

'Do I what?'

'Want to stay out of prison?'

'Yes. Of course.'

I am never going back there, I add silently. *Not ever. Not even for a day, an hour, a minute. Not for you, not for anyone.*

He raises an eyebrow at me and resumes his spiel with the air of a man who has recited these same words hundreds, if not thousands, of times over the years.

'So, just to reiterate, parole is a system that allows prisoners to be released into the community on licence, under the supervision of a probation officer.' He pats a palm against his chest. 'That's yours truly.'

'On licence. Got it.'

'You've served fifty per cent of your term, and as per the guidelines you're to serve the remainder of your sentence in the community, subject to licence conditions. Do you understand, Heather?'

'Completely.'

He finds another sheet of paper, an envelope clipped to the back of it, and scans the page briefly.

'If you don't stick to the rules and requirements you can be found "in breach" of your licence and that will land you right back in Eastwood Park for another nine-stretch.' He gives me a humourless grin. 'Do not pass Go. Do not collect two hundred pounds. Proceed straight to jail.'

'I can stick to the rules.' I give him an emphatic nod. 'I'm sure I can do that, absolutely. There won't be a problem.'

'That's good to hear. Very good.' He comes out from behind his desk and lays the sheet on the small round table in front of me before shuffling back and collapsing into his chair again. 'Rules of the game,' he says.

I scan the page, the blue crest and letterhead of HM Prison and Probation Service at the top, with a bullet-pointed list of conditions. It says:

Any or all of the following may be regarded as a breach of your conditions and lead to an immediate recall to prison:

- *Any arrest and/or charge in relation to a criminal matter*
- *Any contact **of any kind** with any witnesses, jurors, police or court staff involved in your original trial*
- *Any contact with any family members related to the victim/ victims in your original trial*

I knew this was coming – knew the last stipulation would be there and had tried to prepare myself for it. But it still makes my stomach plunge when I read the words, laid out in black and white.

Any contact with any family members related to the victim.

'What about my boys,' I say quietly. 'How do I see them?'

'Yes. About that. How old are they again?'

'Finn's just turned thirteen and Theo's fourteen-and-a-half.'

'Right. Well, as stipulated by your licence conditions,' he taps the letter, 'you're not to have any contact with them.'

'But there must be a . . . a way that I can see them in time, once I've been out for a little while, maybe? It's been so long. They were tiny when I last saw them, last spoke to them, there must be a way—'

'You have no legal right to see them, Heather, at least not without the express permission of their legal guardians. I understand they're being brought up by your late husband's parents?'

'Yes. But they're my *sons*.'

'And they're still minors in the eyes of the law. Once they reach eighteen, they can decide for themselves who they see and don't see. Until then, as I say, that decision is for their grandparents to make.'

'That's still *years* away,' I say. 'So what are my legal options in the meantime?'

Boyle narrows his eyes. 'How do you mean?'

'In terms of challenging this. There must be something I can do in legal terms.'

'I'm afraid not.' He folds his arms over his chest. 'This is the law of the land. It's not the judgement of some court, subject to legal challenge. These are the terms of your parole.'

'So how do I see my children?'

Other than by climbing a tree and spying on them from a distance. I wonder briefly whether my trip to Dormers yesterday would technically count as a breach. I'm guessing it probably would.

He gives me a pained expression, as if I've not been paying attention. 'You don't see them unless you are granted explicit written permission by their legal guardians. Which they are under no obligation to give.'

And will only happen when hell freezes over.

I swallow down the knot of pain in my throat. 'There must be a way.'

'What I advise my clients, Heather, is to focus on today. Focus on the here and now, the present. Take one day at a time and don't think about the future too much. You're out of prison, and that's the main thing.'

'The main thing is seeing my boys,' I say, trying to hold my voice level. 'It's the only thing.'

I look at him, this tired man in his tired office, paperwork overflowing everywhere, and can almost feel the dead hand of probation bureaucracy weighing on my shoulders.

He turns back to his computer monitor, checking his watch.

'Be back here in two weeks,' he says, fingers already clattering on the keyboard. 'And stay out of trouble if you want to stay out of prison.'

Saturday, 13 July, 2013

3.08 p.m., Bath Police Station

They wouldn't let me see the boys.

They wouldn't let me see anyone except the duty solicitor, a willowy grey-suited man in his late twenties who sat with me and talked while I sat and sipped strong, sugary tea from a chipped blue mug. I wasn't really aware of what he was saying, what the words meant, what any of it meant, what I was doing here alone in a police station when I should be with my boys. They'd be frightened. Disoriented. Hungry. They needed me. I needed to be with them. But they wouldn't let me see them. Soon, people kept telling me. Soon, but not yet. I felt as if I was coming apart, stretching, tearing, about to shatter into pieces with only a single frail layer of skin keeping me together.

So I'd just let the solicitor talk in his strange monotone, seeing his mouth move, the gestures he made with his nail-bitten hands, the movement of his biro as he filled in forms, the expressions of his smooth, pale face as we sat together in a little room deep in the bowels of the city police station on Lower Bristol Road, the events of the morning replaying over and over in my head on a horrific loop.

First there had been the ambulance. A pair of green-clad paramedics gently moving me away from Liam's body while they went through the motions of checking for signs of life. Radio calls, static and acronyms and the inert, bloodless language of death. The patient is deceased. *My boys wide-eyed with fear, cowering from these loud strangers in the house, not really knowing what was happening but sensing it was something dark and terrible and unfathomable. The three of us huddled together in the kitchen in our dressing gowns, me fighting with all I had to stop the tears, pouring cereal into bowls, feeding the dog and letting him out into our little back garden. Theo watchful and pale as he spooned Coco Pops into his mouth, question after question that I couldn't answer. Finn wriggling out of my desperate embrace and fetching his dinosaurs from the toy basket, playing an oblivious game with them on the kitchen floor while the paramedics carried on their hopeless task just a few yards away in the next room.*

After the paramedics, the police. Two uniforms, the younger one stationed outside our front door, the other in the lounge talking in a low voice to the paramedics.

Then the neighbours, a little hastily dressed knot of people I half knew and some I'd never even spoken to, arms crossed at the end of the drive in a pretence of neighbourhood concern. And before long, the photographers had started to arrive. First one, then two, slung with cameras and equipment bags and thick as thieves as they angled their lenses towards the house, an ambulance jammed into the driveway in front of my Nissan estate. Then a second police car, and by this time the group of photographers had swollen to half a dozen, and then—

The solicitor was asking me a question.

'What?' I said.

'Is there someone you want to call?' he asked, biro poised over his pad. 'A friend or relative?'

I blinked. Looked into the chipped mug in my hand. It was empty. I was still here, still in this nondescript room, sinking into a low, tired sofa by the single window. A half-empty box of tissues on the table, the wire wastepaper basket already half filled. A scratchy grey office carpet on the floor, generic landscape prints on the wall. It reminded me of the family room at the hospital where I'd sat with *my mum years ago, waiting to be told the inevitable by the doctor in charge of my dad's palliative care.*

'My mum,' I said. 'Can I see her?'

'Soon, hopefully,' my solicitor said. 'She's been in reception since this morning, waiting to see you. I had a quick word with her earlier – she's not going anywhere.'

The thought of my mother sitting alone in the station's reception area for hours brings a fresh lump to my throat. But I knew she would wait for as long as it took until she could see me, talk to me, give me a hug.

I turned my head and saw for the first time that there was another man here, sitting back in one of the chairs by the door. White shirt, sleeves rolled up over brawny forearms, mid-forties, receding hair shaved tight to his scalp. I hadn't even realised he'd come into the room.

'I need to tell her what happened.' It hit me again then, a wrecking ball catching me full in the chest, the overwhelming weight of it forcing the air from my lungs. The pure cruelty of it, the unbelievable, impossible truth of my last sight of him, still lying on the sofa, his face pale and slack. My vision blurred with tears. 'Oh God. Oh God. Oh God. Liam. I can't—'

I broke off, fresh tears streaming down my face. I felt raw, empty, scoured out by grief. My eyes were gritty, my throat swollen and wracked from crying.

The man in the white shirt stood up and brought his chair nearer to mine, pulling a handful of tissues from the box and holding them out to me. I took them and wiped at my eyes, squinting at a lanyard on a blue strap around his neck. DI John Musgrove.

'Why don't you start by telling me?' His voice was gentle, a soft Yorkshire accent that was almost soothing. 'Everything you can remember. And I want to offer my sincerest condolences for your loss.'

'I told the other . . .' Through my sobs, I gestured vaguely towards the corridor outside. 'The other officers, the ones at the house. And *then your colleague who read me the caution and did the DNA swab and all those things.' My voice hitched again, shoulders shaking. 'I don't know why she did that.'*

'Just a formality at this stage, Mrs Vernon. I'm sorry we have to keep going over it, but I want to hear it directly from you so we can find the person who did this and make sure they don't do it to anyone else. Take your time.'

I pulled more tissues from the box, began to tell the story again in as much detail as I could drag from my fogged brain.

When I was finished, Musgrove gave me a pained smile. 'Thank you. You'll let me know if you want a break, won't you?' He pointed to my mug. 'Another hot drink or something to eat?'

I shook my head.

'I just can't imagine who would want to do this to Liam, who would want to . . .' My voice cracked. 'Why would they do this? How did they even get into our house?'

This person had been in our home. *The thought of the killer coming upstairs, to the boys' bedrooms, sent an icy shiver through my whole body. I was torn between wanting more than anything to be back home with my children, and knowing that it could never be our home again. This place where we had been building a life, a place of sanctuary that had been violated in the most unimaginable way.*

'These are all things we're trying to establish, Mrs Vernon.' He flipped to a new page of his notebook. 'I know this is hard to talk about, but I'm particularly interested in any malicious communications Liam may have received at home recently. We're looking at his recent email traffic – thank you for providing the passcode to his phone by the way, it's a real help. But I wonder if there's anything in particular that he may have shared with you.'

'How do you mean?'

'Threats, Mrs Vernon.' The detective inspector spoke softly, almost regretfully, as if he didn't even want to say the word in my presence. 'Against your husband's life.'

10

Findlay & Guy Solicitors is above an estate agent on Newbridge Road. A fine rain starts to fall as I walk across the city and by the time I arrive my jacket and grey joggers have a damp heaviness to them, the smells of prison rising from the wet fabric. I have not been here for many years but the place is just the same, an open doorway beside the estate agent's busy front window, stairs leading up to a first-floor waiting room, a cramped beige space with curling leaflets pinned to a cork noticeboard and a row of hard plastic chairs against the wall.

There's no one else here apart from a receptionist behind a curved front desk, a pallid young man with a nose piercing, talking in a bored monotone into a phone headset clamped over goth-black hair. I stand at the desk and wait. *Everything* about this place is the same as I remember: the worn-out carpet at the top of the stairs, the lingering smell of old cigarettes, the glazed partition through to the two back offices. The receptionist seems to be the only new addition. And he is in no hurry to conclude the conversation, giving me a brief sideways glance before going back to his computer and *click-click-clicking* the mouse.

Finally, he ends the call and turns to me.

'Can I help you?' His tone of voice suggests that helping me is the very last thing in the world he wants to do.

'I'd like to see Mr Guy please.'

'Do you have an appointment?'

'No.' I give him my name, relieved that there's no flicker of recognition on his face. He's barely into his twenties, my conviction was half his life ago. 'But it won't take long.'

His lips turn down at the corners, as if I've just proved him right. 'I'm afraid you'll need an appointment. Mr Guy is tied up at the moment.'

'Honestly, I just need five minutes.'

He taps a small plastic rack of business cards on the front desk between us. 'Like I said, you need to call ahead and make an appointment. This is the number. Should be able to fit you in Tuesday or Wednesday next week.'

'I don't have a phone at the moment.'

He looks at me as if I've just told him I'm an alien newly arrived from another dimension, before turning back to his screen and clicking his mouse again. 'He's tied up all day today and Monday I'm afraid but what time on Tuesday would work for you?'

'Like I said, it needs to be—'

'Don't mean to be rude but are you sure you're in the right place?' He gives me another look, eyes flicking down then up to take me in. 'Mr Guy only handles conveyancing, family law, wills and probate. That sort of thing.'

'I know.'

'He doesn't handle . . . *criminal* matters.'

I feel the heat creeping up my neck, imagining how he sees me and hating my reaction at the same time. 'I'm here about my mother's will. Her estate. Mr Guy handled it some years ago and dealt with the legal side of things when I wasn't . . . able to.' I point through the glass partition, where the angular, balding figure of Alan Guy is currently sitting at a meeting room table with a mug of coffee that says *World's Best Grandad*, the *Daily Telegraph* spread out in front of him. 'He's right there, I can see him through the glass. And I'm not leaving until I've talked to him.'

The young man sees where I'm pointing, huffs out a sigh. 'What did you say your name was again?'

'Heather Vernon. My mother was Carol Merritt.'

He stands and retreats through a wooden door, pulling the blinds on the glass partition fully shut as he goes so that I can't see through to the back office anymore. I'm left alone in the small waiting area, no sound apart from the low hum of morning traffic outside the window. I try to remember the last time I was here, maybe fifteen years ago when I was pregnant with Theo, Mum insisting we both have a sit-down with Mr Guy to alter her will to take account of her grandchildren.

After a few minutes, the receptionist returns, pulling the door shut behind him and taking his seat again at the desk. He is alone. No sign of his boss. Evidently Mr Guy doesn't want to sully his hands by coming out to talk to a convicted criminal.

'Well?' I say.

'Like I said, he's tied up just now.' He gives me a shrug. 'But he said to give you this.'

He puts a plain brown A5 envelope on the desk between us, sliding it towards me as if that's the end of our conversation. There is no label, no name or stamp, nothing written on it at all. I pick it up and turn it over in my hands, the sealed envelope thin and insubstantial, a small weight at one end. Unsure whether this is some kind of fobbing off, a flyer or a form, another way to keep me at arm's length.

My heart gives a sudden leap: or what if it's a letter, a message? Something from my mum, kept in trust at this place in the years since she died? Waiting for this day? I tear it open. Inside is a single sheet of folded paper, a photocopy, the letterhead at the top from a company called Total Storage. Dates and payment details, monthly amounts, bank numbers, an address in town and signature at the bottom that I don't recognise. I don't understand any of it.

'Is there anything else?' I ask. 'I was thinking there might be documents, a letter, something more?'

The receptionist has already gone back to typing aggressively on his keyboard, striking each key with particular venom.

'That's it,' he says without taking his eyes from his monitor. 'That's what Mr Guy gave me, to give to you. Which is what I've done.'

I scan the photocopied sheet again, turn it over. But the other side of the page is blank. *This? Is this it? Is this all?* I upend the envelope onto the counter.

No. There is something else. It tumbles out, clattering onto the counter with a dull metallic *ting*: a key.

11

I walk alongside a smiling, heavyset man in a black and orange Total Storage T-shirt, our footsteps echoing off bare walls. He's in his twenties but has a long beard and a twirly moustache that makes him look a decade older. Big long beards seem to be everywhere: when did that become a thing? Before I went inside? I can't remember. The man, whose name badge says 'Michael', is pushing a trolley and talking amiably as we head deeper into the bowels of the warehouse.

The storage unit, he explains to me, is in their long-term section where rentals are open-ended and can go on indefinitely.

'As long as the direct debit keeps working,' he says cheerfully as he taps his ID against a card reader, a heavy door sliding open for us.

I follow him into a cavernous square room, all four walls lined with metal racks holding hundreds of steel storage units bolted side by side. It looks like the locker room of a gym for giants, each box two feet by three and stacked six high, one on top of the other all the way to the ceiling. Michael checks the number on my key and goes to a wheeled loading machine, the electric motor humming as he parks it in front of a rack in the far corner of the room. Like the young guy at the solicitors' office, he seems not to have registered my name – or if he has, he doesn't care. He elevates the hydraulic platform until he's in front of door 5581, using his own key to open the steel door and haul out a black plastic box. He lowers it all back down again and manoeuvres the loader into the centre of the room, heaving the box onto a large steel table, before reversing the loader back into the corner.

'There you go, Mrs Vernon. Needless to say we advise clients not to leave their possessions unlocked if they leave the room for any reason.' He hands me a black key card. 'This is for the security door, if you can return it to the front desk when you're finished? Toilets are down the corridor on the right.'

I look around for a clock on the wall but there is nothing, not even a window. Only the motionless eyes of a couple of CCTV cameras looking down on us from opposite corners of the room, sprinkler system pipes threaded between the strip lights above us.

'How long do I have?'

He gives me a shrug. 'Long as you like. We close at eight. When you're finished, just re-lock your box and let me know at the front desk, I'll come down and return it to the rack.'

With that, he's gone, whistling a tune, the security door *shushing* shut behind him.

There is bench seating on two sides of the table, privacy partitions evenly spaced along its length. I sit down, shiny bronze key in my palm, just me and the box in the silent corner of this warehouse. I have no idea what's inside. It seemed heavy when he heaved it onto the tabletop, but I can't imagine what it contains. Mum had never mentioned it to me.

It's deep and long, about the size of the plastic crates we used to get our Tesco food shop delivered in, but it's made of some kind of rigid plastic framed with metal, the number '5581' stamped in black on the side next to a barcode. A heavy padlock the size of my fist holding the steel clasp in place.

I push the key into the padlock. It slides in easily, the hasp releasing with a soft *click* as I turn the key. The lid opens on its long edge and creaks back on hinges stiff from lack of use, a release of stale, dusty air that must have been trapped inside for years.

Our house had been sold after the trial, the proceeds going into a trust for the boys, but I didn't really know what had happened to the contents. I knew Mum had been given some of my stuff, personal things that held no interest for Liam's parents. I suppose I should be grateful that all of this didn't end up in landfill.

She must have packed it all up on one of her lucid days, before the dementia really took hold. Before she forgot to safeguard these few precious things, sending them forward instead to the day when I was free again. She had entrusted the key and the payment schedule with Mr Guy.

It feels like a time capsule, a delivery from my old life. A message in a bottle.

The contents are stacked neatly, carefully, but the box is only around half full. Some books, framed photos of the boys, a favourite handbag. A Waterman fountain pen in its box. A cashmere scarf that I'd received for Christmas the year before Liam died. A small box of jewellery, a matching necklace and bracelet, my engagement ring and an eternity ring he'd bought me when Theo was born. A sealed white envelope is paperclipped to the top of a cardboard folder, *Heather* written in my mother's shaky handwriting on the front. But I'm not ready to open it yet. I take it off and lay it carefully on the table in front of me.

I leaf through folders of paperwork in the box; my birth certificate, a hardback envelope holding all of my GCSE and A-level certificates, financial stuff, other forms that perhaps my mum hadn't known what to do with, tucked next to pictures that Theo had painted at nursery, thick lines of red and blue, yellow suns and a house with four stick figures lined up: two big and two small, all of them with big splashy smiles and five stick fingers on each stick arm. Another painting by his brother, this one little more than splats of colour on a page, the paint cracked and faded with age. *Finn Vernon* written in neat round script beneath it by one of the nursery staff. Mum had stuck them to her fridge at home with magnets, in the corner of her little kitchen. A lifetime ago.

I lift items out and put them carefully down on the table. These must have been all the things that either Mum had been given before Liam died, or that his family had not wanted to keep when they sold the house the following year. My framed graduation picture is here, me looking ridiculously young in robes and mortar board, grinning with the dummy scroll they gave to you just for the photo. Various utility bills for the old house. A few years' worth of my old diaries, held together with an elastic band. A glossy photobook that Mum had made of each of the boys when they were first born. Framed photographs of each of them, very young. Finn's first tiny pair of shoes, smart little black pumps with a silver buckle, which fit in the palm of my hand.

A whole house – the three-bedroom semi that had been our home for eight years, the lounge and the dining room, the kitchen and the study, all of it – reduced to this. To one box.

A brown padded envelope has a single word – my name – printed in hesitant capitals on the outside. I tear it open and find a thick wedge of ten-pound notes inside held together with a plastic band. Stuck to it is a Post-it note in my mum's familiar handwriting: *To tide you over xx*. There is also a pre-paid debit card still attached to the issuing letter from a company called MyCash, thanking her for a deposit of £1,000. My throat tightens at the thought of my mum taking this money out of her savings, what should have been her retirement fund, and leaving it here for me to find on some future date. On a day she probably knew she would never see herself. She had planned this, had wanted to make provision for me before the dementia fully took her away. Still looking after me, even now.

My mum's favourite scarf is here. I hold it to my face, breathing deeply, tears threatening as I catch a ghost of the flowery perfume that she'd worn for as long as I could remember. The faintest traces of jasmine and sandalwood persisting after all this time.

There is a shoebox beneath the clothes. Inside I find my driver's licence, expired and with my old address. My passport, expired in 2018. A slim bundle of business cards held together with a fraying rubber band, my old card at the top. *Heather Vernon. Human*

Resources Manager. I flick through the rest. A random selection of tradesmen, financial advisers, former colleagues and a handful of journalists, none of whom I remember. A few things of mine that she must have kept from when I was a girl, not able to part with them: a little pink wristwatch, a sparkly tiara, a tiny white box with a lock of my blonde baby hair tucked carefully inside. I had no idea she had held on to these fading tokens of my own childhood.

I return to the small white envelope bearing my name, turning it over in my hands.

She used to love cards, thank yous and reminders and any little family occasion, *here's a little treat for the boys* with a five-pound note tucked in for each of them. She'd buy the cards in boxes from charity shops, had always liked something you could pin up on a corkboard or a fridge, put on the mantelpiece, use as a bookmark or a reminder long after a text message or email would have been forgotten.

There is a painful hardness in my throat as I tear the envelope open and pull out the card inside. A single 6 × 4 postcard, a soft watercolour image of a grey and white bird poised on the end of a branch, one yellow eye peering out. I read the words, my eyes brimming with tears.

Dear Heather,

Thought you might want a few things for when you get out. Didn't want it gathered up and thrown in a skip with all my stuff when they cart me off to the funny farm.

I love you. I know you didn't do what they said. One day the truth will come out and everyone will know. Whatever you do, I will always be so proud of you, darling girl.

Kiss the boys for me.

Love always, Mum xx

12

The bank manager is a manicured woman in her mid-thirties with a neat bob. She's trying hard to stay professional but I can tell that beneath the facade she knows exactly who I am, her gaze lingering a fraction too long on mine, unasked questions on her lips as we sit in a booth at the back of the branch. Tonight, she'll no doubt relate our meeting to a partner over dinner, an *interesting story from her workday.*

'As you know,' she says, typing as she talks, 'Mr Guy handled your mother's estate – my condolences, by the way – and we were in contact with him regarding the disposal of assets. I understand your mother left quite specific instructions for him, as to how those assets should be made available to her surviving next-of-kin.' She glances at me. 'He made certain arrangements with her and with us regarding her estate, which was deposited in her current account after all the legal processes had been completed. He also arranged for you to be a co-signatory to that account.'

She hits another sequence of keys and turns the monitor towards me so I can see it. An account statement, numbers, codes, dates, and a figure on the top right denoting the current balance: £11,823.

Another wave of gratitude and sadness nudges at me as I stare at the figure. My mother, who had worked hard all her life, had raised me single-handedly after my father died, who had been smart and independent and loving and kind, who had helped me through uni and paid off her mortgage on her own. Who had then seen her beloved house sold to pay for her care as she slowly disappeared into the fog of dementia: this is what all of that amounted to. This was what she had left. It didn't seem fair.

The bank manager gives me a sympathetic smile, turning the screen back towards her side of the desk.

'We did have discussions with Mr Guy about how the funds should be handled, including a suggestion that they might be better in a trust or a savings vehicle that would yield a better return over the medium term. But he was quite specific. Your mother, apparently, was quite specific with *him*.'

She slides a clear plastic folder across the desk to me.

More paperwork, forms to sign. But also a Visa debit card – with my name on it. I detach it from the accompanying sheet and hold it in my hands, turning it so the hologram catches the light, transfixed by my name in silver letters on the plastic. Something so small and everyday – that I had taken for granted for so long, had probably used a thousand times in my old life – but it feels like a talisman, a ticket back to the real world. A sign that I do still actually exist.

I stop at the cashpoint on the way out but it's been so long since I've performed this simple action – card in, keypad, selection, money out – that I have to think about every step of the process, remind myself how it works.

I change the PIN number to 2811. Liam's birthday.

The crisp twenty-pound notes feel different, smoother and more synthetic and they are smaller than I remember, more colourful, the image changed too. Inside it would have taken me months to earn this amount, in the kitchen or the laundry at prison rates of ten pounds a week.

I find a branch of Primark to buy new clothes, inconspicuous blacks and greys, dark blue jeans and a baseball cap. Clothes that would be good for blending in, for disappearing. It's a relief to shed my old clothes – still ripe with the stink and grime of prison, the pallor of too much wear – and I feel like a snake shedding old skin, leaving it behind. I didn't want anyone to look at me the way people had been looking at me for the last twenty-four hours, giving me a wide berth on the street.

In the changing room, I tuck half the fresh banknotes into my jeans pocket and the other half into my right shoe before slipping it on.

Old habits.

I change in the toilet cubicle of a supermarket, tie my hair back and put on the baseball cap, turning up the collar of my jacket to cover more of the ribbon of scar tissue that climbs up the left side of my neck.

I buy a pay-as-you-go phone and fifty pounds of credit and spend half an hour in the park, trying to set it up. My old email password doesn't work; I guess the account must have been consigned to the digital void after my life had stopped like an unwound clock. A quick Google search confirms that I'm about eight years too late – it would have been automatically deleted after two years of inactivity.

When I've started to get the hang of it, I sit for a minute and look at the contacts folder. Empty. *Let's get started!* as the phone puts it. There is no one, no old phone to populate the address book, no old email or apps to trawl for names and numbers to add. I can barely remember my old number, let alone anyone else's.

I go to Google and create a new email address, using my maiden name instead of my married name. Then I head for the hostel, avoiding the crowds and keeping to side streets.

A new energy lightens my steps and pushes me forward.

It's been so long that it takes me a while to figure out what it is.

Purpose. A renewed sense of purpose.

A feeling of forward motion, of momentum: of having a reason to put one foot in front of the other.

Saturday, 13 July, 2013

3.22 p.m., Bath Police Station

DI Musgrove passed me another tissue from the box.

'We need to establish whether there were any threats made to your husband recently, anyone who had made specific or repeated threats against him? A constituent he'd dealt with, perhaps? A disgruntled voter or someone who may have come into contact with him through his parliamentary work? Obviously we're following up with the Parliamentary Safety Office as well but it may be something he hadn't reported yet.'

'He never mentioned anything to me.' I shook my head. 'There have been a few cranks, for sure. Overenthusiastic party members, single-issue obsessives and Liam's own little fan club of women of a certain age, but they all seemed pretty harmless. He had his share of trolls online, of course, but no more than any other MP.'

'Was there a particular issue that he was dealing with, maybe something that was taking up a lot of his time? Or perhaps a particular individual that he'd mentioned to you? Had he seemed particularly bothered or stressed in the last few weeks?'

'He was busy all the time, always going from one thing to the next. Always on his phone or at events or catching up on correspondence. And he did seem particularly preoccupied in the last few months, working very long hours.'

'Preoccupied with what?'

'Work. I don't know exactly.' In truth, I'd had my own suspicions a few times. But now I felt only the heat of guilt for doubting him.

Had I just been too wrapped up in the boys and my job and my own day-to-day battles to notice if something had been bothering him? 'A lot of his work was confidential. He said last night he'd been talking to a colleague about . . . something shady going on, breaches of the parliamentary code or something. But it was all very vague.'

'Did he mention a name?'

'To be honest I thought he might be making it up on the fly to cover his tracks.' *I stare at the floor.* 'I thought there might be another woman.'

'We'll look into it anyway.' *Musgrove made a note on his pad.* 'How about the financial side of things? Were there any debts, did your husband have any money worries, unsecured loans, credit issues?'

'No. Liam's family have always made sure that we're . . . they've always been very generous.'

'I'm interested whether you heard anything last night, anything at all.' *The detective spread his hands, biro clamped between two thick fingers.* 'Perhaps the front door opening, if your husband let someone in? Any kind of conversation, or even a confrontation?'

I groped through the fog of memory, willing myself to remember. But there was nothing.

'I'm a pretty deep sleeper,' *I said.* 'I have pills to help me sleep. I was prescribed them last year alongside some other medication I have for post-natal depression, general anxiety and insomnia. After I had Finn, things were difficult.'

'Can I call you Heather? My name's John, by the way.'

'You have kids of your own?' *I said.*

He shook his head. 'Wasn't to be, unfortunately. Lots of nieces and nephews though.'

I tried to remember what he'd been asking a moment ago. What was it? My brain was scrambled.

'I have the pills to help me sleep,' *I said again,* 'but I only tend to take them at weekends because I don't have to get the boys up and ready for nursery.'

'So you took one last night?'

'I . . . think so. How are they?' I said. 'Are they OK? No one's told me anything.'

'They're being looked after by your in-laws, Heather.'

'I need to see them, to talk to them.' Theo had been crying when he'd been picked up by his grandmother; sobbing and clinging to my leg while Finn watched his brother in white-faced silence, sucking his thumb, white muslin cloth clutched in his little fist. 'I need to explain to them what's happened. When can I go home?'

'Soon.' He opened a fresh page of his notebook. 'The sooner we get this done, the sooner we can get you back to your boys.'

'I can't believe they found their dad like that, it's just . . . too horrific.'

The shock rolled over me again in a wave, the grief so powerful it almost knocked me to the floor. The memory of my last words to him, angry, accusing words, after telling him not to kiss our boys for fear he would wake them.

Now he would never kiss them again.

The guilt was like a punch to my sternum.

Every time I closed my eyes I saw Liam's face, waxy and pale, the slackening of death almost making him look like someone else.

And every time it was like another sharp stab of grief as if I was experiencing the worst moment of my life over and over and over again, that moment when I had pulled down the blood-soaked duvet. The lightning bolt of fear, of panic, of sheer unalloyed terror as I pushed on his chest and put my mouth to his cold lips desperately trying to breathe him back to life. Pushing on his chest, pinching his nose and forcing air into his lungs, blood smearing my hands and soaking my nightie, pushing and breathing and breathing and pushing. One and two and three, breath, one and two and three, breath. Knowing it was pointless but not able to stop.

'Can I see him?' I said softly. 'Can I see Liam?'

'Not quite yet. But soon. If you want to.' He leaned forward. 'Listen, I know this is an incredibly difficult time,' Musgrove said.

'But we need to work up a timeline for last night. What's the last thing you can remember?'

I shook my head, as if to clear it. 'Checking the boys were both asleep.'

'You're sure?'

'Pretty sure.' I frowned. 'It's always the last thing I do before I go to bed myself.'

Now that I tried to recall, I couldn't actually remember many of the details, those routine things that I did so often that memory skated over them. I couldn't recall much beyond that last argument in Liam's study, finishing the washing up, checking on the boys and then . . . nothing. Only a terrifying blankness, a void in my memory as if everything had been wiped clean like a beach swept flat by the rising tide. I couldn't even remember taking one of my pills. But I must have done.

'Around ten thirty?' That was about normal for a Friday night. 'Maybe closer to eleven.'

He checked his notebook again.

'And did your husband often spend the night in the lounge?'

Did he. Past tense.

'His study was just off the lounge,' I said, swallowing the tears down. 'Sometimes if he was working late he'd just stay down there, crash on the sofa rather than coming upstairs to bed. So he didn't disturb the boys.'

I stared at my hands, at my fingers, at a rust-coloured fleck in the corner of one nailbed. Realised with a jolt of horror that it was dried blood, a remnant of the hopeless minutes I had spent trying to revive Liam. I curled my hands into fists in my lap.

'So the fact you were sleeping in separate beds,' Musgrove continued, 'wasn't because you were having difficulties?'

I blinked, looked up into the detective's broad face. 'What do you mean?'

'In your marriage.'

13

Bath Central Library is modern and airy, high ceilings and tall stacked shelves, a wide staircase leading up to the first floor. I head upstairs to find the study section at the back of the main area, where I find what I'm looking for: a long table with six PCs. Only two of them are in use, one by an old gent with a stack of maps on the table next to him, another by a grey-faced man in his fifties, pecking at the keyboard and checking the screen after every stroke. Neither of them look at me as I sit down.

I'd wasted half an hour looking for an internet cafe, but they seemed to have disappeared from the high street. The library was my next best option.

I sit at one of the spare terminals and shake the mouse to bring it to life. Everything seems smaller, the monitor slimmer and more compact, the screen brighter. We had limited access to an email service in Eastwood Park, and some video calling that was set up during the pandemic lockdowns of the last few years, but there was no proper access to the internet, to Google, to social media. I settle my fingers on the keys, index fingers on *F* and *J*, waiting for the muscle memory to return. Willing my fingers to remember the touch-typing I'd taught myself at uni.

But the knowledge is gone. Atrophied over the years, faded away with lack of use like so much else in my life.

I find and peck at the keys instead, like the grey-faced man opposite. It doesn't take long: a simple Google search on Liam's name brings up more than 100,000 results. They're dominated by the court case, my conviction, Liam's life and stellar career and his untimely death, the size and reach of his father's company, Vernon plc. Page after page on the trial and the aftermath, headlines screaming my guilt at the end of it all.

They had all used the same pictures. First a shot of me walking into the police station in sweatshirt and joggers, head down, bird's-nest hair, blotchy face, a female officer leading me by the arm. Not handcuffed, but I might as well have been. Dark rust-coloured stains still visible on my wrists where not all of the blood had come off.

The other image was even worse: a shot of me being led out of my house on Maitland Street, looking up towards a camera, into the morning sun. Squinting at the sudden brightness – but that's not how the picture looked. The moment captured made it look as if I was *smiling*, my lips turned up at the corners as if in some macabre greeting for the gathered photographers. As if I wasn't distraught and heartbroken at all, but actually able to summon a grin for a total stranger.

I had never found out how they had arrived at my house so quickly, barely an hour after the first police vehicle had been followed by another, and then another. There was no way they could have got that picture at my house without being tipped off.

I scan the first lines of the news stories. Some of it was true, some of it was half true, other lines seemed to be the product of either speculation or outright fabrication. My eye is drawn to a few sentences in particular, a hot, painful lump growing in my throat as I see my devastation packaged and wrapped and summarised in a handful of words on the screen.

Liam Vernon, 36, a rising star of the party tipped for a potential cabinet role, was found brutally murdered at home . . .

. . . Heather Vernon, 33, showed no emotion as murder
detectives led her into the police station . . .

. . . their sons, two and four, are understood to have discovered their father's butchered body while she slept off
the effects of a drinking binge in a separate room . . .

. . . understood to have had a turbulent relationship
and were sleeping in separate bedrooms at the time of
his death . . .

I shake my head, feel the heat rising to my face. Clicking and scrolling. Not wanting to see any more, but not wanting to stop. There
were background pieces on other politicians who had died through
violence or suspected foul play. Other stories detailed Liam's life,
his illustrious family and his career in finance before becoming
an MP, his growing popularity and meteoric rise within the party.
Yet more pieces on other MPs who had become embroiled in sex
scandals over the years, brought crashing down to earth by their
own infidelity, from Lord Profumo to Earl Jellicoe, Cecil Parkinson
and David Mellor.

My late husband now has his own Wikipedia page, and I'm
shocked to discover that I do, too. Sketchy details about our lives, the
vast majority of both entries given over to the circumstances of his
death and my conviction. More clicking and scrolling. More pages.
Certain columnists in certain papers decrying the corrosive effect of
working mothers, of marriages overlooked in favour of careers, of
neglected husbands straying from selfish wives and the tragic example of where that all leads, provided by the Vernon family.

I settle into the chair and allow myself to fall deep down the rabbit hole, devouring it all with a masochistic fervour. *Click. Scroll.
Click. Click.*

There had to be doubts out there *somewhere*. Someone who
hadn't swallowed the police's version of events, who didn't accept
the jury's decision at face value. I just had to find those doubts and

follow them, find a loose thread and pull on it until the whole thing started to unravel.

It was the only way I was going to be able to see my sons again, to rebuild a life with them. To be a mother to them.

After an hour, I have two dozen tabs open on the browser. The BBC News website and other outlets had done pieces on the first anniversary of Liam's death, as his parents founded a new charitable trust dedicated to helping victims of domestic violence. I google the Vernon Trust, scanning the pages. The trust, I read, also works to raise awareness of male victims of domestic violence committed by their partner or spouse, 'the under-reported and stigmatised issue of men being the victims of it rather than the perpetrators'.

Elsewhere, there is barely a mention of my failed appeal, two years after the conviction. Just a few short pieces with the barest of facts – but it's confirmation of what everyone already knows. She did it. Not really *news*.

Some years ago there had been a documentary on one of the cable crime channels, and I find it now on YouTube – *Death of an MP* – watching the subtitles in silence as DI Musgrove and various other interviewees, neighbours, ex-friends and parliamentary colleagues are interviewed for the hour-long show. As I watch, it rapidly becomes clear that the police only ever had two working theories during their investigation. The first – a home invasion gone wrong, a struggle in the dark, Liam stabbed by a burglar surprised to find him downstairs – had apparently been discounted through lack of evidence within the first twenty-four hours. What was the thing Benedict Cumberbatch said on that TV show Liam had loved, the Sherlock Holmes series? *When you have eliminated the impossible, whatever remains – however improbable – must be the truth.* Something like that. That was what the police had done: they had eliminated all other possibilities. Which left the only other theory, that someone in the house must have done it. That *I* had done it.

They had never seriously entertained the version of events that I *knew* to be true: that I had been set up. Framed. A perfect patsy for the cold-blooded murder of a popular MP, touted as a future leader of the party.

Reading story after story, it almost seems as if Liam's popularity had worked *against* me, had loaded the dice from the start. As if I was in his shadow from the very beginning, the negative to his positive. Because my husband had been a charismatic, well-liked politician – and God knows, there were few enough of them – so someone had to pay for his untimely death. The cosmic debt had to be settled, somehow. Someone had to be held responsible – why not his cold, ambitious, social-climbing wife, who had smiled for the cameras when she was arrested? Who was paralytic drunk in charge of her kids and who couldn't even cry in court? Who was so consumed by jealousy that she left the poor mites to discover their poor dead father in a pool of his own blood?

It was a good story. But that was all it was.

14

Among all the hundreds of news pages and websites and blogs and comment pieces about my husband's death, I can only find a single dissenting piece, published in the *Guardian* in 2016. Seven years ago. A single contrary voice among the mass of court reports, features and the calls for me to spend the rest of my life behind bars. A single loose thread among the thick tapestry of 'facts' that had been woven since my life became public property.

Questions Remain Over Murder of MP

By Owen Tanner

It was a case that shocked the nation – the brutal death of charismatic MP Liam Vernon.

Characterised at the time as a crime of passion motivated by jealousy, fuelled by alcohol and prescription drugs and carried out by a spurned wife intent on revenge, the killing shone a spotlight on the issue of domestic violence directed against men. Heather Vernon – who has always denied the murder – was handed an eighteen-year sentence and will not be eligible for parole until 2023.

But two years after her conviction, unanswered questions still remain about the circumstances surrounding the case.

Suggestions have even been made of irregularities in the police investigation, or a cover-up that reaches to the highest levels of the British establishment.

I scroll further down the piece, to a series of sub-heads outlining the questions and inconsistencies hanging over my case.

> *– The woman with whom Liam Vernon is alleged to have had an affair – used in court to provide evidence of motive for the killing – has never come forward and was never traced by police.*
> *– Heather Vernon, a human resources manager with a software company at the time of the murder, had no criminal record and no documented history of violence.*
> *– Questions remain over suggestions of corruption within Parliament, and evidence that Mr Vernon was about to blow the whistle at the time of his death.*

I read the third sub-heading again, scrolling through the text in vain for anything concrete. The corruption angle had been floated a few times in the media but never seemed to lead anywhere. All the same, I sit back with a strange feeling of lightness high in my chest. It takes me a moment before I figure out what it is: for the first time in a long time, it feels as if I'm not completely alone. As if I'm not the only one who knows the truth, not a lone voice shouting into the hurricane.

I check the date of the article again: 27 April, 2016. Less than two months before the Referendum vote in June, when the news had been a constant back-and-forth of *Leave* and *Remain* arguments, debates, stunts, claims and counter-claims. A time when everyone had seemed consumed with it, when it had seemed to take over the country like a contagion – squeezing out news of anything else.

The comments below his story are a queasy blend of conspiracy theorists spinning their own ideas on Liam's death – the cover-up of a party scandal perhaps, Russian agents or maybe a rogue IS cell – mixed in with the anonymous misogynists saying I got everything I deserved plus a sprinkling of true crime fans talking about me as if I was a fictional character in some low-budget TV show.

I search Tanner's name and hundreds of other articles come up, going back to the early 2000s. Page after page of hits, everything from crime to politics to some international stuff around corporate fraud, money laundering and high-level corruption. In a 2010 byline picture, he glares through small round glasses, buzz-cut ginger hair the same length as the stubble across his lantern jaw. I combine my name with his in the search box and see, with a sting of recognition, that he had been writing about my case ever since the weekend of Liam's death. The articles that carried those damning pictures of me being led from the house by police, squinting into the sun in a way that looked like a smile.

His 2016 story is the last I can find from the *Guardian*. He has a few subsequent articles in the *Independent*, the *New Statesman* and then it seems to tail off. All I can find from the last few years are pieces published on his blog, www.theylietoyou.co.uk – long rambling stories about Chinese agents and Russian oligarchs, a few from the pandemic about the scandal of government contracts given out to ministers' friends.

Clearly his efforts to reignite interest in my case had not gathered any momentum. I had known that the chance of a successful appeal against conviction was slim without significant new evidence. But maybe this was a starting point. I send the link for Tanner's 2016 story to my new email address, so I can read it again later.

My stomach growls with hunger. My eyes are gritty and dry from so much staring at the monitor, so much reading, so much information swirling and trying to get a firm handle on it all. I'm still getting used to the fact that I can sit here all day if I want to, there is no one to tell me time's up, time to get into the canteen queue, report for work or return to my cell for bang-up and lights out. I blink and tear my eyes from the screen, look around for a vending machine, something to keep me going until later. I've not eaten since leaving the probation office and the—

I stop, a tingle of alarm fluttering low down in my stomach.

At first I think it's the cumulative toxic effect of all those news stories, seeing my guilt repeated so many times in black and white. But the tiny hairs are standing up on my forearms, the way they sometimes did in Eastwood Park after I'd been there a few years. That electric, unnatural calm when something was about to kick off, when someone was about to get jumped and everybody else knew it. Someone out to settle a score or get their retaliation in first. A ripple of silent intent, of warning.

I have my back to a wall of reference books, more stacks lining the other walls, more tables, a seating area scattered with beanbags by the children's books. The clientele seems to be made up of pensioners, parents with pre-school age children, a few teenagers and a homeless man dozing on a sofa in the local history section. The kind of people you'd expect in the library.

Except for one guy.

He's on the edge of my peripheral vision: early thirties, athletic build, dark sweatshirt. Short dark hair, receding at the temples. I've never seen him before but he looks completely out of place. As I turn towards him, his eyes meet mine for a half-second before he slips behind a tall shelf of books.

The library feels suddenly claustrophobic, the book-lined walls too close. I check my route to the exits: the main door straight down the aisle to my front, plus a fire exit to my right, closer, leading out into some kind of courtyard. I can be out of that door in five seconds if I have to.

Pulse drumming in my wrists, I close the browser on the computer and roll my chair back away from the desk, ready to go, ready to run. I keep my eyes on the other end of the shelf where I'd seen the sweatshirt guy, waiting for him to reappear. Waiting to see if he makes eye contact again.

A clock on the wall behind me ticks dully and I count to sixty.

He doesn't reappear.

I count off another sixty and then stand, going the long way round towards the aisle where I saw him, checking my route to the front door is still clear. The tingling is in my stomach, my knees, the light feeling in my chest to *get out of here, just get out,* but I want to get one more look at him before I do. There are people in the library: staff, customers, parents, children. It's safe – I think. I move from shelf to shelf, quickly, quietly, taking the long way around past the front desk and a table strewn with magazines. Coming up on the far side of the aisle, on his blind side. Sliding out a heavy hardback on the way – I don't know why exactly but it just feels better to have something solid in my hands. With my heart in my throat, I step out and scan the aisle, fingers gripping tightly around the hard-edged heft of the book.

But there's no one. The aisle is empty.

15

I take an indirect route back to Southmead House, walking quickly and ducking down side streets, slipping into shop doorways and waiting to see if the man from the library is following. But I don't spot him and after fifteen minutes I feel my heartbeat slowing to something near normal, fatigue creeping up my limbs as the adrenaline drains away. Was it all in my head? Had I imagined it, the way he had been observing me from across the room?

He was probably just a mature student, a book-lover getting out of the house, a guy killing time on a quiet afternoon.

But he had disappeared very fast after I noticed him. And there was *something* about him.

Safely back at the hostel, I sit on my bed and start to go through some of the paperwork I took from my mother's storage box. I had taken as much as I could carry: colour photographs of the boys when they were young, the old address book that lived in a kitchen drawer at the Maitland Street house, my old driving licence, papers and mementos and a stack of my pocket diaries including the last one I had owned – which had somehow survived the worst year of my life. The rest of the contents I left there, under lock and key.

I'm alone in the little dormitory room at the hostel, savouring the quiet after the hustle and bustle and sensory overload of walking around the city all day, seeing so many people. I go through the paperwork – bills and statements, letters and certificates, tax returns, official-looking stuff from Parliament and all kinds of other stuff – sorting it into three piles according to whether it looks *useful*, a middle pile for *maybe*, and a third for *probably not*.

The *useful* pile is the smallest.

My 2013 pocket diary has stylised Cath Kidston flowers on the cover, a Christmas gift from Liam the year before he died. It has everything in it from my old life – work meetings, birthdays, holidays, the kids' playdates, visits to friends, dinner parties, babysitters, reminders and lists and notes to myself. Each week of family life summed up in the faded pencil words on a pair of facing pages, all of it tailing off after 12 July, 2013: birthdays for which I hadn't sent cards, events where I had been absent, work deadlines I had missed. I flick idly through our old address book too, letting the pages tick past my fingers, trying to summon faces to match the names. Old school friends, housemates from university, former colleagues, relatives, neighbours. Many of whom had severed contact pretty much straightaway after Liam died; others who had gradually bled away after my conviction until almost none remained.

I go back to the bundle of older pocket diaries. Six in all, their covers curved with age, pages inside crinkled with fading ink. A different cover design or colour each year but always the same size and always a week-to-view. I leaf through the weeks of the 2012 diary, a bittersweet reminder on every page, a steady pain against my ribcage as I trace the happy minutiae of my old life. The entry for 5 August in exuberant capitals: *FINN'S SECOND BIRTHDAY!* I do the same for 2011 and 2010, allowing myself to slide back into nostalgia for a time that would never be again. To bathe in it like warm bathwater, even though I knew it would make me twice as cold when I emerged.

The one at the bottom of the stack is also for 2013. A duplicate. I frown, trying to remember if I received an extra one as a gift that year. But this one had been used.

And as soon as I open it I realise my mistake: it's not mine at all.

It had belonged to Liam.

A powerful swoop of something like vertigo rocks me with dizziness as I sit cross-legged on the narrow bed.

When we first met, Liam had teased me about my preference for pen and paper until I finally converted him and we got into the habit of buying each other diaries for Christmas every year after. It was our cheesy in-joke, a silly festive tradition before the mass migration of everything to digital that came afterwards. Now, I press my palm against the navy blue cover of this thin book, as if I might be able to feel something of him, sense something of him captured in these pages. A link preserved between the two of us.

I open it carefully to study his once-familiar handwriting, quick and precise, the shock of old memory breaking the surface. It's been ten years since I've seen it but his style is unmistakable, his sharp Ts and looping Ys, the flourish of his capital Bs and the effortless way it all runs together. I'd no idea how this diary had ended up in the stack of my possessions, in this storage box. It must have simply been mixed in with mine. I guess they all looked pretty similar. And just like mine, it is filled until the summer, in the weeks and months leading up to that day in mid-July. I run the tips of my fingers over the lines of his writing, seeing him in my mind's eye the way he would sit at the kitchen table filling in the pages, laptop open, bouncing one of the boys on his knee, giving me that smile as I topped up his wine.

My hand shakes slightly as I turn to the double-page spread for the week commencing 8 July, 2013. The weekdays packed with meetings, committees, votes in the House, a couple of media interviews, conference calls with numbers to dial in. That Friday, the day he'd died, is just as busy as the others. Two meetings, lunch with a journalist, a sub-committee and a reception at 4 p.m., in the terrace pavilion overlooking the Thames.

I flick to the following week, the week he had not lived to see. My first week on remand after being charged, as it turned out.

Allowing myself – just for a moment – to imagine a life in which that terrible day had never happened, a parallel universe in which our lives rolled on undisturbed as they had done for years previously. A life in which there was no terrible fork in the road on 12 July, no intruder in our house, no knife, no murder charge, no trial. No conviction. Would we still be in the same house on Maitland Street? Probably. I would have gone back to work full time after Finn went to school, maybe moved jobs, looked for a promotion; Liam would have carried on rising in the party, a high-flyer for sure and maybe in the Cabinet by now, or maybe—

Stop. This was not helping.

I force myself to focus on each entry for the week commencing 15 July. More of the same, all fairly familiar, if not routine. The patterns of parliamentary life as MPs wound down towards the holidays. It was actually the last week the House would sit before the summer recess. Did that mean something? In the section for Thursday 18th, Liam had written 'House rises', underlined once. The last week of business before September, and if anything it was busier than the previous week. There is only one notation that catches my eye, because it is so short. On Monday 15th, the first entry is just a time, with initials next to it.

8 a.m. – AY

Liam would typically get the 6.02 a.m. train to Paddington on a Monday as he liked to be in his office by eight, with a little breathing space before the first business of the day.

Like this meeting with *AY* that had never taken place.

16

I do a few quick Google searches on *AY*, combined with *Parliament, MP, Westminster*. Nothing seems to jump out.

The next entry for that day is not until midday, a lunch meeting. In the afternoon, long-scheduled parliamentary stuff that he would have added weeks or months before, once his office populated his electronic diary. All specific, clear, unambiguous.

Not at all cryptic. Not like the 8 a.m. entry. I assumed AY were someone's initials, or maybe a place? I flick back through the pages, looking for any other meetings scheduled in with AY. But I can't find any. Then I check against our home address book, but there's nothing that corresponds there either.

The police had had access to his phone, his electronic diary, almost from the start of their investigation. It was one of the first things they asked me, that nightmarish first day when I'd discovered his body. But had they seen this too, his paper diary? I wasn't sure. They were almost the same anyway, with just a few extra personal items added to the hardcopy.

Which might mean AY was something *other* than work.

A personal meeting. Private. Illicit, perhaps.

No.

I don't want to go there, not at this moment. Not when I've only just rediscovered this keepsake from my old life, this little book

that Liam had held in his hands a hundred times, that he had carried in his jacket next to his heart.

The weekend he'd died, the entries look normal, recognisable.
The event he'd been invited to on the Saturday after his morning
constituency surgery. Theo's football match on Sunday morning,
and one other notation for the evening of that day.

Another cryptic one.

8 p.m. – cl N

Cl was his shorthand for *call*. So, a call scheduled for 8 p.m. on
a Sunday. By which time he'd already been dead more than thirty-
six hours, and I had already been charged with his murder. Maybe
N was another colleague? A member of his staff? The only one he
tended to call out of hours was Christine Lai, his office manager.

I flick to the back of his diary. Most of the notes pages are taken
up with more of his handwriting, most of it relating to constituency work, follow-ups and action points to be raised about local
issues. A half-page of text that is mostly crossed out, thick black ink
obscuring the writing below. A few other elements are just about
legible, on one of the lines.

Two more initials, or names, or whatever they are.

AT → NS?? 10/6/13 CUTOFF

Below it I find one further reference to AY. Buried among more
text obliterated with crossings out until a final looping arrow
points to the initials, circled twice in ink so heavy it has almost
torn the page.

It's only as I look closer that I see the ragged leftover where the
next page has been torn out. Not neatly, not cut with a blade, but
ripped away as if in haste or anger. That was weird; it wasn't like
him at all to tear out pages wholesale. Why not just cross it through?
I read back over everything again, trying to discern pattern or
meaning – if there even is one.

Eventually, I close the diary and tuck it carefully under my pillow,
turning to the few other items sorted into the 'useful' pile. The stack

of business cards, wrapped tight in its elastic band, might be interesting. Near the top I find a card for Owen Tanner, the journalist, presumably from an effort years ago to contact my mum for comment on my case or my appeal. There is a mobile number and an email address. The mobile number just gives me an automated voice, *This number is out of service, please check and try again*, so I open a fresh email instead, attaching a link to the article of his that I'd found on the library computer. I used to write dozens of emails a day at work, but it's been so long that I have to concentrate hard to summon the format from memory, like hauling water up from a very deep well. I write the email several times, debating with myself how much detail to include, but decide in the end to keep it simple.

Dear Mr Tanner,
    I was very interested in the story you wrote a few years ago about my case. I'm back in Bath and would like to talk to you. Are you free to meet?
    Heather Vernon

It was time to find out what else Owen Tanner knew about my husband's death.

17

The door to the dormitory room flies open and Jodie bursts in, grinning widely.

'Oy oy!' she says, her voice loud. 'You still here?'

'Still here,' I say.

'No suites available at the Royal Crescent Hotel then?' She gives me a lopsided wink, but I don't think she's drunk. Just a bit manic.

'Overrated.' I shrug. 'And this place has got a much better rating on TripAdvisor anyway.'

'Ha! Yeah right.' She kicks her shoes off. 'Thought you'd be up and out and on your way by now though, missus.'

'I'm working on it.'

'Another night in paradise for us then.' She flops down on her bed with an exaggerated sigh. 'Hey, how'd you get on yesterday anyway? With old whatshisname?'

'Who?'

'You know. Your probation meeting with Boyle.'

'Oh, him. Yeah, he was . . . all right, I suppose.'

'I can't stand him. *Wanker*.' She points to a shopping bag on the end of her bed, an edge of belligerence creeping into her tone. 'What's this? Who's been dumping all their shit on my bed then?'

'It's for you,' I say. 'If you still want it.'

'What is?'

'Open it and you'll see.'

She opens the bag, the grin slowly returning to her face. She pulls out my old jacket, the one she had tried on yesterday morning while I was sleeping, and the trainers too.

'Are you winding me up?' she says. 'For me? Seriously?'

'Sure. If you still want them.'

She shrugs off her own threadbare cotton jacket and delightedly pulls on mine, popping the collar and posing in the little mirror by the door, turning this way and that with her hands in the pockets. She was right – it was a perfect fit. She pushes her bare feet into the shoes, pulling each one on quickly without bothering to tie the laces.

'No offence, but I look better in them than you did anyway.' Seeing my shrug, she bursts out into a hacking laugh. 'Only joking, Heather! Just winding you up, love.'

'There's a few other bits in there as well, if you want them. I was in Boots so I got some stuff.'

She delves further into the bag and pulls out bottles of shampoo and conditioner, shower gel and toothpaste.

'Bit of freetail therapy,' she says. 'Nice. Can't give you nothing for 'em though. I'm completely and utterly skint.'

'I don't want any money for them.'

Her eyes narrow. 'So what *do* you want?'

'Nothing.' I shrug. 'Like I said, I was in Boots anyway. They had some deals on.'

'Deals? Like, you mean, you didn't swipe it? You *paid* for all this?'

'Yes.'

'Seriously?' she says again, her face relaxing back into a smile. 'It's like Christmas! Cheers, mate.'

Jodie gives me an awkward hug, patting me on the back. She smells of smoke and sweat and berry-flavoured chewing gum. Sitting back down on her own narrow bed, she produces an unopened half-size bottle of vodka from her old coat and offers it to me.

'Want some?'

I try to think of a reason to abstain, but can't think of one. The hostel has a *no drugs, no alcohol, no guests* policy, among its other rules, but it doesn't seem to be enforced.

'Why not?'

I take the small bottle from her and unscrew the cap, putting it to my lips. It's been so long since I've had a drink that the vodka is like pure fire going down, lit petrol blazing its way down my throat. I gasp, covering my mouth with a hand.

'Looks like someone's out of practice.' She laughs and retrieves the bottle from me, taking a long slug herself. 'You know what? We should go out, me and you. Get a proper drink one night, I know some great places we could go.'

There's an unfamiliar buzz from the bedside table. My new phone, vibrating against the cheap laminate. *One new email.* It's a reply from Owen Tanner, sitting there in my inbox only minutes after I had emailed him.

> Hi
> Thanks for getting in touch glad to hear you're out.
> A talk would be interesting.
> Out of interest how did you get my email address?
> O

I reply with a quick explanation about finding his card among the possessions my mum had put into storage. His response is a single line. No greeting, no sign-off.

> Email not secure use Telegram instead send me your mobile no

What the hell is Telegram? I assume he doesn't mean an *actual* telegram. Seems a bit old school. After several minutes of fruitless searching on my phone, I go to Google, to Wikipedia and from there to the App Store to download the Telegram app which promises 'fully secure, encrypted end-to-end messaging'. I hastily set up a new account and send him the username and number for my new phone.

Jodie is stretched out on her own bed, still fully clothed, staring at her own mobile between long, slow blinks.

The Telegram app pings with a new message from a user called O$INT17614.

Where did you go on holiday after your oldest son was born?

I frown, thinking that perhaps I don't understand this app and I've stumbled into someone else's conversation by mistake. It takes me a moment to realise what this is: he's *testing* me. Checking I am who I say I am. God only knows how he is aware of this obscure fact about my old life.

I type:

A little place called Appledore. Near Barnstaple in Devon.

Theo had been ill for most of it, colicky and snotty and awake half the night, then it had rained for two days straight before we had to pack for the long drive back up the M5.

The phone buzzes again.

Meet tomorrow 10.30 a.m.? There is a place called Ollie's Cafe in Fishponds.

On the bed across the room Jodie is snoring gently now, mobile on the pillow, the half-empty bottle of vodka cradled against her chest.

I type a quick reply.

OK. How will I recognise you?

There is a pause before he responds, three terse messages arriving in rapid succession, stacked one on top of the other on the phone's small screen.

Tell no one where you're going.
Make sure you're not followed.
Come alone.

Saturday, 13 July, 2013

3.35 p.m., Bath Police Station

DI Musgrove rearranged himself on the chair, turning his body to face me more fully.

'Did you argue when your husband got home last night?'

I frowned. 'What's that got to do with anything?'

'With him sleeping downstairs. Hence my question about any . . . strain there might have been in your marriage.'

'As I said, sometimes he just slept downstairs if he was working late, that's all.'

'It's just that we've had officers going door-to-door today on your street. One of your neighbours said she heard raised voices last night between nine and ten. Shouting, arguing. A woman's voice.'

'Who told you that?'

'Does it matter?'

I felt myself redden, blood rushing to my face, hot tears of shame rising. The regret that my last words to my husband had been angry, accusing. Regret that I already knew I would carry with me until the day I died.

'There was a phone call,' *I said slowly.* 'He said he was talking to a colleague but it wasn't her. It was someone else.'

'Who?'

'I don't know. A woman, calling on his work phone. He said it was some sensitive work thing, a constituent. He wouldn't tell me her name. He told me some other stuff too but I thought he was making a lot of it up as he went along.' *I described the rest of our conversation – as best as I could remember it – up to the point where I had slammed the door and stormed upstairs.*

Musgrove paused to make another note in his pad, tight blocky capitals underlined twice with heavy slashes of his biro.

'So he lied about this mystery caller and then you argued.' It was no longer a question.

I nodded, eyes on the table. 'It was stupid. It was nothing.'

'Have you argued a lot recently?'

'What? No.'

'Had you been drinking last night?'

'I had a few glasses of wine after the boys went to sleep.'

Musgrove nodded slowly. 'How many's a few? Three or four? Did you finish the first bottle and start on the next?'

'Maybe two, I don't know. It could have been three. We don't normally drink during the week, but it was Friday night.'

'I understand there was an empty bottle of wine on the kitchen counter and also an unfinished glass of whisky on your bedside table. A little nightcap, was it?'

The honest truth was that I couldn't even remember pouring a whisky, let alone taking it upstairs. Whisky had always been more Liam's thing than mine: he would usually bring out the single malt if his parents were visiting, at the end of the evening.

'I might have had one.' I shook my head. 'I was tired, it was late.'

The detective lowered his voice. 'I understand you've complained of blackouts before when you'd been taking your sleeping pills, when alcohol is added into the mix. You asked your doctor to lower the dose. Is that right? Do you think you might have blacked out last night?'

'Why are you asking that? How is it helping to find the person who killed Liam?'

'Because if – for example – there is a reason why you might not have heard a struggle, an altercation downstairs, then we need to know about that reason. Do you see? We need to get these questions out of the way and it might as well be now, while it's fresh in your mind.'

There was a rap on the door and a young woman appeared, a police ID on a lanyard around her neck. I had met her earlier – when

I was cautioned and fingerprinted on first arrival – but I couldn't remember her name.

'Boss?' The woman leaned around the door, her tone clipped. 'Can I borrow you for a second?'

Musgrove reached across to the recorder. 'Interview suspended at 15.41.' He hit a button and the red light winked off. 'Excuse me for a moment, Heather. Is there anything I can get you while I'm out? Another cup of tea?'

I shook my head. Musgrove left the small room, heavy door swinging shut against the frame with a percussive bang that made me flinch.

I tried to force myself to focus on practicalities, on the boys, on where we would stay tonight while police forensic teams remained in our house. This afternoon, the boys were with my in-laws, Peter and Colleen, at their house in Bathwick. I would pick them up and take them to my mum's. They would prefer that; they always preferred my mum's house where she would let them eat biscuits and make a mess in the way that small boys did. Rather than the big old house on Cleveland Walk where they were allowed only healthy snacks and football in the garden was forbidden for the sake of the flowerbeds.

It was almost half an hour before Musgrove reappeared, his expression a little darker than before. On the table between us, he placed a clear plastic evidence bag and a brown cardboard folder.

'Interview resumes at 16.04.' He cleared his throat. 'All previous attendees present.'

Sealed inside the bag was a small black plastic phone, smaller than a regular mobile, a basic model with a small screen and a regular keypad. It looked like the kind of phone that had been around when I had been a teenager in the late nineties, when they still had some novelty value.

'Is this your phone, Heather?'

'No. Mine's an iPhone, you took it off me when I came in.'

He tapped the edge of the plastic bag with a thick index finger.

'Not Liam's?'

'He had a Samsung for work and an iPhone for personal stuff.'

'So you've never seen this device before?'

I leaned forward, peered closer at the handset. Smooth black plastic, a small screen, new looking but cheap with it. It looked almost like a toy, a child's phone. I'd not heard of the brand name: Doro.

'No. Never.'

'You're absolutely sure about that?'

'Yes.' I sat back in my chair, an unpleasant tightening in my stomach. 'Why? Whose is it?'

'We believe it's your husband's. His burner phone.' He pushes the evidence bag across the table towards me. 'So you're saying you haven't seen the pictures on here either?'

'What pictures?' I felt a sudden lurch of panic, like a passenger on a platform as my train was starting to leave, hurrying alongside and trying to climb aboard before it picked up too much speed. 'Pictures of who?'

From the folder, he pulled a selection of colour printouts, fanning them out across the desk like a casino dealer with a deck of oversized playing cards. Photographs of a long-haired blonde woman – or women plural, it wasn't immediately obvious – some in lingerie, some semi-naked, all close-up and extremely intimate. All dark or artfully shot, cropped or deliberately blurred so they didn't show the woman's face; all of them looked like selfies.

'Showing Mrs Vernon evidence items numbered JX191 to JX202,' Musgrove said. 'Is this you?'

'What?' I recoiled, frowning. 'No. Of course not. Who is this person?'

'That's what we were hoping you'd be able to tell us.'

I paused, turning a couple of the pictures to see them better. A flash of memory from my last conversation with Liam – the new intern in his office. Could it be?

'There's a junior member of his staff,' I said carefully. 'A young woman, early twenties, blonde. She's an intern.'

'Francesca Walker-Clarke?'

'Yes. I've only met her once but she's—'

'She was the other side of London last night,' Musgrove said. 'At a family gathering in Surrey, with a dozen witnesses.'

I shrugged. 'This is the first time I've seen these pictures.'

'Despite the fact that you sent eleven of them to your phone last night.' He stabbed a thick index finger down onto one of the printouts, which showed the curve of the woman's thighs, the delicate red lace of her suspenders against a nondescript background. A bedroom, maybe, or a bathroom. They looked like the sort of images that might be exchanged by a couple in the first flush of a new relationship. 'Why'd you do that, Heather? So your husband couldn't delete them? Proof that he couldn't deny? For leverage?'

'I didn't send any pictures. There's been some sort of mistake.'

'No mistake. We found them on your phone, sent from your husband's burner. So either he's forwarded them to you in a sudden fit of guilty honesty; or you've found them and want to preserve the proof. So which is it?'

'Neither,' I said again.

'I'm going to ask you again, Heather.' His voice is flat, loaded with menace. 'Have you ever seen your husband's burner phone before?'

'No, never.' I shook my head. 'I swear it.'

'That surprises me,' Musgrove said slowly.

'Why?'

'Because it was found in the master bedroom of your house,' he said, his pale blue eyes on mine. 'Under your pillow.'

18

MONDAY

The train to Bristol Temple Meads is busy with commuters and I stand by the doors all the way, casting a surreptitious eye over everyone in the carriage, people who got on with me at Bath and who come off the train with me. But at Bristol there are hundreds of people, a solid mass of commuters shuffling down the platform together, and it's impossible to look at all of them. If someone *is* following me it would be very difficult to spot them among this crowd.

I get a bus out to Fishponds and find the cafe with twenty minutes to spare, ordering a pot of tea and taking it to a corner table that faces the door and the big front window. The cafe is tired but clean, with plastic-topped tables and a whiteboard menu on the wall in carefully written capitals. It's only after sitting and sipping my tea for ten minutes, watching the door, that I remember I still don't have an up-to-date picture of the man I'm going to meet: the most recent one I can find is from 2010.

But from his article history online I figure that he's late forties to early fifties, educated, cautious, probably lives locally and he'll almost certainly come in alone. I picture a slender, intense, bookish guy with round glasses; I'll know him when I see him.

The cafe is quiet.

I sit and wait, pouring the last cooling dregs from the teapot as I watch the door out to the street. A young mum wrestles a buggy through the door and parks it up by the window, a toddler reclined with her arms thrown back in sleep. A pensioner in a flat cap and raincoat shuffles in and orders a sausage bap to eat while he pores over a crumpled copy of the *Racing Post*.

Half past ten comes and goes.

I double check the location on Google Maps. This is *definitely* the place.

At a quarter to eleven, when Tanner still hasn't shown up, my phone buzzes with another message on Telegram.

Sorry can't meet something came up.

I frown, deflated, and type a reply.

I'm here. I can wait. Or can talk on the phone.

The dots pulse on the screen as he types.

How about same time same place tomorrow?

I type again, pushing down the bubble of irritation.

I'm here. In Bristol. Can meet you anywhere today or talk on the phone.

Today no good – work stuff.

Tanner might have useful information and I need to keep him onside. I sigh and type:

OK. Tomorrow 10.30.

I drain the last of my tea and leave the cafe, heading for the bus stops on Downend Road. While I'm here in the city, there's someone else

I need to speak to. I might as well make use of my visit and I've already found the address on Queen's Square: I can catch him on his lunchbreak.

The day is bright and sunny, the mid-morning air is fresh and my annoyance at being stood up slowly dissipates as I head back out of the pedestrianised area. I decide to get a cab to save time, and take a short cut through the park towards the main road. There is a little play area on my left, slides and swings and climbing frames populated with noisy pre-schoolers charging around. Children seem to be everywhere I look.

I turn away and walk on. The more I think about it, the more Tanner's abrupt change of mind doesn't make sense. *I* had approached *him*, I was surely a tempting prospect for any journalist, the chance to hear my story straight from the horse's mouth. Clearly he thought there were grounds for doubt over my conviction – or at least he had when he wrote that article – so what had changed between last night and this morning?

Maybe he didn't believe I was for real. Or maybe he really *did* have a work emergency.

Back on the road there is another row of shops dominated by a carpet wholesaler, thick rolls stacked up behind a wide pane of glass. As I cross over towards it, the angle of the sun on the glass reflects the view behind me, a row of parked cars, a stand of trees, the fence, the gate into the park—

A guy coming through the gate behind me.

Head down, on his own, hands in his pockets. Angling the same way as me.

Following me?

I feel like I've seen him before, maybe at the train station. Or was he on the bus?

An unpleasant pulse of adrenaline loosens my knees, my stomach, and I quicken my pace, snatching another look at the reflection in the glass as I reach the pavement. My pursuer is bigger than the guy from the library, a little older too, but dressed in the same blandly anonymous way. Dark jeans, sweatshirt, no logo or pattern or identifiable brand anywhere. This one has a beard and a black beanie hat pulled to his eyebrows.

I don't know this part of Bristol well and only have a rough idea of my direction; if I slow down to look at the maps app on my phone he will be on me in a matter of seconds. As my brain floods with more bad news, it occurs to me that no one knows where I am today, or who I'd come to meet. It had been one of Tanner's instructions: *Tell no one where you're going.* Maybe this whole thing had been a set-up. How had I been so stupid? Turning left at the junction, I duck into a side street and break into a run to the end. I'll cut around the side and double back across the park, back the way I came, to throw him off the scent.

I run around a corner to find a chain-link fence. Padlocked.

Shit.

I'm cornered. I haul myself up and over the fence, criss-crossing wire digging into my fingers, arms and shoulders burning with the effort, rolling over the top and dropping down into a loading yard behind the carpet shop. I run over to an alley on the far side, ignoring the shout from a red-faced delivery driver getting out of his van. Keep going. *There.* A patch of green at the end of the alley, the park just in view. I sprint back across the road, threading between parked cars, don't see anyone but if I can get back to the play area where there are people, witnesses, I'll be safe. My lungs are already bursting and I slow to a jog, heading back across the park, when I hear a presence behind me.

Breath, heavy footsteps. A tall shadow falling across mine.

A hand on my arm.

I dodge away and turn, fear flooding my arms and legs, a scream gathering in my throat. Hands curling into fists because suddenly I'm back inside and every prison fight is over in the first five seconds, never mind two people slugging back and forth for ages, that was just cinema crap, in a real fight only one thing mattered: you hit first and made it count. I rear around and cock a fist back at the man, ready to hit and run, ready to—

He takes a step back, both palms up in surrender.

'Whoa!' he says.

'Back off!' My voice is almost a scream.

'Take it easy, Heather.' He keeps his hands up as if he's dealing with a startled animal. 'It's me. Owen.'

19

I notice two things about Owen Tanner straightaway.

First: he's not what I expected. He's younger than me, maybe late thirties, and not the slender bookish type I had imagined but stocky and bearded, more like a rugby player than a deskbound office worker who made his living with words. And second: up close, he's *big*. Bigger than he looked in his reflection. He must be six foot three at least and wide with it, a broad neck and shoulders rounded with muscle.

'Jesus,' I gasp, my fist still raised. 'You scared the shit out of me. What the hell?'

'Sorry, Heather,' he says. His voice is deep, with a flat south London edge. 'I didn't think you were going to run. Didn't mean to scare you, OK?'

'Thought you were too busy to meet today? You texted me, told me you couldn't do it till tomorrow.'

'Had to make sure this was the real deal.' He scans the park, checks over his shoulder. 'That it was really you.'

'Who else would it be?'

He shrugs. 'A random email out of the blue, could have been anyone: Special Branch, MI5, the Chinese, the Russians, the Yanks, take your pick. How was the tea, by the way? They do an excellent full English in Ollie's as well.'

I frown. 'You were watching me back there? In the cafe?'

'Had to be sure you were on your own and you hadn't been followed. Sorry,' he says again. 'This wasn't quite the intro I had planned. Can I buy you a coffee to apologise?'

He gestures towards an outdoor cafe next to the play area and we head towards it. The wash of adrenaline has started to recede, a wave of soft fatigue taking its place.

I study him as we walk. 'How do I even know you are who you claim to be? You don't look much like a *Guardian* journalist.'

He grunts. 'What does a *Guardian* journalist look like then?'

'I don't know.' I gesture vaguely at him, at his size. 'Thinner?'

He pulls out a selection of cards – driver's licence, debit card, library card – all bearing his name. The driver's licence looks genuine enough, although he's clean shaven in the picture. 'The beard is good for messing with facial recognition software and CCTV,' he says, rubbing a palm along his jawline. 'It's the one bit of your appearance that you can change constantly. Makes things a bit harder for them.'

'Harder for whom?'

He doesn't answer my question. 'Did you google the location of the cafe, by the way?'

'Of course.'

He sighs. 'And have you turned off location tracking on your phone?'

'I've only had it a day. Trying to remember how to send an email was tricky enough.'

'Better to be safe – I can do it for you.' He holds out a big hand. 'Do you mind?'

'I do, actually, yes.'

'Oh.' He seems taken aback. 'OK. Suit yourself.'

At the outdoor cafe, he gestures towards an empty wooden picnic table and goes to the counter. I take a seat and watch him as he orders, taking out my phone and snapping a surreptitious picture of him as he stands at the counter. I don't even know why – but I'm still not quite sure about this man, who had watched me, followed me, told me to keep our meeting a secret. It feels better to have something, some record of him.

He returns to our table with two large steaming paper cups and sets one down in front of me. He takes a fistful of sugar sachets from his pocket and proceeds to pour four into his own cup, ripping them open one by one and stirring them vigorously into his tea.

I take a sip from my own cup, the coffee strong and scaldingly hot. 'So you're freelance now?'

'Yeah. Kind of.'

'And this is all off the record, right? You won't quote me, not until I say it's OK?'

'Yup.'

The rest of the cafe is quiet, only one other picnic table occupied by an elderly couple, a white-haired grandfather rolling a pram gently back and forth while his tiny, smiling wife keeps a wary eye on the play area where toddlers run and slide and swing.

'I read your article,' I say carefully. 'The one about questions remaining over my conviction. Thank you. It was an excellent piece.'

'For all the good it did.'

I lower my voice. 'I didn't kill my husband.'

He gives an almost imperceptible nod. 'I know.'

'You do?' Hearing it out loud, from someone else's mouth, is still like a shock of cold water poured over me. 'You believe me?'

'Yes,' he says. 'I do, as it happens.'

'You might be the only one.'

'Wouldn't be the first time.' He takes a sip of his tea, a big hand wrapped around the cup. 'Blew up my career over your case, actually.'

'What?' I say. 'How? What happened?'

He waves a hand, dismissively. 'It's ancient history, I'll tell you later. What matters now is that you're out, and this is the best chance you're ever going to get to clear your name. To get your conviction quashed.'

My blood is suddenly humming with a current of hope I haven't felt in years. I still don't entirely trust this man but I have a hundred questions, crowding and jostling and all trying to get to the front of the queue first.

'So you know who really killed Liam?' I check over my shoulder, lean a little closer to him. 'Do you know what actually happened?'

'Bits of it, yes.' He fixes me with dark brown eyes. 'You were just in the way, that's all. A part of the problem, until you became part of the solution. You were used to create a narrative, a story for the police. But there were still so many holes in the prosecution I was amazed when your appeal fell through. Like, what about this *other woman* who was never found? Is she connected to allegations about corruption in Westminster? And how often do you have a crime of passion, of hot blood, of a spurned spouse, where there's not a multitude of wounds, not a sustained attack carried out in the heat of high passion, but only a single wound? A single, fatal stab wound directly into the heart?'

'I don't know.' I look away. Even after all these years, the horror of Liam's final moments is still raw, a wound of my own that will never heal.

Owen doesn't seem to have noticed. 'Never. Or at least hardly ever. A single wound says *professional*. Not personal. Not passion, not anger. It says deliberate, almost clinical. With a domestic murder you'd almost always have ten, twenty, thirty injuries, defensive injuries, bruising, signs of a struggle. But this—' he taps the rough wooden table with a big finger '—was more like an assassination.'

'The press called me the ice queen.' I remember the tabloid coverage at the time. 'A cold-blooded bitch.'

'That line was fed to me and a few others. Because it fit the facts the police had.'

'Leaks from inside the investigation?'

He shifts in his seat. 'Bits and pieces, yeah.'

'All those negative stories – somebody out there wanted to paint me in the worst possible light, to make me look like this cold, calculating killer. The *black widow.* '

'That line came from a different place, I don't know who. I got a phone call a few hours after the story broke. It was a crazy day, and, like I said, a lot of rumours and theories and leaks were flying around, it was—'

'A phone call from another police contact?'

'No.'

It's the answer to a question I had asked myself over and over again in the run-up to the trial. Only a small piece of the puzzle, but a piece nonetheless: proof that there might be much more to find. 'Who was it then? Man? Woman?'

'A bloke. But it was a long time ago, Heather.'

'Could we find him? Could we trace that caller, do you think?'

It's the first time I've used the word *we* since we sat down, an implication that we would work together, that we have a common interest in finding the truth. But if Tanner is surprised, he doesn't show it.

'Truthfully? Tracing the caller now would be a tough job.' He shrugs. 'And it could have just been someone with a grudge. Maybe some work colleague you'd pissed off years ago? An old flame? A random internet troll with an agenda?'

I study him for a moment.

'But you don't believe that, do you?'

'No,' he says carefully. 'I think whoever made that call wanted to stack the deck against you as quickly as possible.'

'What about the blonde woman, in the pictures on Liam's burner phone? If she *was* having an affair with him, like they said, she might have killed him out of jealousy? Then she would have wanted to steer the attention towards me.'

He shakes his head, looks away for a moment.

'I don't think she was who she was made out to be in court, during the case.'

'What do you mean?'

'And I think there was a good reason why the police couldn't track her down ten years ago, or any time since. The same reason why finding her now would be almost impossible.'

'Why?'

'Because I think she was probably dead within a few hours of your husband being killed.'

20

His words fall like a hammer blow striking the table between us. Even after so many sleepless nights in prison, lying awake staring into the dark and constructing a thousand scenarios of what might have happened, it had never once occurred to me that the blonde woman might be something other than a perpetrator of this crime, a part of it. Perhaps a *cause* of it. It had never occurred to me that she might be a victim too.

'*What?*'

'It's entirely possible that she was used as much as you were, to create this false narrative for the police.'

'I . . . don't understand. So she wasn't his lover after all?'

'Not sure either way, to be honest. My gut instinct is that her role was more complicated than we think, but ultimately she was just more collateral damage, like you. Because why leave a living witness who might contradict some of the narrative that's been created? Why leave that loose end, take that risk? Because if you could find her, you could start to unpick the whole thing. And yet she wasn't found, despite one of the most exhaustive police searches of recent years. Contrary to popular belief, it's incredibly hard to just disappear for that long, and never make a mistake, never be found. Statistically, it's *much* more likely she's dead.'

My mind is spinning. 'You're talking about it like it was planned, an organised conspiracy to mislead the police and public and the jury and everyone else. Who could do all that, who could put it together, who could carry it out?'

'*Now* we're getting to the real question.' He taps the wooden tabletop with a big palm. '*Cui bono?*'

I frown. 'My Latin is a little rusty.'

'Lucius Cassius?' He raises his eyebrows. '*Cui bono* means *Who benefits?* As in, who benefits from your husband's death.'

The idea strikes me as obscene, that someone could have actually gained from Liam's murder, that any benefit could have been derived from my sons losing their father. But if Tanner registers my discomfort, he doesn't show it.

'Financially?' I say.

'In any way at all.'

'I just . . . I always assumed that it was to do with her, this blonde woman. That she did it. She was the one, perhaps because she was obsessed and maybe Liam was trying to be diplomatic with her, trying to treat her with kid gloves but she wouldn't leave him alone. And so when he got tough with her, told her enough was enough, she flipped.'

I think about the entries in Liam's diary, about *AY* and *N*, a meeting and a call that had never taken place. But I don't know if I can trust this man with that information yet.

Tanner seems not to notice my hesitation, his eyes shining as he gets into his stride.

'But if not her,' he says, 'then who? When I'm building a story I try to forget everything I've been told, ignore all the agendas and start from scratch. Build it from the ground up, only with facts, nothing else. And always keep in mind that the purest definition of news is telling a story that someone, somewhere, doesn't want you to tell.'

'Is that Lucius Cassius too?'

He shakes his head. 'Lord Northcliffe.'

He describes his unsuccessful attempts to reignite interest in my case; various threats made by parties unknown trying to warn him off. He tells me about Christine Lai, Liam's constituency office manager, and an article that he had written about her that had landed him in the libel courts – a case he had lost and that had ruined him professionally, financially and personally. All traces of that story had been expunged from the internet by court order – all except one password-protected page on his blog, a link he emails to me and tells me to read.

'Even by emailing the link to you, technically I'm breaching the terms of the court order so please don't share it any more widely. But there's some stuff in there you need to know.'

In return, I tell him what little I've learned myself in the last three days. He's particularly interested in the locker tucked away at Total Storage, and we arrange to meet there tomorrow to go over the contents in the search for a new lead. By the time I'm finished, the dregs of my coffee are cold and the weather is turning cooler too, a strong wind whipping across the park.

'If we pool resources,' he says, 'we can come at this story from a whole different direction, Heather.'

'It's not a story,' I say, trying to keep my voice level. 'It's my life. My family. Justice for my husband.'

'I know.' The skin of his cheeks reddens above his beard. 'I'm sorry, I know. I didn't mean it like that.' He fiddles with his empty cup, finally draining the last of it and setting it down at the end of the table. 'Listen, if we're going to do this, there's something else I need to ask you first.'

There's something new in his tone, his baritone dropping even deeper.

'OK,' I say.

'I need to know how far you're prepared to go. To find his killer.'

'As far as we have to, as far as it takes.'

'Even if it means bending a few rules?'

I remember the warning from my probation officer, the breaches that would send me straight back to jail to serve the rest of my sentence. *Any arrest and/or charge in relation to a criminal matter.*

'I've got to be careful, Owen. I can't afford to get caught.'

'Understood,' he says. 'And you know we could find out things about your husband that you might not like? Things that you'd rather not hear?'

I look down at my left hand, twisting the platinum wedding band I put back on my finger two days ago and still haven't got used to. It turns easily, the metal loose against my skin. *This is the only way, the only road. My only way back.*

'Yes,' I say. 'As long as it's the truth. Whatever the truth might be.'

He nods, as if I've passed some test, and launches into a brief explanation of mobile phone security and how to fly under the radar of what he calls the 'surveillance state'. He tells me to buy a cheap pay-as-you-go burner phone and use that number only if I need to call him, and the Telegram app for messages. I should assume that the phone I bought yesterday has already been compromised, he says, and that any calls, text messages, emails or voicemails might be read or listened to by what he calls 'bad actors'.

'Compromised by who?' I ask, looking over my shoulder without even realising I'm doing it. The idea that someone might be spying on me already, within days of my release from prison, sends a pulse of unease through my stomach. Perhaps I'm already out of my depth and just don't know it yet.

'By the people who set you up ten years ago.' He says it as if it's the most obvious thing in the world, leaning forward on the table and lacing his fingers together. 'One more thing you need to know. After you were convicted and I was digging into your case, certain things . . . happened. To me.'

'Like what?'

'I was followed, on and off, for a few months,' he says. 'So was my ex-wife. Had tracking devices put on my car. Numerous attempts to hack my email, my laptop, mess with me at work.'

I tell him about the guy in the library yesterday, the one who'd seemed to be watching me. He nods grimly.

'And there were a couple of times,' he says, 'when they went a bit further than that, trying to warn me off.'

'You were threatened?'

He turns his head, points to a faded scar behind his ear, another curving into his hairline. Lifts his lip to reveal a chipped front tooth.

'They fractured a couple of my ribs, too,' he says. 'The point is, I'm big and ugly enough to look after myself, but if we start digging all of this up again and they come after you . . .'

'Nine years in jail, Owen,' I say to him. 'I've learned to have eyes in the back of my head.'

'I'm not doubting that for a second, but you can't fight these people, Heather. The guys that came after me were both twice your size and I only got away because I got lucky. I mean it: they're serious.'

'So am I.'

He frowns, as if I'm not listening to him.

'Whoever did this to your husband,' he says quietly, 'whoever came after me, they'll do it again. You need to be careful, do you understand me?' He lays his big hand on my forearm. 'You need to watch your back.'

21

I catch a city-bound bus and sit on the back row, mulling over what I had learned as the double-decker winds its way through Mayfield Park and Speedwell. A young mother sits in front of me, a child opposite her in a yellow waterproof and wellington boots. The little girl is perhaps four or five years old and has strawberry-blonde hair tied in neat bunches. I give her a smile but she just frowns back at me before putting her thumb in her mouth and clambering up onto her mother's lap.

I'm still not quite sure what to make of Tanner. He had clearly invested a huge amount of time and effort into investigating my case and my conviction, even if he did come across as borderline paranoid and distrustful of almost everyone. Perhaps that was inevitable when you had worked hard to expose the truth but ended up being sued for libel instead, ridiculed, reviled and bankrupted.

The meeting has stirred up more thoughts that I have tried to keep locked away for the last few years. The knowledge that someone had stood over me with a knife that night, could have killed me just as easily as they killed Liam. A single thrust to the heart. For that matter they could have killed all four of us, the boys included. The thought makes me shudder. But the killer hadn't done that. Why?

The answer seems as obvious now as it had done on the day I was charged: to provide a fall guy. A patsy. A convenient suspect to take the blame. A double murder, husband and wife, would throw it wide open in terms of potential suspects. It would turn into a national manhunt. On the other hand a domestic murder – one partner kills the other – was absolutely part of the regular grim routine for every police force in the country. Granted, a woman was the victim in the vast and overwhelming majority of cases, but it was still within the realm of policing experience. It was what they *expected*: a suspect known to the victim, because they were a current or former partner.

The bus is not even half-full but I study each of my fellow passengers in turn, the journalist's warning still ringing in my ears. *Watch your back*. Only when I'm satisfied that none of them seem to be a threat do I take out my phone and click on the link he sent me, to the news story that landed him in court. It had been a follow-up to his first article casting doubt on my conviction, intended to be part of a series, an investigation that would win him a British Press Award. Instead, it had ruined him. The story that had been taken down by order of a judge and now only existed in one place – on a strictly restricted page of his website. I enter the password and the text and headline appear, a date from 2017.

CAMPAIGN FUNDING CONCERNS LINKED TO MURDERED MP

By Owen Tanner

A close colleague of murdered MP Liam Vernon is linked to a foreign firm that was at the centre of corruption allegations, the Guardian *can reveal.*

Christine Lai, Mr Vernon's constituency manager, is believed to have received a six-figure sum funnelled through a shell company registered offshore in exchange for confidential information.

Serious questions remain over her connection to a US company thought to be at the centre of 'cash for access' allegations in Parliament.

Mr Vernon, the popular MP for Bath, was found dead at his home in July 2013. He was thirty-six. His wife, Heather Vernon, was convicted of his murder at Bristol Crown Court and sentenced to eighteen years imprisonment in April 2014.

The total of the sums said to have been received by Ms Lai have not been disclosed but are believed to be in the low six-figure range, channelled through an anonymous shell company registered in the Cayman Islands. Efforts to trace ownership of the shell company have so far been hampered by labyrinthine legal and financial structures spanning three continents.

An investigation by this newspaper has also revealed serious concerns over key aspects of the police case that led to the conviction of Heather Vernon.

A source close to the investigation said . . .

I come out of the story and back to his main website, where a series of blog pieces document his long legal battle and the devastating effect of losing the case. He had effectively been a freelancer, and had ended up having to shoulder the cost – and the risk – on his own. Losing his house as a result. Losing his job. Losing his reputation and his livelihood.

They had shut the story down with ruthless efficiency. They had shut *him* down.

I knew that Owen had his own reasons for talking to me: finding out the truth about Liam could get him his career back. We were both looking for redemption, one way or another.

The bus wheezes to a stop on Union Street and the engine shudders into silence. I wait for everyone else to get off before following them out and turning right onto Wine Street, heading south and west. There are new shops I don't recognise, new names, the old ones seeming to have disappeared while I've been away. Familiar facades have moved or vanished, their places taken by newcomers.

There are street cafes crowded with people enjoying a Monday lunchtime drink with colleagues, autumn sunshine providing a last gasp of summer. I cross Baldwin Street and pass the Old Vic, then cut down a side street towards the leafy green space of Queen Square, rows of handsome four-storey Georgian townhouses converted into smart city offices.

There was one person who had never spoken to me about Liam, had never given evidence in court, never replied to the dozen letters I wrote to him while I was in Eastwood Park.

One person who had known him almost as well as I had.

Sunday, 14 July, 2013

11.16 a.m., Bath Police Station

The night had felt as if it was never going to end: a cycle of star-ing up into the darkness beneath a threadbare blanket, of jangling exhaustion that made sleep almost impossible, shouted obscenities from other prisoners, a pervasive stench of drains and the clockwork regularity of footsteps outside the locked steel door of my cell. I had entered some parallel universe in which everything was turned on its head and it was all my fault, everything good in my life had been taken away and I wanted more than anything to step back through the looking glass into my old life.

In the morning I found myself back in an interview room with DI Musgrove and his colleague DS Gilbert, a sharp-faced woman in her early thirties, dark hair pulled back severely from her forehead in a tight ponytail. Dark shadows lay below her eyes; Musgrove's own face was grey and speckled with salt-and-pepper stubble. He smelled of coffee and sweat, the crisp white shirt he'd worn yesterday now rumpled and creased.

'OK, Heather,' he said without preamble. 'Let's go back to the burner phone. The one found under your pillow. I'm wondering if you've remembered anything overnight, now you've had a chance to think about it?'

I shake my head, saying nothing.

He opened his file and extracted a sheet, turning it around for me to see, a computer printout with one number highlighted in yellow.

Dozens of calls spread over the last two weeks, both outgoing and incoming, all to and from one single number.

'There's just one number in the call history, another mobile. Do you recognise it?'

I frowned, trying to make sense of it. 'I don't know . . . who that is.'

'We've cross-referenced it with all the contacts in his regular mobile, his work mobile, his office manager's list, and your phone too. No matches. All very mysterious, don't you think?'

'I'm sure there's an explanation.'

He sighed in frustration. 'Oh, and by the way, this phone, that you've supposedly never seen before? We found your fingerprints on the back of the case. Index and middle fingers of your left hand.'

My forehead began to pound, a steady drumbeat thrumming just above my eyes.

'That's not . . .' *The words tangled in my mouth.* 'The person who was in our house, who put this under my pillow. They must have somehow put my fingerprint on the phone . . . touched my hand against it when I was sleeping.'

It sounded ridiculous, even as I was saying it.

Musgrove was shaking his head in a short, exasperated motion as if to say, Not good enough.

'You see, here's the thing, Heather. We've had forensic teams in and out of your house for the last twenty-four hours now, going over every inch. There's no sign of forced entry. No keys missing, no doors or windows unlocked or damaged, no physical evidence of locks being tampered with or your alarm being disabled. No suggestion from your neighbours that you had any visitors last night, no evidence of a third party at all, no sign of anyone else being in the house apart from you and your husband. And your boys.'

'Somebody must have put the phone there.'

The detective let my words hang there for a long moment.

'How about we talk about your husband's iPhone for a minute? His regular phone.' *He pulled out another sheet of paper from his green file and slid it across the table: black text on white, a few short paragraphs in a familiar format. 'Thank you for giving us the passcode. This is a printout of an unsent email we found in his drafts folder.'*

I studied the message. It was addressed to me, the subject line left blank.

'What is this?'

'From what our digital guys can gather so far,' Musgrove said, tapping the sheet with his index finger, 'the message was first created five days ago and has been edited and re-saved multiple times since then. But it was never sent; hence why they found it in the drafts folder. Have a look and see what you make of it.'

I scan the text quickly, a chill creeping over my skin as I read.

Heather,

I need to write this down first so I get it right. Just the facts about what I've done. I've been writing this and deleting it, rewriting, deleting, just trying to get the words straight in my head. Trying to find the courage to actually tell you face to face.

The truth is that I have done something incredibly stupid, something I will regret for a very long time. Maybe for the rest of my life. My main concern is for you and the boys and what it might mean for us as a family. I've been a coward up until now. And worse. I've betrayed everything, I've let you down, I've let our sons down and that is something I never wanted to do. I need to tell the truth. I'm not excusing what I've done, or asking for you to understand, but I hope one day you will be able to forgive me.

    L

I read it twice, feeling all the eyes in the room on me. Heat burning in my cheeks as words and phrases land like blows.

Musgrove sits back, studying me. 'Have you seen this before, Heather?'

'No.' My eyes were still fixed to the words on the page. 'Never.'

'He didn't talk to you about this on Friday night?'

'No.'

'He didn't hint at what he'd done, this secret he was going to tell you?'

I shake my head, a hard lump forming in my throat. 'No.'

'Because it looks to me as if he's rehearsing what he's going to say, getting himself ready to tell you everything. What do you think?'

I push the sheet back across the table to him, images flashing in my head of my last conversation with Liam. The phone call, the woman's voice, the lie that had sparked our last argument. Our last words to each other.

'He didn't say anything like this.'

Instead of returning the sheet of paper to the green folder, Musgrove leaves it between us on the desk.

'What do you think it is?'

'I've already told you,' I said quietly. 'I don't know.'

'I think it's pretty obvious, isn't it? It looks to me an awful lot like an admission of guilt.' He stabbed his index finger into the sheet again. 'A confession.'

22

The reception area of Beckett, Weaver & Fox is light and airy, an echoing glass atrium with a high ceiling and a welcoming square of leather armchairs around a low table in the corner. But there is nothing welcoming about the blank-faced receptionist, dark auburn hair piled on top of her head in a complicated updo.

'Mr Chopra is not available unless you have an appointment.'

Not *this* again.

'I know he'll want to see me.'

'As I said, he's *extremely* busy today and doesn't have any time in his diary.'

'Look, I'm an old friend of his, we—'

'Mr Chopra was *quite clear* that he does not wish to see you today or at any other time.' There is a quiver of anger in her chin. 'Now, madam, I'm afraid I'm going to have to ask you to leave.'

'Five minutes,' I say, 'that's all I'm asking.'

She picks up her phone and I can hear her summoning security as I turn and walk away, shaking my head.

On the way out there is a corporate family tree of faces on the wall, smart head-and-shoulders shots of all the lawyers in the company in their respective divisions. I study the images, photoshopped smooth and perfect, until I find him. *Nishan Chopra, Commercial Division*. His dark brown hair is cropped shorter and he's carrying a little more weight in his face than when I last saw him a decade ago.

He had always looked younger than his years. Right back to our first day at university, when he'd been the skinny intense kid who sat next to me in Medieval Britain 400–1200 AD.

I head out through the sliding glass doors and back into the weak September sunshine. The tree-lined street that is home to Beckett, Weaver & Fox overlooks an elegant Regency garden, a square of green in the middle of the city bordered with tall plane trees, leaves already turning golden brown for autumn. Eight straight paths lead into the centre of the square, converging on the bronze statue of some long-dead king on horseback.

I find a bench facing the building and settle down to wait. After forty minutes, when he's still not emerged for lunch, I dig out the business card I found in the storage locker and dial his direct line. There is a momentary flutter of silence when I give him my name, the sound of an office door being hurriedly shut.

'What are you doing, calling me?'

'I'm OK, thanks Nish,' I say. 'How are you?'

'I'm hanging up. Don't call me again.'

'Please, Nish.' There is a moment of silence on the other end of the line, and I dive into it. 'I need to talk to you about Liam, about the weekend it happened.'

'What the *hell*, Heather? This is my office, I've got colleagues upstairs, clients coming in, my boss on the top floor!' His voice is hushed, horrified, as if he's just witnessed an accident and is trying to process what he's seen. Or just received a call from the person convicted of killing his best friend.

'I could camp out in reception, if you prefer?' I squint at the Georgian townhouse through the trees, as if I might be able to see him through a window. 'Make a proper scene for your colleagues to see? Or we could just have a conversation now, and then I'll be gone.'

'I'm hanging up,' he hisses. 'This is crazy.'

'Please,' I say again. 'As a friend. Five minutes, that's all I'm asking. Then you'll never hear from me again.'

He huffs out a breath. 'I'll give you two,' he says. 'What do you want?'

'If you'd read my letters, you'd have a good idea. Why did you never reply?'

'Do you even need to ask?'

'I didn't do it, Nish. I'm not guilty.'

'If you've called just to tell me that, you're wasting your—'

'And I need to find out who did, to have any chance of seeing my children again,' I say. 'Your godsons. You understand that, don't you? Imagine if you could never see Meera again. Think about what that would be like – paying that price for someone else's crime.'

Mention of his daughter seems to give him pause, but only for a moment.

'Not someone else's crime, Heather. *Your* crime.'

'Don't pretend you didn't have doubts, you know I couldn't have done it.'

'What I think now is irrelevant,' he says tersely. 'You were convicted by a jury of your peers. Your appeal was thrown out. The best thing you can do now is move on, move forward with your life.'

'That's just it, I *can't* move on. Don't you care about catching the person who actually did it? The one who's actually responsible?'

'Raking it all up again now is the last thing those boys need.'

I try to recall the friendly guy I had shared a student house with in second and third year, who'd pulled all-nighters with me in the library before exams, who'd been there for countless nights out at the students' union. Who had introduced me to his schoolfriend Liam Vernon and been Liam's best man at our wedding. I wonder where that man has gone.

'You were his best mate, Nish,' I say quietly. 'You knew him better than anyone.'

He sighs, some of the fight seeming to go out of him. 'Maybe.'

'I need to ask you about something I found in his diary.'

'From ten years ago?' he says dismissively. 'Sounds like you're clutching at straws. I can barely remember what I was doing—'

'The weekend he died, Liam was planning to call you on Sunday night, wasn't he?'

I say it as if it's fact; as if I know it for sure. Rather than guess-work inspired by a few scribbled letters in an old diary. But there is something almost palpable in the silence that follows, and I know straightaway that I've guessed correctly.

'What?'

'That weekend, on the Sunday evening, he was going to call you at eight o'clock. He'd even put a reminder in his diary.'

'So?'

'Seems a bit weird that it was in his diary, as if he'd scheduled it and didn't want to forget. You were his best mate, why would he do that? Why not just call you, if he wanted to?'

Nish considers this for a moment, another long stretch of silence between us.

'We hadn't spoken properly for a while, we were both so busy. Just messaging back and forth, you know? Maybe it was on his mind to have a good catch-up.'

'Did you tell the police?'

He nods. 'Yeah, I told them he wanted to chat on Sunday night, but I didn't know what about. There wasn't really much to tell, or anything for them to follow up.'

'You're sure he didn't give you a clue what it was about?' I close my eyes. '*Please*, Nish. I know you're loyal to his memory, to the man he was. But I need the truth now, whatever it is. It might be important. I've spent so many years trying to figure out what was going on with him in those last few weeks, why he was so distant.'

'He . . . had messaged me earlier in the week, I think. He'd been elusive, we'd been missing each other's calls and hadn't had a proper chat in a few weeks, like I said. I thought he just wanted a catch-up.' His tone softens slightly. 'Look, it's a long time ago, right? That's all I can remember.'

'That's it? You're sure?'

'Something was definitely on his mind but I've always assumed it was extra work to do with the select committee.'

I let out a sigh of frustration. 'What about the initials AY? Do you know who, or what, that is?'

He repeats the letters to himself, seeming to give it genuine thought. But eventually grunts a negative.

I explain the mention of AY in Liam's diary, a meeting or *something* scheduled for Monday morning that had never taken place. Twelve hours after a catch-up with his best friend that had likewise never happened. Could there be a connection between the two? A link with the message he had drafted to me and never sent? To the anonymous blonde on his burner phone? To hushed-up allegations about corruption in Parliament?

He sighs, his tone hardening as if he's just made a connection. 'Oh God, you haven't been talking to Owen Tanner, have you? Was he wearing his tinfoil hat, telling you the Chinese were after him? The Americans? Or was it the Martians this time?'

'I just want the truth, Nish.'

'The truth is never as interesting as you want it to be, in my experience.'

'You still didn't answer my question.'

'And your two minutes is up. You want my advice? You have to accept what you did before you can learn to get past it. Otherwise you're going to spend your whole life going over and over it, again and again, instead of accepting responsibility. Everyone else has moved on – it's time for you to do that too. Don't contact me again.'

He hangs up without waiting for a reply.

23

The letter is waiting for me when I return to the probation hostel.

I'm jumpy and strung out again by the time I make it back there, after being recognised at Bristol Temple Meads as I waited for the train back to Bath. Out of the corner of my eye I'd become aware of a couple, a man and woman dressed for the office, holding their phones up in my direction. On instinct I had turned to look – instantly regretting it – before turning in the opposite direction and heading further down the platform, digging the baseball cap out of my bag and trying to disappear into the crowd.

It's almost a relief to get back to the hostel, the one place where I don't feel judged. The manager calls me over as I walk past his little office, handing me an official-looking white A4 envelope bearing my typewritten name and address on the label, *STRICTLY PRIVATE & CONFIDENTIAL* in heavy red print across the bottom. Another sticker indicating *guaranteed delivery* and *signature required*. I take the envelope up to my room. Jodie is not there but one of the other women is sleeping on her bed at the end of the row, snoring gently even though it's mid-afternoon.

I tear open the envelope and pull out several thick, heavy sheets of typewritten paper, my name at the top with the hostel details beneath it. So someone other than HM Prison and Probation Service knew I was here. The letterhead is from a Bath legal firm with an expensive Great Pulteney Street address, a name on the covering letter that I recognise. I scan the text with a dull ache in my chest, phrases and sentences burning themselves into my brain.

Acting on behalf of our clients Mr and Mrs Peter Vernon . . .

Further to your conviction, sentencing and subsequent release on parole . . .

In the interests of the family and the deceased's two children in particular . . .

We have been authorised to make you an offer . . .

Help with accommodation, arranged in Wick . . .

A financial offer to aid with rehabilitation . . .

Plus ongoing assistance to secure a new passport with a view to permanent relocation overseas after completion of your parole . . .

Subject to your signed agreement to specific terms listed below . . .

All communication to be handled through our office . . .

A one-time offer valid for forty-eight hours from date of receipt . . .

A section at the foot of the page has been left blank for my signature and the date. My father-in-law's signature already beside it, slashes of sharply angled black ink.

I read the letter again, running through the twenty-three specific terms: the expensive London solicitors had been very thorough. They had thought of everything. On my phone, Google Maps confirms what I had already suspected: the place referred to in the letter is not the Wick just down the coast from Bristol, but Wick in Caithness – near the northernmost tip of Scotland. Only a few miles from John O'Groats.

Basically as far away from Bath as it was possible to get, within the UK.

I feel the swell of jagged pain against my ribcage, pushing its way up into my throat as if I'm being gripped by invisible hands, squeezing all the air out of my body. Squeezing tighter and tighter until there is nothing left to keep me alive. As if every trace of my life, everything I've been, every link to my last remaining family, is about to be extinguished.

I shove the letter back into its envelope and head back out into the afternoon drizzle.

My parents-in-law still live in the same house in Bathwick, an impressive three-storey Georgian pile that has been in the family for several generations. I sit in the taxi for a moment, aware of what has changed – very little – and what has stayed the same. The handsome frontage lined with large windows and finished in creamy Bath stone. A line of beech trees screening it from the mansion next door. Peter's Jaguar, reversed neatly into the open double garage beside his wife's more practical Audi estate.

I can picture the spacious lobby, coats on hooks and a spray of umbrellas in a tall brass holder, shoes lined up in a rack. Trainers, school shoes, rugby boots that belong to my sons. A memory returns to me: of standing here on this very doorstep half a lifetime ago, not long after Liam and I had started going out. The first time I had met his parents, invited to their house for Saturday brunch, ringing the ornate brass doorbell as butterflies danced in my stomach and Liam's big hand enfolded mine.

As I watch, the front door swings open and I find myself looking at Peter Vernon. He appears to have aged twenty years in the last ten; maybe both of us have. His face is grooved with new lines, his salt-and-pepper hair turned completely white and thinning back from his forehead. He goes to his car, fetches something from the driver's side before he turns to the street, his gaze seeming to fix on my taxi as it idles by the pavement. He stares for a moment, eyes narrowing, almost as if he's waiting for something to happen. Then he turns and disappears back inside the house.

I pay the driver and open the door of the cab, ready to march up the gravel drive and tell Peter Vernon I will never accept his blood money. My pulse is racing, thrumming in my ears, ready to face my father-in-law for the first time in ten years, since that last day in court when he had looked at me with such burning hatred—

I stop, with one foot already on the pavement.

Wait. Think.

Every instinct I had was telling me to walk up to the house, to hammer on the door and make it clear that I wasn't going anywhere. To stake my claim on the boys' lives, however marginal.

But it's exactly what they'd *expect* me to do. What Peter Vernon had been waiting for me to do.

And it was expressly forbidden under the terms of my licence.

Any contact with any family members related to the victim.

I swing my leg back into the taxi and pull the door closed again. Hand the driver another ten-pound note.

'Actually,' I say to him, 'could we just wait here for five minutes? I need to make a phone call.'

The driver, a taciturn young guy with a few days' ginger stubble, gives a grunt of approval as he accepts the cash and pulls out his mobile.

I take out my own phone and look for the name and number on the letter. Michael Hammond has been Peter's legal counsel for decades, I've even met him a handful of times at company events and launches. I'm pretty sure he even came to our wedding reception at Dormers. He picks up after the fourth ring and I introduce myself.

'Yes?' There is no familiarity in his tone, no hint that we know each other at all when I introduce myself. It's as if he's talking to a stranger. 'Mr Vernon has authorised me to act on his behalf in this matter. Can I help you?'

I glance at the white envelope on the seat beside me.

'My answer is no.'

'In that case, I suggest you reconsider. It's a very generous offer, in the circumstances.'

'I don't agree and I'm not going to sign. Not today, not ever.'

He sighs. 'That is ... regrettable. It's a chance to start again, to start fresh, where no one knows you. Where you won't have to hide.'

'In the northernmost tip of Scotland, six hundred miles away from my children.'

'It's a very beautiful part of the world. You could do a lot worse.'

'My home is here.'

'Not anymore. And don't pretend that lingering around here is to anyone's benefit other than your own. You're just stirring it all up again and it's the *last* thing those boys need.' I can hear a shuffling of papers at his end of the line. 'Mr and Mrs Vernon are willing to help you relocate, to start afresh. It's the best thing for all concerned, for them and for you.'

I shake my head. 'Ceasing all contact with my sons and living hundreds of miles away? I can't do it. I *won't* do it.'

'You have no legal right to see them in any case,' he says. 'They've moved on. They don't remember you – you're in the past for them.'

The lawyer's smooth tone is a weird echo of my father-in-law, his manner, his figures of speech. Maybe that's why they got on so well. Liam's dad has always been like this too: measured, analytical, lawyerly, gauging and judging a situation and how he and his family can best emerge from it. A firmly established member of the upper echelon in this part of the world, a man who had taken considerable inherited wealth and multiplied it several times over with his own company diversifying into telecoms and green energy. The confidence of wealth and status, of connections in the city and beyond.

'What happened to Liam ...' The words catch in my throat. The same words I had written so many times from prison, the letters to Peter and Colleen that had never been answered. 'It destroyed me. But I'm innocent. It's only the thought of the boys that's kept me going.'

'Every time you deny it,' he says, his voice hardening, 'you make it worse for his parents. You tear open the same wound again, make it impossible for their son to rest in peace. Do you understand that?'

'It's the truth. I didn't do it. And I'm going to get my life back.'

'You think you deserve that, do you? You think you should get your sons back too? It's because of you that Mr and Mrs Vernon will never see *their* son again. You certainly don't deserve a second chance like the one in that letter, but they think it'll be worth it if they never have to see *you* again.'

'I loved my husband,' I say. 'And I'm going to get justice for him, for the whole family.'

There is a long silence on the other end of the line before Hammond speaks again.

'The offer is valid for forty-eight hours, I suggest you take another look in the meantime. Make the right decision for Theo's sake, for Finn's sake.'

As he ends the call, a sharp tap on the window makes me jerk in my seat. I turn and buzz the window down to see my sister-in-law standing beside the taxi, a deep frown of recognition dawning on her face.

'Heather?'

Seeing her for the first time in a decade – this woman who had been my friend, my confidante, my bridesmaid all those years ago – steals the words from my throat. There are a million things I want to say but all of them are out of reach.

'Amy.' My throat is suddenly dry.

'What are you *doing* here?' she says, arms crossed tightly over her chest. She's dressed in jeans and a white sweater, dark hair loose to her shoulders, the same chestnut brown as her brother's. The years have taken their toll but she's still an attractive woman, with high cheekbones and kind, soulful eyes.

'I was . . .' I indicate the sheaf of white paper on the seat beside me. 'Talking to your father's head of legal. About the letter.'

Her frown deepens, as if a decade of grief and pain and loss is settling there.

'What letter?'

'The offer.' I hand her the papers through the open window and she studies the text, something passing across her face that I can't identify.

'You got this today?'

'By courier,' I say. 'You didn't know about it?'

She shakes her head, handing the letter back to me through the taxi window.

'And I take it you said no?'

'I did.'

'I could've told Dad you'd say that,' she says. 'Saved him the trouble.'

'Amy, can I—'

'You should go, before he comes out of the house again. You shouldn't be here.'

'I need to talk to you.'

'He's never going to forgive, you know. It's not in his nature.' She crosses her arms again. 'I don't think I can, either.'

I open the door and climb out of the taxi so we can talk face to face. 'I'm not asking for forgiveness. Just for you to hear what I've got to say.'

'What makes you think I want to talk to you?'

'*Please*,' I say, 'just ten minutes. There are things you need to know.'

'Don't think that's such a good idea in the—'

'He's still out there, Amy. Still walking around free. Whether you want to accept it or not, I'm *telling* you that your brother's killer got away with it. He was never punished, never had to answer for what he did to your family. And mine.'

My sister-in-law is already shaking her head but I cut her off.

'If I'm wrong, what have you got to lose? I'm already convicted of the crime so nothing will change. But if I'm right – and I think deep down you might have always had a doubt, otherwise you wouldn't be out here talking to me now – then we can finally get justice for Liam. Finally let him rest in peace.'

She glances towards the house, but her expression has softened a little.

'All right,' she says finally, quietly, as if worried about being overheard. 'But not here.'

Besides Liam, she had always been the member of the Vernon family to whom I felt closest, and there is a little lift in my stomach at her words. It is the faintest glimmer of hope, but it is there nonetheless.

'Thank you, Amy.'

'Where?'

I think for a moment, dredging memories until I hit on a neutral venue, a place nearby that we have in common.

'Remember that place in Alexandra Park, where we used to take the boys when they were little?' I open the door of the taxi. 'Tomorrow morning, nine o'clock. I'll look out for you.'

24

The house on Maitland Street is just as I remembered it. A semi-detached, double-fronted Edwardian with big windows faced in white. The same small black garden gate at the front, same cherry tree on the left, same purple wisteria climbing the side of the house on the right. Even the front door is the same fire engine red that I remember. It had been a place of so much joy – where I'd brought both the boys back from the hospital as newborns; where Theo and Finn had spent their first birthdays, first Christmases; where they'd taken their first steps, uttered their first words. A place of tragedy too, of unimaginable heartbreak, the place where Liam's life had been taken and mine had been shattered forever. Where our boys had lost both their parents in one terrible night.

The last time I'd been here there were strangers in the house who had started to arrive as soon as I had made that first panicked 999 call, who had arrived all day and tramped through the hallway, the kitchen, going up and down the stairs. Scenes-of-crime people pulling on their white boiler suits on the drive, filing in with bags and cameras and lights and all kinds of equipment. Our home invaded, our private space violated, not once but twice. First by a silent intruder in the night, and now – as if the nature of Liam's death had suddenly turned the house into public property – to be photographed and swabbed and picked over by anonymous strangers.

A VW people carrier pulls into the drive as I watch, disgorging three chattering teenage girls who are followed into the house by a dark-haired woman in a smart raincoat. As she's closing the front door she catches sight of me across the street and pauses, eyes narrowing as if to say, *I see you, and you don't belong here,* before pushing the door fully shut.

On the way back into the city I stop at a 24-hour garage and follow Tanner's advice, buying a cheap pay-as-you-go mobile with twenty pounds worth of credit and stashing it in the bottom of my backpack. I buy a small notebook too, conscious of his instruction to keep things out of the digital domain if at all possible. I walk with the hood of my sweatshirt pulled up over the baseball cap, stealing glances into restaurant windows where families eat and drink together, talking and laughing and enjoying a meal out on a Monday night. I haven't eaten since breakfast and hunger gnaws at my stomach, but the idea of sitting down alone in one of these places with a dozen pairs of eyes on me is impossible, unthinkable.

There is a volunteer food kitchen at the Methodist church hall on Nelson Place – free meals every Monday, Wednesday and Friday at 6 p.m., according to Jodie – and I head there instead.

It's the tail end of dinner by the time I arrive but the place is still busy, full of low chatter and the fug of warm bodies, long tables lined with people of every age, prematurely old men bundled up in heavy coats, skinny boys barely out of their teens, women with young children and others closer to my own age, alone and watchful as they eat. Jodie had suggested we meet here for dinner but there's no sign of her. I get a few stares from people as I wait in line at the serving hatch, a few who give me that double-take I've started to notice more and more over the last few days. *I know you. Don't I?*

Each time, I look away and shuffle forward with the queue.

The food is hot and filling, a rich vegetarian stew served with hunks of wholemeal bread and mugs of strong tea. It's the best food I've had in years, a whole world better than the slop we had been served in prison. While I eat, I send Owen the number of my new burner phone and jot notes in the pad. I also send over a series of questions on Telegram asking him about Christine Lai and the detective who had led the murder investigation, Inspector John Musgrove.

He replies quickly with an address on Woodford Avenue, Weston Park, a suburb on the north-west side of the city. A message saying it is the last address he has for Christine, with a couple of other messages following straight after.

Handle with care. She has restraining order against me.
No idea about Musgrove, retired 2018 and dropped off the radar since. Will have another dig around.

Once upon a time, Christine and I had been friends, of a sort. She had worked closely with Liam for some years, by his side as he first won the seat in the 2007 election and then built on his majority in 2010. She ran things for him in the constituency, handling all aspects of his work as the MP for Bath. But that was before she had given evidence for the prosecution at my trial, before she had been embroiled in Owen's own investigation into parliamentary corruption, before she had sued the journalist for libel – and won.

She no longer works for Liam's successor, who still occupies the Bath parliamentary constituency office on London Road.

She doesn't have much of an online presence and gives the impression of someone who takes their privacy seriously, the only hits on Google linking through to a LinkedIn page and a handful of local news stories around the time of the last election, where she's pictured in a grinning line-up with various other party workers.

A Twitter account seems to have been dormant since 2020. There doesn't seem to be anything personal online about her at all, no Facebook or Instagram, at least not under her own name.

She would not want to see me now, of that I'm sure. But I need to see her.

The dinner crowd at the church hall has started to thin out as I finish my meal. Taking my empty plate up to the servery, I recognise one of the other women from the probation hostel. She's in her mid-twenties with dark hair cut very short and a line of piercings in one ear.

I give her a nod of recognition.

'Haven't seen Jodie, have you?'

'Not since this morning,' she says. 'She'll probably be down the Arches by now.'

'Is that a pub?'

She snorts. 'The old railway arches? Off Station Street.'

'Right.'

'With all the other alkies.'

'Got you.'

I grab my jacket and head back out into the darkening city.

* * *

The Arches are little more than a line of soot-stained brick openings beneath the London-bound railway line, a couple of dozen dark semicircles beneath the track that seem to extend back into the hillside behind them. About a mile from the city, away from the tourists, away from the Roman Baths and the Royal Crescent and all the pretty architecture, they might once have been home to stables and warehouses and working yards. But now they are dark and derelict, at the far end of a dead-end road, the tang of woodsmoke and burnt plastic hanging in the air.

The blood drums a little quicker in my veins as I approach, an unpleasant flicker of adrenaline in my stomach, my fingertips. I peer into the first of the arches, a graffiti-sprayed cavern littered with rubbish and a torn red sleeping bag discarded in the corner, heavy smells of earth and rain and human waste. In the next one, split-open black bin liners are piled beside a grubby green tent zipped tightly shut, used syringes scattered in the dirt. A hugely bearded man in the third arch is warming his hands by a small fire. When I ask him if he's seen Jodie, he gives a brief jerk of his head towards the further reaches of the crumbling structure.

It's another six arches further down when I spot my old jacket, draped over the back of a shopping trolley. A soft sobbing reaches me from the darkness within. I flick my phone light on and make out a shape in the shadows of the corner, a prone figure sprawled on sheets of dirty cardboard. Shining my light closer, it reveals my room-mate groggily propping herself up on her elbows.

'Jodie,' I say, my voice a flat echo in the enclosed space. 'It's me, Heather. Are you OK?'

She shields her eyes against the light.

'Too bright,' she slurs.

On the torn blanket next to her is a half-empty bottle of super-market vodka and scattered blister packs of pills. The sharp sour smell of vomit is somewhere close by.

I angle the phone torch towards the pill boxes. Paracetamol.

'Did you take these? How many?'

She mumbles something I can't make out.

'How many, Jodie?' I crouch down and grip her arm, the first pulses of real fear arcing through me like an electric current. One of my first cellmates at Eastwood Park, Caitlin, had overdosed after saving up all her meds for weeks, her body already stiffening and cold to the touch by the time I realised the next morning and began screaming helplessly for a guard. It was difficult to overdose in prison but it still happened, rules circumvented, drugs hoarded by the most determined. Jodie reminded me of Caitlin in some ways: the same sweeping, manic highs and deep, dark lows that left her mute and inconsolable, the swing from dizzying exuberance to black despair.

'The pills,' I say to Jodie again, holding up an empty box of pain-killers in front of her face. 'Did you take all of these?'

She nods, her voice catching in another sob.

'Two . . . two boxes.'

'Then we need to get you to the hospital,' I say, pulling her upright. 'Can you walk?'

I try to pull her to her feet but she pushes my hand away, mumbling an objection.

'Jodie, listen to me, we have to go *right now* and get you to a doctor.'

'No.'

'I'm not asking you, I'm telling you.'

She bats my hand away again.

'Couldn't keep them down.'

'What?'

'The pills. Couldn't keep them down.' She collapses back against the dirty brick wall. 'Sick everywhere. Couldn't even do that right.'

The sharp smell of vomit hits me again, hanging pungent in the air.

I kneel down next to her on a piece of flattened cardboard.

'Let me help you, Jodie,' I say. 'Talk to me. What's going on?'

'Just wanted to be on my own.'

I find a bottle of water in my bag and hand it to her.

'Here, have some of this.'

She tips the bottle back and takes a long drink, before finally seeming to focus on me for the first time. 'What are you even doing here?'

'Missed you at the food kitchen,' I say. 'I wanted to ask you about something.'

'Everyone always wants something.' She sits up and rubs her face with both hands. Her eyes are puffy and bloodshot from crying. 'You know, no one's going to give a shit about me when I'm really gone. I'm going to be like one of those old fogeys who dies in their flat and no one realises for months until the stink gets bad. Eaten by my Alsatian or something.'

'No chance,' I say gently. 'You haven't even got an Alsatian.'

She snorts, but there is the ghost of a smile too. 'You know what I mean, smart-arse.'

'What's happened?' I indicate the pills and vodka bottle next to her on the ground. 'Why did you think you wanted to do this?'

She looks away, her face creasing in pain, a tear cutting fresh tracks through the smudge of dirt on her cheek.

'She's gone.' Her voice is little more than a whisper. 'He's taken her away.'

'Who?'

'My ex.'

'Who's he taken away, Jodie?'

She sniffs. 'My Holly. My little girl. First, they said I couldn't see her anymore and now he's taken her and he's gone. To Ireland, back to his parents.'

'How old is Holly?'

'Fifteen in November.'

'Let me help you,' I say. 'I'm sure there's something we can—'

'No,' she sobs. 'There's nothing. There's no point anymore, no way to get her back.'

I cover her hand with mine. 'There's always a way, Jodie. We just have to find it.'

'Leave me.' She goes to lie back down again on her makeshift mattress of flattened cardboard. 'Just leave me. I don't wanna . . .'

'You can't stay here, it's not safe,' I say. 'You don't know who might be hanging around.'

The hostel closes its doors at 10 p.m., which means we have barely half an hour to return before we're in breach of the curfew. I put a hand under Jodie's armpit and hoist her to her feet. She's unsteady, swaying as if she's on the deck of a ship in heavy seas.

'Come on,' I say. 'Let's get you back.'

25

TUESDAY

The view from Alexandra Park is breathtaking, all of Bath laid out in the valley below. From the lookout, the city is a graceful mass of pale stone and dark roofs, church spires and tall Georgian row houses marching up the hill, the railway line curving up and around like a spine running through the middle. Across the valley, the streets rise towards Larkhall and Charlcombe, wispy September clouds above the ridgeline on the far side.

I'm early for my meeting with Amy. I hadn't slept well, checking on Jodie every few hours to make sure she was still OK, rolled onto her side in the recovery position. She had still been asleep when I left the hostel this morning, pale and still beneath the scratchy grey blankets, her breathing deep and slow.

Amy is early too. She approaches from the path and sits down at the other end of the bench, leaving plenty of space between us. She's dressed for work in a pale grey trouser suit, her long dark hair tied back. We exchange brief greetings and lapse into an awkward, loaded silence, both of us staring out at the view.

'Wasn't sure you'd come,' I say finally.

'Neither was I,' Amy says.

'I'm glad you did.'

She doesn't reply and we fall back into uneasy silence again.

'I wanted to thank you,' I say, without looking at her. 'For what you've done with the boys. For being there for them while I was . . . away. It was a comfort to know that you were still part of their lives, that they've had that continuity at least.'

She is quiet for a long moment.

'Being an auntie to those two is the best thing that ever happened to me.'

On the hilltop behind us, the air is thick with the shouts and laughter of children in the little playground, and I'm glad of the background noise, glad this is a neutral venue. It had been here where Liam had first told me he wanted to become an MP, to take his life in a new direction and make a difference in the lives of others. A Sunday afternoon walk here on a frosty winter's day so many years ago, the sky a perfect blue from horizon to horizon, the air sharp and cold enough to sting our cheeks as we huddled together with hot chocolates looking out over the city. And Liam had suddenly come out with it, this idea he had been working up to, a change of direction that he would only commit to if I agreed. Only if I gave my blessing. Neither of us with any idea of the dark trajectory our lives would take from that day onward.

Amy turns to me as if to say something else, then stops.

'What is it?' I say.

'I need to say something to you. To get it out.'

'OK.'

'I hated you. For a long time.'

'I understand.'

'No,' she says, more forcefully. 'I really, *really* hated you. It didn't seem like enough, what you got. You were in prison, but I knew you'd get out eventually, you'd carry on with your life. I prayed every day we'd get the news that you'd fallen down the stairs or been attacked in your cell, beaten to a pulp or scalded or stabbed.'

'Well,' I say slowly, 'most of your prayers were answered.'

I still remembered the first time, my first week inside, catching the wrong kind of attention as a celebrity inmate whose trial had made all the papers. When I discovered my status as the infamous newcomer to B Wing who deserved to be taken down a peg or two. *A stuck-up bitch who thought she was better than the rest of us. Killed her husband in cold blood and let her kids discover their dad's body.* My first trip to the sickbay with a black eye and a sprained wrist, a clump of hair gone from the crown of my head and a cracked rib that sent shooting pains into my chest every time I coughed.

Amy looks down at the hard-packed dirt beneath our feet.

'I know it was wrong for me to wish for those things.'

'But it wasn't you that did them,' I say with a shrug. 'It was other women. Other inmates, most of them just as messed up as me.'

'What I mean is, it felt like jail time wasn't enough for what you'd done, not nearly enough. It felt like a betrayal, first by you, then by the system that was supposed to punish you. A betrayal twice over. That's how I felt.'

I let her words settle between us, choosing my response carefully.

'Do you still feel that way?'

'When he . . .' She clears her throat. 'When it happened, I don't know what you heard, but I was in a really bad place for a long time.' She trails off, breathing hard through her nose.

I had heard second-hand that she'd had some kind of breakdown after her brother's death, had spent time in a treatment facility.

'There's no shame in it,' I say quietly. 'In seeking help, in admitting you need it. I wish I'd been brave enough to do the same.'

'I was going to visit you once,' she says, drumming a nervous fingertip against the rough wooden bench seat. 'In prison. But only because . . . I wanted to see you suffering. I wanted to see you paying for what you'd done to my brother, to see with my own eyes what your life had become. To focus all my anger and pain and grief on you like I could pass it on, get rid of it.'

It had been six or seven years ago but I remembered the visiting order, my surprise that she had responded. Then waiting in the visitors' hall for the full hour, alone at a table with a red tabard like all the other prisoners, even when it was obvious Amy had changed her mind.

'I sat in the car park,' she says, 'just sat there in my car, going over and over it, trying to work out what I was really doing there. How I could possibly have thought it would make things better, sitting in my car crying and shouting and cursing you. Eventually, I just turned around and drove home again, didn't tell Mum or Dad where I'd been, didn't tell anyone.'

'Do they know you're here now?'

'*God* no! They would freak out if they knew I was talking to you.'

'What about your dad's offer, yesterday,' I say. 'Paying me off, setting me up in the north of Scotland, was it for real? Or just a set-up to lure me to their house and get me arrested? Stitch me up for breaching the terms of my probation?'

'Both, I think,' she says quietly. 'If you'd taken the offer, you're gone and he wins. If you refuse, there's a decent chance you'll want to tell him that to his face, make it clear that you won't be bought off. And then you end up in the back of a police car anyway. So it was a win-win for him.'

'He figured I'd probably come to the house.'

She leans forward, elbows on her knees. 'Why did you ask to meet, Heather? What did you want to tell me?'

I've thought about how much to share with my sister-in-law, how much to reveal about what I'm planning to do, about what I've *already* done since getting out of Eastwood Park. We'd got on well from the beginning, since she'd been a bridesmaid at my wedding. After my mum, she had been the closest I had left to family beside the boys. The closest I had to a sister. I'd even had her on my prison paperwork as next of kin, alongside the boys.

'I'm not going to Scotland,' I say softly. 'I'm not taking your dad's money. I'm going to stay and find out what really happened that night.'

'How, though? Not being funny, Heather, but I don't see how you're going to find something new, ten years on.'

I describe my conversations with Owen and Nishan, the unexplained notations in Liam's diary and the stranger in the library who had been following me. The storage box left by my mother, filled with memories from my old life.

'I'm sorry,' Amy says suddenly. 'About your mum.'

'Thank you.' The weight of tears is heavy behind my eyes. 'I know you were kind to her when you didn't have to be. Helping her sort out the house and everything when she started to struggle.'

'None of it was her fault.'

'Well, I appreciate what you did for her, and I'm sure she did too.'

We fall into another long silence before Amy turns to me again. 'So what happens now?'

'Someone knows something about what happened ten years ago,' I say. 'They're out there, somewhere, I just have to find them.'

'You're asking for my help?'

'No. I just wanted you to know, that's all. To hear it from me. And I don't want you to get in any trouble.'

'Why would there be trouble?'

'Because . . . whoever set me up is not going to like me digging into it again. Who knows what lengths they might go to. Lines are probably going to be crossed.' I lean an elbow on the back of the bench to look at her properly. 'And if that happens, I need to know you'll still be there for Theo and Finn.'

'Of course.'

'My card is already marked with the probation service, the police, with everyone, and if things go sideways for me I need to be sure you'll still be there for your nephews. To look out for them if I end up back inside.'

She's nodding, looking away from me, all her earlier anger seemingly spent.

'I see so much of Liam in the boys, you know? So much of his light, his energy. Theo reminds me so much of what my brother was like, when he was fourteen.'

'The age gap between you and Liam must have seemed much bigger when you were growing up.'

'Not to me.' She shrugs, cuffing a tear away. 'I always idolised him. Right from when we were kids, I always knew that he was special, that he'd do great things. He would always play with me and make sure I was included even though I was probably *really* annoying at that age.'

'You looked very sweet in all the family photos.'

She gives me a sad smile. 'I mean, Mum never wanted there to be a seven-year gap. She had a few miscarriages.'

I knew, from long-ago conversations with Liam, how desperate his mother had been for a girl to complete her little family. His earliest memories were of his mother crying and crying, of being sad all the time, Liam being unable to console her and being told simply that *Mummy was sad because the baby went away.* Not understanding what it meant or knowing how to make her better. And then finally: a miracle. A little girl, a sister, with white-blonde hair and a beautiful sunny smile and the youngest sibling's ability to get away with almost anything.

Her mother had doted on Amy, and Amy – in turn – had doted on her brother.

'I always looked up to him,' she says, 'but it wasn't just me. Everyone loved him.'

'They did.' My throat is thick. 'Everyone.'

A train creeps into view below us, pulling slowly to a halt in the station. We are too far away to hear the engine and the whole thing happens silently, as if in an old movie.

We exchange numbers and I tell my sister-in-law that I'll keep her updated with what I find. She wipes more tears away with the sleeve of her top.

'I should probably go,' she says abruptly, checking her watch and standing up. 'I have a million meetings today.'

'I'm glad you came, Amy.'

She nods, turning away and walking back up the hill without another word.

26

Owen buys coffees from the vending machine in the reception area of Total Storage and the two of us sip them as we lay out the contents of the big plastic box once it is retrieved from the rack. It would help to get a handle on anything significant, he tells me, if we can see everything laid out in one place, sorted according to whether it's likely to be useful. We have the cavernous room to ourselves, and before long the big central table is almost completely covered with documents, books, photo albums, letters, cards, keepsakes and other assorted things from the bulky storage locker.

'Can't believe there's this much paperwork,' I say. 'Thought most of it would be digital, stored in the Cloud or on a hard drive somewhere.'

Owen doesn't look up. 'Ten years ago, remember? Much more paper-heavy then, especially parliamentary business. And digital copies of anything incriminating will probably have been erased years ago, that's why hard copies are probably our only chance.'

'So what are we actually looking for?' I gesture at the collection of stuff laid out in front of us. 'In here?'

'Inconsistencies,' Owen says. 'Anomalies. Wrong notes. Basically any document in among this stuff that might contradict the police's bullshit theory of what happened.'

He describes the concept of 'noble cause corruption', a term he had first come across coined by American defence lawyer David

Rudolf. It can happen when police lose sight of their real role as investigators, Owen explains. Detectives stop trying to solve the crime and instead focus all their energy on proving the culpability of a single suspect – because they believe they are doing the right thing.

'It's not that they're trying to frame you,' Owen says. 'More that they have this total faith in their own ability to know "*what really happened*". When you throw confirmation bias into the mix and their desire to ensure the suspect doesn't walk away scot-free, they get totally focused on proving guilt, rather than looking at the whole picture. It's one of the ways innocent people end up in prison.'

'What about the evidence?' I say. 'The phone, the fingerprints, the pictures?'

'The police found the evidence that corresponded with what they *thought* had happened,' he says. 'If you're trying to fool someone, that's half the battle, isn't it? Tell them a story they want to believe.'

I pick up an old paperback book from the box, *Into the Woods* by Tana French. 'So what are we hoping to find?'

'Any mention of money changing hands, or of the select committee inquiry Liam was chairing at the time of his death. Or anything relating to a US company who might have been paying for information and influence in Parliament – *that's* what I think Liam was about to blow the whistle on, before they silenced him. This thing has been stitched up for so long already, and lots of people want it to stay that way. We're the only ones who actually want the truth.'

'But won't all the useful stuff have been taken by the police as evidence? It'll still be in a box in some police warehouse, won't it, can we get access to that too?'

'Not without a formal appeal process against the verdict,' he says. 'Which was already thrown out. And besides, a lot of the police evidence went missing last year.'

'*What?*' I stare at him.

'Evidence storage was contracted out to the private sector. Loads of it ended up in landfill by mistake – *allegedly* – and not just from this case. But that's another story, for another day.'

'That's bloody outrageous.'

'And all the more reason for us to be careful with whatever new leads might come our way.' He gestures at the assortment of material spread out on the table. 'And in any case, the police mostly went over documents from his office. But Liam kept a lot of the most sensitive material at home, according to a source that I trust.'

I sip my coffee. 'Who's your source?'

'You don't need to know.'

'And why would Liam even do that?' I say. 'Keeping files at home would be a breach of the rules, wouldn't it?'

'Technically yes,' Owen says, 'although it does happen. The question is, why do we think Liam kept the most controversial, potentially explosive stuff at home?'

I frown, reaching back a decade and more to recall any conversations Liam and I might have had on this topic. We had talked about our jobs often enough over the kitchen table, but he had never gone into specifics about the confidential aspects of his work. I'd always assumed he was merely being professional, discreet, and in any case it had been that time in our lives when the two of us never seemed to actually finish a conversation – or a bottle of wine, a meal, a film – without being interrupted by the demands of looking after two small children, of work and housework, meetings and messages and calls, a new puppy and everything else. I had always longed for more time, more hours in the day to do things properly rather than bouncing from one task to the next, feeling as if I'd not done any of them properly. Until that dark Rubicon in July 2013, the dividing line between my old life and my new one. After that day I'd had only time. Nothing *but* time, and nothing with which to fill it.

I shrug, scanning the assorted paperwork. 'Liam had so much work on, he could barely keep up. I guess he brought some of it home because . . . he had to plough through it in the evenings and at weekends? Or perhaps because the office wasn't secure?'

'Maybe the office. Or maybe the staff *in* the office.'

'Christine?'

'That's my guess,' Owen says with a nod. 'He had to keep it away from his constituency manager.'

'Where exactly does Christine Lai fit into all this?'

'That,' he says, 'is what we need to find out.'

27

Two hours later, we're still looking.

I've been going through a thick stack of newspaper cuttings from around the time of my arrest and trial. Mum had even managed to get parts of a court transcript of my case, dog-eared pages held together with fraying treasury tags, many of the sheets annotated in her handwriting, phrases in the witness testimony circled or marked in yellow highlighter, question marks and looping arrows in fading black ink. I had no idea she had taken so much time, going back over what was said in court.

Owen has been on his laptop, combing through one of the USB memory sticks we found in the box.

Finally, he snaps the laptop shut, his big shoulders slumped.

'Shit,' he says. 'I thought it might be here.'

'What?'

'I don't know.' He blows out a breath. '*Something*. But this all seems to be pretty routine stuff. We need to keep looking.'

He's taken his black sweatshirt off to reveal a Clash T-shirt and a selection of swirling Celtic tattoos up and down strongly muscled arms. My eye is drawn to the biggest of the tattoos, on his inner forearm, stretching from his wrist to the crook of his elbow. A bearded figure in robes, with a staff and a medallion around his neck.

He sees me looking. 'Don't tell me – you didn't think a *Guardian* journalist would have so much ink?'

'Just didn't have you pegged as the religious type.'

'Lapsed Catholic. Got my first tattoo in Cardiff when I was doing my postgrad.' He taps a stylised dragon beneath the swell of his right bicep. 'Did a bit of door work on weekends to pay the bills, got friendly with some of the other guys and just got into it. Been adding them ever since.'

I point at the robed figure on his forearm. 'That one looks really familiar but I can't place it.'

'St Jude,' he says.

'Patron saint of journalists?'

He shakes his head. 'Lost causes.'

'Is that what I am?'

'No cause is ever truly lost, Heather.' He says it quietly, holding my gaze. 'If even one person can hold on to hope.'

I'm about to tell him I don't agree – that hope is for gamblers and dreamers, that losing all hope in prison had been almost a release for me, a freedom, because it was the moment I stopped expecting things to get better on their own, the moment I realised I had nothing and no one left to rely on except for myself – but Owen has already broken eye contact. He picks up a greeting card from the pile in front of him. This one blank inside apart from the words 'Dear Heather' in familiar handwriting, as if my mother had forgotten to write the rest of it. I've no idea what it's doing in this box but there had been Christmas and birthday cards like that when I was in jail, more signs of the disease progressing, cards with just my name, some left completely blank. One year I had received three separate Christmas cards a few weeks apart, all from my mother.

He holds up the front of the card to me, an image of a grey bird on a branch.

'Your mum liked cuckoos, did she?'

'I thought it was a hawk.' I'm glad of the change of subject. 'She liked all the birds of prey, all those watercolour prints.'

The early signs of Mum's illness were there even before I was sent away, but it is still unbearably painful to think that she'd had no one to be with her at the end, in the last few years and months, no one to visit her and talk to her, to sit with her and drink a cup of tea on a Sunday afternoon, to talk about everything and nothing, to listen to her in those lucid moments or just to sit with her in silence, holding her hand the way she had done when I was poorly as a girl, my mum sitting by the bed and holding my hand, stroking the hair away from my face.

I blink the memories away. 'Any joy with the memory stick?'

'Not yet,' Owen says. 'Most of it's pretty standard parliamentary correspondence. Is it OK if I take it away for a couple of days? Need to cross-reference with some other documents I've got at my house.'

The contents of the box still feel precious, like an unexpected gift, and I don't like the idea of handing over any of it to a virtual stranger who may or may not have another agenda.

'Actually,' I say, 'I'd rather you didn't do that.'

'Oh,' he says, as if surprised by my refusal. 'OK. No problem.'

We both go back to sorting, sifting and reading.

I work through an old leather-bound Moleskine notebook, the pages yellowed and creased, the ink faded but still legible, page after page of my old life. Half the *Notes* pages at the back are taken up with various lists I've written, shopping and to-do lists, Christmas presents received and thank-you cards sent, of nursery closure days and holiday packing lists. A list of birthdays too, more people lost to me a decade ago.

'Heather?' Owen holds up a single sheet of A4 paper, lines of black text below a green header. 'This could be something.' His eyes flick back and forth across the page. When he's finished, he checks the other side before laying the sheet flat on the table and taking three quick pictures of it with his phone, his bearded face alight with fresh interest. 'Looks like minutes of a meeting, with a specific mention of some confidential arrangement, here in black and white.'

'The one you wrote that story about?'

'Maybe,' he says, handing the sheet to me. It has the familiar green House of Commons portcullis header at the top and is numbered as page four of four, the twin holes left by a missing staple visible in the top left-hand corner. A faded red watermark across the top denotes the document as 'STRICTLY CONFIDENTIAL'.

The page looks like actions from the meeting, collated with corresponding initials to show who's been nominated to do what.

'There are four sets of initials here,' Owen says. 'CL for Christine Lai against three actions. I guess it's no surprise she didn't see fit to mention this in court.'

'Are the first three pages there too?'

He shakes his head. 'Just this last one, page four, in among a load of unrelated stuff. It was stuck in between your son's one-year progress report from nursery and some paperwork from the Kennel Club.'

One of the actions reads 'CL to coordinate with NS Joint Endeavour team re: approval/authentication prior to forthcoming issue, under the agreed terms.' A note is written next to it, in Liam's distinctive handwriting: 'What is this??? Ask CL ASAP'. The acronym ASAP is underlined twice.

The initials NS appear four times in the text and look as if they might stand for a company or organisation. The other attendees at the meeting are designated 'PB' and 'YJ'.

Lower down on the page, next to one of Christine's actions, he's written something else in his trademark fast-flowing red ink: 'Call Phillipe ASAP!'

Owen has already pulled a small notebook from his pocket, leafing through pages thick with an unintelligible scrawl.

'Did Liam ever mention these names to you? Anything with the acronym "NS" or these other initials?'

'I don't remember,' I say. 'I don't think so.'

'It would really help to have the cover page of this, might give a full list of attendees, a venue and the date it took place.'

I point to the very bottom of the page, an italicised footnote that has faded with time to almost nothing.

'We have the date it was created at least. Look.'

The footnote contains a long file path full of forward slashes denoting the computer folder on which this document was stored. At the end is a six digit number: /030713.

'The third of July, 2013,' Owen says.

The two of us look at each other as the significance of the date becomes clear. But I'm ahead of him. I'm already there.

'That was nine days before it happened,' I say quietly. 'Before Liam was murdered.'

For a moment, neither of us speaks.

My eyes linger over a single phrase, four words loaded with meaning. *Under the agreed terms.* The suggestion of money changing hands seemed clear.

'Christ,' Owen says finally.

'So what does it mean?' I say. 'That it's turned up here?'

'That he chose to remove this from his parliamentary office, from his constituency office, and keep it at home among his personal stuff? And that this meeting happened nine days before he died? I'm not a big believer in coincidences.'

'Neither am I.'

'I'm thinking if your husband was going to blow the whistle on this, he'd want to keep this document safe – away from Christine Lai. At home.'

I look up from the page. 'Does it help?'

'Maybe,' he says. 'It's a record of the meeting and who was involved at least. A new piece of the puzzle.'

'So, what now?'

'We need to find the rest of this document,' Owen says. 'If the first three pages are not in this box, where could they be? We can assume that Christine would have disposed of any other copies years ago, if they were in his office. What about your in-laws' house?'

'I could ask Amy.'

'Do you think you can trust her?'

'Why do you say that?'

He shrugs. 'Just asking the question, that's all.'

I describe our conversation at Alexandra Park this morning.

'I'm trusting you, aren't I?' I shift in my seat to look at him. 'And I've only just met you. Me and Amy have known each other more than fifteen years.'

'Fair enough,' he says. 'Obviously we need to take a closer look at Christine Lai too.'

'We?'

'Not me, I can't go within five hundred feet of her according to the restraining order.'

'In theory I'm supposed to stay away too,' I say, 'according to the terms of my probation. She gave evidence against me at the trial. But maybe it's worth the risk?'

'I'm thinking we could just give her a nudge.' Owen indicates his open laptop. 'And then see what she does next.'

Sunday, 14 July, 2013

2.59 p.m., Bath Police Station

Musgrove was relentless.

There were dark shadows under his eyes but he showed no sign of easing off or bringing the interview to an end. If anything, he seemed to grow more determined with every passing hour.

'Let's talk about the argument again,' he said, arms crossed over his chest. 'How did it start?'

'We talked about . . . who he was on the phone to.' I couldn't bear it, speaking ill of my husband. 'About him being secretive. It was stupid, it was nothing.'

'A neighbour heard raised voices, a man and a woman. An argument.' He indicated the lurid printouts fanned out across the table between us, pictures found on the burner phone. 'You confronted him about the pictures, didn't you? You argued and it escalated from there – you'd both had a few drinks. You'd mixed the red wine with your pills, and you weren't thinking straight. But you were angry with him, you're working your guts out and looking after the children while your handsome husband is running around taking advantage of whatever young flesh is on offer.'

It was all too much, coming at me too fast. I felt as if I was dodging traffic in the fast lane of the motorway and wasn't quick enough to see the next thing bearing down on me.

'No,' I said again.

'You believed he was having an affair. He's pretty much owned up to it in writing.' He taps the email printout on the table. 'You argued and that's why he slept downstairs. He'd been sleeping down there quite a bit, hadn't he?'

'This is insane. You can't possibly think that I . . .' The sentence was too awful to complete. Too horrible to contemplate. 'Can you?'

'You had a row, confronted him, things got out of hand. You snapped. You were sorely provoked and—'

He was interrupted by a sharp knock on the door.

'Boss?' DS Gilbert said, holding it open. 'Have you got a minute? There's an update from forensics.'

Musgrove suspended the interview and left the room, leaving me and my solicitor to sit in awkward silence. I think of the boys and what they're doing today, if they have any understanding of what's happened and what I'll say when we're reunited. How I will try to explain the inexplicable.

It was fifteen minutes before the detective inspector finally returned, Gilbert taking the seat beside him. There was a new energy about them, a buzz that only served to underline my own exhaustion.

'I've just had an update,' Musgrove said. 'From the forensic team working at your house.'

'What is it?'

'It looks as if they may have identified the murder weapon, Heather.'

'What?' I felt a swoop of nausea and gripped the arms of the chair. 'Where?'

'It's a Sabatier that matches the set in your kitchen. A carving knife with a ten-inch blade.'

I always kept the knife block high up on the shelf next to the wine rack, so the boys couldn't reach it. In fact anything sharp, anything with a point or a blade or a serrated edge – I always dried them straightaway and put them away out of reach of small, inquisitive hands. The knife the police had found was the longest, sharpest of the set.

'How do they know it was the one that—'

'Do you know the knife I'm talking about?'

'They were a present.'

'I'm sorry?'

'That set. It was given to us as a wedding present, can't remember who from.'

'I see. Is there anything else you want to tell me, Heather?' He laced his thick fingers together. 'Anything at all?'

'The knife.' A fresh tear spilled down my cheek. 'Where did they find it?'

Musgrove crossed his arms. 'Back in the knife block with the others – hidden in plain sight, you could say. Looks as if there had been some hurried attempts to rinse the blade but traces of blood are still there. Preliminary work has also identified something else, on the handle. You're right-handed, correct?'

My throat felt tight, as if it might close up at any moment. 'Yes.'

'Can you speak up please, for the tape?'

'Yes,' I said again.

'Only one set of fingerprints on the knife, Heather. Right thumb and index finger.' His unblinking pale blue eyes fix me like the beam of a searchlight. 'Your fingerprints.'

The silence was absolute, as if all the air had been sucked from the room.

No. No. This wasn't happening, it wasn't real.

And yet it was. Here we were, the four of us around a table, talking about the knife that had ended my husband's life. The shaped, sharpened piece of steel that had separated us forever.

The hand that last held it.

DS Gilbert spoke for the first time since entering the room, her rapid Wiltshire vowels a contrast to Musgrove's slow-and-steady Yorkshire intonation. 'Did he threaten you with the knife first, Heather? Was it self-defence?'

The female detective's words reached me as if through a wall, as if I was standing in the next room and had to strain to hear her.

'What?'

'Had your husband been physically abusive?' Gilbert leaned forward and put a hand lightly on my forearm, the gesture surprisingly intimate in the cramped confines of the interview room. 'It's a lot more common than you think. Did he get drunk and threaten you, push you around, hit you? And you were fighting back? How long had it gone on for?'

I felt the tears brimming in my eyes again. The words were so far away from the man Liam had been that it was almost laughable, if it hadn't been so utterly tragic.

'No,' I said. 'He was never like that. He would never do anything to hurt me, or the boys.'

'But you were angry, you were furious, it's not the first time he's betrayed you, is it? You're deep in shock – of course you are – you're under the influence of alcohol and prescription drugs, you're not in your right mind. So you got the knife to protect yourself.'

'No.' It felt like the hundredth time I had said it. As if it was a test of my fidelity to the story, a test of whether I could keep steadfast hold of the truth. 'I would never do that. Maybe I used it to make dinner, that's why my fingerprints are on there . . .'

The words tailed off as Gilbert withdrew her hand from my arm. Musgrove's phone buzzed in his jacket.

He took it out and checked the screen, tapping, scrolling, reading, scrolling, taking his time. Angling it briefly towards DS Gilbert before turning it face down on the table.

It's over, I thought. A flare of hope in the darkness. They had covered all the questions, jumped through all the hoops, filled out all the forms. I had sat and listened, I had cooperated and answered all their questions, tolerated all the hypothetical scenarios pulled together in this little room. And now I could go home, to be with my boys again.

Musgrove leaned forward and laced his fingers together on the table.

'Heather Vernon, I'm charging you that on or around the twelfth of July 2013 you murdered Liam Fitzpatrick Vernon in the county of Somerset contrary to common law. You do not have to say anything but it may harm your defence if you do not mention now something which you later rely on in court. Anything you do say may be given in evidence. Do you understand?'

28

The garden of 44 Woodford Avenue is long and neat, waist-high rose hedges separating it from the street. A tidy gravel path leads to the front door of a handsome three-storey Georgian row house built of creamy-clean local stone. Quite a contrast from the two-bedroom terrace Christine had lived in a decade ago.

Owen and I are waiting in his ancient VW Golf, which smells of fast food and leaking oil, floor carpets worn through to the metal beneath. He's parked at the kerb across the street, where we have a view of the front door. I observe for half an hour, watching Christine as she comes back from a run, goes upstairs before re-emerging in the front room in jeans and a loose shirt. She settles herself in the large bay window with a laptop and a tall glass of water. The last ten years have treated her well – she looks slimmer and more stylish somehow, more confident in herself, as if she very much belongs in this upmarket neighbourhood with its wide, clean streets. Liam and I had looked around here after we got married, but it had been out of our price range.

I send Amy a text describing the document we found in storage, asking if there might be any more of Liam's things from his office that had ended up in the attic of his parents' Bathwick house after he died.

While I resume my watch of the house, Owen continues working on his laptop.

I don't ask where he got Christine's number from, and he doesn't volunteer it – other than saying it wasn't hard to get hold of.

'Christine's done well for herself,' I say quietly. 'Has she got kids? A partner?'

'No kids. I think there was a partner a while back, but I don't know what happened with him.' He continues typing. 'When did you last see her, before today?'

I think back to that day in April 2014, the third day of the trial, watching her in the witness box. Calm, considered and devastatingly effective as a witness for the prosecution.

'Bristol Crown Court, nine years ago.' She had related the argument she had overheard between Liam and me on an open phone line, the night of his death. Helping to build the case that I had been jealous, aggressive, angry, that I had discovered his affair that night and it had spilled over into violence. 'The jury loved her.'

Owen puts a finger to his lips. From his laptop comes the sound of a phone call dialling out, the ringtone filling the small car. After two rings the call is answered with a click.

'Hello?' A woman's voice. Southern. Educated. Familiar.

Owen keeps his finger on his lips. Neither of us speak.

'Hello?' the woman says again, then a third time before hanging up with a sigh of frustration. The entire call has lasted perhaps ten seconds, if that.

Owen hits another series of keys on his laptop, the percussive clicks forming their own kind of rhythm.

'OK, we're good to go,' Owen announces. 'I'm in.'

I turn to look at him. 'In her *phone*? Just like that?'

'She helped to put you away, so she's fair game in my book. Probably best if you don't know too many details though.'

'I'm probably an accessory to whatever crime you just committed, Owen,' I say. 'So I'd rather know, if it's all the same to you.'

He reddens slightly. 'Suffice to say if she makes contact with anyone now, if she takes the bait we're about to throw her, we'll know about it.'

'How?'

He clears his throat, indicates the MacBook on his lap.

'An adapted Pegasus trojan using a zero-click exploit.'

I frown. 'You lost me at "adapted".'

'Pegasus,' he explains, 'is a piece of spyware originally developed by an Israeli company that has since been pirated and adapted by hackers, for sale on the Dark Web. "Zero-click" meant the target didn't even have to click on a malicious link in a text or email – accepting an incoming call was enough to infect the device.'

'You just hacked her with a *phone call?*'

'Listen, there's no possible way she can detect it and—'

'You'd better be right about that.'

'And even if she does,' he finishes, 'there's no way to trace it back to us. Back to me.'

'You're absolutely certain?'

'One hundred per cent.'

I study him for a moment, this big guy crammed into the driver's seat of his car with a laptop on his knees, who had been a stranger until twenty-four hours ago. Who had no doubt also been *absolutely certain* about the story that had ruined him and wrecked his career. Now, I was risking my freedom, my one chance to get the boys back, just by associating with him.

But I couldn't walk away, not now. The only way through was to keep going forward.

'OK,' I say finally. 'Let's just hope this gives us an opening.'

'Remember what you need to say.'

I get out of his car and cross the street, walk slowly up the path of number forty-four and ring the bell. From somewhere inside I can hear the soft strains of classical music, a violin concerto. The door swings open to reveal a high-ceilinged hallway, all smooth white lines with no clutter anywhere. No coats on hooks, no shoes lined up, no umbrellas, no bags. Minimalist perfection.

Christine stands in the doorway, pen in hand, and for a second there is no hint of recognition.

Then the expression dissolves on her face, the practised smile melting away.

'Heather?'

'Hello, Christine,' I say evenly.

'What—'

'I'm sorry to drop in on you out of the blue like this.'

'You're . . . out.'

'Yes. I am.'

'What are you doing here?'

'I was hoping you might have a few minutes to talk.'

'What? Now?' She seems to recover her wits, looking over my shoulder to the street behind. 'I'm right in the middle of something.'

'Just a few minutes, that's all. It's to do with Liam and why he died, who really killed him. New evidence has come to light and I wanted to—'

'What *evidence*?'

'Corruption. Bribery. Sensitive information sold to the highest bidder.'

'You shouldn't even be here,' she says, shaking her head. 'You know that, don't you?'

'Just five minutes, Christine. That's all I'm asking.'

She pushes the door half closed, her slim body filling the gap between the frame.

'I don't want to talk to you.'

'We know you were talking to an organisation outside Parliament, probably receiving money from them as well. Liam found out about it, didn't he?'

The door shuts with a solid *click*, the steel rattle of the chain being slid into place before her footsteps retreat towards the back of the house.

I give her my parting shot through the ornate brass letterbox.

'We're not going to stop until we've found the truth, Christine.'

Owen has reversed the car back out of sight. I climb back into the passenger seat as he pulls headphones off his ears.

'Well?' he says.

'She wasn't very pleased to see me.'

'You gave her the line about having new evidence?'

'I did.'

'How did she react?'

'She shut the door in my face.'

'And how did she look?' he says. 'When you told her that?'

'Spooked. She tried to hide it but I could see it took her by surprise.'

'Good. That's good.'

We had discussed a strategy, an approach, and agreed it before the short drive to this smart street in Weston Park. Now we just had to see whether she'd take the bait.

'It seems like a long shot,' I say. 'She's not going to run scared now, is she? You think she might crack, after all this time?'

'Ten years of guilt,' Owen says, 'is a lot to hold inside. Ten years of thinking you've got away with something.'

'So what do we do now?'

Owen shifts position in the driver's seat and I get a hint of his aftershave, sharp like cold ocean water, chewing gum on his breath

'Now,' he says, without looking up from his screen. 'We wait.'

29

Owen continues to tap at the laptop while I study the document again, eyes lingering over every word. I've read it a dozen times now, trying to squeeze the last drop of information from it. I'm still trying to digest the fact that this single sheet of paper has been hidden in a storage unit for so long, remaining undiscovered for a decade, and might now be the key that unlocks everything.

. . . CL to coordinate with NS Joint Endeavour team re: approval/ authentication prior to forthcoming issue under the agreed terms.

Liam's handwritten note: *What is this??? Ask CL ASAP.*

I've already googled every possible name, every acronym, trying to find a relevant connection. There are millions of search results for 'Joint Endeavour' but none with an obvious link. It seems to have been the name of a NATO operation in Bosnia in the 1990s. Could there be something in that? It didn't seem likely. Or could it relate somehow to the unsent message the police had found in Liam's email? The message intended for me, that he had composed but never sent? The police had built their theory on the assumption that his email was a confession, an admission of adultery. But I had never wanted to believe that was true, despite the mystery female caller on the night of his death and what the police had discovered afterwards. What if his email was something else instead?

Beside me in the driver's seat, Owen grunts and angles his laptop's screen towards me.

'You should probably see this, Heather. It's . . . you've been spotted.'

I look at the screen and my stomach drops. It's a story on the *Bristol Live* website, a phone picture of me on a railway platform, my face caught in half-profile just as I'm turning towards the camera. Ugly red scar tissue climbing the side of my neck. Beneath it is the headline:

MP's Killer On the Streets Again

CONVICTED murderer Heather Vernon is out of prison and planning to start a new life in Bristol, we can exclusively reveal today.

Vernon, 44, was jailed in 2014 for the brutal murder of her husband, charismatic Bath MP Liam Vernon.

She was spotted at Temple Meads railway station yesterday just DAYS after being released from prison, where she has served half of her eighteen-year sentence.

An onlooker said: 'Her hair was longer but you could definitely tell it was her. She was just sitting there waiting for a train. When she saw me taking a picture, the look she gave me – it was cold as ice. Makes me shiver just thinking about it.'

Vernon was dubbed the 'ice queen' during her trial for her detached and unemotional testimony when confronted with the evidence of her husband's death from a single stab wound . . .

I scan down further through the text, but there's nothing else of note, nothing new. The comments from readers are all along the same lines. *Should be doing the full eighteen years. Life should mean life. Sentencing is a joke in this country. Hope she rots in hell for what she did.*

I hand the phone back without reading the rest. I knew it would only be a matter of time until I was recognised, but I didn't realise it would happen quite so fast. If it kept on happening, it might become a problem. I pull on a baseball cap from my bag and tug the brim down low.

The *ting* of an electronic bell comes from his laptop and he returns his attention to the screen, clicking an icon on the desktop.

'We're in business,' he announces after a minute.

He turns the computer to face me again. On the screen is a short message thread from Christine to an unknown number.

Need to speak to you. Urgent.

Can talk now?

Not on phone. In person.

A drink for old time's sake? Usual place, 2 p.m.

'The other number,' I say, 'the recipient. Can you find out who that is?'

'Depends on how careful they are. I'll see what I can do.'

I point through the windscreen. 'Or we could find out the old-fashioned way. She's on the move.'

Christine emerges from her house in smart jeans and a fitted tweed jacket, striding down her garden path with a handbag over her shoulder and big designer sunglasses on despite the September clouds. She gets into her car, a spotless white Lexus, and pulls quickly away.

Owen starts the car and follows her.

We tail her Lexus as she heads into the city centre, Owen staying one or two cars back so we are not spotted. He doesn't seem fazed by it at all, keeping his distance in the traffic but staying with the Lexus through turns and junctions, pushing through a couple of orange traffic lights to make sure we keep the target in sight.

'You've tailed people before?'

He gives me a lopsided grin. 'No comment.'

After a ten-minute drive into the middle of Bath, Christine pulls into a multi-storey car park and Owen finds a spot in a lay-by a little way down the street. After a few minutes, she heads out on foot, crossing the road behind us and into a side street, against the one-way traffic.

'Stay here,' I say, opening my door. 'I'm going to see where she goes.'

He gives me a reluctant nod. 'OK. Keep your distance.'

Christine walks quickly and I have to keep my eyes on her retreating back to make sure I don't lose her among the afternoon shoppers and tourists on St James's Parade. She's already thirty yards ahead of me when she ducks left into a bistro with two large windows at the front and a scarlet sign displaying its name: The Harlequin. I walk by, throwing a casual glance into the window as I pass. Christine is being led by a waitress to a booth at the back, an intimate corner of this chic little bistro.

A man is waiting for her, standing as she approaches. He's tall, distinguished, handsome in an expensively cut dark-grey suit, heavy watch at his wrist. He's perhaps in his mid-fifties – at least a decade older than Christine – with flecks of silver in his dark hair. They air-kiss their greetings and she sits at the table opposite him.

I carry on walking past, pulse thudding in my veins, heading up the street to another side street leading into a small park. From here, I can keep an eye on the door of the bistro.

Counting off ten minutes on my watch before making another pass, I pretend to loiter a moment to look at the eye-wateringly expensive menu in the window. From under the brim of the base-ball cap I glance towards the back booth where the two of them are deep in conversation now, heads close together, coffees untouched on the table between them. Her posture is animated, uncomfortable, whereas he is grim-faced and attentive. I can't quite work out the dynamic between them – friends? Or colleagues? Lovers?

I watch for a moment longer, wishing powerfully to be a fly on the wall listening to their conversation. But one of the waitresses catches my eye and I move away, back to the side street where I can keep my distance.

It's another twenty minutes before Christine emerges, alone, turning smartly away from me and heading back down St James's Parade. She seems entirely preoccupied and doesn't look in my direction.

I take out my phone and dial Owen's number, giving him a brief summary of what I've seen.

'Can you stay on Christine? She's on her way back to you now.'

'What about you?'

'I'm going to follow the guy in the bistro.'

'Let's divide and conquer, then.' At his end of the line I hear the old VW's engine grumbling into life. 'Stay in touch. And be *careful*, Heather.'

Phone still in my hand, I snap a couple of pictures of the man in the grey suit as he walks out of the bistro a few minutes later. A chauffeur in a peaked cap is already waiting next to a long black Mercedes Maybach parked on the double yellows outside. But Grey Suit waves the chauffeur away, saying something to him as he strides off down the pavement away from the city centre. The sun has emerged from behind wispy autumn clouds; it seems he prefers to walk.

On the other side of the street, I follow him. He talks on the phone all the way to an anonymous office building on New King Street. It bears no company name or logo, just a large number '125' over the entrance, six storeys of dark mirrored glass that show nothing of what lies behind it, discreet cameras covering every approach.

The man in the grey suit steps into a revolving door at the front and disappears inside.

30

It's been four days since I was released and my boys seem further away than ever. When I was locked up I could pretend they were somewhere in my future, but now I'm back in the world there are reminders at every turn of how distant they have become. We occupy two separate worlds now, and I'm starting to wonder whether I will ever see them again.

I leave New King Street behind and take an indirect route to Bathwick. I knew enough to know where I needed to be and by 3.30 p.m. I'm in position, leaning on a bus shelter on the other side of North Road with a good view of the entrance, the brim of my baseball cap pulled low. I see Amy as she arrives, walking up from the bus stop with Jet trotting along beside her. She strolls up onto the main drive of King Edward's School, towards an imposing Victorian building of honey-coloured stone common to so much of the city.

I shift my position, taking in the smart cars pulling into the kerb. BMWs, Mercedes, Teslas, Audis. Women and men of about my age, talking listlessly on phones or drumming steering wheels, not a single one of them aware of how lucky they are to be here. How lucky they are to be doing something as mundane and everyday and wonderful as the school pick-up on a warm Tuesday afternoon. There is a churn of nerves in my stomach again, the reminder that

I'm an outsider looking in – I have forgotten how to do this, how to *be* this person.

Pupils start to wander out through the gate and I study each face in turn. *Is it you? Or you? You?*

Amy emerges with two boys in smart navy blazers, backpacks on their shoulders, the three of them chatting easily as they walk down the drive. Much closer than they had been at Dormers a few days ago.

Hot tears brim behind my eyes.

I feel my throat closing, a pressure in my chest as if my lungs are being squeezed tightly together in a vice. Willing myself not to cry, not to make a sound, not to give myself away. Fists curled tight in my pockets, nails digging into the palm of each hand.

My boys.

Theo and Finn.

So much time has been lost. It has been almost ten years since I was this close to them. Three thousand, five hundred and twenty-two days: we've been apart far longer than we were ever together. I've been a mother for fourteen years but have never done the school run. Not even once.

Finn is in front with Jet's lead in his hand, Theo behind, talking easily to Amy. Theo is a teenager now, brushing a long dark fringe out of his eyes, the resemblance to his dad so strong in his face, the line of his jaw, the confidence of his stride. He's already taller than Amy and even from across the street I can tell his voice has broken. It seems impossible. *My little boy's voice has broken.* Finn's blond toddler hair has darkened to a sandy light brown, cut short at the sides and a mass of curls at the front. He has my eyes, the same dimple in his chin. My baby, always the one who took after my side of the family, who looked more like me. Born Thursday the fifth of August at 6.41 in the morning, six pounds and eleven ounces, after seventeen hours of labour and *lots* of gas and air, lots of swearing on my part. Fifty-three centimetres long from the crown of his head to the wrinkled tips of his tiny toes, soulful blue eyes that have never changed colour since the day he was born.

A good feeder right from the beginning, not such a good sleeper to start with but we got there in the end. Back then I knew everything there was to know about him, I knew him better than the doctors and the nurses, the midwives, the grandparents, better than Liam, even. Better than anyone.

I wonder how I would appear to him now: a stranger, just hanging around at the end of a school day. A woman on her own, watching from a distance.

The only picture I had of them in prison was from seven years ago and they look completely different to how I remember them, but also the same. They are strangers who have taken the place of my children – and yet, I know them better than I know my own face.

Finn turns to his brother and gives him the same lopsided smile he's had since he was a toddler, the same mischievous grin as when he would bump down the stairs on his bottom, when he would splash water out of the bath, when he would run laughing circles with Jet in the back garden.

They turn left out of the gate and walk up the hill, then left again towards the fields above the school.

OK. I wanted to see them close-up, and I've done that. I've seen them. Now it's time to go. I shouldn't push my luck. And there is work to do.

I know all this.

But I follow them anyway.

By the time I've turned the corner they are already disappearing through a wooden gate and into the field, a rough stretch of grassland bordered by a screen of trees, with a golf course on the far side. I follow at a distance, taking my time, walking behind a group of sixth-formers as they make their way slowly up the hill.

I linger by the gate, waiting until the trio are halfway across the field before I follow, angling left and taking care to stay within the shadows of the treeline. I find a bench beneath the heavy branches of a broad-spreading oak and sit down. It's a sunny day and the grass is newly cut, the warm clean smell of it fresh in the late summer air. Finn is throwing an old tennis ball for Jet, who trots off happily to collect it. The field is wide and long and there aren't many people around, just a few dog walkers and a handful of other King Edward's pupils talking and laughing, a rugby ball thrown back and forth. Theo flops down on the grass, retrieving a mobile phone from his backpack and squinting at the screen. Amy sits beside him, leaning back on her elbows, face up to the sun. She's changed but could be mistaken for a big sister rather than their aunt, dressed casually in jeans and a cotton jacket, the thin leather strap of a handbag across her chest. When I first met her she had been a fragile, rather brittle teenager who had been in the shadow of her older brother. Now in her thirties, she has matured into a strikingly pretty woman who still looks younger than her years.

It seems like a familiar routine for the three of them. Just as she'd often done the nursery pick-up for me, when the boys were little.

When the boys were little.

They weren't little anymore. All of that was gone. Theo was a teenager on the cusp of manhood, and Finn wasn't far behind.

But I feel another surge of gratitude towards my sister-in-law for maintaining this little bit of continuity, some small consistency with their old lives, with the world as they knew it before the catastrophe of losing both parents on the same terrible night.

I had come here just to look. Just to see them, that was all. The probation service letter is still in my pocket, the words seared onto my memory.

No contact of any kind with relatives of the victim.

Boyle had been quite clear about that. And not for the first time, I wonder whether the best thing for my boys would be if I just left this place and never came back. If I got on a coach or a train and went somewhere far away, changed my name and disappeared, let them carry on growing up without me, rather than trying to force my way back into their lives. Rather than trying to prove that everything they had been told about their father's death – everything they had come to believe – was a lie, turning their lives upside down for a second time. Was that what was best for them? Or for me? Was I just doing it for myself?

No. The truth had to come out. Liam deserved the truth; we all did. And if nothing else, the real killer was still out there. Undiscovered and unpunished.

I'm startled out of my thoughts by the soft clink of metal on metal, a once-familiar sound that I had almost forgotten. A sound from another life: the collar of a dog, links clicking together.

Jet is sitting beside me, dark brown eyes looking up at me expectantly as his black tail swishes a slow back-and-forth in the patchy grass.

There are flecks of grey around his whiskers, his muzzle dotted with white. But it's him, same old Jet, the collie who had come to us as an eight-week-old puppy, a companion for the family. His pink tongue lolls from his mouth as he catches his breath, the old tennis ball at his feet.

'Hello, boy.' I lean towards him, touch the silky black fur on his head. 'Hello there.'

A memory emerges from somewhere deep, a long-forgotten time when I had brought this puppy home, fed and walked him, groomed and looked after him as he became a part of our family. Bought him his dog bed and lined it with an old picnic blanket, even though he preferred to fall asleep curled next to me on the sofa. I had trained him, but he probably wouldn't remember. I lift my right hand and tap my left shoulder blade twice, giving the signal.

He holds a paw up.

He *did* remember. The trick we had taught him when he was still a pup. *Shake hands.* I hold out my right hand and shake it, the pads of his paw rough in my palm. He whines quietly in his throat and edges closer, rests his chin on my thigh. I cuff tears away as I scratch the top of his head, the way he'd always liked.

I keep my voice low. 'Have you been looking after them?'

He blinks again, still looking up at me.

Finn's high voice cuts through the trees, the softest hint of a West Country accent creeping through.

'Jet? Where are you? Have you lost your ball again?'

The collie's ears prick up at the sound but he doesn't move, chin still resting on my lap. 'I have to go now.' I stand, giving him one last stroke. 'Stay, Jet. Good boy.'

He does as he's told, his eyes on mine, tail swishing slowly in the grass.

I turn and slip away quickly into the trees.

31

'So who is he?' I say quietly into the phone to Owen. 'Have you ever seen him before?'

I've sent him the two long-distance pictures in the hope that he might recognise Christine's companion from the bistro. My first instinct had been to follow Grey Suit into the mirrored glass building but there were too many cameras, and the risk of being captured by one of them was too high. I spent an hour watching the building instead, the comings and goings of smartly dressed staff, expensive cars nosing out of the underground car park. Grey Suit didn't reappear.

'His face doesn't look familiar,' Owen says. 'But a reverse image search might work. I'll look at the address as well, see if I can find the owners or companies based there. What was your take on him and Christine, their body language?'

'They were quite familiar with each other. Maybe close colleagues.'

'Or perhaps more than that?'

'Not sure,' I say. 'Maybe in the past?'

'And yet he's willing to come and meet her at the drop of a hat, without even knowing what it was about. To me, that says more than just good friends.'

There is a silence between us for a moment, broken only by traffic noise at his end of the line.

'You could be right,' I say. 'Where are you, anyway?'

'Parked up on London Road.'

Christine, he tells me, had driven there and spent fifteen minutes in a nondescript two-storey building that used to be very familiar to me: a place that had been like Liam's second home. The parliamentary constituency office.

'What the hell was she doing *there*?' I say. 'She left years ago.'

'I was wondering the same thing. Maybe she's still got friends on the team, giving them a heads-up that you were out and about.'

'They'll see it on the news soon enough. Any more calls or messages on her phone?'

'Just the usual kind of stuff.' I can hear the distant pecking of keys on his laptop. 'Nothing that seems urgent or out of the ordinary.'

We end the call with a promise to keep each other updated. I pull my hoodie up over the baseball cap as I make my way to the bus stop, trying to cover as much of my face as possible. There's an optician on the way and I pick up a cheap pair of lenseless glasses with thick black frames, paying with cash and leaving quickly. I've never needed glasses before and they feel weird, fake – they *are* fake – but they also feel like another little piece of my armour, another thin barrier between me and the world. There's more I need to do, to change my appearance, but this will have to do for today.

When I get off the bus near the hostel, Jodie is waiting for me on a bench.

She looks rested, better, her hair washed and tied back, and for the first time since I met her a few days ago her eyes are clear of the manic sheen of alcohol. The terror and tears of last night now buried deep, no doubt, along with all the other traumas she has suffered over the years. But the sight of her, sober and straight, gives me a lift I wasn't expecting and I find myself smiling as the double-decker pulls away in a belch of diesel. Here was the woman she *could* be. And would be again, I was sure of it.

She grins back at me. 'Just the lady I wanted to see.'

'Hey, Jodie, how are you feeling?'

'Peachy,' she says, linking her arm into mine and leading me across the road. She's still wearing the jacket I gave her. 'Nice specs by the way. Come on.'

'Where are we going?'

She taps the side of her nose. 'You'll see.'

We fall into an easy stride, the sun warm on our faces. For a moment it feels almost like my old life, catching up with a friend on a nice afternoon, going shopping or maybe just for a coffee while Liam took the boys to the park for a kick-about. Almost as if the last ten years had never happened. But the moment is gone almost as soon as it arrives.

I glance over at her. 'You sober?'

She holds three fingers up together, like a Brownie salute.

'As a judge.'

'Do you want to talk about it?' I wait a beat before adding: 'About what happened last night, I mean?'

'Not really.' She sniffs. 'Same shit, different day, that's all.'

'I meant what I said, you know, I want to help you. With your daughter.'

'You've got enough on your plate already, lovely.'

'I mean it, we could look into—'

'There were some blokes at the hostel earlier,' she interrupts me. 'Looking for you.'

'What?'

'Three of them.'

I stop walking, withdraw my arm from hers. 'What are you talking about?'

'Seemed proper keen to get hold of you, if you know what I mean.'

There is the familiar loosening in my stomach, the liquid feeling of adrenaline and fear pulsing out to every nerve ending. I check over my shoulder, back towards the bus stop. Normal weekday traffic. Parked cars. Two teenagers on bikes. A young mum with a pushchair.

'Tell me *exactly* what happened, Jodie. Everything you can remember.'

'So, I went out to get a few bits at lunchtime. Up the shops. Had a chat with Linda in the bookies. Then when I came back I see this black van with tinted windows parked across the street from the hostel. I'm thinking someone was in the shit over something, because it looked dodgy, right? So I'm just minding my own business, thinking I don't want nothing to do with any of that, when two blokes get out of the van and come across to stand in front of me, blocking the pavement so I can't get to the front door, and I'm like, 'Excuse me, lads, do you want to get out of a lady's way?'

'How do you know they were looking for me?'

She is animated now, gesticulating with her hands as she relates the story.

'The big one gets right up in my face and literally blocks my path, and he's like four feet wide and eight feet tall, a real hatchet-faced bastard, you know? And then the other one, the smaller one, says, "Hello, Heather, how are you doing?"'

My heart starts to bump painfully in my chest.

'I tell him my name's not Heather,' she continues, 'and he's got the wrong person and all that, and he's like, "Yeah, we just want a chat, Mrs Vernon, just five minutes that's all, there's someone who wants to talk to you and it would be better if you just do as you're told."'

'And so I'm like, "First off my name's not Heather, and second off, I'm not getting in the back of your rape-mobile even if you pay me a million quid." The smaller one – the American feller – he didn't like that at all and he tells the—'

'He was American?'

'Sounded like it. And there was another one waiting in the van, I think.' She screws her face up, trying to remember. 'I mean, dunno if they *were* American or not but he had like an accent. The massive guy was white but I never heard him speak, he looked proper inbred. Anyway the little one kept going on at me and I'm telling him he's got the wrong person and eventually he's like, OK then, I'd better tell him where you were and when you'd be back. And maybe we should go sit in his van while we waited for you.'

'God, are you OK?' I touch her arm. 'Did they make you—'

'No,' she says. 'Had this on me, didn't I?' She produces a small serrated knife from her pocket. 'Borrowed it from the kitchen after last night. Told the little one I'd scream the place down and stab him in the balls if they didn't just f—'

She catches the swear word just in time, as a young mum pushes a toddler past us in a stroller.

'I told them to do one,' she says, giving me a grin. 'And they let me get into the hostel. Then I slipped out through a storeroom window in the back and came to find you. Been waiting ever since.'

'How long ago was this?'

'Couple of hours.' She fixes me with her pale blue eyes, tiny blood vessels visible against the white. 'What's going on, Heather? Who were those guys?'

'I don't know.'

'Right.' The disbelief in her tone stretches the word out.

'Sorry that happened to you, Jodie.'

She shrugs. 'Why'd they want to talk to you, anyway?'

'I think maybe I've been asking too many questions, said the wrong thing to the wrong person.'

'Sounds like the story of my life.' She points down the road. 'Come on. I know another way back.'

32

The back way takes us across a park, over a fence and through someone's overgrown garden, but the black van is gone by the time we return to the hostel and peer out of the first-floor window in our shared room. Whoever they were, they had tracked me here and I feel certain they will be back. I pull the thin curtain across the window even though the dusk is still a couple of hours away.

Jodie and I grab an early evening meal from the canteen – luke-warm vegetarian lasagne – before returning to the room. Neither of us wants to go out again today. I try to talk to her about last night, about the situation with her daughter, but she shuts me down every time. Instead, she curls up on her narrow bed for a post-dinner nap while I unload the backpack onto mine, taking out everything I removed from the storage locker earlier.

I find my 2013 diary and turn to the third of July. Each double-page spread covers a whole week so there is only room for the basics. The third of July was a Wednesday and I've marked three things in hurried blue biro: early drop-off for T+F, Tesco delivery 6 p.m. and choir 8 p.m.

An early nursery drop-off for Theo and Finn probably meant a 9 a.m. work meeting for me, but I couldn't check because my work diary back then was all electronic and would be long deleted by now. After work there would have been the usual Wednesday evening scramble to get the boys picked up from nursery and fed, the dog walked, the shopping delivered and put away, the boys in the bath, pyjamas on and bedtime stories done before bolting some food for myself and run-walking down to the church hall for fort-nightly choir practice with the Liberty Singers. I had no memory at all of when Liam had returned from work that day, but he must have been back for 7.45 so that I could go singing.

All in all, it looked like a totally unremarkable day in my old life. An unremarkable, wonderful, beautifully mundane day, full of everything that I had lost. I rest my fingertips on the page, the paper dry and yellowed at the edges, stabbed with a painful pang of nostalgia for those days when a hectic evening routine had been the most I had to worry about.

I put the diary to one side and pick up the court transcript, the dog-eared pages thick with my mother's notes in the margins. I had no idea she even had a copy of this document. Perhaps she'd been waiting to find a breakthrough, an opening, a piece of good news that had never come. She hadn't found it, but perhaps I could.

I leaf through the dozens of pages containing the prosecution's case, forcing myself to look properly at the back-and-forth of evidence that had been presented at my trial. Remembering the persuasive tones of the prosecution barrister, Christopher Gorsky, a neat, unassuming Scotsman whose approach had been quietly devastating.

Mr Gorsky: In this morning's session you described the find-ings of your post-mortem, Dr May. You outlined to the court that you found no defensive wounds on the victim's body, no bruising beyond the fatal injury. No cuts on the hands or fingers to suggest that he may have tried to fight his attacker off.

Dr May: That's correct.

Mr Gorsky: And what conclusions did you draw from that?

Dr May: I would suggest there are two main possibilities. The first being that Mr Vernon was completely surprised by his attacker and had no time or opportunity to react before the fatal injury was inflicted. The second possibility being that he may have been awake but he knew and trusted his attacker – and did not perceive any threat from them for this very reason.

Mr Gorsky: Or perhaps both?

There is a hard, painful wedge in my throat. I flick back a few pages, steeling myself to continue reading the grim, horrifying banality with which my husband's death was described in court. Strangely, I have only the vaguest memory of what I'm reading, as if I had blocked it out while I sat there in the dock.

Mr Gorsky: I'd like to turn to the contents of the victim's study. A police search revealed something unusual, did it not?

DI Musgrove: It did. A listening device disguised as a plug-in air freshener. A fairly basic piece of surveillance equipment that could be purchased from various retailers.

Mr Gorsky: And who put it there?

DI Musgrove: Our investigations suggested it was put in place by Mrs Vernon when she became suspicious of her husband and came to believe he was having an affair.

Another throwaway prosecution line that had turned into a newspaper headline and from there into an unchallenged truth. Despite the fact that the first I'd heard of any listening device was in the police interview room.

There is a swirl of nausea in my stomach and I flick forward through the pages again. It was so long ago but I feel sure there *was* some mention of Parliament, of potential links with Liam's role as an MP – the threads that Owen would eventually pick up a few years later. At the time, the media had paid it scant attention, viewing it as a dirty defence tactic to muddy the waters around motive and distract from the much juicier and more familiar story: that *Hell hath no fury like a woman scorned.*

The police and the CPS had taken the same view.

DI Musgrove: We did pursue alternative leads, yes.

Mr Welsh: It was just a cursory look though, wasn't it, Detective? Rather than a detailed and proper investigation of possible links to the victim's job as an MP?

DI Musgrove: As I said, we followed everything up in a thorough and professional manner. Nothing was ignored. We simply went where the evidence took us.

Mr Welsh: But is it not the case that—

Judge Singleton: I can see little merit, Mr Welsh, in asking the same question over and over again, albeit in slightly different ways, when the answer remains the same. We have much ground to cover. In the absence of a solid basis for such speculation, I suggest we move on.

It was only after my conviction and failed appeal that Owen really started digging properly into other possible motives for the murder. What was that thing he had said about detectives developing tunnel vision? *Noble cause corruption.* When investigators zeroed in on one theory to the exclusion of all else. I wondered if DI Musgrove still felt the same way now, with the benefit of ten years' hindsight.

There are two more notes at the foot of the page, a single word in my mother's small, neat capitals: 'ARTEMIS??' An arrow next to it pointing to a set of initials I have seen before: 'AY', followed by a question mark.

I feel a jolt of recognition at these two familiar letters, the same as the notation in Liam's desk diary. *AY.* The 8 a.m. meeting – or phone call, or whatever it was going to be – scheduled for the Monday two days after his death. It reminds me that I'm no closer to knowing who or what the initials belong to, and how they might have related to his murder. A Google search on Artemis throws up 175 million hits, on the Greek goddess of the hunt, on numerous companies, a NASA rocket programme, and on and on, page after page of results. I close the browser window in frustration.

There is finally a reply from Amy on Telegram, a good four hours after my earlier message about the strange document we'd found in the storage box.

Will try to get a look at boxes up in attic. Some marked with Liam's initials.

I reply to thank her and ask if she's ever looked through them before.

No. Was stuff that came back from his office, assumed it was personal items, pictures etc.

Owen has also responded to my earlier message.

No joy yet on Grey Suit guy. Am looking into 125 New King Street.

I ask them if Artemis means anything, but both reply with question marks. I don't tell them about the strangers here at the hostel, looking for me. Because I know Owen will get worked up and worried on my behalf, he'll tell me it's too dangerous for me to be out there. And besides, Jodie has promised to watch my back.

Her voice gives me a start.

'You know,' she says, studying me with sleepy eyes, one palm tucked under her head, 'you're not what I expected at all.'

'What did you expect?'

'Dunno, bit frosty and posh, I suppose. Up your own arse. But you're not really.' She gives me a slow grin. 'I mean, not *all* the time anyway.'

I give her a small smile in return. 'Thanks. Maybe I'll put that on my CV.'

'You're very welcome.'

She yawns hugely and I go back to the diary, flicking through the days and weeks before Liam's death, trying to dredge up memories to go with them. But it's so long ago that it's like they're at the bottom of the ocean, fathoms deep and lost in the dark. I give up and pick up my phone instead, trying some new searches on Google.

Jodie's voice breaks the silence again.

'Heather?'

'Yes?'

'I've been thinking.'

'OK.' I look up at her.

'Those blokes today,' she says. 'How did they know where to find you? Loads of halfway houses you could have been placed, and you've only been out a few days.'

'Honestly, I've got no idea.'

'Because, as much as I like your company, staying here might not be such a good idea anymore. They'll be back.'

'I know.'

'Is that what you're looking for on your phone? Somewhere else to crash?'

I drop the mobile into my lap. 'Before that, I'm going to need transport.'

'Why?'

'There's a particular police officer I need to find.'

'Eurgh.' She pulls a face. 'Why?'

'Because he knew more about my case than anyone else. He's the one who sent me down.' I point to Liam's old diary, the court transcript, the page from the storage locker. 'He might know something that will help me put these pieces together, and maybe he doesn't even realise it.'

'Can't you just go to the station where he works?'

'He's retired and it's going to take some legwork to track him down. So I need a car.'

Jodie raises an eyebrow. 'Except you haven't got a permanent address and your credit history is knackered?'

'Exactly,' I say. 'And my driving licence expired while I was in prison. So I don't know where to start. Google doesn't really help either when it comes to buying a used car with no questions asked.'

She sits up, rubbing her face with both hands.

'You got cash?'

I think of the envelope of twenties my mum left for me, most of it still untouched.

'About a thousand.'

'Well then, Mrs Vernon.' She gives me a conspiratorial wink. 'Lucky for you, I know just the place.'

33

WEDNESDAY

The car is a scratched black Vauxhall Corsa with squeaky suspension and 85,000 miles on the clock. The seats are pockmarked with cigarette burns and there are two hubcaps missing, but the engine starts first time and it seems to run OK as I drive tentative laps around the potholed car park.

The dealership is an out-of-town place, tucked away in the backstreets behind some industrial units. Jodie's cousin's friend works here, fixing up the second-, third- and fourth-hand cars that come their way. I don't ask too many questions. Neither do they – which is the reason we're here.

In the tiny office, Jodie makes small talk with the manager while I count out nine-hundred and sixty pounds in cash onto the counter, twenty pounds at a time. The manager is a wiry man in blue overalls, the palms of his hands dark-lined with engine oil.

'You know,' he says to me in a broad Bristol accent, 'you look really familiar.'

I continue putting twenties down, trying not to lose count. 'Yeah, I get that a lot.'

'Have you been on the telly?'

'Nope.'

'You sure?'

'I just have one of those faces.'

He frowns, as if trying to remember the answer to a tricky quiz question. 'You *are* really familiar though.'

Jodie interrupts to distract him, hustling us out of there as soon as the money is counted – twice – and the manager hands over the keys.

As we're climbing into the old Corsa, she says: 'Looks like you're going to need more than fake specs, love.'

Driving again is a shock to the system. I stall it three times before I'm a mile down the road, and quickly realise that I have to keep the revs up constantly – even when I'm waiting at traffic lights – to stop the engine from spluttering into a stall. I guess that might be why there was only a couple of weeks left on the MOT. But after a few miles more I've started to get used to it.

We make a quick stop at a retail park on the outskirts of Bath. I tell Jodie what I need and we hit one shop each before making a hasty exit, Jodie getting the radio working and finding a nineties station blasting out old anthems as we pull onto the dual carriageway. She turns it way up and winds her window down, sticking her arm out and letting her hand bounce in the slipstream like a teenager as I ease the gearstick into fourth and push down hard on the accelerator. There is something about driving, about having my hands on the wheel, with the freedom to go wherever I want, that feels like another small liberation. Another step towards normal life.

'So where are we going?' she half-shouts to me, as 'Parklife' blasts from the speakers.

'Like I said,' I reply. 'To the police.'

She does a double take. 'You were serious?'

'Kind of.'

I explain to her what I mean, handing her the folded sheet of paper that Owen had provided from the electoral register. Six addresses in and around Bath. Owen himself has said he's going to spend the day shadowing Christine Lai and monitoring her phone activity.

Jodie turns the music down a notch. 'You sure about this, Heather?'

'It's got to be worth a shot. I've got to try.'

'What if you get recognised again?'

'You're going to help me with that,' I say. 'And anyway, it's all about context.'

'It is?'

'Sure. People see me on the street, and I'm a stranger who might look familiar, but if I'm knocking on their front door, the context is totally different.'

'If you say so.' She takes a battered smartphone out of her jeans pocket and types the first postcode into Google Maps. 'Take a left here.'

It's a half-hour drive to Keynsham and I wind my window down too, wind whipping through the car. 'Learn to Fly' by the Foo Fighters comes on the radio and Jodie cranks the volume all the way back up again as we head west on the A36. It occurs to me that I don't have insurance and had completely forgotten to ask about road tax – but then I don't have a valid driving licence either, so there seems little point in worrying about any of it right now. Not when we have places to go and people to see.

* * *

I park a few houses down from the first address that Owen had found for me, switching off the engine and turning to my passenger. There is a missed call from Trevor Boyle on my phone, a voicemail asking me to call him. I'll do it later.

'You're going to need to help me with the next bit,' I say. 'It's been such a long time.'

Jodie opens the Boots bag from the retail park and produces lipstick and blusher, eyeliner and mascara. I clip my hair back and we turn to face each other across the cramped front seats while she goes to work.

'I really appreciate your help with this,' I say to her. 'I honestly don't think I'd remember how to—'

She shushes me dramatically with a raised mascara brush.

'Pleasss.' She adopts some kind of mangled European accent. 'Not vile ze artist ist virking.'

As she works, turning my face this way and that, the soft-edged fragrance of new cosmetics is almost overwhelming. I'm transported back to the bedroom of my old house, makeup and perfume arranged beside a little mirror on top of the chest of drawers, high enough so the boys' small grasping hands couldn't reach.

Ten minutes later, she turns the rear-view mirror towards me and I almost don't recognise myself. It's subtle, as I had asked her, but I look like a different person, colour in my cheeks, my lips fuller and my eyes darker, more defined.

'What do you think?' she says, snapping the lipstick shut.

'Thank you,' I say, swallowing the lump in my throat. 'It's just right.'

'You're welcome.' She winks. 'Anyway, it's the first time I've paid for cosmetics in years.'

I slip off my windbreaker and open the other bag from the retail park. Inside is a smart linen jacket and I rip off the price tag, easing my arms into it. There is a matching handbag as well, a new pair of brown loafers to wear instead of my boots.

Jodie spends a moment straightening the jacket, gives me a thumbs-up. 'Sure you don't want me to come with you?'

'This will only work if I'm on my own.'

'All right.' She nods. 'What's our code going to be then?'

'Code?'

'If you get any bother.'

'I'm sure I can handle—'

'How about this?' She holds her phone up. 'You text nine-nine-nine to me if anything kicks off, or you want to get out, OK? Just those three digits. Then I'll come up and start banging on the front door.'

'All right,' I say. 'Three nines. Got it.'

'And take this as well.' She produces the small serrated knife she showed me yesterday, the one she'd brandished when the men had come looking for me at the hostel. 'For emergencies.'

'I don't need that.'

She flips it around, holds it out to me handle first.

'Better to have and not need, than need and not have.'

'You read that in a fortune cookie?'

'Tarantino. My ex was a fan.' She taps the wooden handle against the gearstick. 'I insist.'

I slip the knife into the new handbag and get out of the car.

34

The first house is a neat end terrace in Keynsham with a front door that opens right onto the pavement. The door is opened by a young woman in an apron, a baby on her hip, the sweet smell of baking reaching me from the kitchen behind her.

'Hi,' I say with a smile. 'This is a bit awkward and I'm so sorry to bother you, but my name's Helen, I'm looking for someone and thought you might be able to help . . .'

She bounces the baby on her hip as I continue with my spiel. I've thought of a couple of different stories to try, depending on who answers the door.

I knew that tracking down John Musgrove was not going to be straightforward. The first time we'd met, in the police station after Liam's death, he'd told me a few things about himself. I realised later, of course, that these were simply tactics to lower my guard and encourage me to open up. But nonetheless he *had* said he was only a few years from mandatory retirement after completing his thirty years' service. He'd told me he had one sister plus some nieces and nephews. Most likely she had a married name, which was not much help to me. I knew he'd be around his mid-fifties now, that he'd lived in or around Keynsham and would have retired from the police. As an ex-detective who had put numerous unpleasant people behind bars, Musgrove would be careful with his privacy to guard against ex-convicts who might like to pay him back with their fists.

I'd spent hours googling him anyway, finding dozens of news stories and police press releases quoting him about various cases in which he had been the senior investigating officer – including my own.

But in terms of anything personal, I'd drawn a blank. His online footprint was strictly professional, no personal accounts, no sports team, no hobbies, nothing. Not even a rough indication of where he lived, and no listing in the phone book either. Clearly he was ex-directory and probably had been for years. But just because he kept a low profile, it didn't mean his extended family would too: hence the six addresses Owen had sourced from the electoral register.

Five minutes later, I'm back behind the wheel of the Corsa.

'Where's the next address?' I say to Jodie as I put the key into the ignition.

'Willsbridge. Do a u-ey and head back up to the roundabout.' She looks over at me. 'No joy?'

'We can cross that first address off, I think.'

The second address is a first-floor apartment in a smart new development near the river. The name by the intercom is *Musgrove, D.*, flat 109. The main door buzzes open as soon as I press the call button and I head upstairs.

The guy who answers the door of 109 is a tall, slim guy in his twenties. He's in grey sweatpants and a white T-shirt, a small fluffy dog cradled in his arms.

I launch into my lonely-hearts patter about trying to reconnect with John Musgrove, my old boyfriend. Before I can finish the small dog starts barking, loud and sharp, regular as a metronome, showing me his little teeth.

'Stop it, Perce!' The dog lapses into silence. To me, the slim guy says: 'I'm so sorry, he's getting a bit grumpy in his old age. Who is it you're looking for again?'

We go around in circles for another few minutes. He seems desperate to help, to give me *something*, and is still apologising to me as I back away from his flat and head for the stairs.

Jodie is in the driver's seat of the Corsa, engine running, radio off, when I walk back out to the car park.

I switch to the passenger side instead. 'Fed up of my driving already, are you?'

'Put your seat belt on,' she says, her voice flat. 'And listen to me.'

'What's the matter?'

'Just keep looking straight ahead. Don't look over your left shoulder. There's a van back there that pulled up a minute ago. I'm pretty sure they're the same guys who came looking for you at the hostel yesterday.'

I snap the seat belt into place, a wash of fear low down in my stomach. 'What are we going to do?'

'Quick question,' she says, jerking a thumb towards the apartment building I've just left. 'Is this the place?'

'No. Another blank.'

She doesn't reply but pulls smoothly away as if nothing's wrong, indicating and turning left back onto the main road. Traffic is light and I keep an eye on my wing mirror. After a few moments I see the black van appear behind us, two cars back.

I glance over at Jodie but she has her eyes on the road, hands on the wheel at ten and two, a serious set to her face that I've not seen before. She drives steadily, as if she has all the time in the world, shifting lanes and indicating to make a right then another right, turning onto a route that takes us back the way we came, sticking strictly to the speed limit.

They follow us all the way back to Bath, and my eyes stay on the wing mirror the whole time.

'The van is still back there.'

'Yup,' she says tersely.

'What's the plan?'

'Just give me a minute.'

We lapse into silence as Jodie turns down a side street. The van turns in to follow and now it's directly behind us, big and dark and high up off the tarmac. There are three men in the cab. We join the four lanes of another main road and approach an elongated roundabout with a large island in the middle, Jodie working down the gears as we slow and look for a gap in the traffic.

The van fills my wing mirror.

At the last second, Jodie slams the car into first and punches the accelerator, the little Corsa shooting out into the roundabout amid a blare of horns and squealing tyres from other drivers. She weaves in between cars, slamming into second gear, and it's all I can do to hang on to the handhold above the door, my other hand braced against the dash as she careens around the roundabout.

The van driver is surprised but only for a moment.

'They're coming!' I shout as he swerves into traffic behind us.

Jodie waits until we're on the far side of the roundabout before she pulls hard to the left lane and stamps on the brake. The car behind almost clips us as he skids out of the way amid a chorus of angry hooting. Jodie shoves the stick into reverse, leans around her seat to look behind and stamps on the accelerator again, the engine hitting a high-pitched whine as she backs up *into* the oncoming traffic. I try to speak, to warn her, to tell her we're going to get hit and is she crazy? But all I can do is swear, a long continuous string of swear words one after the other as my heart jackhammers in my chest.

The black van rounds the turn and has to swerve to miss us – Jodie flipping the driver a middle finger salute as they fly past – and then he also screeches to a stop, trying to follow us back around. But we're small and nimble and the van is big and ungainly, twice as long as our little Corsa, and I can hear the *crump* of metal on metal as it backs into a blue city bus and comes to a shuddering halt.

Jodie reverses into the nearest exit and keeps going, more cars swerving around us until she backs into a side road, does a U-turn, and heads off calmly in the other direction.

'You all right, Heather?' She gives me a grin. 'You look a bit pale.'

I take my shaking hand away from the dashboard, nerves still jangling with adrenaline.

'Think I just aged ten years in the last two minutes.'

She laughs and switches the radio back on, turning the volume up high.

35

Two hours later, we grab a late lunch at a drive-through McDonald's in Melksham, eating it in a church car park further down the road. It's good to spend time with Jodie when she's sober, she's thoughtful and kind, and I start to realise that the jokey banter is just a part of the armour she wears to deflect from the harsh realities of her life and her past. She tells me about her own stints in prison, for drugs and shoplifting. I tell her I wish we'd known each other back then, thank her again for her help today.

'Obviously I'm up for this, Heather,' she says through a mouthful of cheeseburger. 'You know that, right? Afternoon cruising, listening to some tunes, grabbing a Maccies. Me and you doing the Sherlock thing, solving your own cold case or whatever – it's miles better than sitting in the bloody hostel being bored to death.'

'But?'

'But . . . I don't really get what you're expecting to happen. Do you think this guy's just going to hold his hands up and say "Oh yes, you got me, I knew it was a stitch-up and I never said nothing. Please put me in the cuffs and take me away." I've been arrested more times than I can remember, and most of them cops wouldn't piss on you if you were on fire. Let alone cough to banging up an innocent person.'

She's right, of course. It's a slim hope. But it's not nothing.

'He might not even realise he knows it,' I say. 'We add what we've discovered to what he found out back then, maybe it throws a whole new light on Liam's death. Maybe something that was overlooked.'

'OK.' She shrugs, and I can tell she's just humouring me. 'Like a missing link or something.'

'Exactly. And in any case, I just want one chance to look him in the eye and ask him. Just the two of us. I want to see if there's *anything*, even a flicker of a doubt. Then I'll know.'

'You think you'll be able to tell?'

My job feels like it was a million years ago; the psychology degree even longer ago than that. But I had a few skills that had not been dulled and deadened by prison life – a few abilities that had been sharpened instead. Like the ability to read people, to judge them.

'I used to interview people for a living, in my old life. I was good at it. I've interviewed hundreds of people, maybe more than a thousand, and after a while you get to know body language. You know when someone's bending the truth a little bit, when they're making things up on the fly and when they're flat-out lying. You know who can be trusted and who can't. It's the one skill I've got that had plenty of use in prison.'

'*Everyone* lies in prison,' she says. 'The truth is too bloody depressing.'

'Sure. But I have to try everything,' I say. 'This guy, he's retired, he's done his thirty years and he's got his nice police pension, he's safe. All he's got now is time – time to think. Time to reflect on all his cases. He's had ten years to think back on what happened.'

She considers this for a moment, slurping thirstily on her Diet Coke. 'Or there is the other option.'

'What's that?'

'We could just threaten to cut his balls off.'

I snort into my own drink. 'I'll try the talking option first.'

* * *

There is only one address left on the list of Musgroves that Owen had compiled from the electoral register. Jodie's map reading takes us to the picturesque little village of Neston, to a bungalow tucked away at the end of a cul-de-sac that peters out into a farmer's field. A twenty-year-old Volvo saloon sits on an overgrown drive, rust clustering around its wheel wells.

I have to ring the doorbell three times before it's answered, a thin female voice floating up from behind the frosted glass, her words unintelligible. A moment later, the door is opened by a tiny white-haired woman in a flower-patterned housecoat, a pair of secateurs in her hand. She's rake-thin and in her early eighties, the skin of her cheeks like fine crepe paper.

'Yes?' Her pale rheumy eyes are magnified behind large purple-framed glasses.

'Hi,' I say, putting my phone away as I launch into my patter again. 'Mrs Musgrove?'

'Yes?' She looks me up and down, taking in my jacket, my bag, my shoes.

'This is a bit awkward and I'm so sorry to bother you, but my name's Helen, I'm looking for someone and thought you might be able to help.'

She cocks her head, like a bird hearing a sound, but doesn't respond. So I continue with my lonely-hearts spiel about my relationship with John, our unintended break-up and how I'm desperate to re-establish contact.

'We were seeing each other for a bit,' I say, 'and we got along so well. We had such a lovely time together. But there was a bit of a misunderstanding on my part and . . . I'm not proud of what I said to him.' I purse my lips in what I hope is a suitably sad expression. 'We lost touch. I'd love to get back into contact with him again but I've lost his number. Saw you in the phone book and just thought I'd give you a try.'

It's not perfect but it was the best I could come up with at short notice. I knew Musgrove hadn't worn a wedding ring, and had said he didn't have children. Ten years ago, anyway.

Mrs Musgrove blinks slowly, twice, her eyes magnified by the big glasses.

'What did you say your name was again?'

'Helen,' I say. 'Eastwood.'

'And you were in a relationship with . . . ?'

'John.' I say it a little louder, wondering if she's hard of hearing. 'It was only after we split that I realised he was one of the good ones.'

'Close, were you?'

'For a time, at least.'

'Is that right?'

'Yes. I'm just so sorry about how it ended.'

She glances down the drive, to where Jodie waits in the car, before her small, sharp eyes return to me.

'Is this some kind of joke, young lady?' Her voice suddenly has an edge to it that wasn't there before.

'No,' I say, trying to work out where I've gone wrong. This had started well but it seemed to be going downhill fast. 'No, of course not.'

'Because if it is, it's in extremely poor taste.'

I hold a placatory hand up. 'I . . . didn't mean to upset you, Mrs Musgrove, I'm sorry if I have. To be honest it's been a little while since I've seen John, is everything OK?'

Her face darkens.

'You've got a damn nerve coming here.' She points a bony finger at me. 'In fact . . . I know who you are. Who you *really* are.'

I brace myself for the familiar refrain of a total stranger, the stare of recognition that says, *I know you. I saw you on TV. You killed your husband.* Clearly the glasses and the new jacket, the makeup and the handbag and the good shoes are not enough to disguise who I am.

'Honestly, Mrs Musgrove.' I clasp my hands in front of me, as if in prayer. 'I'm only trying to—'

'You're another one, aren't you?'

'I'm sorry?'

'Another one of those blasted nurses, you've seen an opportunity and you're just out for what you can get.' Her eyes are blazing now behind the purple-framed glasses. 'Just like the other one was.'

'No,' I say gently. 'Just a friend, that's all.'

'A *friend*.' She spits the word. 'My son doesn't need friends like you.'

'If I've offended you, Mrs Musgrove, I'm—'

'Think you can wheedle your way in so you can get your hands on his money, his pension? Get your name in his will for when the time comes? You're disgusting, that's what you are.'

I open my mouth to respond but she cuts me off before I can even get a word out.

'That's it, isn't it?' She jabs the finger again. 'Another bloody gold-digger? Well, Green Acres will be hearing from me again, you can be sure of that.'

She slams the door so hard the frosted glass panes rattle in their frames. I stand there for a moment longer as if she might open the door again to continue our brief conversation, the sting of her anger mixing with the exhilarating sense that *this is the place*. She's the right age to be his mother. I ring the doorbell again, willing to face her fury if it means uncovering even one more scrap of information. But the sound of a TV reaches me from deeper inside the house, the volume rising as if she's trying to blot out the sound of the doorbell. I ring a third time but there's still no answer.

Back in the car, I take out my phone and do a quick search, clicking on the first result that comes up.

'She seemed nice,' Jodie deadpans. 'What was all that about?'

'Not sure yet.' I hold the phone up to show her the screen. 'But she mentioned somewhere nearby. It could be worth a look.'

She nods and puts the car into gear. 'Let's go and pay a visit then, shall we?'

36

I'm wrong about John Musgrove.

He doesn't have time.

And he's not at Green Acres, either.

We pay a visit to the purpose-built facility on the outskirts of Corsham, posing as cousins up for a visit from London. Jodie is friendly and disarming and utterly charming with the young woman on the front desk – *Kathryn*, according to her name badge – and within a few minutes they're chatting away like old friends while I eavesdrop, pretending to peruse the leaflets in a rack about bereavement services and bequests.

Mr Musgrove, Kathryn tells Jodie apologetically, *was* a resident here but is not anymore. She lowers her voice, telling us that his mother had him moved to another facility not far away after complaining the staff at Green Acres were 'over familiar'. One agency nurse in particular – since dismissed, we are told in hushed tones – who tried to develop a relationship with John that 'went beyond the professional'. And even though Kathryn's 'not really supposed to give out forwarding addresses, not without permission,' – it would be such a shame if we didn't get a chance to see poor cousin John, especially since we've made the trip all the way from London.

Forty-five minutes later we're pulling into the car park outside Willow House, a grand old manor on the edge of Bradford-on-Avon with a large modern extension surrounded by lawns and trees. Like Green Acres, it's a hospice, although the place itself is older and more expensively decorated, more like a country club than a care facility. Visiting hours are until 7 p.m. so we have a little bit of time. Jodie gives the reception manager the same story as before and we are directed down a corridor towards the south wing and room seventeen.

'Didn't know you were such a good liar,' I whisper to her as we walk the echoing corridors, the soles of our shoes squeaking on the tile flooring.

'Never trust a former addict, Heather.' She gives me a wink. 'We lie to *everyone*. Including ourselves.'

A carer in dark blue scrubs is coming out of room seventeen as we walk up. She's carrying a clipboard and gives us a sympathetic smile as she passes by.

The door is open. Jodie stands back to let me go in first.

And then, for the first time in nine years, the first time since he'd stood in the witness box at Bristol Crown Court and helped to secure my conviction for murder, I'm face to face with former Detective Inspector John Musgrove. He's in a navy dressing gown and pyjamas, dozing in an armchair by the bay window, bathed in early evening sunlight. The view out into the gardens is stunning, manicured lawns rolling gently down to a lake, paths and benches dotted here and there with visitors pushing patients in wheelchairs. But Musgrove is turned away from the window, away from the light, and doesn't stir when we come in.

I hardly recognise him.

Whereas before he had been broad, with thick forearms and heavy shoulders, now he seems shrunken away to half the man he had been a decade ago. The dressing gown swamps his thin frame and he's completely bald, a greyish tinge to his mottled skin. There's an oxygen mask in his lap, a tube snaking to a tank on a wheeled trolley beside the chair. The air in the room is warm, a sharp tang of disinfectant layered with the thick dull smell of air freshener.

Jodie and I exchange glances. She pushes the door shut with a *click* and Musgrove stirs in the chair, eyes half opening, his head moving slowly to take in the two of us. He blinks slowly, frowns at me, checks the watch on his thin wrist as if unsure how long he has been asleep. He reaches for his glasses and puts them on with unsteady hands, studies us again. Studies *me*.

And then, finally, there is a dawn of recognition on his face. He stiffens and his eyes flick momentarily to his bed, where there is a large red call button on a unit perched on the bedside table.

He sees me seeing it too, and his body sags back into the armchair.

'Don't worry,' he rasps. His voice is familiar, that Yorkshire accent curling around each word, but as weak as if he's just climbed a mountain. 'It'd take me five minutes to get over there anyway. And besides, you're the first visitors I've had all week.'

I have imagined this moment a thousand times, thought about what I would say to him if I ever got the chance. What I would ask him, shout at him, how I would pour out all my anger and frustration and pain. But now the man is here in front of me, my mind is as blank and quiet as a fall of fresh snow.

'Hello, John.'

'How'd you find me, Heather?'

I shrug. 'Knocked on some doors. I had help.'

'I don't suppose it matters.' He coughs, a dry hacking wheeze that seems to exhaust him even further. 'You're here now.'

'This is my friend Jodie, by the way.'

'Welcome to the departure lounge, both of you.'

Jodie is still standing with her back to the door, hands thrust into the pockets of her jeans. She gives him a nod but says nothing.

Musgrove puts the oxygen mask to his mouth and takes a long puff, then another, before dropping it back into his lap.

'Wondered if you might come looking for me when you got out. Don't suppose there's much point asking how you've been?'

I ignore his question. 'How long have you . . . been here?'

He snorts, and it sets him off coughing again. 'That's the question people ask when they really want to know something else. They don't *really* want to know how long you've been in, what they're actually asking is how long you've got left.'

'And?'

'A few weeks, they say. Maybe a month if I'm lucky. Seems like you got here in the nick of time.'

The place is comfortable enough, I suppose. A suite rather than a room, with a big TV on the wall and a tasteful kitchenette off to the side, a sink and cupboard, a fridge, a small dining table extending out from the wall with a chair on either side and a laptop plugged into the socket. There is little to distinguish the cream-painted room from any other, only a handful of personal items. A hardback biography on the bedside table, a couple of framed pictures on the bookshelf, one of his small white-haired mother – who had slammed the door in my face earlier this afternoon – and the other a photo of a much younger John Musgrove in a grey morning suit with a white carnation in his lapel, hand in hand with a fair-haired man dressed identically. Both have broad *just-married* smiles.

I realise, as I study the wedding photo, why Mrs Musgrove didn't buy my lonely hearts story.

'Me and Gavin are separated,' he says. 'In case you're wondering.'

'Sorry to hear that.'

'So what are you going to do now you've found me, Heather?' He fixes me with his sharp blue eyes. 'You going to get the thumbscrews out? Wire me up to the mains, a dose of payback for the copper who got you sent down? I'm afraid lung cancer has beaten you to it. And I'm sure you're aware that coming here is a big black mark against the terms of your parole.'

I sit on the bed. It's high and firm, neatly made with a thick patterned blanket over the duvet.

'I just want to talk. About my case.'

He shrugs his thin shoulders. 'So, talk.'

I give him a summary of our investigation so far, Owen's work to uncover a conspiracy, unanswered questions about Christine Lai and the three men who have been looking for me since I was released.

'There's also the fact that I didn't kill my husband,' I add.

Musgrove takes another puff of oxygen from the mask.

'What do you want from me?'

'I need to know, John. I need to hear it from you.'

'Hear what?'

'The truth.'

'The truth is that I'm fifty-six years old and I'm dying, Heather.'

'And I'm sorry about that, I genuinely am. I think you were a decent man trying to do a difficult job ten years ago, with a lot of pressure on you from all sides.' I lean forward on the bed. 'But *surely* you had doubts back then, didn't you? Alternative suspects connected with his parliamentary work? With the benefit of hindsight, do you think it's possible you got it wrong? The fact that I'm here ten years later, still telling you I didn't do it, isn't that enough to make you wonder—'

'You know the worst thing about this place?' he says, cutting me off. 'Apart from the staff trying to be relentlessly bloody cheerful all the time?'

'What?'

'No booze. Not a drop. Not allowed in case it interferes with the delicate balance of my palliative care regime, or whatever they say. I mean, if you can't enjoy a dram in here of all places, what's the point of it all?'

'No booze in prison either.'

'Touché.'

'So what's your point?'

'Listen, we both want something, right?' He lets out a long, sad sigh. 'You want to know what was wrong with your conviction. I want one last bottle of fine single malt, to take the edge off.'

Words stall in my throat, the blood starting up a *thud-thud-thud* in my ears as his words sink in.

What was wrong with your conviction.

37

Finally, here in this moment, in this place, I had found what I had been seeking for the last ten years. I had found the key, the secret to unlocking all of it – to redeeming my past and finding a new future. A future in which my sons could be a part of my life again. And now that I was here I didn't want to wait another minute, not a second longer. Musgrove had *known*, he had known the conviction was unsafe and if we hadn't tracked him down he would have gone to his grave without telling a soul. He *owed* me this.

'So you'll tell me?'

He gestures at his surroundings. 'Haven't exactly got much to lose now, have I?'

The thud of blood in my ears is getting louder. 'If you've got something to tell me, just say it now. It's to do with corruption, isn't it? I know what happened to Liam was because of his job. And Christine Lai's tied up in it too. Just *tell* me instead of dancing around it, I don't have time for that.'

'You have more time than me.'

That brings me up short. 'True, I suppose.'

'Quid pro quo, Heather.' He gives me the ghost of a smile. 'Consider it a condemned man's last request. Put a glass of Talisker in my hand and I'll tell you everything.'

I stand up, blowing out a frustrated breath. 'Seriously?'

'I want a drink, and you want to know.'

His eyes hold mine with a quiet intensity, daring me to say yes. Knowing that I can't say no.

'Deal,' I say.

'I'll go,' Jodie says. It's the first time she's spoken since we walked into the room, and I get the sense she's eager to leave, to get away from this man if nothing else. 'I know a place nearby.'

I hand her my payment card and she's gone without another word, pulling the door shut behind her. I'm left alone with John Musgrove.

He indicates a wheelchair, folded next to the door.

'In the meantime, Heather,' he says, 'how about you and I get some fresh air?'

* * *

I wheel him out to the garden, along a path bordered by pink and purple hydrangeas, the sweet-soft scent of their blossoms heavy in the air. We find an empty bench down by the lake and he manages, with an effort, to lever himself out of the wheelchair and onto the wooden seat.

We sit in silence for a moment, the only sound between us the wheeze of breath forcing its way in and out of his shattered lungs. The sun is still warm but he's bundled up in an overcoat and scarf, thick slippers on his feet and a flat cap on his head. And still, he seems to shiver as if there is a coldness set deep in his bones.

'Would you ever have told me?' I say finally. 'Would you ever have told anyone, if you hadn't been here? If I hadn't come to find you?'

He folds his arms across his chest, shoulders hunched.

'I'd be lying if I said I hadn't thought about you over the last ten years, Heather. I've thought about you a lot, from time to time. You retire, you think you'll put it all behind you, but certain cases . . . Yeah. They stay with you.'

'You got promoted off the back of my conviction.'

'It wasn't only that.'

'How long has it been since you've known? Just since you've retired, or was it longer ago? Did you know even at the trial that it wasn't right, it wasn't me, but everything was too far gone by that point?'

'The thing about police work, Heather, the thing no one understands outside of the job, is that no case is watertight. No prosecution case is one hundred per cent perfect. If you're lucky you might get it to ninety per cent, or eighty, or maybe seventy-five, and God knows I've seen people convicted on less. And acquitted on more. There's always going to be an element of doubt, that's just how life is.'

We gaze out across the lake as a trio of ducks make a splashy landing on the water.

'But why did you wait so long?' I say.

He shrugs. 'Always thought there would be a better time. That I'd have more time.' He curls into another fit of hacking coughs, bending almost double at the waist. 'And now I've got secondary tumours in my liver, and up here too.' He points an index finger at his bald head. 'Short-term memory's going, can't even remember my own bloody phone number but I *can* still remember the details of cases from ten, twenty years ago.'

I'm surprised to find that my anger has dissipated almost completely, replaced with a heavy grey melancholy that wraps itself around me like a shawl. Both of us are losers here, both of us beaten by life.

'How long has it been, John?' I say quietly. 'Since you were diagnosed?'

'Christmas.' His voice has dropped to barely a whisper.

'I'm sorry,' I say. 'I had so much anger in prison, towards you, towards the system, towards all of it. But I'm sorry this has happened to you.'

He doesn't respond straightaway and I think emotion might have finally got the better of him. It's only after a minute that

I realise his eyes are closed, his chin dipping down to his chest with fatigue.

We're still like that – at opposite ends of the wooden bench, him dozing and me staring out at the lake – when Jodie finds us half an hour later with a couple of plastic bags clinking in her hand. Together we ease Musgrove back into the wheelchair and the three of us return to the hospice's main building, down the long corridor to his room, helping him back into the big armchair by the window.

Jodie has outdone herself. Not only has she got exactly the single malt whisky he asked for, she has bought cut-glass tumblers too.

'No point buying the good stuff,' she says, 'and then drinking out of the crappy little squash glasses you've got in your cupboard.'

Musgrove has perked up considerably since seeing the unopened bottle of Talisker.

'Quite right,' he says. To me, he adds: 'I like her.'

Jodie unpacks her purchases in the little kitchenette, a soft *pop* as she twists the cap off the whisky and then half fills a small jug with water from the tap.

'Just a little dash of water,' Musgrove calls to her, licking his lips. 'Not too much, love. A drop or two to break the meniscus and open up the taste, that's all.'

While she's pouring and he's distracted, I slip my mobile phone from my pocket and hit *start* on the voice recorder app, placing it on the side table next to his armchair. Jodie emerges from the kitchenette with a loaded tray and hands a tumbler to Musgrove, and then one to me. She takes the last one for herself.

'So what are we going to toast?' she says.

Musgrove stares longingly into the pale amber liquid in his glass. 'How about justice?'

The three of us clink the heavy glasses together and murmur the toast. I take a small sip, the smoky, peaty liquor burning my throat as it goes down, too nervous to really enjoy it. Jodie knocks hers back in a single gulp, like a shot. Musgrove holds the glass beneath

his nose, inhaling deeply before taking a slow, considered mouthful, closing his eyes in rapture as he swallows and exhaling with a
sigh of delight.

'A fine single malt is all you really need in this life,' he says, taking another mouthful. 'And that is God's honest truth.'

He pushes his empty glass towards Jodie and she obliges, filling
it with another generous measure of whisky and topping it up with
a splash of water. She pours another half-inch into her own tumbler as well. There is a tremor in my hand as I raise my glass. *Just a
sip. Need to focus, need to be straight for this, to remember exactly
what he says next.* I glance at the screen of my phone to double-
check the voice recorder is going, seconds ticking onwards.

'So, John,' I say, leaning forward. 'We made a deal.'

'Indeed we did.'

'Now I need you to tell me.'

He takes another hefty swallow of Scotch from his glass.

'And you're sure you want to know?' he says.

'I am.'

'You're absolutely *certain*? Because some things can be very
hard to hear.'

'Yes.' My heart drums painfully against my ribs. 'Whatever it is,
just tell me.'

'OK, Heather. I'll tell you what was wrong with your conviction.' He looks me right in the eye. 'Nothing. Absolutely *nothing
at all.*'

He raises the whisky tumbler towards me.

'Cheers.' He takes another deep sip, letting out a little gasp of
pleasure, his head falling back against the armchair. 'That's the
stuff all right. Oh *yes.*'

For a second I'm too stunned to say anything.

There is a sick, hollow feeling in my stomach as if I've been
cheated or tricked, as if I've opened a longed-for gift and found
nothing inside but an empty box.

'I don't understand,' I say. 'What are you talking about? What do you mean, *nothing*?'

'Exactly and precisely that, my dear.'

'We made a deal, you said you'd tell me the truth. You said you'd tell me everything.'

'I *said* I would tell you what was wrong with your conviction. Which is exactly what I've done. Your conviction was entirely safe and justified and correct, and that's why you did those nine years. That's why your appeal was dismissed. To be honest, I'd hoped by now you'd accepted the consequences of your actions, taken responsibility for them. It's the only way you're ever going to move forward.'

38

I'm gripping my glass so tightly the knuckles are white ridges of bone beneath the skin, and I have a sudden urge to hurl it at his head. I slam it onto the table instead, whisky slopping out onto the polished teak.

'You bastard. You tricked me.'

Musgrove shrugs. 'What did you expect?'

'You were talking as if you'd changed your mind. As if you had regrets. I know I didn't kill Liam, and I hoped you'd want to put the record straight.' I gesture at the surroundings. 'Especially considering you're here.'

His forehead bunches with angry lines for the first time since Jodie and I had arrived.

'What?' he says. 'You thought that just because I'm dying, I'd fall to my knees and confess that it was all a stitch-up? That I'd unburden myself with some great revelation about how me and my team turned you over?' He is breathless again, his chest rising and falling with the exertion, and he reaches for a puff on the oxygen mask next to his chair. 'That I *knowingly* got an innocent person sentenced to eighteen years? That I'd take my whole life, my whole career – a career that has been everything to me – and blow it all away just because you turned up on my doorstep?'

'You never considered any other suspects,' I say. 'Not after that first day. You got tunnel vision, you were totally fixated on me and you couldn't see the bigger picture, all the things that didn't fit.'

He shakes his head. 'I tried to tell you earlier. Every case has its rough edges, the little pieces that don't quite fit. The odd things that don't quite chime with the rest, or don't slot in one way or the other. People nowadays watch so much *CSI* and *Sherlock* and *Silent Witness* on telly and they think that everything is tied up neatly with a bow. But real life isn't like that. Real *cases* are not like that either, there's never a case that's one hundred per cent watertight, that's why we let the jury decide one way or the other.'

'And what were the *rough edges* in my case?'

'It doesn't matter now. Not with your legal options exhausted and—'

'It matters to me! If there were weaknesses in the case I deserve to know.'

'You haven't been listening to what I'm saying to you. You're a convicted murderer, you've had your due process and you deserve whatever—'

'*Wrongfully* convicted.'

He grunts and shakes his head.

I stand up, move nearer to his chair. 'Were you leaned on by the chief whip's office to get a quick result?'

'No.'

'Was there pressure on you to ignore any connection with corruption in Parliament, cash for access, sensitive information being sold to big corporates?'

'There was pressure to get a result. The *right* result. Full stop.'

'Does the name Artemis mean anything to you? Is it a company? A project name?'

There is the slightest pause in the passage of the glass to his lips, before he takes another sip of whisky.

'Never heard that name before.'

'I don't believe you.'

'Believe what you like,' he says. 'I'm dying.'

'Why has most of the case evidence been lost by the police?'

'Nothing to do with me.' He shrugs. 'I was already retired by then.'

'The blonde woman in the photos on Liam's phone, how come you never found her?'

'Rough edges, like I said. But we still had enough to get over the line.'

For some reason, the sporting analogy stokes the fire of my anger even higher.

'That's what you call it, ruining my life? *Getting over the line?*'

'You killed your husband, Heather.'

'No!' I lean down towards him, close enough to smell the sour whisky on his breath. 'No, I didn't. And I really thought you'd have the guts to admit you had doubts. Especially when I found out you were in this place.'

He doesn't move this time, doesn't flinch.

'In that case, I'm pleased to be able to disappoint you.'

I blow out a sigh of frustration and turn to Jodie who has been leaning against the wall, glass in hand, observing the whole exchange. Her raised eyebrow says, *I told you so.*

Without a word, she turns and moves back to the kitchenette, rattling through cutlery in the drawer loud enough for him to hear.

'Some decent knives in here, Heather, if you want to go with my approach instead.' At my quizzical look, she adds: 'Remember – we threaten to cut his balls off unless he gives us the info?'

Musgrove freezes, the glass halfway to his lips again, eyes flicking between the two of us as if he's not sure whether she's serious.

Jodie pulls out a wicked-looking carving knife with a silver handle, testing the blade against her fingertips. She grips it easily, checking the weight, the balance, the point, as if to familiarise herself with the knife. She seems quite comfortable with a blade in her hand.

'I reckon this one's the sharpest.' She points it casually at Musgrove. 'What do you reckon, *John*? Do you want to play the yes–no game?'

For a second, the temptation is there. I don't think Jodie would actually hurt him but *he* doesn't know that. Maybe it's worth a try, just to see if he gives us anything more.

But it's not right. Not when he's defenceless. Whatever he's done or not done, he doesn't deserve this.

I shake my head. 'We're wasting our time here.'

'Pity.' She stabs the carving knife down into a chopping board with a *thud* instead, leaving it embedded upright in the wood. She comes out of the little kitchen and points at the three-quarters-full bottle of whisky. 'Do you want it?'

I look at Musgrove, at the tremor in his hand as he pours another generous measure into his glass.

'Leave it,' I say, grabbing my phone up off the side table. 'Let's go.'

I throw one last glance back at former Detective Inspector John Musgrove, but he won't meet my gaze. The door swings shut.

Jodie hurries to keep up with my angry strides as we head back along the corridor towards the reception desk.

'It was worth a go, Heather. Not your fault he's an arsehole.'

'You were right,' I say through gritted teeth. 'Should have listened to you.'

In the car park, she guides me to the passenger side of the little black Corsa. I wait until both doors are shut before I let it out, a sob of rage and frustration so loud it makes my ears ring.

Jodie takes my hand, gives it a squeeze.

'That's cops for you, isn't it?' she says. 'They're all bastards. All the bloody same.'

'I really thought . . . when we found him and he started talking to us.' I shake my head. 'He could have called for help, raised the alarm somehow, but he didn't. Thought he had something to say to me, to get it off his chest after all these years.'

'Not too late for us to go back and have a go with the knife.'

'Don't think he'd have budged anyway, he seemed pretty adamant to me. Can't believe we've wasted a whole day on this.'

She makes a small sound in her throat. 'Maybe it wasn't totally a waste.'

'What do you mean?'

'You say you can spot a liar? OK. But I know cops. Dealt with a million of them in my time, and I know the difference.'

'The difference between what?'

'Between him trying to convince *you* of something, as opposed to trying to convince *himself* just by saying it over and over again. Repeating the same bullshit until it seems like the only possible version of the facts. Polishing the bullshit until it turns into gold.' She squeezes my hand again. 'There *is* something that he's not telling you. And you know what else? I was watching him, watching his body language from when we walked in, and the one time he really flinched, like you'd struck a nerve, was when you asked him about that Adonis thing.'

'You mean Artemis.'

'Artemis,' she says. 'Yeah. That was the one time you caught him off guard, like he wasn't expecting it. It really landed.'

'Only problem is, we don't know what the hell Artemis is. Or was.'

'There was definitely something there, though. We could go back in and show him the knife again?'

'I'm not going to threaten a dying man, Jodie.'

'Had a feeling you'd say that.' She produces her phone from her jacket pocket, shows me the screen. 'Took a picture of this in the kitchen, while I was looking for a water jug. Maybe it might help?'

It's a close-up shot of a Post-it note, looping blue biro in the large rounded handwriting of a teenage girl or a young woman. Maybe a member of staff. The first is an email address, jmus4519@flashmail. com. The second looks like it might be a password. *Tyke$1967.*

'Where did you see this?'

'Above the little kitchen table, pinned to the noticeboard.'

I remember his words as he drowsed on the bench by the lake. *Short-term memory's going, can't even remember my own bloody phone number.*

'His email address,' I say, taking out my own phone. 'I'll try to log in now.'

She reaches into her other pocket, holds up a small silver device the size of her little finger. 'Swiped this as well, it was just like poking out of his laptop. It's one of those sticks, isn't it? What do you call it?'

'A USB memory stick. You stole it?'

'Never trust an addict, Heather.' She drops it into my palm. 'We'll nick anything. Got to be worth a look, hasn't it?'

I turn the little silver stick over in my hand, the polished metal smooth and still slightly warm from her pocket. There is nothing on it apart from a manufacturer's engraving denoting its memory capacity: *32GB*.

'Looks like I'm going to need a laptop too.'

Jodie turns the ignition key and the Corsa's engine coughs into life.

'First things first,' she says, 'I need another drink.'

39

We find a pub in Winsley with tables in a timber-beamed dining room, Jodie working on a large glass of red wine while I sip a Diet Coke and open up the browser on my phone to log into Musgrove's email account. I wondered if he would suspect anything, whether he might have already changed the password to keep us out and maybe called an old colleague in the police for good measure. Then I think about the open bottle of whisky we'd left behind, the enthusiastic third drink he was pouring as we walked out, and nurture the hope that it might be a while yet. I have another missed call from Trevor Boyle, but no message this time. I'll get back to him later.

Jodie sees it first.

'Oh shit,' she says quietly, swallowing a mouthful of wine.

'What?'

She points across the other side of the room. A collection of newspapers stuffed into a wire rack for pub customers to read and return. Among them is today's edition of the *Bath Echo*, my face filling half the front page, my throat tightening as I read the headline. 'Killer Wife Walks Free'. We're sitting barely twenty feet away from a blown-up picture of me, taken yesterday by a random stranger on a train platform. Presumably the local press have picked it up from the Bristol paper. It was spreading like pondweed.

'Christ,' I breathe. A real-life pariah in my hometown: so this is what it felt like.

'I hate to say it,' Jodie says, 'but every idiot is going to be trying for a shot of you now, to put up on their social media.'

I retrieve the baseball cap from my bag, pulling the brim low over my face.

'Better crack on then, hadn't we?'

At the email login page, I type in Musgrove's details from the Post-it note.

In a detached way, I feel bad about doing it; I'm basically hijacking his account. Snooping on the personal correspondence of a dying man. But I don't have space for those kinds of scruples any more – they are a luxury I have not been able to afford for a long time.

Musgrove hasn't changed his password.

There are more than five thousand emails in his inbox, a counter at the bottom of the page indicating that almost four thousand of them are unread. I scroll back. It doesn't look as if he's been checking the account for a while and the unread emails seem to date back to the end of last year, about nine months ago. Around Christmas, the time he said he'd been diagnosed. The kind of news that must have meant staying on top of his inbox suddenly became an extremely poor use of his time. I wonder how long after that the doctors told him there was nothing more they could offer but palliative care.

There are more than a hundred sub-folders too, listed alphabetically, everything from 'AA/car' to 'Wales'. Maybe thousands more emails filed away in these folders too.

It was going to take a while to go through all of it. But before any of that, I needed to lock the door behind me. I find the account details and click on the option, typing in the existing password into one box, pausing to look up at Jodie across the table from me.

'What was your first pet called?'

She smiles at me over her glass. 'You trying to figure out my porn name?'

'Just humour me.'

'Butch. She was a rescue cat with half a tail.'

'She?'

'I didn't know she was a girl when I named her.'

'And what was the number of your first house?'

She shrugs. 'Dunno. We moved around a lot, different council places. Didn't stay anywhere very long.'

'Ok, doesn't matter.'

I type 'Butch2023' twice into the two empty boxes, and then that's it: the password is changed and Musgrove is locked out of his account.

Jodie finishes her wine and orders another before our food has arrived: steak and fries for her, Caesar salad for me. She tucks hungrily into her steak while I pick at the salad with a fork as I continue to scroll through his emails.

Fifteen minutes later, Jodie lays her cutlery on her empty plate and signals to the waiter for another round of drinks.

'Come on now, Heather.' Her tone is playful, relaxed, a passable attempt at a posh Home Counties accent. 'You know the rules, darling.'

I don't look up from the phone. 'What rules?'

'No devices at the dinner table.' She picks up the phone and moves it away from me, next to her own plate. 'Eat up your rabbit food, there's a good girl.'

I give her a small smile. 'OK, Mum.'

'You eat and I'll look.' She taps at the screen of my phone. 'What are we looking for again?'

I have to admit that I don't actually know, not precisely. He's been retired for a couple of years and his email might contain a whole lot of nothing, but if Jodie's instincts were right – and he *was* hiding something – it wasn't a bad place to start.

'Anything that might relate to his work as a detective, on my case or any other. Anything from Avon and Somerset Police, anything that looks official or confidential, anything that's to or from former colleagues on the force. You'd be surprised at the kind of stuff people put on personal email.'

'Nothing surprises me anymore,' Jodie mutters, scrolling through his inbox.

The salad is good, tasty and filling with big chunks of chicken and a delicious creamy dressing. I hadn't realised how hungry I was, how good it feels to be able to sit and eat a meal in my own time, in a cosy pub, rather than at a long bench table with inmates crammed to my left and right.

Jodie narrates as I eat, clicking into emails, scanning them, looking at the next one. After a few minutes, she makes a little sound in her throat.

'What is it?' I say.

'Found his address.' She holds up the phone to me, an order confirmation email for a set of speakers from John Lewis. A Bath address for Mr J.T. Musgrove listed in Rockliffe Road, Villa Fields. 'We could have a look?'

'But we know he won't be there.'

'Exactly.'

'And even if we did, how would we get in?'

She frowns at me as if I'm slow on the uptake. 'Duh?'

*   *   *

Back in Bath, I park the car a few streets over from the hostel and we use the back way in Jodie had showed me yesterday. It's dark by the time we're climbing the park fence and we approach slowly, taking our time, in case the three men have returned. Jodie goes in first, alone, and texts me an all-clear message a minute later. There is no black van parked in the street out front.

'Thanks,' I say later, as we get ready for bed in the cramped dormitory room. 'For today.'

She shrugs. 'It was fun.'

'But I'm glad you were there. That we were together.'

'I like being busy,' she says, looking down at the floor. 'Takes my mind off everything else. And besides, us screw-ups have to stick together, right?'

* * *

The two of us head out early on Thursday morning to buy a laptop. After a quick visit to Currys we decamp to a nearby Starbucks and I get it unpacked and plugged in while Jodie fetches coffees and pastries for breakfast. I had assumed she'd want a lie-in this morning, but she was up at the same time as me; she seems newly protective after the time we spent together yesterday, and doesn't want me to go off on my own.

By the time she returns with the coffees, I've finished setting up the laptop and logged onto the free Wi-Fi. I also have another missed call from Trevor Boyle, to add to the two from yesterday. He leaves another irritated voicemail asking me to call him back as soon as I can to arrange a meeting at his office. We're already scheduled to have a two-week progress meeting next week so I delete the message and switch my phone to silent.

As I'm sliding in the memory stick Jodie took from Musgrove's room at the hospice, I wonder again whether he'll file a complaint, go to the police or otherwise come after us for stealing it. Or maybe that was the reason for Boyle's call? All the more reason for accessing the contents, copying them, and getting rid of the memory stick as soon as possible.

Clicking on the icon to look at the memory stick, listed as the E-drive on my screen, I say a silent prayer that it's not password protected.

Please just give me a break, just this once.

It's not.

And I'm in, the screen filling with small yellow directory icons, dozens of them.

A quick scan suggests there are years' worth of folders here, maybe the entire contents of his laptop and a previous one, documents going back five, six, ten years or more.

Jodie leans over to peer at the screen. 'Any good?'

'There are masses of files here, it's going to take me a while to plough through this lot.'

'What are we looking for this time?'

'Same as with his email.' I take a sip of my Americano. 'I'll tell you when I find it.'

My phone buzzes on the table and I answer it without checking the display.

'Finally!' Trevor Boyle talks over my greeting. 'So you've not died then? Why are you not returning my calls?'

'Sorry, some trouble with this new phone, I can't seem to set up the voicemail properly—'

'Whatever,' he says, irritation snapping in his voice. 'I need you to come in as a matter of *urgency*. Not this week, not tomorrow. *Today.*'

I look at my watch. 'I'm seeing some people at noon but I could come to you after that?'

'People?' he says. 'What people?'

'Some . . . old friends.' I glance over at Jodie. 'And new ones.'

'Two p.m., and don't be late. Do *not* miss this appointment unless you want to find yourself on your way back to HMP Eastwood Park. Am I making myself clear?'

40

The College Arms is an old-school pub that Owen assured us would be less busy than the more modern bars and gastropubs around the Rec. He's at a table in the low-ceilinged saloon bar at the back, where yellowing real ale posters adorn the wall and a small TV in the corner plays silent coverage of the horse racing. We're the only people in there. I make the introductions and go to order a round of drinks at the bar, alcohol for Owen and Jodie, soft for Amy and me.

As the barman fills our glasses, I lean against the polished wood and look over at my strange group gathered around the ring-stained wooden table in the corner, grateful and humbled and most of all amazed that there is even one person left in the world willing to sit down for a drink with me, let alone three. Jodie is on the left, still wearing the jacket I gave her a few days ago, talking animatedly to Owen about how she and I met. He nods and listens, his back to the wall, keeping a wary eye on the door. Amy sits off to the right in a jacket and blouse, a little stiff and separate from them, awaiting my return from the bar.

My crew. My little team, all of us broken in our own ways: the recovering addict, the disgraced reporter and the bereaved sister. And me, the worst of all of us. And yet, the three of them are here *because* of me. Because of Liam.

All of us looking for a way back, perhaps.

I pay for the drinks and carry them on a tray to the table, where Jodie is trying to coax Amy into the conversation.

'You know,' she says to the younger woman, 'you don't look much like I thought you would.'

Amy raises an eyebrow. 'How'd you think I would look?'

'Dunno,' Jodie shrugs. 'Maybe a bit older. Our age.'

'There was a gap between me and Liam,' Amy says, apparently unfazed by Jodie's directness. 'Our mother didn't want to give up trying for a girl.'

Owen clears his throat. 'Right,' he says. 'Updates. Heather, you should go first.'

I give them a summary of the last thirty-six hours, running through our travels yesterday to track down John Musgrove and our subsequent conversation with him at the hospice. Our suspicions about his behaviour and our initial work to trawl through his email and the memory stick Jodie took from his laptop. At her prompting, I also mention the appearance of the mysterious black van over the last two days and its occupants' apparent interest in me.

Owen, who has been writing rapid shorthand into a spiral-bound notebook, looks up to ask if I'm OK.

'How about that 2013 memo from the meeting with Christine Lai,' I say to him, changing the subject. 'Any luck tracking down the other two people who attended it?'

'Maybe.' Owen holds up an image on his phone of the man in the grey suit she had met on Tuesday. 'I did a bunch of reverse image searches on this guy. Despite a lot of deliberate obfuscation online, a lot of scrubbed data and deleted pages, I finally got a match.'

Jodie leans closer to study the picture I snapped as he came out of the Harlequin bistro two days ago.

'So who is he?' she says. 'Looks proper rich.'

'As best I can tell, his name's Philip Boivin,' Owen says. 'French-Canadian CEO of various companies registered overseas and extremely protective of his privacy. His online footprint is virtually non-existent. I'm still trying to dig more stuff up.'

I take another look at the image of the tall, distinguished-looking man, his dark hair flecked with grey.

'PB,' I say. 'The initials from the memo.'

Owen nods. 'It would be a hell of a coincidence if he *wasn't* the guy from that meeting.'

'I spook Christine by turning up on her doorstep, and he's the first one she runs to.'

Jodie drinks a third of her vodka and Coke in one long pull.

'Or maybe she's sleeping with him?' She sets her glass down heavily on the table. 'He's a good-looking fella.'

'There's got to be more to it than that,' I say. 'There's *got* to be. We have to figure out their connection back then, how and why they both ended up in that meeting.'

On Christine herself, Owen says, there was little activity on her phone over the last couple of days that aroused his suspicions apart from a single text message from an unknown number, which he reads out to us:

As discussed, you can reach me on this number in emergency.

Christine had sent a single thumbs-up emoji in reply but there had been no other traffic between her and this number, nor to the number she had messaged on Tuesday about *needing to speak urgently, in person* – a number we now believed belonged to Philip Boivin. Owen tells us he had followed Christine again yesterday with the help of the spyware he had installed, but had found nothing more interesting than the gym she belonged to and the food delivery company she used.

'Thanks, Owen.' I turn to my sister-in-law, who has waited silently through all of this. She still looks a little uncertain, as if she's not sure what she's let herself in for. 'And to you, Amy, I just want to say thanks again for coming along today.'

'Not sure how much help I'm going to be.' Amy indicates a stack of dusty black A4 box files in a plastic bag by her feet. 'But I went up into the attic too, like you asked. Had to wait until my mother and father were out at the gala dinner last night. There's *so* much of Liam's stuff up there, boxes and boxes of it, I had no idea they had kept so much. It was quite hard to know where to start.'

She describes the contents she's found so far: pictures and certificates, his old exercise books from school, folders of university notes, old clothes and toys and model aircraft from his boyhood bedroom. Plus some work-related material, including notebooks and files from his time as an MP. An initial sift of the material has yielded three box files of papers which might be relevant, she says.

'I had a look at some of it but there wasn't really time for a deep-dive,' she says, tucking a strand of hair behind her ear. 'A lot of the stuff they could just never bear to part with, I suppose. And it's been there ever since.'

Owen leans forward. 'Any chance you could get me in there to have a better look at it all? Or Heather?'

'Too risky for Heather.' She shoots me an apologetic glance. 'They're rarely out at the same time so probably too risky for you, too. These box files are a start, and I'll go up to the attic again for another look the next time I get a chance.'

She pushes the plastic bag full of box files towards Owen with her foot. He lifts one of the heavy black folders out and blows dust off the top, easing off an elastic binder holding it closed.

'Oh,' Amy says, 'I found this as well. Thought you might want to have it, Heather.'

She takes something square out of her shoulder bag and puts it on the table in front of me: a plastic CD case. I recognise it immediately, heat rushing to my face. A home-made CD cover, a composite of four pictures of Liam and me taken in a photo booth in the King's College student union one night, me sitting on his lap, both of us grinning, laughing, half drunk, in that first fierce full bloom of love. Liam had printed a copy as the cover for this, the mixtape he had made for me after a long conversation about favourite bands on our first date. I turn it over, where the track listing is handwritten in faded capital letters. Radiohead, Manic Street Preachers, Lauryn Hill, Faithless, Oasis, Massive Attack and a dozen others, love songs and ballads and anthems that he'd wanted us to share. The first gift he ever gave me.

'Thank you, Amy.' I brush my fingertips across the scratched plastic cover. 'Thank you. Never thought I would see this again.'

I open the case and the silver disc inside still bears Liam's handwriting, in black marker pen.

For Heather
Enjoy!
L x

It's like a message in a bottle, washing up from my old life. An aching, bittersweet reminder of what Liam and I had really meant to each other. Not the public narrative that had been created by others over the last decade. The *truth*.

'Just wish I had something to play CDs on.'

'I could burn you a digital copy of that playlist?' Owen says. 'If you like?'

I nod my thanks and he takes a picture of the track listing on the back.

'OK,' I say, taking a deep breath and clearing my throat. 'What about Christine Lai?'

Jodie, who has sat silently through all of this, raises her hand.

'I could follow her,' she says, finishing her drink. 'I want to do *something*, I mean as long Heather doesn't need the Corsa tomorrow. Different person, different car, Christine won't have seen it before and it's just a beaten-up old thing, wouldn't stand out anywhere. Good at blending in. Just like me.'

Owen is nodding. 'It's not a bad idea. Heather?'

The three of them turn to look at me.

'Sounds like a plan,' I say. 'I'll stay at the hostel. I've got a ton of stuff to trawl through on Musgrove anyway.'

I take a sip of my lime and soda and summarise the plan of action. Owen would work through the box files retrieved from the Vernons' attic; Jodie would keep tabs on Christine Lai, where she went and who she met; and I would scour the material we had obtained from John Musgrove to figure out what he might have been hiding all these years. If she had a chance, Amy would check if there was anything else that might be useful stored in her parents' house.

We were a team. A good team. For the first time, I feel a glimmer of hope that we're actually making progress. That all of this might actually *mean* something.

I'm still thinking this as I follow the three of them out, into the main bar at the front of the pub. It's busier in here with lunchtime customers eating and drinking, people in work clothes mixed in with the tourists. At a large table near the door, a dark-haired woman is carrying drinks over from the bar, two at a time to a group of colleagues all sporting photo ID lanyards around their necks.

She turns to collect the last of the drinks off the bar and we almost collide.

'Oh,' she says absently. 'Sorry.'

'Sorry,' I reply automatically.

She reaches for the last two drinks – a pair of pint glasses full of lemonade and ice – and then stops, meets my eye and does a rapid double take that I've seen too many times already in these last few days.

There is a moment of frozen recognition on her face. Her mouth goes slack, but no words escape. She takes a small step back as if I might be contagious.

'Sian,' I say. 'Hi.' When she doesn't reply, I add: 'How have you been?'

She has changed little since we shared an office; her hair is shorter and there are a few more lines at the corners of her eyes, but that's about it. We had been close colleagues and good friends, once upon a time. Had worked together, been in the choir together, had lived in the same neighbourhood and sent our kids to the same nursery. We'd even been on holiday to Devon together when Theo was a baby. Her two were around the same age as mine.

'Heather,' she says finally, as if dredging the name up from the depths of her memory. 'My God. I didn't even realise you were . . . that it was . . .'

'Yeah. Last week.'

Amy, Jodie and Owen have gone on ahead of me and are already back out on the street, so it's just the two of us standing awkwardly at the bar. Sian hurriedly puts down the last two drinks on the table in front of her colleagues and a couple of them look up expectantly, as if she's going to introduce us. She looks utterly horrified at the prospect.

'How are . . . things?'

'I'm getting there.' I force a smile. 'Just glad to be home.'

Sian's pretty face darkens in confusion. 'Home?'

'Well, you know . . . Here. Bath.'

'Right. Of course.'

Another awkward moment of silence.

'We should . . .' I trail off, realising that I have no idea what I'm actually going to say to this woman. *We should do what, exactly? Go for coffee? Grab dinner and drinks to talk about old times? Or about the fact that you pretended I didn't exist for the last ten years?* 'How are Callum and Paige doing?'

'Good.' She takes another step back, looking as if she wishes the ground would swallow her up. 'Really good, thanks.'

Jodie reappears in the doorway. 'You coming?' she says.

I give Sian a nod. 'It was good to see you.'

Relief washes across her face.

'You too.'

The whispered chatter starts up at her table before the door has even swung closed behind me.

41

'Help me out with this,' Trevor Boyle says. 'Which part of our conversation last week did you not understand?'

I'm back in his office, back in the stuffy room with the big desk and the small meeting table, and he is already out of his chair and pacing the patchy carpet. He has spent the last ten minutes going over in fine forensic detail the specifics of my probation, the conditions on which I have been released from prison on licence and the process of a possible recall to prison.

'It's normally the men who struggle with this,' Boyle says. 'The men who can't adhere to a few basic rules and end up going back inside. But you want to be the exception, do you?'

'No.'

'So I'll ask you again: which part of our conversation last week did you not understand?'

There's no right answer to his question, so I don't reply.

'To be specific,' he says, sighing with exasperation, 'which part of "no contact with witnesses, jurors, police or court staff involved in your original trial" did you not understand? You do remember being in this room less than a week ago, sitting in that chair, reading the terms of your licence agreement and signing your name at the bottom?'

He holds up his copy of the document as if to prove his point.

'Yes,' I say. 'I remember.'

'Well thank *goodness* for that.' He drops the paper back to his desk. 'I'd started thinking I had imagined the whole thing.'

A formal complaint, he tells me, had been made to the probation service. That complaint had attracted the attention of his boss, the regional director, who was only too aware of the high profile nature of my original case and *extremely* keen that the current situation didn't blow up in his face.

'What am I supposed to have done?' I say.

'You've been knocking on doors, Heather. Telling stories.'

'According to who?'

He leans forward across his paper-strewn desk.

'You know I'm not going to tell you that.'

But he doesn't need to. Former DI John Musgrove must have made a call after my visit yesterday. It hadn't occurred to me that it would come back to bite me so fast; I assumed the wheels of probation service bureaucracy moved more slowly.

'Hard for me to respond to an allegation if I don't know the details.'

'But you deny it anyway?'

When I don't answer, he launches into another monologue about the fact that he's been obliged to start work on a 'recall dossier' that could be submitted at any time, and I wait for him to hit me with the *coup de grâce*: the fact that I'd already broken the rules not just *once* but *twice*, by talking to Amy. If Boyle knew about Musgrove, perhaps he knew about that too. I brace myself, thinking of ways I could explain, defend or deny my actions.

Boyle carries on with his lecture: he is a man who likes the sound of his own voice.

But after a few minutes I start to suspect that maybe he *doesn't* know about me seeing Amy. Because she's kept it a secret – to protect *me*. I feel a new surge of gratitude towards my sister-in-law, who had shielded me with her silence. Who had talked to me, listened to me, had searched a dusty attic for information that might help me find the truth.

My probation officer is still talking, his initial anger seeming to have burned itself out.

He leans back in his leather swivel chair, putting a fleshy hand on each armrest like a king on his little throne.

'Listen,' he says. 'This is serious, Heather.'

'I know. I'm sorry.'

'All it takes is one phone call from me,' he says, 'and before you know it, you'll be in that secure van on your way back to Eastwood Park. No waiting, no hearing, no long drawn-out process, you just get sent straight back while we work out what to do with you. You never know – maybe your old cell will still be free.'

As if his words trigger a memory of that place imprinted on my skin, the scar tissue on my neck starts to itch. Angry red flesh left by scalding water thrown into my cell, sugar mixed in to make a paste that sticks to skin and intensifies the burns. It had happened in my first year in prison and I couldn't even remember exactly how the dispute had started. I *could* remember that my attacker had never been punished – I had known enough by then to stay quiet when the screws asked me who did it. To bite down on the pain and keep it inside, because being known as a grass would be to fall even lower in the grim hierarchy of prison life.

I'd been out for barely a week but every day of freedom that passed, every hour, made the thought of a return to life behind bars even worse. The thought of losing my foothold back in the world, however tenuous, was unbearable. To have glimpsed justice in the far-off distance – only to have it snatched away – would be more than I could take.

'I understand,' I say through gritted teeth.

'Because you should be absolutely clear that there's no flexibility here, Heather. You only get *one* warning.' His eyes challenge me not to look away. 'And this is it.'

42

I tell Jodie what I need and she says she knows just the place, telling me on the way about her own brushes with Boyle in the past. She drives us west and south, bypassing the city centre and heading into Twerton. It's not an area that I know well but she seems very familiar with it, navigating effortlessly among long rows of pale post-war terraces packed tightly together and unloved four-storey blocks of flats.

'Heather,' she says, as we wait at a traffic light. 'Can I ask you something?'

'Of course.'

'Not being funny but . . . how did you meet that journalist guy?'

'Owen?'

'Yeah.'

I explain how I had found his articles online and then come across a business card in the storage unit that had led me to him.

'When I first saw him in the pub earlier,' she says, 'I thought you'd taken a leaf out of my book.'

'How do you mean?'

The light turns green and she pulls smoothly away, going up through the gears.

'You know,' she says. 'I've always had a thing for deeply unsuitable men too.'

I shake my head. 'It's nothing like that.'

'But you didn't, like, go to his office first?'

'He's freelance.'

She pulls a sceptical face.

'You just sent a message to this random email address and this big tattooed guy turns up the next day and says his name's Owen Tanner?'

'Well, there was a bit more to it than that but—'

'Are you sure you can trust him?'

'Don't you?'

Her brow creases into a frown. 'Dunno. There's something . . . odd about him, but I don't know what it is.'

'Like what?'

'It's weird. I can't put my finger on it.' She indicates right and turns across a junction leading deeper into the housing estate. 'Maybe it's because he doesn't quite look like I thought he would look.'

I remember when I had first met him, my surprise at his physical appearance. At his size, the way he dressed.

'I know what you mean,' I say. 'But if he's not Owen Tanner, who is he?'

'Don't know that either,' she says quietly. 'Just . . . don't let him spin you a line, OK? Seems a bit obsessed to me and he sets off my weirdo radar big time.'

Finally, she pulls the car to a stop outside a short parade of shops and points to a larger unit at the end, which houses a community library.

'Free Wi-Fi,' she says as I get out. 'And not as many rubberneckers as in town, wanting to take your picture. You should be safe as long as you stay right here. Don't go wandering off anywhere.'

'Where are you going?'

'To see a friend.' She gives me a wink. 'This is my old stomping ground. Won't be long.'

'Jodie?'

'Yeah?'

'You know if you get found with booze at the hostel they'll kick you straight out?'

She pulls a shocked face, a palm to her chest. 'Booze? *Moi*? Can't believe you'd even suggest such a thing.'

She grins, reversing the Corsa back out onto the street before I can reply.

I head into the library, past rows of bookcases to an empty table at the back. It's late afternoon and it's not busy, a couple of primary-age children with their parents, a few pensioners and a solitary teenager hunched over his own laptop, headphones clamped over his ears. I take my new laptop out of the backpack and log into the Wi-Fi, using a password given to me by a friendly older guy on reception. I *could* trawl through Musgrove's email account on my phone, but I don't want to burn through my data and it's just easier on the laptop's bigger screen because I can see more messages at once.

On the email welcome page I enter his username and the new password – *Butch2023* – the inbox appearing with its mass of unread emails. There are a dozen or so new ones that have come in during the day, mostly promotional spam about holiday destinations, pensions, credit cards and the like. It looks mostly like a lot of junk to me, with frequent Google Alerts mixed in here and there.

I feel like I've forgotten most of what I knew about email over the last decade, so I just click on the most recent alert, from today. It's set up to flag any new web pages that mention someone called Andrew Carney. The name doesn't ring any bells. I scroll down further, spotting more alerts scattered here and there among the forest of unread emails. More names flagged – including my own – and I realise what the alerts are for: these were some of the many people who had crossed paths with Detective Inspector John Musgrove. Clearly he liked to keep tabs on the people he'd sent to prison. It made sense. He was retired, without access to police resources, but still wanted to know if they were making the news again for any reason. If they were back in circulation or had moved in down the street.

It also helped to explain why he'd not been that surprised to see me yesterday.

I click on a folder with the title 'Convicted' and it drops down to reveal dozens of sub-folders, surnames and a first initial arranged in alphabetical order. Scrolling down, I find 'Vernon, H.' near the bottom and click on it with a tingle of anticipation. Perhaps there would be case files in here, emails from the original investigation, notes or documents from 2013, but my heart sinks when I see there are only four emails. All four are Google Alerts, the oldest from three years ago, a retrospective about MPs who had been the victims of violent crime. Musgrove had retired three years ago. OK. I click on the other two. More passing references to my case that added nothing new. If there was anything useful to be found, it wasn't among these automated alerts.

I check down the main folder listing for anything else with my name attached to it. But there is nothing so obvious. What I needed to find was a mention of my trial or appeal. A private conversation with a friend or colleague that he assumed would stay between them, an aside or a passing comment – that could be the key. A chink of daylight that could be levered wide open.

Unfortunately, Musgrove seems to be the king of the one-line email.

His messages are brutally short and to the point. No greeting and often no sign-off either. No 'how are you' or 'hope you're well', no small talk, no personal stuff, barely any punctuation. Only the words needed to convey the message, and not a single consonant more.

I spend an hour going through the contents of his inbox anyway, trawling for personal messages and replies. There is some contact with friends and former colleagues, arranging nights out and trips to the rugby, a local cricket team for whom he was the wicketkeeper. A group of half a dozen ex-cops who went out drinking every once in a while. I take a picture of the email addresses on my phone in case I can figure out a way of following up with that little group. I bet they had some stories to tell. There is very intermittent contact with a brother, Anthony, whose email address indicates that he lives in Spain. None that I could find with Gavin, Musgrove's ex-husband.

The former DI also seems to have done some consultancy work since retirement and there are threads that look like professional correspondence with a university, a conference centre and a construction company to advise on security matters. A few others with corporate entities that – again – are brief to the point of brusque, so short that it is difficult to discern what they even relate to. Some kind of consultancy or troubleshooting perhaps, talk of documents and confidentiality and contracts signed. A sub-folder marked 'Broadcast' holds the back-and-forth correspondence with a TV production company that made the documentary about my case, which had aired on the fifth anniversary of Liam's death. Musgrove had had a starring role.

I look up from the screen. My eyes are gritty and dry, and I rub them with the heels of my hands, standing up to pace for a minute and get the circulation going in my tired limbs. How can it be that I have access to all of this, to the private correspondence of the man who put me in prison, and not find *something*? Not find anything that relates back to what must have surely been one of the highest-profile cases of his career? I grab a plastic cup of water from the dispenser and wander the aisles for a few minutes more, letting my eyes drift over the titles on the shelves. They have an employment section and I'm intrigued to find a few textbooks I recognise from my own long-ago professional training with the Chartered Institute of Personnel and Development.

The open laptop draws me back to the desk.

In my work life, in the roles I held in HR, I'd had some experience of disciplinary procedures where emails had been used as evidence. Sent items, I knew, tend to be overlooked by people trying to cover their tracks on email. I had dealt with one case of fraud in which a member of staff had got rid of thousands of received emails, diligently deleting whole threads and expunging them permanently from his trash to cover his tracks, but had forgotten to apply the same care to his *Sent* folder.

I sit back down and select Sent items: more than eight thousand emails.

This could take days. Weeks. With a sigh, I make a start anyway. Clicking through the messages one by one, page by page, month by month. Looking for an elusive needle in the electronic haystack.

43

I'm so cross-eyed with staring at the screen an hour later that I start in surprise when someone pulls up the chair opposite. But it's only Jodie, looking mischievous and quite pleased with herself. I pack up the laptop for the short journey back to Southmead House. There is a plastic bag in the footwell of the Corsa, and she tells me to look inside as we drive through Twerton and back up to the main road. Inside is a shoulder-length dark blonde wig.

I hold it up. 'Really?'

'You'd look amazing as a blonde.' She nods encouragingly at me. 'And everyone knows they have more fun.'

'You're actually serious?'

'Try it. You said you needed a better disguise.'

'Yes but not like . . . this.'

'Proper job, that is, not just any old fancy dress rubbish. Got it from a mate who does them for cancer patients.'

Reluctantly, I tuck my own hair back and pull the wig over the top, shifting and straightening it in the car's mirror until it's sitting more or less naturally, dark blonde instead of my natural brunette.

'I look ridiculous.'

She grins. 'You look like a proper cougar.'

'I don't *want* to look like a cougar.'

'I mean,' she says, 'you don't look like you anymore. You look different.'

It's true enough, I suppose. Close up, a keen observer would probably be able to tell; but from any kind of distance it would help me to hide in plain sight. And I'm touched that she's even gone to the trouble.

'Thanks, Jodie. How much do I owe you?'

She waves my offer away and makes it clear that she won't take my money.

We follow our usual routine as we near the hostel: parking up a few streets distant and going in the back way, Jodie checking it's safe first then texting me an all-clear. The staff are in the middle of doing room checks, a periodic sweep of all the dormitories to check for drugs. Jodie has kitchen duty this evening so I find a spot in the corner of the communal area and set up my laptop to continue working. By the time we break for dinner at 7 p.m. I've ploughed through forty-seven of the folders on the stolen memory stick, now copied across in its entirety to my new laptop. So far this search has yielded a grand total of: nothing. Or nothing that's useful to me, anyway.

Dinner is a thick vegetable soup, the one hot meal the hostel provides each day, and I head up to the dormitory afterwards while Jodie finishes her work in the kitchen.

There are 129 different folders in total, most of it personal: financial stuff, pension, holidays. Photographs catalogued by year, mostly of holidays, parties, rugby matches and skiing trips. A handful of work pictures that seem to show Musgrove with a number of other officers, all in full dress uniform, at some kind of formal ceremony. For the first time in hours I feel a little tick in my blood, a stirring of recognition jolts me out of the monotony of so many hours of clicking and reading, clicking and reading. In the picture, Musgrove is smiling next to a short guy in a double-breasted suit, both of them with champagne flutes in hand. I recognise the other man immediately: Neil Walls, a Wiltshire MP and one of Liam's contemporaries in the House of Commons who had risen rapidly through the Home Office and gone on to become Minister of State without Portfolio. He and Liam had been friends, or acquaintances, at least. I right-click on the image to bring up the attached information. The date on it was December 2012.

Here was something, finally. But what did it mean? That Musgrove had connections in the party hierarchy that predated Liam's murder? That Walls might have applied pressure during the investigation, to avoid embarrassment for the party? I save the image to my desktop and make a note to check into him more closely when I have Wi-Fi again. I pick up my phone and fire off a quick message to Owen.

Did Neil Walls MP ever come up in your investigations?

He replies immediately.

Not sure. Will need to check my files. Why?

Just wondering. Found a pic of him chummy with DI Musgrove back in the day.

Jodie wanders into the room and flops onto her bed with a sigh of exhaustion.

'Bloody washing up,' she says. 'They should splash out on a couple of dishwashers, I reckon. Did you find anything?'

'Not sure yet. Give me another month and I'll let you know.'

'God,' she says, 'aren't you bored of looking at that stuff all day?'

'It's not as if I have much else to do.'

'I dunno,' she says, 'we could go and see some people I know, get ourselves sorted for the night. Could be a right good laugh.'

'Thought you were staying sober?'

'I *am*.' She puts her hands on her hips. 'Just messing with you, Mrs Goody Two-Shoes.'

After a while she finds the blonde wig in the plastic bag and puts it on, pouting in the mirror and practising different poses. It looks better on her than it does on me, and I tell her as much.

By half past ten she is asleep on her bed, fully clothed, the wig askew and half covering her closed eyes. The only other occupant of our room, Natalie, is sleeping too. All she seems to do is sleep. Looking at the two of them makes me even more tired, the fatigue tugging on my eyelids like an invisible weight.

But lights-out is not until eleven. I'll do another half an hour, then call it a night.

I am three-quarters of the way through the personal folders that had been backed up onto John Musgrove's USB stick, my vision blurring with exhaustion. The next folder is designated 'T&S'. One of the other things I've learned about the former detective is that he's a big fan of abbreviations and acronyms, of any way of shortening a message even further. They crop up everywhere.

I double click to open the 'T&S' folder, the way I've done for the last hundred like it.

It contains five Word documents, listed as 'MS' V1 to V5.

Every single one of them is password-protected.

I right click to check for a date, or file size, or author, but it asks again for a password before I can see any of the associated information. Five documents, all in the same folder. The only ones I've found so far that have been locked behind a password.

I do a file search for 'T&S'. Nothing else. No matches, no other corresponding documents. A Google search on my phone throws up a bunch of random acronyms: the medical term 'type & screen' to do with blood tests, 'travel & subsistence', 'timing & synchronisation', a local plumbing and heating service, a car dealership and many more random hits below that. No obvious police service acronyms apart from 'training & simulation', although I can't see how that would fit in here.

But there *is* something ringing a vague bell. Something from earlier today. Not here, not this evening. 'T&S'. When I was at the library, paging through his email account on the free Wi-Fi?

I haven't paid for much data on the phone but I need to check something. Remembering the way Jodie has showed me, I set up a Wi-Fi hotspot for the laptop and quickly log back onto Musgrove's email.

It's only when I delve back into the email folders, where old messages are archived for safekeeping, that I stumble across a string of emails from last summer. In a folder named 'Truman & Shaw', some correspondence that I had assumed related to his consultancy security work, some brief discussions of contracts, timescales and confidentiality. I page back further, going through each response in a long, convoluted and, at times, rather bad-tempered email thread between Musgrove and someone called Felix Shaw, Director and CEO at the company Truman & Shaw.

And slowly, something else starts to become clear. Something else Musgrove had not thought to mention on Wednesday afternoon. Because he had more than just a passing interest in me, more than just a decade-old memory of my case. He had neglected to mention something rather important.

He was writing a book about it.

44

I remember his words at the hospice, as we looked out across the lake.

I've thought about you a lot, from time to time.

That strikes me now as something of an understatement.

It looks as if he's tried to cash in on the appetite for true crime books, the insatiable demand for behind-the-scenes stories of notorious murders that seemed to have become so popular while I was in prison. Or had they always been popular? I couldn't remember. But there is a sick rolling in my stomach at the thought of a book written about my husband's death, of money being made and enthusiastic readers turning the pages. Thousands of words about the investigation and the court case, with a horrific tragedy as its starting point.

And yet, I *need* to see it.

Going back more carefully through the emails filed in various folders, I can trace the correspondence between Musgrove and various publishers that he had approached directly. He seemed to start out more than a year ago talking to three or four different companies, well-known London publishing houses, abortive attempts to approach them directly for meetings to discuss what he describes as 'the *real* inside story of a crime that shocked the nation'. His tone is direct and to the point, requesting non-disclosure agreements to be signed up front and an indication from each one as to their willingness to be part of a bidding situation for the rights to his 'explosive' manuscript. He comes across as a bit of an arse; the same as he had been with us yesterday.

Over the course of a few weeks, all the large publishers politely decline.

They cite various reasons – mostly anodyne – one saying too much time had elapsed since the original crime, another that they weren't sure it was the right 'fit' for their list, a third citing 'issues of tone and format' with the manuscript. Did it mean something, that none of them want to touch it? Probably not. That was just wishful thinking on my part. They were probably nervous because of the huge libel action that had spun out of my case following Owen Tanner's article, which seems to hover in the background like an unwelcome guest at the banquet.

I dive back into his emails. It is at this point, in October last year, that Musgrove seems to concentrate his efforts on a single, more specific target: a smaller, independent publishing house in Enfield called Truman & Shaw. A quick Google search on my phone reveals they have more of a focus on non-fiction and true crime, with a small staff and smaller budget. A search of their backlist reveals no title by John Musgrove, nor any indication that his book is forthcoming.

The emails back and forth between Musgrove and Felix Shaw become more intermittent over the next few months. But they continue to be maddeningly oblique, referring to phone calls that have already taken place and documents to which I don't have access. There are never any attachments so presumably he used a secure document transfer service. Unless he was sending hard copies. But does anyone still do that, hundreds of printed pages in a padded envelope instead of a single electronic document? It seems unlikely.

I sit back from the laptop and rub my eyes. I'm propped up against my thin pillow with the blanket gathered around me. It's gone midnight and the hostel is quiet, lights-out has been and gone, the other residents are asleep. The only light in our small dormitory is a cold grey wash of light from the screen of my laptop, glowing in the blackness of this room as if it is the only light left in the world.

But sleep can come later.

I go back to the five Word documents in the T&S file, double clicking on the first one to bring up the small box in the centre of the screen again. *Please enter password.* It was only luck – and Jodie's thieving instincts – that had got me this far. A helpful member of staff had probably written down his email and password on that Post-it note as a reminder, and he had not thought to protect the memory stick because ninety-nine per cent of it was of no interest to anyone but him. But he *had* taken steps to encrypt these documents, which might prove to be the single most important material we have found so far. I had to get access, one way or the other.

The cursor blinks in the empty password box, taunting me.

I try the email password first – *Tyke$1967* – typing it carefully before hitting return.

The little box shakes from side to side, red text appearing beneath it: *The password you have entered is incorrect.*

Of course it wasn't that. Too obvious.

After twenty minutes of combing through more emails I find his date of birth on a membership renewal form for the squash club.

I type it in as a six digit number, day–month–year, and press return again.

Again it tells me the password is wrong, some additional red text appearing beneath it.

Please be advised that one more incorrect password attempt will LOCK this document for 72 hours during which time it will be inaccessible to ANY AND ALL further attempts.

I take my hands off the keys, not wanting to risk another incorrect guess that locks me out of the document. Although . . . there were five documents. Maybe five different versions of the same manuscript? In which case I had not just three tries but *fifteen*. It stood to reason that V5 would be the most complete, most up to date, so I should start with V1 – *version 1* – and work my way up from there.

Half an hour later, I've burned through thirteen of my password attempts and four out of five of the documents are now locked.

Shit.

Shutting the laptop, I stare into the dark. It had been stupid, trying to guess his password. I don't even have a hint or a place to start, a number of characters or a way to narrow down possible options. There were probably only two people in the world who actually knew the password, and I'd stolen these documents from one of them.

The ghost of an idea comes to me.

I pick up my phone and compose a new message directly to Felix Shaw, from my own email account. In the Cc line, I add Musgrove's own address so that he will be copied into the message.

Dear Mr Shaw,

You don't know me but I believe you have been in discussion with John Musgrove about a book concerning my trial and conviction.

I've been in touch with John since my release from prison and we've agreed to collaborate on a new and expanded version of his manuscript in which I will be a co-author, bringing my own insights to the tragic events of 12 July 2013 and telling the story of my own journey through the UK prison system. As you may know, John's having a very difficult time with his health at the moment and has asked me to liaise with you direct. He has advised me that you will be able to provide me access to the latest version of the manuscript.

I certainly understand if you wish to contact John to verify our agreement and have cc'd him into this message to expedite the process. Alternatively, you can reach me at the email above if you wish to discuss or clarify any of the issues raised.

In the meantime, many thanks for your help in this matter.

Heather Vernon

I press send, a tiny *whoosh* from the phone as my lie flies off into the ether.

Shaw would not know the email account had been compromised, that it would be *me* replying as Musgrove to confirm that this new arrangement was all OK. If he phoned the ex-detective instead, well then ... I'd have to think of something else. But the acrimonious nature of their relationship suggested Shaw might want to keep the whole thing at arm's length.

I lie down in the narrow bed, staring at the dark outline of a water stain on the ceiling. Sleep eludes me. My body is exhausted but my brain is still in high gear, racing thoughts of John Musgrove and Christine Lai, of Philip Boivin and Neil Walls. Of Owen and Jodie and Amy, all four of us deep in the forest now. A forest of lies.

Of Theo and Finn, on the far side.

I'm finally drifting off, the laptop closed on the bedside table beside me, when my phone buzzes under my pillow: a new email.

Felix Shaw, it seems, is also a night owl.

Dear Ms Vernon,

Thank you for your email but I'm afraid I can't help you. All electronic copies of the MS have been permanently deleted at my end and all physical copies returned to Mr Musgrove, as per the terms of the non-disclosure agreement. Also as per the terms of that NDA, I'm afraid I can't discuss anything further with you in relation to this matter.

I wish you both well for the future and the success of your project.

Sincerely,

Felix Shaw

Director and CEO

Truman & Shaw Publishing

I read the email twice, a sag of disappointment in my stomach. But then my eyes snag on four words in particular.

... *all physical copies returned* ...

Physical copies of the manuscript, returned to Musgrove when negotiations finally ground to a halt. Which meant it didn't matter if I couldn't get into the documents on the memory stick; it didn't matter if I couldn't guess the password.

Because there would probably be a hard copy at his house.

45

FRIDAY

My head is still fuzzy with sleep when Jodie shakes me gently awake on Friday morning. She is already dressed and sitting on the end of my bed, cradling a steaming mug of tea. She points to another one, next to me on the bedside table beside a slice of jam on toast on a small plate.

'Late one last night, was it?'

'A bit.' I raise myself up on one elbow to check the time on my phone with one bleary eye. Almost nine o'clock already. I haven't slept this late in longer than I care to remember; morning unlock in prison was always 7.45 a.m. I had assumed I'd lost the ability to sleep beyond that time, but maybe there were already changes happening within me, subtle changes of which I wasn't aware.

'Heard you tapping on that keyboard until God knows what time, interfering with my beauty sleep.' She sips her tea. 'You look rougher than I feel.'

I nudge her with my toe. 'Thanks. Where are you off to?'

'Christine Lai's place. See if I can catch her with her hand in the till.'

I tell her about Musgrove's unpublished book and my hope that he'll have a full paper copy of the manuscript at his house.

She narrows her eyes at me. 'You're not going to his house on your own, are you? Not going to try to get inside?'

'No.'

'You sure about that?'

'Although it *is* empty, with him being in Willow House.'

'Is it though? What if his mum turns up? Or you bump into the cleaner or the lodger or the next-door neighbour?'

'I might just have a look from the taxi, a drive-by, nothing else. Check if anyone is there.'

'We'll go and have a look together. Later. You don't want to be wandering around on your own with those three nasty bastards still out there, driving around looking for you. They could turn up here again, for all we know. Not to mention the risk of you getting arrested.'

'I know.'

'*Together*,' she says again for emphasis, pointing a slender index finger at me.

I dress quickly once she's left and check for any more messages from Felix Shaw, or anything of note that has landed in Musgrove's inbox since last night. But there is nothing. After another two hours, I've finished the search of his inbox and failed to come up with anything else that seems relevant.

I go back to Shaw's email response to my query, an itch gathering in my palms as I read the words again.

. . . *all physical copies returned to Mr Musgrove* . . .

We already knew the ex-detective's home address; it was one of the first things that Jodie had found when we'd started the trawl of his email on Sunday evening. Villa Fields is a safe neighbourhood in one of the safest cities in the country, maybe a ten-minute drive from the hostel. I could be there and back inside half an hour: a cab to get me there, just sit and look, take it all in, and back here again without even leaving the back seat of the taxi. Door to door. No danger, I wouldn't even get out. No time out on the street on my own. And Jodie won't be back for hours yet.

I pick up my phone.

* * *

The taxi driver is happy to wait as long as he can keep the meter running, and I ask him to pull up at the kerb opposite number 117 Rockcliffe Road. It's a world away from the hostel, well-kept Edwardian houses with small gardens in front, a quick online search suggesting you wouldn't get much change from £750,000 for one of these properties. Perhaps Musgrove had been here for years, or had bought it with his husband before they split.

It's not a main road but a quieter, suburban street, just the occasional cyclist or student, a pensioner pulling her shopping in a wheelie cart. The blonde wig is surprisingly comfortable after I've had it on for half an hour or so. I'm wearing the same stuff I bought on Wednesday – shoes, bag, good jacket – in case of close encounters.

Number 117 is at the end of a terraced row of four houses joined together, each with its own gabled roof over an upstairs bedroom. There is no driveway, just a small iron gate and a rather overgrown front garden, a bush spilling over the low wall and stubby weeds pushing through near the front door. A path at the side leads around the back of the house.

There are not many cars parked outside the houses; presumably most are out at work. I've read the stories about people working from home a lot more since the pandemic, but hopefully things have gone some way back to normal since then. I was locked up myself during every single lockdown and I don't really have any-one to ask. From here I can see through the front lounge windows and a little of the master bedroom upstairs, although the elevated angle makes it impossible to see the whole room.

My phone buzzes in my bag. It's a Telegram message from Owen.

Re: your question on Neil Walls MP.

What have you got?

His messages drop in, one on top of the other.

> *Big influx of jobs into his constituency in 2017 from a US mul-*
> *tinational called . . . North Star*
> *North Star built a UK distribution hub on a site called Dakota*
> *Park near J15 of M4*
> *Big phoenix-from-the-ashes story after North Star almost*
> *went bust in 2014.*

I frown, trying to work out how this relates to my question last night. By 2014, my world consisted of only three things: remand, Crown court, prison. I send back a quick reply.

> *???*

> *Can you guess who was an executive director on the board at*
> *North Star?*

> *?? Don't know. Never heard of them before.*

> *Here's a clue: you took his picture the other day.*

> *Philip Boivin???*

> *Yup. Found an old mention online.*

I stare at the text string for a moment, trying to discern the pattern. Philip Boivin, who clearly knew Christine Lai and also had connections in Westminster. The confidential memo we had found in the storage locker. *NS*. North Star. It had to be.

> *What does it mean though?*

> *Boivin linked to Neil Walls. Walls had met Musgrove at least*
> *once. Walls also worked with Liam*

Is Walls still an MP? Worth tracking down?

He died in a helicopter crash in Florida last year.

Owen's bluntness brings me up short. He messages again to ask me if I can talk now and I tell him it's not a good time.

> *Out at Musgrove's place at the moment. Good work though.*
> *Let's catch up later.*

I put my phone away and watch the house for ten more minutes, looking for any sign of movement, shadows shifting behind the windows or the frosted glass top of the front door.

But the house looks empty. Musgrove hadn't lived here for weeks, or maybe months; he was divorced, his brother lived overseas, his mother tiny and frail and ten miles away.

And I was *here* now.

The driver, a polite young Eastern European guy with a pony-tail, has kept the engine running.

'Actually,' I say to him, checking my watch, 'think I'll nip and see my friend quickly, to pick something up. Could you come back here in half an hour? Should be all done by then.'

I hand him a couple of notes and he nods, assures me he'll be back here at 11.40, and gives me the change. I can't have him around while I do what I'm about to do.

He pulls away and I do one last check up and down the street before pushing open the little iron gate and walking slowly up the path.

I ring the doorbell, listen to the dull clang of the bell inside. There are no cameras that I can see. The view into the front bay window reveals a fairly unremarkable lounge, sofa and armchairs, big TV, bookcases, a large Impressionist painting over the fire-place. No signs of life.

A second press of the doorbell has the same response as the first. I give it another minute and walk around the side, down the path into the back garden. It's small and more overgrown with bushes and weeds than the front, a hedge on one side and a fence on the other. A barbecue covered with a black canvas raincover. Green plastic garden chairs, stacked against the wall. A frosted half-glass back door next to the kitchen window; no plates or cups out, no dishes drying in the rack, no mail on the counter.

Most importantly, the back garden is not overlooked. I find an empty stone plant pot, a sizeable thing with thick square sides and six inches of green-tinged rainwater in the bottom.

I had spent almost a year padded up with Courtney, a chatty ex-burglar who had done hundreds of houses together with her then-boyfriend, who liked her mainly – she told me ruefully – because she was small enough to fit through windows that he couldn't. There were a few basics. *Don't carry any tools on you, just use what you find in the garden or shed and leave it behind afterwards. Easy options are best, always check for open windows and unlocked back doors. Don't spend more than five minutes inside. Wear gloves. Don't get greedy.*

I was particularly struck by one thing she'd told me: *alarms didn't matter.* People, she'd said, had one of three reactions when they heard a house alarm: irritation if it's in the day, anger if it's at night, or embarrassment if it's your own alarm and the neighbours are cursing you for letting the cat set off the motion detector *again.* No one is actually *alarmed* any more when a house alarm goes off. Even if it is connected to a rent-a-cop company or the police, it's never a priority because ninety-five per cent of the time it's a false alarm. They know it, you know it. Everyone knows it.

I snap on a pair of cheap yellow Marigolds I'd taken from the hostel kitchen and heft the stone plant pot in both hands, tipping out the rainwater onto the patio.

Moving to the back door, I wait for the next car to pass by on the street out front and when the engine noise is closest, I heave the heavy pot straight through the frosted glass.

46

The shattering glass sounds like a bomb going off and for a moment I think everyone on the street must have heard it, but then the car passes by and suburban silence returns, broken only by the disinterested chirping of birds in the trees nearby. I reach through the broken pane and find the latch to the back door, turn it with a *click* and I'm in, my loafers crunching on broken glass as I step carefully into the kitchen, adrenaline pulsing through my veins at a hundred miles an hour.

OK. I check my watch: 11.13 a.m. Need to find it and get out.

The air in the hallway is still and stale. A hanging plant on a side table is parched completely brown, long fronds hanging lifeless and scattered on the tiled floor beneath. There is an alarm panel by the front door but there's no beeping or flashing light, no message. Just three green LEDs at the top. I guess the house was being looked after by Musgrove's elderly mother, who probably didn't want the trouble of setting and disarming the system every time she visited. I ignore it. To the right is the lounge that I could see through the front window. Staying out of sight from the road, I peer in, but there's nothing on the low coffee table or in the bookcase that looks like an A4-sized manuscript. It's not a workroom.

I move to the stairs, taking them two at a time and opening doors off the landing: master bedroom at the front, spare room on the side and then the third one – the box room at the back. Desk, chair, computer, filing cabinet, shredder, more bookcases squeezed into the small space. The desk is clear apart from a keyboard, mouse and monitor, stationery and a stack of unopened mail. Every surface covered in a fine layer of dust.

Musgrove's study.

I find what I'm looking for almost straightaway.

It's in the top drawer of the filing cabinet, a thick stack of printed A4 paper, hole punched and bound together with treasury tags. The front page bearing Musgrove's name and former police rank below the title: *Death of an MP: the inside story of a murder that shocked Britain*. Below this is text indicating this is 'Version 5, incomplete draft not for circulation or quotation and STRICTLY CONFIDENTIAL' across the bottom of the page in heavy red capitals.

This was it. His unpublished non-fiction book about the case. As a way of getting inside the head of the man who had put me away, it was a potential goldmine.

With a surge of anticipation I take it out of the drawer and lay it on the desk, flicking through the stack of paper. It's hundreds of pages thick, full of red track changes and handwritten annotations, Post-it notes sticking out haphazardly here and there. There is *so much* here, the sheer weight of possibility in this document feels like a tiny victory all on its own. I had no idea his account would be so exhaustive but I know Owen will absolutely *love* a chance to go through it in painstaking detail.

I should just take it and leave, but the temptation to have a quick look is just too strong. I find the Contents page at the front, a listing of all the chapters. 'Liam Vernon MP'. 'That Night'. 'The First Call'. 'Forensics'. 'Day One'. 'Zeroing In'. And so on and so on, all the way through to the conviction and epilogue. So much to go through. I have an idea and flip to the back. A glossary of police terms, followed by an index which runs to ten pages. My eyes flick across the index entries, looking for one of those loaded words that people liked to hide behind: 'challenges', 'issues', 'problems', 'inconsistencies', 'weaknesses', 'inconclusive' or 'contested areas' or perhaps 'disputed evidence'.

None of these terms appear.

I go back to the top of the index and start again, going by subject, looking for defence theories, any mention of corruption, of Philip Boivin, of Liam as a potential parliamentary whistle-blower. The first interesting entry I come to is on the fourth page, an index entry entitled 'Lines of enquiry, alternative'.

The word 'corrupt' features in the second of three.

Lines of enquiry, alternative	– parliamentary aspect, 58, 61
	– allegations of corrupt behaviour, 99
	– discounting of, 167

Blood is pounding so hard at my temple that I'm getting a headache. My watch says 11.19 a.m. I flick to page fifty-eight, my hands shaking, searching the page for the first reference to other possible suspects in my case that had been discounted too early. My eyes fall on a particular sentence in the third paragraph down:

It was at this point, when forensic material had been analysed and began to come back to the investigating team, that several alternative lines of enquiry were developed including the relevance or otherwise of the victim's role as a Member of Parliament. Although it was later determined that none of these alternatives were significant in a wider evidentiary sense with regard to the overall thrust of the investigation . . .

I flick forward to page sixty-one.

The intensity of media coverage was not a surprise, given the nature of Mr Vernon's role as MP for Bath, and all of us in the Major Incident Team were very much aware of the

strong focus of public attention and their justified expectation that we would pursue the perpetrator with the utmost
vigour. We devoted significant resources to the investigation of all aspects of Mr Vernon's personal and professional
life, and where his public role may have exposed him to an
elevated level of risk . . .

I shake my head in frustration and flick back to the index, then to
the mention of corruption on page ninety-nine.

As we had already established, our work threw up a number of potential lines of enquiry during the early phase of
the investigation. One such line emerged as my team con-
ducted background interviews in which it was suggested
that Mr Vernon had been at least aware of unethical and
possibly corrupt corporate behaviour on the part of US
company North Star, which had been seeking entry into the
UK telecoms market. Ultimately, however, investigation of
these allegations did not bear fruit and no further relevant
information came to light. Subsequently, the line of enquiry
was not deemed relevant and did not form part of the prosecution case that was built over the subsequent months . . .

North Star. That name again. But the rest of it seemed about as clear
as mud; I was beginning to see why this manuscript had been on
its fifth version. Maybe publishers were worried about being sued.
More to the point, I couldn't remember anything like this being
mentioned at my trial. Why was it deemed 'not relevant' by the
prosecution? I shake my head, flicking back to the index to find the
next page reference, when my eye falls on three words near the top.
Another entry that stops me dead.

Artemis Tech, 99

That mysterious word my mother had written on a page of the court transcript. *Artemis.* Where she had heard it, I would never know. But it had been enough to spook Musgrove when I'd repeated it back to him at the hospice. And now here it was in the index of his unpublished book. With shaking hands, I'm trying to find the page when I jerk at a noise from the street right outside. The slam of a car door.

It is almost ten minutes since I'd broken in. Time to go.

Jamming the manuscript into my bag, I creep into the front bedroom, dropping into a crouch as I move towards the four large bay windows looking out over Rockliffe Road.

A car is parked on the other side of the road, a silver Toyota Land Cruiser. A tall black man is standing by the open passenger door, on the pavement side, a cluster of shopping bags in one hand. As I watch, an elderly woman shuffles out slowly and takes his arm, a walking stick in her other hand. He helps her down from the big car and closes the door behind her, then leads her slowly up the drive to the house opposite. Mother and son back from a shopping trip, that was all.

I feel the tension in my body relax slightly. *False alarm.* I watch the street for a minute more, checking it's clear, the breath halting in my throat as a police car turns into view at the far end of the road. *Keep going. Keep going.* I hunch down further so I'm only just looking over the windowsill. The police car is cruising slowly, daw-dling up the road at maybe ten miles an hour, a pair of uniformed officers in the front scanning left and right as if they're looking for something. Or some*one*. It comes closer, slowing even further as it draws level with the house. The car windows are down, the driver with his elbow resting on the sill, his colleague on the radio.

The police car crawls past and pulls to a stop, two houses further down. My heart rises up into my throat. Should I run or stay? Take a chance or hide in the house?

Neither of the officers gets out of the car.

They just sit there.

They'll almost certainly see me in their mirrors if I go out the way I came in, around the side of the house. Or if I leave by the front door I could just brazen it out. I don't *look* like a burglar. Unless they've got my description and they're already looking for a woman. *Shit*. Are they here for me, for this, or is it just coincidence? If they catch me in here, it's game over. I cannot get caught.

Stay or go. Stick or twist.

A minute ticks by. Then another. Still, they just *sit* there.

I decide to go out of the back door, find a way over the fence and through another garden, aiming for the nearest gap between houses. Not a perfect plan but it would bring me out on Forester Avenue, give me a head start at least. Thank God the house is on this side of the street; the gardens on the other side back right onto the River Avon.

As I'm about to crawl back to the landing, the police car's blue lights start flashing and it pulls away abruptly from the kerb, accelerating hard up the street. Within seconds it's out of sight and all I can hear is the shrieking wail of its siren as it fades into the distance.

I let out a painful breath. Another bullet dodged.

I go quickly downstairs and out through the back door, crunching over broken glass again, pulling it shut behind me. The street is quiet now the police have gone but it's another fifteen minutes before my taxi is due to pick me up. I text the driver to give him an alternative pickup point, at the junction around the corner, and start walking in that direction. Gripping the strap of the shoulder bag tightly, I try to look as if I belong here and am simply out for a morning stroll to the deli or the coffee shop.

The manuscript feels heavy in my bag. Loaded with possibility. The dates on the computer files suggested Musgrove had been working on the book for several years, but still hadn't managed to find a publisher. It was a high-profile case, so why did no one want to publish it? Was it because of the stink surrounding the libel trial that had sunk Owen's career, or was there something else?

I take out my phone and fire off a message to the group chat that Owen set up for the four of us on Telegram.

Anyone know the specifics about allegations of unethical/corrupt behaviour relating to North Star? Mentioned in Musgrove's unpublished book.

Putting some distance between myself and 117 Rockcliffe Road feels good. I'm impatient to be back at the hostel, to be able to read the document in its entirety, to tease out the secrets that lie hidden within its pages. It feels like progress, like forward motion. Never mind the fact that burglary is a clear and obvious violation of my licence conditions. It was worth the risk.

My phone pings with a new message on Telegram. I'm retrieving it from my bag and am about to unlock it, when I see him.

A man on the other side of the road, smoking a cigarette.

A man I recognise.

47

It takes me a second to work out where I know him from and then it hits me like cold water in the face: Bath Central Library, two days after my release. The slim balding guy who had been watching me as I worked on the computer. Who had disappeared when I tried to confront him.

He doesn't look as if he's going to disappear again today. He is leaning against a tree on the opposite corner of the crossroads of Powlett Road and Forester Avenue, perhaps thirty metres away, dressed in a dark green canvas jacket and black jeans.

As I watch, he takes one last drag on his cigarette before flicking it into the gutter and starting towards me. He crosses the junction, keeping his eyes on me the whole time, arms loose by his sides. My taxi is not here yet and there is very little passing traffic, no cars to flag down or drivers to see me. I reach the junction, aware of him closing in on me from the left side so I turn right, picking up my pace. I seem to remember there's a fire station very close, an ambulance station too. If I can get to one of them I'll be safe.

The phone is in my hand. Should I call the police? And tell them what? *Hello, I just burgled an ex-policeman's house and now I'm being followed?* What if this guy *was* the police, and they had been watching me ever since I got out?

I type another quick message into the group chat instead.

Being followed. Forester Ave.

I drop the phone into the shoulder bag and feel around for the handle of the little knife that Jodie had given me, my hand scrabbling underneath the manuscript, bumping up against everything else, pens, keys, purse, cosmetics, other random stuff I had accumulated over the last few days. His footsteps are still behind me, quick and confident. A grassy bank rises up to my left, houses on my right, a DEAD END sign straight ahead. *Shit.*

The knife is not in my bag.

I look behind. The balding man is closing on me, perhaps twenty metres away now, his eyes on mine as I turn. My phone pings twice in quick succession in the bag but I don't have time to look down at it. Instead, I turn right into Forester Court and break into a run, a high wall on my left, trees on the right, the road opening out into a small parking area bordered on two sides by flats, sandy three-storey blocks with scrubby lawn in front. A communal door shared by all the residents, I'd be caught for sure before anyone opened it up for me. I run straight between the two blocks and out the other side, my arms pumping but there is no way through, only a row of lock-up garages and a high hedge bordering the site. Running feet are coming up fast behind me, the *slap-slap-slap* of footsteps on concrete getting closer.

I cut hard left down the side of the building, across the grass, the river right in front of me now and I wonder for a second whether I should just jump the low wall and take my chances swimming it, see if my stalker would be willing to follow me into the water. Then I remember the paper manuscript in my bag. Besides which, it's been ten years since I was last in a swimming pool and I'd probably drown.

I scramble left again at the corner, my lungs starting to burn as I sprint along the rear of the block of flats, doubling back on myself. I'll head out to the street the way I came in and return to the junction, flag down a passing car or – I say a silent prayer – jump in my taxi if he's already waiting for me.

There is a thin strip of grass at the back of the flats, a couple of benches and a low wall that drops down into the dark roiling water of the River Avon. My legs are getting heavy but I keep going, keep sprinting, turning the last corner around the long block of flats and out into open ground again, dodging between wheelie bins and out onto the tarmac before I realise I can't hear my pursuer anymore. I throw a glance over my shoulder but there's no one there, he must have fallen back or stopped or changed his mind, but I don't slow my pace, I have to keep going until I'm out of this enclosed complex because it only has one exit back to the main road and I can't let myself get trapped here, getting caught is not an option—

A black van is pulled across the width of the street.

My exit is blocked.

I skid to a stop, pulling up so hard that I almost fall forwards. I will have to take my chances with the river: I will hide my bag, stick it in one of the wheelie bins and come back for it later, in the car. With company.

I turn to retrace my steps and collide with something solid.

This time I do fall over, bouncing backwards and jarring my backside on the hard ground. But it's not the balding man. It's a huge white guy in a black sweatshirt and jeans, with a neck as thick as his head, bowling-ball shoulders and hands as big as frying pans. Staring up at him from the floor, he looks absolutely *enormous*. His cheeks are pockmarked, his eyes as flat and lifeless as two old pennies.

My heart threatening to punch a hole through my chest, I remember Jodie's words from Saturday. *He's like four feet wide and eight feet tall, a real hatchet-faced bastard.*

And somehow, he had found me.

Before I can scrabble away, he grabs the scruff of my neck with one meaty hand and drags me to my feet, pinning my wrists together with the other. I aim kicks at his crotch, his knee, but both seem to bounce off without any noticeable effect.

'Get off me!' My voice echoes off the flat blank wall behind me. 'Help! Somebody help me!'

He lets go of my jacket and clamps the hand over my mouth instead, my nose filling instantly with the smells of sweat and onions and cigarettes. He starts to frogmarch me towards the black van, looming over me from behind. The balding man appears on his other side but neither of them speaks.

A third man emerges from the van, stepping down lightly onto the tarmac. He has very short jet-black hair and high cheekbones, with the muscular build of a dancer or a boxer. He puts his hands in the pockets of his dark suit trousers, watching me as I approach.

'Hello, Heather,' he says. 'We meet at last.'

48

The handcuff bites into my wrist.

It's attached to a metal bar welded to the side of the van at head height, so I have to keep my left arm up. There are no windows in the back of the van, just a dim strip light and bench seats along both sides, a collection of assorted tools and rolls of plastic, grey duct tape and rope, a mound in the corner covered by a tarpaulin. It smells strongly in here of sweat, oil and diesel and something else that is more animal, ripe and sour. They've taken my bag with my phone, frisked me quickly and efficiently for everything else including the manuscript, the blonde wig torn off and discarded on the floor.

The huge guy, who the dark-haired man called Rennick – I'm not sure if it's his real name or a nickname – sits on the bench opposite me with his fists on his knees. He doesn't speak, doesn't move, barely blinks. Just stares at me with his flat alligator eyes.

My pulse has settled to a canter, the first spike of adrenaline fading to cold, blank fear, like a falling tide revealing the terrain beneath.

We've been driving for about ten minutes before the van rolls to a stop and the dark-haired man comes through the door from the cab, closing it again behind him. He takes a seat on the bench beside Rennick, crossing one leg over the other and considering me for a full minute. His clean-shaven features are Asian, perhaps

Chinese, and beside the huge man next to him he seems slender, almost skinny.

'Now then, Heather,' he says. 'You've been a busy girl, haven't you? Nice wig, by the way.'

'Whatever it is you want, I can't give it to you.'

'Oh I think you can,' he nods slowly. He has an American accent, wide and confident. 'And you can call me Mr Jones, by the way. Not my real name, but it's as good as any.'

'If you let me go now, I'll just walk away. I won't report this to anyone, no police, no one else has to get involved.'

He actually laughs at that, a short bark that echoes loud inside the cramped confines of the van.

'OK, let's get one thing out of the way from the get-go.'

With his index finger, he indicates to Rennick. The big man stands up, towering over me, and backhands me hard across the side of the face. It happens so fast I have no time to brace myself before his big knuckles smash into my cheek, my head bouncing back against the metal side wall, explosions of hard hot pain inside my skull.

I raise my right hand to try to ward off another blow, blinking away white stars blurring my vision, but Rennick simply sits back down on the bench seat opposite, fists on his knees as before.

Mr Jones studies me for a moment. 'So, Heather, just to be clear? This is not a negotiation, not a conversation. I'm going to talk, you're going to listen, and if you manage to give the right answer at the end *then* you might get to walk away. Or you might not. Do you understand?'

'Yes.' The coppery taste of blood is in my mouth.

'Good. Glad we've got the ground rules out of the way.' All traces of humour are gone from his voice. 'So I'm here to deliver a message. Are you listening?'

'Yes.'

He leans forward, bringing his face nearer to mine, close enough for me to smell his aftershave, musky and expensive.

'Stop,' he says. 'Stop what you're doing. Stop asking questions, stop stirring things up that should be left alone. Stop trying to rewrite history. Stop it *now*.'

My voice is barely a whisper. 'I can't.'

'Can't, or won't?'

'I can't let my boys be brought up by someone else. They're my sons. *Mine*.'

'If you had your boys' best interests at heart, you'd let the past go, Heather. Let them move on. Imagine how hard it is for Theo and Finn to deal with the fact that their mother killed their father. Losing both parents in one night. How many years it takes to process, to get your head around it? To come to terms with it? Now imagine you're little Finn and your mother won't let you do that. She refuses to let you come to terms with it. She's too selfish, too self-absorbed, too self-obsessed to do the right thing for her own children. To do what's best for them.'

The pain in my jaw has settled into a hot, burning ache where Rennick's blow connected.

'It's not selfish if I didn't do it.'

'Everyone and his wife knows that you did.'

I let that go without comment.

'My children need me.'

'I'd say the last ten years is clear and definitive proof that is *not* the case.'

'Who do you work for?'

He doesn't answer. Instead, he takes his phone from his pocket and holds it up so I can see, scrolling through a series of pictures. The first is of me coming out of the probation office after a meeting with Trevor Boyle, then a shot of me and Jodie at the second-hand car place, me driving the black Corsa, me again on the street outside the Vernons' big house and then a shot of us walking into the hospice where Musgrove was a patient.

'All you need to know about my employer is that they don't give three strikes before you're out. They only do *one* strike so you should consider this your first and only warning. There will not be another.' He slips the phone back into his pocket. 'It would be so easy to get you sent back inside to do the second half of your sentence. By the time you come out your boys will be men – Theo will be what, twenty-three? – they'll be out in the world probably looking to get as far away from here as possible. You won't even be a memory to them. *You'll* be so far behind in the rear-view mirror that you'll be all but invisible. You'll be a myth, a rumour, a cautionary tale best forgotten.'

'No.' My throat is thick. 'That's not true.'

'Failing that . . .' He leans closer. 'You do have one other option.'

I look up. 'Which is what?'

'Put it this way: how many people do you think will look for you if you disappear? How many will grieve for you?' He shrugs, the shoulders of his expensive jacket riding up. 'Who would actually miss you? The ripples might last a day, a week, then they'd be gone. *You'd* be gone.'

'There's more than just me now. And the truth is going to come out, one way or the other.'

'You have literally no idea what you're up against.'

I weigh up, for a second, the risks of fighting fire with fire. Of throwing something back in his face – even if it is half guess, half bluff.

'I know North Star was involved in what happened to my husband,' I say. 'That they were paying off parliamentary staff for information, including his constituency manager, and Liam found out about it. He was going to blow the whistle, to blow the whole thing wide open. So North Star had him killed, and put the blame on me to cover their tracks.'

Jones crosses his arms, a deep frown darkening his features. 'You haven't been listening to me, have you?'

'We're on to you.'

'We? Do you mean your little crew of screw-ups and misfits?'

'Was it you?' I say. 'Were *you* the one who killed my husband?'

There is a certain bitter irony to it: I had been looking for these men, but they had found me first. Because this was what they *did*. To have got in and out of our house without trace, to have knowledge of my sleeping pills, family timings, Liam's movements, to have framed me so completely to divert attention away from the real perpetrators. It was well thought out, a professional job. And now they had come back.

Jones signals to Rennick again, the big man standing up and cuffing my right hand to another bar so both my arms are up now, spreadeagled to each side. I'm completely defenceless and my heart starts to crash painfully against my ribcage as Rennick goes to the tarpaulin in the corner and retrieves a pair of thick black rubber gloves. He snaps them onto his big hands, then takes something else from a toolbox and begins to work on it. His back is to me so I can't see it.

Jones stands up and moves to the side as if he wants a good view of what's about to happen.

'You were asking,' he says, 'what your other option was in all of this. Do you still want to know?'

My eyes flick between him and Rennick, who still has his broad back to me in the corner and is working on something, the rustle of plastic, the hard *clink* of metal on metal. The big man turns to loom over me and I flinch back in expectation of another blow, but instead of a punch there is the rough brush of plastic against my hair, my scalp, my ears, my face, and the world turns opaque.

A tightening around my throat to secure the thick clear plastic hood that's been pulled over my head.

A rush of pure liquid panic.

A breath that only pulls thick plastic against my mouth.

Moisture misting in front of my eyes as I exhale. Rennick's big hands are at my neck and I feel the ligature pulled even tighter, cutting into the skin and I have no way to reach it with my cuffed hands, no way to release the pressure. I try to bite into the plastic but it's too thick and I can't get any purchase on it, can't get it between my teeth.

'Forensically,' Jones says, his voice muffled to my ears now, 'plastic is quite hard to beat, in my experience. Not especially glamorous but it means no messy blood spatters, no follow-up cleaning. No penetrating injuries to match to a weapon, no ballistics, easy to dispose of and about as cheap as you can get. All you need is a few minutes.'

Rennick is standing back now, arms crossed over his chest, a spark of interest in his eyes for the first time. There is a pressure building in my chest, my head, a dizzy sickness as I try and fail to pull in more oxygen. I slam my fists against the side of the van, knuckles flaring with pain as I try to attract the attention of anyone who might be nearby.

Jones shakes his head. He's still standing there, still watching, still talking to me.

'Hypoxia, Heather. It's when your body's not getting any oxygen, just the carbon dioxide you're breathing out, so your blood can't carry enough oxygen to your tissues. Including your brain.'

I try to slow my breathing but it's almost impossible. Every heave of my chest is greeted with a mouthful of the plastic, no release, no let-up, no *air*. My body screams for oxygen.

'Your breathing and your heart rate are speeding up,' Jones continues, with an air of academic interest. His voice sounds as if it's coming from a long way away. 'Blood vessels in the lungs are constricting while your peripheral vessels in your arms, legs, hands and feet are dilating. That's the tingling sensation you can feel.' He holds a hand up, waggles his fingers as if to demonstrate. 'Pretty soon it leads to an inability to communicate, general confusion, unconsciousness and coma.'

A greyness is starting to cloud the corners of my vision, pressure building in my skull as if my head is about to split wide open. It feels as if I am drowning in my own hot, toxic air. The pain in my chest is unbearable.

Don't black out. Don't quit.

'Brain cells are *very* sensitive to lack of oxygen,' Jones adds. 'Doesn't take long before they start dying.'

This is it. This is the end. I think of Theo and Finn, and I'm glad that I got to see them after my release, even if it was from a distance. Then I think of Liam, unavenged, his killer never caught, justice never found. The greyness crowds to the centre of my vision and it feels as if I'm sinking, falling backwards, falling into the deepest black hole and knowing that I'll never be able to climb out—

The ligature around my neck loosens and a rush of pure, sweet air floods into my nose and mouth as the plastic hood is pulled away. I suck in a huge breath so painful that my lungs feel as if they might burst.

'One warning, Heather. That was it: ninety seconds in the bag. Next time, I let him leave it on for ten minutes and then we put you in a hole in the ground somewhere no one will ever find you.'

Rennick unlocks first one cuff then the other, and I collapse to the floor, retching and gasping, coughing and sucking in air on my hands and knees.

Jones leans down to my level.

'So,' he says. 'Do we understand each other now?'

49

Owen's face drains of colour when I walk into the pub. There is a yellowing bruise on my cheekbone and another at my hairline where the blow had slammed my head against the wall of the van; an angry red mark around my neck where the plastic ligature had been pulled tight. The four of us had arranged to meet up at 4 p.m. to compare notes on the day's work, back in the College Arms. He's with Jodie, at the same table in the back room where we had met yesterday.

'Jesus Christ,' he says, getting up so fast he almost knocks his pint over. 'Are you OK?'

Jodie stands up too, and without saying a word she pulls me into a hug, her thin arms wrapped around me, rubbing me gently on the back like a mother comforting an errant daughter. For the first time since I had been pushed out of the back of the van I feel my eyes brimming and before I know it I'm crying properly, all the shock and pain and fear pouring out of me in a hot rush of tears.

She hands me a couple of serviettes from the bar and instructs Owen to buy me a large brandy, which he duly presents to me as the three of us sit down.

I wipe my eyes and explain what had happened, where I had been and what I'd found when Jones and his men had cornered me.

'Got your message on the group chat,' Owen says, 'and I was messaging you back, calling you, but you didn't reply so I jumped in a cab down to Forester Avenue. By the time I got there, I guess the van was already gone.'

'They took my phone off me,' I say. 'Drove me God knows where. They took Musgrove's manuscript too.'

'Shit,' Owen says, his face falling.

'Yeah.'

I tell him what little I had learned from my quick reading of the document, the mention of corruption and North Star. He nods and takes notes as I talk.

Jodie is shaking her head at me.

'I bloody *told* you not to go off on your own. If I'd been there, you wouldn't have got hurt.'

'If you'd been there, they would have got both of us.'

'Or,' she says, squeezing my shoulder, 'I would have given them a taste of their own bloody medicine.'

I take a sip of the brandy and it burns my aching throat, but numbs it too.

'Sorry,' I say. 'Next time I'll listen to you. Just can't work out how they found me, how they knew where I was going.'

Jones and his two men had dumped me in a potholed cul-de-sac of lock-up garages in Southdown, with no phone, no bag and no money. I had walked back into town.

'What about the police?' Owen says tentatively.

'No way,' I say.

'But they could have killed—'

I hold up a hand. 'And say what, Owen? That these guys told me to back off, to stop doing something I'm not supposed to be doing anyway? To admit I've already committed multiple breaches of the terms of my parole?'

'We don't have to tell them that, we could just say . . . you were attacked by these guys. Get it on the record at least.'

'And how do I explain *where* I was? Around the corner from their ex-colleague's place, that coincidentally has just been broken into?'

'They won't necessarily connect that to you.'

'No. Cops,' I say.

'Agreed,' Jodie says.

Jodie describes her day following Christine Lai, who had gone first to the gym, then to her office, then to an unknown house in Combe Down for an hour and a half before returning to her office for the rest of the afternoon. Owen was chasing down an owner's name for the Combe Down address, he said, and there had been one further interesting text from Philip Boivin's number to Christine, six words only:

All being dealt with as discussed.

To which she had replied, simply:

OK.

She had also reached out to her solicitor to enquire about a new restraining order – against me. From the excited gleam in his eye it seems there is more to tell, but he says he wants to wait until Amy gets here so we can all hear it together. I finish the brandy and he asks if I want another while we wait, but I decline.

'Where is Amy, anyway?' I say, checking my watch. 'Has anyone heard from her today?'

'I tried ringing her a couple of times,' Jodie says. Messaged her too, but she's not been answering.' She sips her vodka on the rocks. 'Maybe she's stuck in the office?'

A cold finger of nerves traces its way down my spine – it's not like Amy to be out of contact.

Owen asks me again about Musgrove's unpublished manuscript but we're interrupted almost immediately when his phone rings with an unknown number. He frowns at it, answers and has a brief conversation before ringing off.

'That was her,' he says, his face grim. 'Asking if we could pick her up.'

'Where is she?'

'At the hospital. In A & E.'

50

The Accident & Emergency department at Royal United Hospital is busy. It's always busy, in my experience, always too many patients and not enough staff, not enough time and space, and this early Friday evening is no exception as the three of us hurry through the hospital's main reception area. Owen has not left my side since he arrived and almost squares up to a guy who accidentally bumps into me as we turn down a corridor.

Amy has had it worse than me.

We find her sitting in a plastic chair outside A & E, cradling a plastic cup of machine-dispensed tea. Her bottom lip is split and swollen and she has dark bruising along her jawline. She too has the telltale red ligature mark around her neck, nasty bruises coming up around both wrists where the cuffs had held her tight and more marks of violence darkening the skin of her lower arms. Her top – a pastel yellow V-neck – is streaked dark with dried blood. She looks utterly traumatised, still in shock, as if it has taken today's near-death experience for her to fully appreciate the stakes of the game we're all playing.

She struggles to her feet as we approach and I fold her into a hug, a rush of relief that she's *alive*, she's here, we've got her. She cries into my shoulder and I pass her a tissue as Jodie and Owen look on, their faces creased with concern.

'Thought I was going to die,' Amy whispers. 'I thought that was it.'

'Me too,' I say. 'Those bastards. Can't believe they did this to you as well. I'm so sorry.'

'It's not your fault.'

I disagree. But I let her talk anyway as we walk back out to the car park, Owen and Jodie taking the lead and the two of us following, looking as if we've come out the wrong end of a very one-sided fight.

Amy had been coming out of a client meeting in the city, she tells us, when she was grabbed in the car park and bundled into the back of a black van. The descriptions match – Jones, Rennick and the balding man who had chased me on the street. The treatment the same, the handcuffs, the plastic bag sealed tightly around her head and ninety seconds of excruciating suffocation before the reprieve – and a final warning to stop digging into the circumstances of her brother's death. A nurse had checked her over, stitched her up and done a precautionary X-ray of her wrist, where she had been pushed out of the van onto the pavement. It was a nasty sprain but it wasn't broken.

The four of us climb into the little Corsa, Owen and me up front, Jodie and Amy in the back.

'Thanks for coming to get me,' Amy says. 'Didn't want Mum and Dad to pick me up here, to see me like this before I've got myself together a little bit. I just can't understand how those men knew where I'd be.'

'They're smart, well resourced,' I say. 'And they must have come for me straight after they were finished with you. Took your phone so you couldn't warn me.'

She nods, her face dissolving into tears again. 'I was so scared. I've never ... I really thought that was it. When I couldn't breathe and they were just watching me gasping and gasping, the plastic against my mouth ...'

Jodie turns around in her seat, squeezes the younger woman's arm. 'You'll get through this,' she says. 'You'll be OK.'

Amy turns back to me.

'Heather, I'm so, so sorry.' Her voice catches in a sob. 'All this time ... how wrong I've been about you. How wrong we've all been. Seeing those men, listening to them, what they said they were going to do to me if we didn't back off Liam's case. I can't believe that all this time, the police and the courts and the jury and the media, all of them have got it wrong for so long. I got it wrong too.'

'It's me that should apologise,' I say to Amy again. 'I never thought there was a risk they'd come after you too. You should stop, this is too dangerous for you. Besides the boys, you're all I have left. You're the closest I have to family.'

She wipes her eyes with a sleeve.

'Are *you* going to stop?'

The same question had been bouncing around in my head since the moment I thought I was going to die a few hours ago. But there had only ever been one answer then, and there was only one answer now.

'I can't.'

'I lost my brother,' Amy says quietly. 'I can't lose you too. And I have to find the people who took him away. Find them, and make them *pay*. Get justice for Liam.'

'At least take a step back for a few days, stay at your parents'. Promise me you won't go out on your own.'

'What about you?'

'I'll be extra careful. I promise.'

I tell Owen and Jodie that they need to be careful now too – because they will probably be next. Owen shakes his head and Jodie is indignant, insisting that she can take care of herself. I'm not convinced that either of them is taking the threat seriously enough.

Jodie goes to start the car but Owen holds up a hand. None of us, he says, have asked what he's been doing today. He delves into his messenger bag and pulls out a curling cardboard folder – one of the files Amy had found at her parents' house, boxed-up paperwork that had lain undiscovered in the attic for the last ten years.

'Before we go,' he says, his eyes lit with excitement, 'you all need to see this.'

51

It's a bank statement.

He hands it to me first, a single sheet that looks like a faded photocopy with the bank's logo and corporate address across the top. The date of the statement is 20 May to 19 June 2013, page number two of four. I don't recognise the account number or sort code but the account holder's name is very familiar. Listed down the page are a series of small deposits and withdrawals for shopping, food and drink, petrol, train tickets. Nestled among them, circled twice in biro and underlined, a single deposit for £75,000 from a company called BD Holdings.

Seventy-five thousand pounds. A significant sum that should have raised multiple red flags with party head office, the overall parliamentary watchdog and probably the police too. And yet it had gone completely under the radar, completely unreported at the time or since. There had been no mention of it in the trial which surely meant the police had been unaware. I kick myself again for the loss of Musgrove's manuscript.

I look at the account holder's name again.

Christine Lai.

The date of the deposit is 28 May. Liam had been killed on 13 July, around six weeks later.

Was this the start of it all, the start of the countdown that had ended with his death? How long had he suspected, and how had he got hold of her bank statement? Had he confronted her, or reported his suspicions to anyone else? The questions were multiplying, answers still elusive.

'Spent most of today going through the paperwork in those box files from your parents' attic, Amy.' He gestures at the sheet of paper in my hand. 'Found that stashed in among some unrelated stuff, committee minutes and meeting agendas from around that time.'

I hand the paper to my sister-in-law. 'As if he had hidden it there, where it wouldn't be found?'

'Tucked away for safe keeping,' Owen says. 'BD is Black Dragon Holdings, a shell company registered in the Cayman Islands,' he says. 'And guess what? It's a subsidiary of North Star.'

We all sit in silence for a moment, digesting the implications of his discovery.

I find myself shaking my head. Seventy-five thousand pounds doesn't seem like enough, somehow. Not enough to destroy a family. Not enough to kill for. It's too small, too insignificant in comparison to how much devastation it has caused.

'Is that all?' I say finally. 'Is that what cost Liam his life?'

'You know what they say,' Owen replies. 'The cover-up is always worse than the original crime.'

'So this is it, then? This is the smoking gun, surely?'

Owen nods slowly, an eyebrow raised. 'I remember Christine in court during the libel action. She stood up in front of the judge, the jury and all those people, and she swore blind that no money ever changed hands. She was so convincing, she convinced everyone. I mean she was really, *really* good at it.'

Jodie takes her turn to read the photocopied sheet. 'Still a bloody liar though, isn't she?'

'They know we're getting close,' Owen says. 'I think that's why you two were attacked today – they're upping the ante.'

Amy leans forward in her seat, reading the document again over Jodie's shoulder. 'We should go to the police with this,' she says. 'It's clear evidence of criminality.'

'No,' Owen says. 'Not yet.'

'What are you talking about?' Amy says. 'This is what you've been looking for, isn't it? The connection you've been looking for since the beginning?'

'It's not enough,' he says. 'This is one more piece of the puzzle, for sure. But on its own, it's not enough. We could go to the police with this but what are they going to do? You think they'll prioritise it after ten years, at the request of a paroled murderer—' he raises a hand in apology to me '—on the basis of a single photocopied bank statement of unknown provenance?'

'*Not* unknown,' Amy says. 'We found it in my brother's things.'

'Yes, but the police will want to establish a clear chain of provenance from the actual bank account to the recipient, they'll need to apply for various warrants of access to the banks, to establish that a law has been broken in the transmission of funds, etcetera. All of that will take time, which will give our bad guys ample time to get their lawyers to wrap everything in red tape while Mr Jones and his asshole friends destroy any remaining evidence, burn the electronic trail and intimidate or kill remaining witnesses.' He looks at me with this last comment.

Amy is shaking her head. 'You're saying we just *sit* on this?'

'I'm saying we need the other piece – the piece that connects the seventy-five grand payment to Liam's death – and then we present the whole thing to the police so we can show them the complete picture. We have to follow the money. And in the meantime, we get a couple of new phones and we get the two of you somewhere safe.'

Amy finally relents, sitting back in her seat with a shrug of her shoulders. She says she will stay at her parents' for a few days, use concealer to cover the bruises on her face and hide the other injuries with long-sleeved tops and scarves.

Owen suggests it would be a good idea to lie low until next week in any case. The hostel is no good, as Jones clearly knows we're there. A hotel seems like the next best option, but I don't particularly like the idea of living on top of a hundred other people while my picture is making the news.

'You can stay at mine tonight,' Owen says. 'It's actually my dad's old house in Larkhall. We'll find you a little B & B tomorrow.'

Jodie starts the car. 'I'm coming too.'

Owen looks hesitant, as if this was not what he had in mind.

'It's not really . . . I mean there's only one spare room, the other one is full of stuff.'

'Got a sofa, hasn't it?'

'Well, yeah. But—'

'There you go then. Or we can top and tail in the spare room. Don't mind, do you, Heather?'

I shake my head. 'What about the hostel rules?'

'Your life is in danger.' She fixes me with a stare. 'Probation service has to make an exception for that, right? As long as we let Boyle know.'

We go to the hostel first, Jodie going in to collect up what little we have from our room, emerging with the sum total of our possessions shoved into two plastic bags a few minutes later, my backpack over her shoulder. She drives us to a Sainsbury's on Green Park Road, Amy waiting in the car while we buy two cheap pay-as-you-go phones with cash. Then we drop her at the big house in Bathwick before heading up to Larkhall following Owen's directions.

His father's house is a small detached with chunks of greying render flaking off the walls and weeds poking up through the cracked paving of the driveway.

'Inherited it last year,' Owen says as he lets us into the wood-panelled hallway. 'Haven't really got around to . . . doing any DIY stuff yet. Wi-Fi password is on the noticeboard in the kitchen. If you want to put your stuff upstairs, I'll put the kettle on. Spare room is on the left at the top of the stairs. The left one, OK? Don't bother with the box room on the right, it's absolutely chock-a-block with stuff.'

There is a slightly musty odour to the house – the smell of an unloved house in need of some TLC, of a single man living on his own – and Jodie raises an eyebrow at me as we reach the landing and take our meagre possessions to the spare room. The room is hung with dusty paintings of old aeroplanes and there's a queen-sized bed with an old knitted comforter on it that looks like a family heirloom; I haven't slept in a double bed for a decade and it looks enormous. Jodie goes off to find the bathroom.

I plug my laptop in to charge it up and check for any new emails. But before I can log in, I hear my name in a dramatic stage whisper and find Jodie on the landing gesturing to me, waving her hand in a *come on* motion.

She's standing in the open doorway to the box room, the one Owen told us not to bother with, a strange expression on her face. She pushes the door wide as I approach. The box room is tiny and impossibly cramped with a desk, a computer, a bookcase heaving under the weight of hundreds of books. A baseball bat leans against the wall next to it, 'Boston Red Sox' stencilled along its length. A single bed in the corner is completely obscured under a foot-high stack of papers, books, magazines and assorted items of clothing flung haphazardly on top.

But the desk is clearly the focal point of the room and it too is piled high with papers, files and bound documents. In front of the desk, the entire wall is plastered with newspaper cuttings, stories on curling, yellowing paper covering it from floor to ceiling. News stories, features, columns and editorials, even a couple of front pages. The images are a mixture of people walking, police mug-shots, family group shots and court sketches. But all of them have one thing in common.

They're all stories about my case. About me.

52

Neither of us admit to looking in the box room.

Instead, we drink tea and talk in the sparse lounge, with its flattened carpet and faded flock wallpaper. Owen orders in a Chinese takeaway and the three of us eat at the kitchen table, and it almost feels like being a normal person again, eating a normal meal in a normal house. No bars, no locks, no canteen rules and no curfew. Just indulgent food and conversation, a welcome distraction from the little aftershocks of fear that hit me every time my memory snags on that windowless black van. Owen opens a bottle of red wine, which helps a little.

It's not until later, after he bids us goodnight and goes to do another couple of hours in his study, that Jodie raises it again.

She and I lie in the queen-sized bed, talking in the dark like a couple of teenagers at a sleepover. We talk about our children and she tells me about her daughter, Holly, about the abuse they'd both suffered at the hands of her partner and the breakdown of their relationship. He had manipulated their daughter and used Jodie's drug addiction, her convictions, to his advantage in the custody battle that followed their split. I tell her about the boys, about seeing them at the park a few days ago after they'd come out of school. All the while, the intermittent *tap-tap-tapping* of a computer keyboard is just about audible through the wall. Eventually, the two of us fall silent and she props herself up on one elbow, the street light leaking through the curtains casting a soft glow on her face.

'Do you think Owen is a bit . . . I don't know.'

'A bit what?'

'Don't tell me you haven't noticed.'

'You're being a bit cryptic, Jodie.'

'What's that, like a crossword?' She lowers her voice, but only a little. 'I mean he's a bit of a weirdo, isn't he?'

'He might be a little bit obsessive.'

'*Might* be?' She snorts. 'You saw that box room of his. Pictures of you all over the wall, from floor to ceiling. Pretty freaky, if you ask me.'

Our room is right next to his study – we're only a few feet away from where Owen is sitting at his computer right now – and I wonder how thick the walls are.

'Keep your voice down,' I whisper. 'He'll hear you.'

'I'm just saying, he's obsessed with you.'

'He's obsessed with my case.'

She raises an eyebrow. 'Is *that* what they call it nowadays?'

I put a finger to my lips. Something has changed: the house has fallen completely silent around us. In the little box room, the tapping on the keyboard has stopped.

'When I first met Owen, he told me something.'

'That he wants to take you for his bride and lock you in his sex dungeon forever?'

I give her a look.

'Sorry,' she says sheepishly, glancing at the red weals on my wrist. 'Bad taste.'

'He told me that every journalist ends up having one big story in their career that outshines all the rest, that sort of defines them. The first one they mention if someone asks them what they do for a living. The story they can't stop thinking about, usually because it's the making of their career.'

'OK,' Jodie says slowly.

'The thing is with Owen, he thinks that story is *my* case. It should have been the making of his career, an award-winner, a brave investigation that overturned a terrible miscarriage of justice. Except it did the opposite – it wrecked his career. Pretty much bankrupted him, made him *persona non grata* in the profession. He thinks he screwed up and he's never stopped thinking about it. He can't let it go.'

'*And* he's weird.'

'Single-minded, maybe.'

She grunts as if she's not convinced. 'Didn't want me coming here to his house though, did he? That was pretty obvious when we were leaving the hospital. Wanted to drop me back to the hostel so he could have you all to himself.'

'That was more about the sleeping arrangements, I think.' I stifle a yawn. 'Anyway, he's probably got a girlfriend.'

'Has he *mentioned* a girlfriend?' She pulls a face. 'Doesn't seem the type, to me. For all we know he could be watching us right now.'

'Stop it,' I say, staring up into the dark as if I might spot a red LED light blinking in the corner. 'Hang on, is that why you shoved the chair up under the door handle?'

'There's no lock. It's better than nothing.' She lies back down on her pillow, still facing me. 'Seriously, didn't you think it was a bit strange when he was telling us about this bank statement he's found?'

'Strange in what way?'

'Like, someone takes a massive bribe and he's got the evidence right there in his hand, and you tell me he's supposedly obsessed with this story and getting to the bottom of everything. And he's been looking for this proof or whatever for years and years, but once he finds it, all of a sudden he *doesn't* want to go to the cops?'

'Like he said, he wants to be sure before he takes the next step. He doesn't want to go off half-cocked, that's all.'

'Hmm,' she says. 'Seems a bit *cryptic* to me.'

Eventually, we lapse into a comfortable silence and I turn onto my side, my eyelids heavy. I try to think about tomorrow, about what we need to do next, even as more barriers appear at every turn. Images flash in front of my closed eyes. My in-laws, the Vernons, who once welcomed me into their family and now had only hostility and threats. Trevor Boyle, relishing the power to snatch my freedom away at any moment. Musgrove, a dying man who might soon take his secrets to the grave. The police car outside his house today, when I was sure I was about to be caught. Christine Lai's corruption unpunished, Jones's chillingly straightforward brutality. *This is your only warning.*

So many reasons to stop what I'm doing. Only one reason to keep going.

Finally, I can feel myself falling, sliding backwards into sleep, when I hear Jodie's voice soft beside me in the darkness.

'Heather?'

'Mmm-hmm?'

'We're going to get your boys back, you know. I promise you.'

I answer without opening my eyes.

'And then we're going to get you back into Holly's life. That's a promise too.'

53

SATURDAY

My sleep is plagued with dark dreams in which I am drowning in plastic, my mouth and nose filled with it, my whole body surrounded by it, entombed in an opaque sea of thick, liquid plastic that wants to drag me to the bottom and there is no oxygen, no air, I can't—

Someone is saying my name.

'Heather?'

Jodie is at my bedside, in jeans and a T-shirt, barefoot, her small calloused hand resting lightly on my arm.

'It's OK,' she says. 'You're OK.'

I blink, trying to remember where I am, this strange bed, this room, this place, before it all comes back to me in a rush. My throat is raw, my voice still somewhere else.

Jodie gives me a concerned look. Her hair is wet. 'Bad dreams?'

I nod and she points to a steaming cup of tea on the bedside table next to me before padding wordlessly back to the other side of the bed, sipping her own cup of tea and looking at her phone.

It's almost nine o'clock. The room is bright with morning sunshine and the sheets, on my side at least, are soaked in sweat. I gather what fresh clothes I have and take a quick shower, dress and towel-dry my hair as best I can. Owen is already gone by the time I come downstairs but he's left bread and cereal, milk and eggs out for breakfast. He's also left a Post-it note stuck to a memory stick; the note says simply 'Heather playlist' and is signed off with a single capital O.

It takes half an hour to configure my new phone, setting up email and messages and signing back into my Telegram account so I can talk securely to the other three. I message Amy privately to ask how she's doing after yesterday. She seems to be OK although I get the impression she's putting a brave face on it.

Owen returns laden with shopping bags from the supermarket which he proceeds to unload onto the side in preparation for lunch and dinner. He'd not had much food in, he explains sheepishly, and didn't often have visitors.

'You've been pushing too hard, Heather, you need to rest,' he tells me, unloading paracetamol, ibuprofen, antiseptic cream and various other treatments onto the kitchen side, urging me to help myself. 'And lay low, at least for today. Did you sleep OK? Injuries keep you awake?'

He insists on making me a cup of tea and leaves food out for lunch before asking me for the second time if there's anything he can get me while he's out. There are some other leads he wants to follow up, he says, including the house in Combe Down that Christine Lai had visited yesterday.

He heads out again just after 10 a.m., leaving Jodie and I alone in the house. I lay out the sum total of my possessions on the bed. A couple of changes of clothes. Basic toiletries. My mum's old watch, phone, bank card, laptop, backpack with assorted paperwork from the probation service.

Zipped into a side pocket of the backpack, I find the key and receipt for Total Storage. Another thing that feels like unfinished business; at some point I needed to find a home for the contents of that big locker. The open laptop reminds me there were some memory sticks to check too – I'd left them behind on Tuesday as I didn't have any way to look at them; but now I do. And I didn't have access to a car then either, to move the contents out to somewhere more permanent.

But now we have the Corsa, parked on the drive outside.

I go downstairs to find Jodie putting her trainers on in the hall, car keys on the side table beside her.

'I can't sit around here all day,' she says, 'so I was thinking about the stuff still at the storage place.'

I give her a smile, holding up the key to locker #5581. 'You must be a mind-reader. Hey, how about I come with you?'

She pockets the key and turns towards the hallway.

'You need to rest up and be safe, Mrs Vernon.' She flashes me a smile as she's pulling the door shut. 'And anyhow, I move faster on my own. Won't be long.'

I open my laptop and copy across the playlist Owen has compiled for me on the memory stick, all twenty-two songs from the home-made CD that Liam had created for me all those years ago. The first song is 'Street Spirit' by Radiohead and a sense of melancholy settles on my shoulders as I listen, a heavy ache, but I don't want it to stop.

I spend a fruitless half-hour googling Christine Lai, combing over all the search results brought up by her name in the hope of finding something useful. She had been close to Liam in those last years, spending as much if not more time with him than I did. She would have *known* if he was having an affair, I feel sure of it, she had run his diary and his office with a comprehensive efficiency that had always impressed me. It had impressed the jury too, when she gave evidence for the prosecution at my trial. She had been a very persuasive witness.

I already knew that she had left the constituency office – discreetly, without announcement or fanfare – a few months after my trial ended. According to her LinkedIn profile she then went to work for an international software company with an office in Bristol, moving jobs twice more before the most recent move last year had brought her to the Ministry of Defence, a few miles up the A4 in Corsham. Five different jobs in the last ten years. Was that unusual? It seemed like a lot of moving around. Her social media profiles were scant, to say the least. Almost nothing that was personal. I knew from Amy that she was single, unmarried and lived alone; whether there had been boyfriends along the way, I didn't know.

I'm still annoyed that I had managed to lose the manuscript of Musgrove's book, that we had worked so hard and risked so much to find, only for it to be snatched out of my hands so soon afterwards. I should have stayed to read about the mention of Artemis Tech, to see why it had been an area of interest in the investigation and maybe even why they had been steered away from it. What might have emerged over the last decade to give an overlooked line of enquiry new relevance.

Instead, I'm back to square one.

54

My phone buzzes with a video call from Amy.

I accept the call and she apologises for not coming out to see me in person. Her parents, she said, had been very upset to see her injuries from yesterday and had insisted she stay at home for a few days to rest and recover. She still looks pale, drawn, a traumatised victim trying to put a brave face on it.

'Mum's gone completely overboard,' she says. 'Feel like I'm sixteen again, getting grounded for breaking my curfew.'

I nudge the subject into more neutral ground, asking her how the boys are doing. She spends a few minutes telling me how Theo and Finn are getting on at school and at home, living in the big Bathwick house with their grandparents and their aunt. Theo is a keen footballer and captain of the cricket team too, she tells me, with a gift for maths and in the top groups for all three science subjects. Finn is more arty, more bookish, into his films and video games – Amy reels off a string of titles like *Elden Ring* and *Dragon Age*, none of which I've ever heard of – and is practising for his grade four piano exam.

She glances over her shoulder and edges nearer to the screen. It looks as if she's in the annex of the big house, the extension that had been built to accommodate her apartment. Finn, she says more quietly, has been asking about me for the first time in years. A warm glow spreads from the base of my throat as my sister-in-law describes a conversation with the son who I doubt would even recognise me. *What happens now?* he had said. *Is she out of prison for good? Is she still my mum? Will Granny and Grandpa ever talk to her again? What happens if she comes to the house?*

I listen in silence, drinking it all in, absorbing every detail and not wanting her to stop. I have missed so much of their lives. Their grandmother will have done her best but she had always been distracted, in her own world half the time, more enamoured of the *idea* of having children than the actual day-to-day work of raising them. I have a strong sense that Amy has been more of a mother to the boys, a listener, a guide, a patient helper and someone who would always have time for her nephews – who would always be there for them. She has even acquiesced to Theo's requests for a couple of aunt-and-nephew driving lessons on the private drive at Dormers.

After ten minutes, the conversation returns to Jones and his men.

'You need to be more careful,' she says. 'Protect yourself. Do whatever you have to do.'

'You too, Amy.'

We end the call and I look out of the front window of the lounge as a fine rain starts to darken the concrete. The street is clear, but I pull the curtains anyway. I think about Amy's words. *Protect yourself.* Jodie had said something similar a few days ago when she gave me the knife to carry in my handbag. The knife that had disappeared when I was cornered by Jones's men. I go upstairs and do a quick search of the spare room, through what little stuff I possess in case I've inadvertently left it in a pocket or a coat. I check my backpack and a couple of plastic bags that I've accumulated along the way. Nothing.

Jodie's cheap vinyl backpack is in the spare room, propped against her side of the bed, so I go through that too. Perhaps she had borrowed the little knife back without me realising. Inside are a few tops, a cap, a phone charger, a small framed picture of a teenaged girl in school uniform – her daughter, Holly, I assume – and a few random toiletries. Right at the bottom of her bag, my fingers brush against a pair of walking socks but as I push them aside there is a little more resistance than there should be. A solidity beneath the wool; something inside. I pull the sock from her backpack and reach a hand into it.

Smooth plastic.

A clear Ziploc bag full of money.

Sealed inside is a thick wedge of banknotes, folded once. I take them out and hold them, the red-purple fifty-pound notes slick and smooth in my palm. A quick count reveals there is more than fifteen hundred pounds here.

A lot of money. Especially to an ex-offender newly released from prison.

I sit back against the radiator, the money spread on the patterned carpet in front of me, trying to figure out what I'm missing.

Because Jodie had no money when we met. She'd told me as much, that first day in the hostel. She had no job, very little family. No visible means of support beyond benefits. Savings from a bank account? It seemed highly unlikely she'd have this stashed away and not tell me about it. My thoughts keep circling back to the same point, like a compass always returning to true north no matter which way I turned.

Since the moment Jones's thugs had grabbed me off the street, I had been trying to figure out how they found me. It made a certain kind of sense that they might track me to the probation hostel: it was where I was supposed to be, according to the terms of my licence. If they knew my release date – and they seemed pretty well informed on matters like that – it was logical for them to look for me at that address. But the house on Rockliffe Road . . . it should have been safe. I was almost certain I hadn't been followed, and yet they had been there in the same neighbourhood at the same time as me, ready to manoeuvre me into a dead end. Ready to pounce.

And there was one person who had known exactly where I would be.

Jodie.

She was the one who found his address, when we first started looking through his emails. She had told me not to go there on my own – insisted we go together instead.

She'd known I would probably go alone anyway.

And there was that echo of her voice, the thing she kept saying to me one way or another.

Never trust an addict. We lie to everyone. Those had been her exact words. Perhaps it was always dangerous to put your faith in someone who had no faith in themselves.

The black van had turned up three days ago as we tried to track down John Musgrove. I had been knocking on doors, leaving Jodie to her own devices in the car, and *somehow* the van had found us. I only had her word that it had even been at the hostel the previous day.

It makes a certain kind of sense. And yet it's still hard to believe that she sold me out. Jodie and I had talked last night, for a long time, about the things that mattered most to us in the world. I felt like I *knew* her on a deeper level, even though it had been barely a week since we'd first met.

I repack the money and replace it inside her backpack.

Perhaps she had already given them this address, and I should leave right now. Just get out and leave it all behind. Go far away. Hide. Disappear.

But I had come too far to walk away now. I had to keep going if I was ever going to get home.

Instead, I go downstairs to the kitchen, find a small sharp knife in Owen's kitchen drawer and slip it into my back pocket.

55

Jodie is not back from the storage place until mid-afternoon, reversing the Corsa almost to the front door and giving the horn a double toot to let me know she's arrived.

'I got all of it,' she says. 'Asked that nice young lad to help me get it on a trolley and out to the car. Pretty much filled the boot, but we managed in the end.' She looks around, points at the front windows. 'Why are the curtains closed?'

She's taken a lot longer than I thought – almost three hours – but I decide not to mention it. I watch her carefully as we cart everything inside, looking for her to betray any hint of deception, any clue that someone has bought her loyalty for fifteen hundred pounds. But she seems to be the consummate actress.

Finally, we have it all stacked haphazardly on the lounge table, with every inch of the stained teak covered. I give silent thanks again to my mother and her decision to store these things away, these fragments of my old life, probably all she received from the Vernons after the house was sold. An entire house, a life, the whole of *my* life, and there was barely enough of it to cover the surface of this small dining table.

I make us both tea and bring it through to the lounge, handing a mug to Jodie. She's looking through a small stack of framed photographs, presumably unwanted by my in-laws because I was in them. One from our wedding day, another from a New Year's Eve party, a third one that Liam had taken on a beautiful summer's day, in the garden of an old pub in Lacock. It's a selfie and we're both wearing sunglasses and giddy-happy smiles, Liam looking like a tanned, chisel-jawed Hollywood film star, like Ben Affleck in his prime, even though he never behaved as if he believed it. I had teased him about the picture relentlessly afterwards. The fact that he never seemed to acknowledge the way he looked, never played on it or exploited it, was one of the things I had loved about him.

Jodie nods in approval. 'Proper handsome fella, your Liam.'

I take it from her and look at the picture, a painful ache deep in my chest. We'd been to Dyrham Park that day, just walked around the grounds of the old country house, holding hands and taking it all in, happy to wander through the Perry Orchard and the herb garden and the park, happy to be anywhere as long as we were together. I didn't know it when the picture had been taken, but a week or two later I found out I was pregnant with Theo.

'Yes,' I say quietly. 'Yes, he was.'

We spend half an hour taking things methodically from the pile and laying them out on the floor of the lounge to go through them again, checking paperwork, studying everything with fresh eyes, trying to catch any clue that might have been missed.

At four o'clock, I go to put the kettle on again but Jodie holds a hand up.

'Enough tea,' she says. 'How about something a bit more worthwhile?'

I shake my head. 'Bit early for me, Jodie.'

'Owen's booze cabinet is sadly lacking,' she says. 'As in, non-existent. So I thought I'd get us something to crack on with, as it's the weekend.'

'I should probably stay sober, thanks.'

But I know what she's really saying. She has that restlessness, that twitch-fingered, wide-eyed look of withdrawal that I'd seen so many times among new arrivals at Eastwood Park.

'Come *on*.' She gives me a grin. 'Weekend, isn't it?'

I put a hand on her arm. 'Just drinks though, right? Nothing else, no drugs?'

'Just drinks.' She gives me a little salute.

She goes to the front door, shrugging her jacket on and scooping up the car keys from the side table. In her haste, she knocks them to the floor and sends them skittering across the tiles. She bends and snatches at them, fingers grasping.

She is in a hurry.

I have a flash of my discovery earlier – *how much do I actually know about her?* – and a horrible, creeping sensation takes hold of me that she's trying to get away, to leave here, to get away from *me*.

'Jodie?'

'Yeah?'

'We're friends, right?'

'Of course.' She winks. 'We've shared a bed now, so we must be.'

'I just wanted to say thanks,' I say. 'For being there. For helping me. And I meant what I said last night.'

'Me too,' she says, pulling the heavy front door open. 'See you in a bit.'

And then she's gone, pulling out of the drive and straight onto the road without hesitating to look or indicate.

I find four more memory sticks in among the mass of other stuff, and go through them one by one.

The first I vaguely recognise, and it turns out to be one of mine. Random documents from my old life, work stuff, presentations, reports and memos. All kinds of meaningless stuff that I had thought, once upon a time, was actually important. The images folder is harder to look at. Hundreds of images of the boys when they were babies, and toddlers, days out and holidays and pictures taken in the garden of our old house in Maitland Street. About a million pictures of Theo when he was newborn – tiny, pink, and slightly squashed from the Caesarean – most of which looked almost identical. The mania of new parenthood, I guess.

The other three belonged to Liam. Two work and one personal.

I spend a further hour going through each document stored on the three sticks, clicking and reading, clicking and reading, hope slowly leaching away as I discount the first dozen, then the next and the next.

There is nothing here.

Nothing that was worth saving, keeping, storing away for a decade. Nothing that makes any difference.

I slam my laptop shut in frustration.

I need some air; need to walk, to get out. Being cooped up in this small pebble-dashed house all day feels a little too much like being in jail, staring at the same four walls. Even though I can go outside and walk around in the small, overgrown garden at the back, it still gives me that same claustrophobic sense that I'm stuck here against my will. And I can't even go out the front because I don't have a key. Jodie has the only spare and she seems to have double-locked it when she left. So I'm basically a prisoner in this house.

It's already creeping into early evening when I realise something else: there was no discussion about finding a B & B for us to move on to. Owen hasn't mentioned it since we picked Amy up from the hospital yesterday, and in any case he's been out most of the day. I guess we'll be staying here under his roof, for one more night at least. Perhaps that was his plan all along.

Eventually, I find myself back in the lounge, staring angrily at the stack of belongings spread across the floor and the dining table. It all seems so pointless now, almost cruel, these things salvaged from my old life that can only remind me of what I've lost. They can't help me move forward, can't give me what I need more than anything else in the world.

There is nothing left untouched apart from a stack of paperback books. Perhaps a couple of dozen – novels that Liam and I had both loved and passed between us. *Gone Girl*, *Postmortem*, *The Silence of the Lambs*. Others by Patricia Highsmith, Margaret Atwood, Stephen King. My original old copy of *Harry Potter and the Philosopher's Stone*, battered and creased and read many times over.

Books that had sat on the shelf of our house on Maitland Street since the day we moved in. Books that the Vernons had presumably thought were too lowbrow to be worth saving, to be worthy of their son's memory. Books that my mother had known I loved.

I pick up *In the Woods* by Tana French and flick through the pages, dry and slightly faded. Inside, I run my fingers over the title page, over the looping inscription in my husband's confident handwriting.

Paper for our first anniversary!
Hope you like this one,
L xx

It had been a good choice, a great book that I had found in the prison library and reread twice while I was inside. There is a bookmark in the pages of this copy, as if someone has reached the middle and given up or run out of time. I flick idly to the page to take it out but it's not a bookmark, it's an envelope jammed between the pages, addressed to Liam in handwritten capital letters at our old house. A letter that seems to have gone astray.

Inside the envelope is a single sheet of A4 paper folded twice into a rectangle. I unfold it, the paper stiff and unyielding with age, creases scored into the paper over many years.

My eyes flick over the text, the image, the note scrawled beneath it. Trying to make sense of what I'm reading.

56

The sheet of paper looks like a printout of a news story, a screen-shot of a webpage. The picture is of a middle-aged man in a white jacket, harassed, sweating and red-faced at the centre of a melee of dozens of people, a mob of photographers and cameras, uniformed police in the mix too.

The headline reads:

THE END OF 'MR CLEAN'.

At the bottom of the page, six words have been written carefully in heavy black biro:

BE CAREFUL – OR YOU ARE NEXT.

I don't recognise the middle-aged man in the picture, or the place, or any of it. The story, the headline, the uniforms – none of them look familiar. A closer look at the web address and a quick Google search reveals it to be a Brazilian news website, the text a slightly haphazard web translation from Portuguese to English. I scan the first few paragraphs: some kind of scandal involving a Brazilian member of the Chamber of Deputies, their equivalent of our Parliament. A deputy by the name of Hector Macedo, who had built a reputation as 'Mr Clean', campaigning against corruption and big business, fighting for social justice and dedicated to his family.

A fearless campaigner who had made powerful enemies when he delayed a large infrastructure project over concerns about bribery and national security.

His career, however, had ended years ago in shame and ignominy.

Accusations of tax fraud and a police search of his property which had uncovered something much worse: compromising pictures on a phone hidden in his study, dozens of images of young boys. Naked. A couple of them have been reprinted alongside the news story, the boys' faces obscured and other details thankfully blurred out.

Macedo had denied it. The phone had been planted, he insisted, and he knew nothing about the pictures: he was a family man who loved his wife and family and would never do anything to hurt a child. He was not a paedophile – the whole thing was a set-up, he said, by enemies determined to silence him.

But it didn't matter what he said.

As soon as the story got out, the images leaked to the media, his denials didn't matter. His career was over. Hence the picture above this story, which showed him being arrested outside his house and escorted away by the federal police amid a maelstrom of publicity.

But this story is *old*. More than a decade ago. The date on it is 25 February 2012, more than a year before Liam died. How could it be related?

Then I read the story right to the very end, and find the answer.

There in the last paragraph is a mention of several large companies for whom Macedo had been a thorn in the side, asking difficult questions and calling for full transparency over the way projects were being run, how government contracts had been issued and who might have been paid off along the way.

One of the companies is a US multinational called North Star.

I look at the note at the bottom of the page again, handwritten in the same blocky black capitals as on the envelope.

BE CAREFUL – OR YOU ARE NEXT

The envelope is addressed to Liam at our old home address but has no stamp, no postmark. Must have been hand-delivered. There is a handwritten date in the bottom right hand corner in faded red ink, the numerals in a strange order: month, day, year: *July-8-2013*. Less than a week before his death.

Facts and dates coalesce, a picture sliding into focus as it starts to come together in my mind. Liam had suspected Christine Lai was being paid off: he had seen her bank statement and threatened to blow the whistle. North Star had counter-threatened him with *this* warning, with blackmail, with the destruction of his reputation – not to mention his family, his marriage – and somehow it had escalated in the most terrifying way possible. It had ended not just in blackmail, but in murder.

With a convenient narrative that put the blame on someone else. Me.

The modus operandi was old school: compromising pictures to guarantee compliance or if not, to ruin a career. Only in this case they had served a second purpose for the prosecution, turning me into the spurned wife who had killed her cheating husband in a spasm of jealous rage.

Liam had kept the blackmail threat at home. Away from the office, away from Christine. And the fact that it was here, having been hidden in a bookcase, was why it had never been found by the police, had never been available to my lawyer as evidence of a wider conspiracy. A hard copy, just old-fashioned paper and printer ink, so there was no electronic trail to lead back to the sender.

I was more sure than ever now of how it had all gone down, the sequence of events slowly becoming apparent as every piece of evidence was discovered. My husband had been a threat to North Star and they had killed him; they had demonstrated very clearly that they were willing to kill again to maintain our silence. Amy and I had the injuries to prove that.

The need to talk about this with someone, to share and discuss and analyse this latest development with a member of my crew, is almost overpowering. But I'm alone in the house. Instead, I take a picture of the printout on my phone and send it to the Telegram group chat shared by Owen, Amy, Jodie and me.

We need to talk about this ASAP. Found it among storage locker stuff. Similarities with Liam. North Star in the mix too.

I feel breathless, light-headed and I have to pace the length of the lounge to calm my racing heart. I go up to the bathroom to splash some cold water on my face, just letting it wash over my skin while I try to think. We had found it: evidence of blackmail, of corruption, of a conspiracy. Surely this was enough? We needed to sit down as a team, put all of the evidence together and discuss next steps. Figure out how we could present it to the police in a way that didn't expose us to more legal jeopardy, and decide which of us should make the first approach. I turn off the tap and reach for a towel. Amy. She would be the best choice. She would have the most clout, her words would carry the most weight, assuming I could persuade her to—

There is a knock at the front door.

Three polite raps on the wood that puncture the silence. I ignore it. Whoever is knocking is here for Owen, and in any case it's double-locked and I don't have a key. I couldn't open it even if I wanted to. Or maybe Jodie has forgotten her key. I finish drying my face and go into the spare bedroom to see who it is.

The knock comes again, slightly louder this time. No longer polite, more of the thudding made by a closed fist.

Not Jodie. Instinct makes me flatten myself against the wall and inch along it to get a better view of the drive. There is no black Corsa. But the street is busy: a police van, a squad car with blue lights flashing and an unmarked saloon pulled up onto the pavement outside Owen's house.

I curse under my breath. *Not now, not when we're so close.*

There are two people in suits at the front door below me. A dark-haired woman standing back, and a bearded man who is doing the knocking. He raises his fist and the hammering comes again, hard enough to rattle the door in its frame. Behind the two suits are four police officers in protective gear, with pads and helmets and extendable batons. The biggest of them, at the front, grips the red handles of a steel battering ram the size of a fire extinguisher.

'Heather Vernon,' the bearded man says, his voice muffled by the double glazing. 'Open the door please.'

Should I stay? Do as I'm asked? Trust the police?

No. Not again. Not this time.

I grab my bank card and cash from the bedside table and go out onto the landing, pulling the door shut behind me. I pull the door of the master bedroom and the little toilet shut too, then take the key from inside the bathroom door, shutting it and locking it from the outside, slipping the key into my pocket. *Closed doors add time.* I run down the stairs, flinching at the creak of wood under my weight and hoping they can't see movement through the frosted glass. Barely three metres from where the male detective is standing and with just a wooden front door to separate us, I hurriedly pull on my boots and grab my jacket from the banister, trying to creep on the balls of my feet so the floorboards don't betray me.

He hammers again. 'We're coming in one way or the other so you'd best open this door, Heather.' The letterbox flap opens, a gloved hand visible. 'It's concerning your probation officer, Mr Boyle.'

Shit. So Boyle had followed through on his threat.

The bearded man's voice is louder now.

'Mr Boyle is in a critical condition right now at the RUH.' He pauses a beat before adding: 'We know you were there at his office, Heather, we found your phone at the scene. But we just want to talk, OK? For your own safety as well as everyone else.'

Boyle was in hospital? What?

There's no time to think about what he's just said. The blackmail threat and its envelope are still on the dining table and I have a flashback to yesterday, finding the manuscript and then losing it almost immediately. That was *not* going to happen again. Hide it or take it? The front room curtains are still closed from earlier, so the police can't see in. I run into the lounge and grab the printout, shoving it into my backpack along with the laptop. There's no time to pick up anything else.

More hammering on the front door, the sound betraying an increasing frustration.

'Easy way or hard way, Heather,' he shouts. 'Last chance.'

I run into the kitchen, hoisting the backpack over my shoulder and checking the little knife is still in my pocket as I hurry to the back door. From behind me comes a colossal *crash* as the steel battering ram is swung into the front door with great force, once, twice. The back door key is still in the lock from my walk around the garden earlier and my hand shakes as I turn it, sweat slipping on my fingers, then it *clicks* and I heave the door open, stepping outside into the cool evening air, pulling it shut – *quickly quickly, another crash from the battering ram* – and locking it again to buy a few more seconds. I hurl the key into a bush and there is a huge, splintering *crack* as the front door gives way and smashes back on its hinges into the hall, followed instantly by a crescendo of shouting male voices almost exultant as they swarm into the house behind me, all screaming the same thing at the top of their lungs.

'Police! Stay where you are! Stay where you are!'

I'm not going to do that.

And so I do the only other thing I *can* do.

Run.

57

I sprint towards the hedge at the end of the overgrown back garden, hurdling a low bush and ploughing through a flowerbed thick with weeds, praying that if there is a fence behind the hedge it is as rundown as everything else. But if there was a fence here in the past there's nothing left now but rotted stumps of old wood, sticking unevenly out of the ground like rotten teeth. I drop to my hands and knees and push my way through, twigs and branches scratching at my skin, snagging on my jacket and trying to pull me back, ignoring the splinters digging into my palms and then I'm through the other side and at the bottom of a shallow slope.

Owen's house backs onto a raised footpath, an old railway embankment that at some point in the past has been converted into a nature walk lined with trees and bushes on each side. I scramble up the bank, still on my hands and knees, nettles blazing a path across the skin of my wrists. My foot catches on a tree root before I reach the top and I sprawl face-first into the dirt, the wind momentarily knocked out of me. I wince, catching my breath and looking around. The footpath – poker straight, like the railway line that preceded it – extends for a few hundred metres in either direction.

A uniformed police officer is on the path.

He is lanky and young and highly visible in his bright yellow jacket, presumably posted behind the house as a backstop in case I bolted. Perhaps fifteen metres from where I am, peering through

the bushes and trees as if he can't identify which house he's supposed to be looking at. It's a long road and a lot of the gardens
must look very similar. He seems to be alone and has his back to
me, talking earnestly into his radio in between squawks of agitated
static from his colleagues in the house.

I scramble back down the bank and work my way further from
him, along the lines of garden hedges, trying to be as silent as I
can as branches and brambles claw at my jeans, my backpack. The
officer's hi-vis jacket is good for one thing at least: it means I can
make him out even through the undergrowth. He's still talking
into his radio, peering into the bushes close to where I was just
moments ago. From further behind, from the garden of Owen's
house, there is a series of shouts and calls from the other officers that indicate they have cleared the house already and are out
through the back. The only positive is that I haven't seen or heard
any dogs; but they'll be here before long if they think I've gone to
ground close by.

The breath is hot in my throat. I have to get away, down the far
side of the embankment. But to get there I'll have to cross the path –
where I'll be in the open, with no cover – without being seen by the
young uniform. The path is three or four metres wide, a second or
two in which I'll be completely exposed if he turns around.

Lying completely flat in the bushes, with my cheek pressed to the
dirt, I watch the officer's progress as he works his way along the footpath towards me, pushing branches aside to squint down the bank.
He's getting nearer, close enough for me to make out the traces of
acne on his chin. The voices from the garden are getting nearer too.

He steps out onto the path again and stops, squinting in my
direction and for a second I'm certain he's seen me, certain he's
about to call it in, but instead his eyes slide over my hiding place and
then he turns as a dog appears at his side, its tail wagging furiously.

Not a police dog. A large and enthusiastic golden retriever off its
lead, sniffing around him and panting, tongue lolling. The police

officer bends to pat the retriever on the head and talk to its middle-aged owner, turning his back for a moment. Turning away from me.

I sprint across the gap and launch myself down the embankment on the far side, but it's steeper here, a longer slope, low trees and dark earth made slippery with the early evening rain and in a second I've lost my footing, I'm falling forwards, hitting and rolling, wrists crackling with pain like an electric current, tumbling faster and faster, my vision spinning – *earth then trees then earth then trees—*

The dark twisted base of an old oak coming up to meet me and I try to bring my hands up to brace before—

* * *

When I come to, my vision is full of tree branches and sky. There is a pulse of hot pain in my head, above my left ear, and dark smears of dirt caked on my palms, my elbows, the knees of my jeans. Blood in my mouth, the skin on my hands criss-crossed with scratches.

I've no idea how long I was out cold – five minutes? Ten? Or maybe just a matter of moments, but it all comes back to me in a rush. The gnarled old oak tree that stopped my descent towers above, a collection of rusting beer cans at its base around the blackened logs of a small fire. I'm at the bottom of the bank, on the other side of the path from Owen's house. Another line of back gardens, of hedges and fences all connecting to each other on this side of the embankment. *Wait. Listen.* Voices at the top of the bank. The static squawk of a radio, but it's too far away to make out the words.

As quietly as I can, I work my way along the bottom of the slope for a few hundred metres, staying away from the path until it rises up and ends where it meets the road. I pick my way through the trees and find a place to observe the road in case they have patrol cars stationed here to grab me when I emerge. The road seems clear but it's too main for my liking, too obvious; side streets will be better. I need to put some distance between myself and this place, need to think, to speak to the others.

I pull the hood of my sweatshirt up and check the phone as I set off. There is a crack across the screen from my tumble down the embankment, but otherwise it seems OK. Our group chat on Telegram is still silent, no responses to my earlier message about the blackmail note. I know Owen said we should stick to the app for security, but I thought this was probably an exception.

I call Amy first but it goes to voicemail. Jodie's too. Owen's phone doesn't even ring; as if it's switched off.

What the hell?

I type a message in the chat instead.

Need to talk ASAP. Owen's house raided by police, I only just got away. My probation officer attacked and they think I did it. We need to meet, call me.

There is a dark, niggling doubt as I read back my own message on the cracked screen of my phone. Something is worming its way through about the events of the last few hours, the last few days. Whatever had happened to Trevor Boyle – someone was trying to set me up. They had done it before, and they were doing it again.

I press *send*.

We would figure this out together. Until then, I needed somewhere to lie low for a few hours. Somewhere safe, where no one wouldn't think to look for me. Not the hostel – the police would know to look there. Not somewhere public either, where a beat bobby might spot me. Somewhere it would be easier to blend in while I wait for the others to resurface and get back in touch. My stomach growls with hunger and it gives me an idea.

It was true that lots of people were looking for me, for lots of different reasons.

But they were going to have to catch me first.

58

An hour later, I'm sitting at the end of a bench seat in the Methodist church hall on Nelson Place, the brim of the baseball cap pulled low beneath the hood of my sweatshirt, a mug of steaming black coffee in front of me. The place is crowded again for this evening's free meal, and I glance sidelong at the other tables hoping that Jodie might be here among the desperate and the destitute. But there's no sign of her.

My phone, too, remains silent on the table beside me. I've sent another message asking them to get back to me without any response. Had they been detained, or hurt, had they been together for some reason? I knew that Amy was traumatised from yesterday and Jodie was struggling with her own demons, but where was Owen? The silence is getting beyond weird and I need to gather all of the evidence we've got – the bank statement, the meeting minutes, Owen's research and everything else – if we're going to get any traction with the police. Not to mention that I need Amy to help me present it to them. I can't stop thinking of how she had looked when we picked her up from A & E, and I'll never forgive myself if Jones has taken out his anger on her. What if she was back in hospital again? What if . . . No. Don't think about that.

Outside, evening is settling on the town as workers head home and others start to fill the bars and restaurants. I would wait until it was fully dark, then do a quick pass of my in-laws' house to make sure Amy was OK. After that, maybe I would just have to push forward on my own. Go to the police with what I had, what I knew, and show them where to find the rest.

The headache from the oak tree has settled down to a low throb. When the coffee's finished, I clean myself up as best I can at the sink and small mirror in the toilet, before making my way back out onto Nelson Place. Backpack over my shoulders, baseball cap on, phone in my hand and the small knife from Owen's kitchen tucked into the back pocket of my jeans. There is a taxi rank on Walcot Street which is only a few minutes' walk from—

I see him almost immediately.

The balding man who had driven the black van.

As before, he's across the street, smoking a cigarette. And as before, he takes one last drag and flicks it into the gutter as he starts crossing the road towards me.

Jones's words come back to me in rush. *One warning, Heather. Next time we put you in the ground.*

My stomach turns over with a kick of adrenaline, every nerve and muscle urging me to *go*, to get away from him, to lose myself in the crowds because the police will be no help to me this time, the police are hunting me too, they're not on my side and maybe never have been. I'm on my own. Every instinct is screaming at me to take off, to run in the other direction and keep going as long and as far as I can in the hope that I'll be able to lose him among the city streets.

Instead, I do the opposite.

Not this time.

This time I go straight towards him, walking slowly across the pavement and onto the road with my head slightly down, eyes lowered to the tarmac. We come together in the middle of the street and he puts a hand on my left arm to restrain me, to lead me away, a small, arrogant smile of victory on his face as if I've finally admitted he's the boss and that this time there will be no running, no pursuit, no attempt to evade the inevitable. That this time I'm going to do what I'm told like a good girl should.

At the last moment I pull the knife from my back pocket and jam it hard into the top of his thigh.

The point is very sharp and it slides in surprisingly easily, like pushing through the skin of a watermelon, just a small *pop* of resistance and then I feel the warm liquid on my thumb and index finger. I pull it out and shove it in again, all the way to the hilt.

His eyes bulge with shock, a strangled cry caught in his throat.

'What the—'

I lean in close and speak softly into his ear. 'Try chasing me down now, you bastard.'

I wrench the blade free in a spray of blood and he collapses back into the road. There is a hooting of horns behind me as I sprint away, into a side street, then another, running as hard as I can for a full minute then ducking into an alleyway behind a row of high-end clothes shops, panting, heart thudding, crouched next to a tall stack of wooden pallets. I wipe the blade and handle of the knife with a piece of old newspaper, wrapping it inside the pages and dumping it in an industrial-sized bin in the alley.

It was no longer a surprise that he'd known where to find me; from now on, I'd have to assume they would be able to track me anywhere. For a moment I think of ditching my phone in the bin alongside the knife, but then how will the other three get in touch? I switch it off instead, shoving it back into my pocket.

I wait for another twenty minutes, listening for any sound of sirens in the neighbourhood. When there are none, I find my way to Walcot Street and climb into the back seat of the first taxi on the rank. The driver simply grunts and nods when I give him the address, hitting a button on the meter. He slouches way back in his seat, the lightest of grips on the steering wheel at the three o'clock position as he heads for Bathwick.

On the way there, we pass by the probation office on Sudbury Street. Boyle's cramped office is on the ground floor. There is an Avon and Somerset Police Scientific Support van in the car park, crime scene tape across the front door and a bored-looking uniformed officer stationed in front.

I slide a little lower in the back seat of the Prius. A churn of nerves starts low down in my stomach, as we ease through stop-start evening traffic on the way to the Vernons' house. A needling fear that this is too risky, that if I get caught one more time it will be the end – of everything. Jones's henchman had underestimated me this evening but he wouldn't make the same mistake twice.

When we're nearly there, I lean forward between the front seats to talk to the driver.

'Actually,' I say, 'could you drive past the address, to the end of the street? I just want to check something first.'

The driver grunts an affirmative and maintains his finger-and-thumb grip on the steering wheel as we turn the corner onto Cleveland Walk.

It's a wide, well-appointed street of large houses and even larger gardens backing onto fields. Lots of trees and manicured lawns, long driveways which means barely any cars are parked on the street itself. It makes vehicles parked on the street stand out more, makes them easier to spot.

Like the black van parked opposite the Vernons' house.

59

'Keep going,' I say to the taxi driver quickly. 'All the way to the end of the street please.'

I lie down flat across the back seat as we pass the Mercedes van, glad of the darkness and the subtlety of the street lighting in this exclusive neighbourhood. I don't need to look twice to know it's the same vehicle that came for me and Amy yesterday. Before we're out of sight of the big Georgian house I risk a single glance up and see lights blazing in most of the windows. All three of their cars on the drive behind a closed gate. My in-laws were there; that was good. Amy should be safe as long as she stayed home.

'Actually,' I add, 'can I give you a different address?'

But as expected, the hostel is another dead end. There is a patrol car parked up outside the hostel with a uniformed officer on either side of the street, one of them showing a head-and-shoulders picture to a passer-by. Again, I tell the cab driver not to stop but to keep going, down to the end of the street where he can make a turn back towards the city centre.

Nowhere is safe. Amy was trapped in her house; Owen and Jodie were missing in action. I was alone again, with nowhere to go.

I ask the driver to drop me at the train station and I turn my phone back on to call Amy, but again it goes to voicemail. I message her instead, about the Mercedes van parked on her street. After a moment the handset beeps with a new message from Jodie, sent only to me, rather than our little group of four. Delivered forty minutes ago. Thank God for that – *one* of them at least has got back into contact. I click to open her message.

Really need to talk to you URGENT. Can you meet me where you helped me Monday night?

Another message below the first sends a pulse of fear through my stomach. It had arrived twenty minutes after the other message: no words, just a three digit number.

999

Our distress code, our call for help. I don't know the street where I have to go, just the nickname of the place but the driver nods, turning his Prius across the width of the street and accelerating hard when I offer him an extra twenty quid if he can get there in under five minutes. Jodie's phone is still going to voicemail.

Come on, come on. Pick up.

As the taxi swings through turns and speeds through dark streets I think about Jodie's message, my senses still on alert. It could be that this was a trap of some kind, a lure to get me out on my own. The thought returns from earlier today: *how much do I actually know about her?* The answer is: *not very much.* Only that she had been a loyal friend over the last week, had helped me and looked after me when I needed it. We had looked after each other.

But that didn't explain why she had a grand-and-a-half in smooth new fifty-pound notes.

The driver drops me at the Station Street turn-off and I thrust three twenty pound notes at him before jumping out of the cab and setting off towards the Arches. The soot-stained brick openings are only vague shadows in the darkness, a couple of dozen half-circles beneath the London-bound railway line that seem to disappear into the hillside behind. Most of the nearby street lights are broken, the acrid smell of burning plastic hanging in the air.

Where the dead-end road becomes impassable with a scattering of rubble and the stripped-out carcass of an old car, the Corsa is parked haphazardly across a broken kerbstone as if it has been dumped. I squint into the driver's side window. Empty.

There is a noise from the shadows behind me, maybe the scratch of a footstep in the dirt. Maybe a rat. Maybe the wind. I tap my back pocket for the little knife, before remembering I had dumped it in town after the encounter with the balding man outside the shelter. *Damn.* I scan the ground for something to replace it but there are only stones and bits of cracked tarmac. I pick up a jagged piece of brick, heft it in my right hand. Better than nothing.

'Jodie?' I keep my voice soft, calling into the first couple of arches, semicircles full of darkness. 'Are you there?'

No answer. My foot catches on the wheel-less frame of an old bike, half obscured beneath a pile of black bin liners and a torn sleeping bag. The clink of a bottle draws me to the next arch, but there is no answer when I say Jodie's name. I move on, to the third, fourth, fifth spaces. The stink of decay is stronger here, of rotting rubbish and wet wood and human waste, a pungent mix that stings the eyes and sticks in the back of my throat.

There is a wet, phlegmy cough from the next arch. I move along to it and can just about make out a small green tent, tucked right into the corner, the faintest of lights visible from within the canvas. I call Jodie's name again and receive a volley of curses in reply. A man's slurring voice that dissolves into another wet, hacking cough.

I keep going, heart fluttering hard in my chest. My eyes are starting to adjust but it's still so dark, too dark to make out more than vague shapes and outlines. The next arch is the one I found Jodie in five days ago, the same rusted shopping trolley still jammed up against the side wall.

'Jodie, are you here?' I take out my phone and turn on the torch, shining it into the darkness. 'I got your message. It's me. Heather.'

There.

At the far end, in the deepest shadows. A dark-haired figure motionless on a dirty blanket. I say her name again but she doesn't move, doesn't respond. I run to her side, kneel down, say her name for a third time, keep on saying it because I can't think of what else to say. Propping the phone up, its bright torchlight casting eerie shapes on the wall.

Jodie's mouth is slightly open, eyes shut, head tilted slightly to the side. Boxes of painkillers scattered beside her.

The blister packs of pills are all empty.

Oh God. Oh no.

There is an open bottle of gin lying on its side, barely a half-inch of it left. There's no time for an ambulance. I search for a pulse in her neck, her skin cool and clammy to the touch, trying to gather the fragments of first aid training I could remember. Grabbing the torch up again, I ease open her mouth and check her airway before leaning over her to listen for any kind of breath, anything at all, crossing my hands over her sternum and talking to her as I frantically pump her chest.

'Come on, Jodie, come on, please, you're going to be OK, please wake up, come on now.'

I don't know how long I keep going with compressions, how many times I try to fill her lungs with the air in my own. How many times I tell her to wake up, to breathe, to come back to me, the tears wet on my cheeks.

But there is no pulse, no breath. No life.

She's gone.

60

I sob in the dark, holding Jodie's hand. Kneeling amid the dirt and debris of my friend's chaotic life and lonely death.

Finally, reluctantly, I make one last fruitless check for a pulse beneath the cooling skin of her neck. But I had known right from the start that it was too late. I had not been here for her when she needed me most. I had doubted her, let her down, made her a promise that hadn't been kept.

It is impossible to believe that she is gone, that I won't see her grin again, hear her talk or laugh or tell an off-colour joke. She had been the first friendly face I had found after leaving prison. Who knew what life was like inside because she had been there herself. Who knew how hard it could be returning to the outside when you'd already lost everything that mattered.

I think back to her prediction in this place, five nights ago, her fear of dying alone where no one would find her. It had come true – and it feels now like a glimpse of my own future. My own path, which a decade ago had been worlds apart from this but had come closer and closer until now our lives were almost interchangeable. Ex-convicts. Broken by the system and denied access to our children. Hopeless. Destroyed. It is so easy to imagine that my last hour will be like this too. Hunted by Jones, sought by the police, chased into a hole so deep that I can't climb out. Looking for oblivion and finding it in an overdose, accidental or otherwise.

Maybe she *had* taken their money.

Maybe she had taken her own life.

Or maybe someone had killed her, as a warning to me.

Jones's words come back to me too, a sick echo from that windowless black van.

How many people do you think will look for you if you disappear? How many will grieve for you? Who would actually miss you? The ripples might last a day, a week, then they'd be gone.

You'd be gone.

It was a sick irony that Amy and I had received his threat, his warning, but somehow it had been Jodie who ended up as the embodiment of his words. Because who would grieve for her, besides our little group? Who would look for her? Not her ex-husband. Not her daughter, a child taken to another country. Jodie was no longer in touch with her own mother and had never mentioned siblings.

The ripples she had made on the world would flatten so fast, fading to nothing as if she had never existed at all. And Jones was right, I was just the same: if I died now, who would know? Who would care?

A day, a week, then they'd be gone.

You'd be gone.

A single tragic postscript added to the ghoulish Wikipedia page of my life. My boys left to grow up without me. Liam's killer still out there, as free as a bird.

Jones had said it himself: I'd be gone.

It repeats in my brain, like the percussive rattle of a locomotive coming down the track.

Jones was right.

Jones was right.

I'd be gone.

Gone.

The idea hits me with such force that there is a roll of nausea in my stomach and I have to sit back on my haunches, blinking into the dark.

Gone.

But it was mad. It could never work. A mad idea, for sure.

Was it?

Or was it the only chance I had left?

I had crossed so many lines already since walking out of East-wood Park. Theft. Criminal damage. Burglary. Assault. Wounding with intent. Plus whatever had happened to Trevor Boyle since I was being hunted for that too. I had done some terrible things, but this would surely be the worst of them. I didn't know how my boys would even recognise me, if I ever managed to get back to them. Whether I might have already travelled too far away from them, gone too far over the horizon.

But there *was* a way I could carry on. Keep going. Keep searching, with the ultimate disguise. Keep looking for the truth, and make sure the search for me was called off. Otherwise what had all of this been for?

Once the idea takes hold, I can't think of anything else. I sit for a few minutes looking out at the night sky, a half-moon appearing and disappearing behind racing clouds, working it through in my mind. Trying to find the flaws. Listening for any sound nearby, any movement, any hint that I'm being observed. But there is nothing except for the hint of woodsmoke and the rustling of plastic bags caught in the chain-link fence outside.

It *was* a mad idea. Risky and wrong and unethical on so many levels, not to mention illegal.

But it might be my only hope.

I cuff the tears from my cheeks and turn out my pockets, laying the contents on the ground in front of me. Expired driver's licence. A roll of banknotes plus a bank card, a pre-paid card and some loose change. My backpack, which contained the laptop and a few keepsakes from my old life, Liam's mixtape CD among them. My phone. The letter from the probation service featuring my name and address, outlining the terms of my licence. The letter and contract from Peter

Vernon offering me a pay-off to move to Scotland, far away from his grandsons. I tear both in two and lay them next to Jodie's body.

All of it will have to be left behind in this dark place, except for the cash and the blackmail threat I had discovered today. I figured I could keep the bank cards as well, at least for the time being.

I ease the jacket off Jodie's shoulders and switch it with the one I've been wearing for the last few days. As gently as I can, I search her pockets for her phone and switch it with my own. My mobile will have to stay here; hers has to leave, as if she has left too.

In Jodie's other pockets are the key to the Corsa along with a handful of coins. A slim purse containing a few loyalty cards and a picture of a girl, perhaps fourteen, dark hair in bunches and eyes just like her mother. A fresh shaft of guilt pierces me as I look at the picture in the light of my phone. I had promised Jodie that I would help her find a way back to her only child, but now they were lost to each other forever. I had let them both down. What I was about to do next might be unforgivable.

I make a silent promise to do the right thing by Jodie's daughter when all of this is over.

There is a platinum American Express credit card in her purse in the name of a Mr Caspar Wagstaff – what *that* is doing here, I can only guess – and a driver's licence in her own name. She also has a silver bracelet that I recognise as one of Amy's. A gift, or something else? I slide the silver bracelet onto my own wrist, take the rest of her things. We would switch everything.

I take off my mother's slim gold watch, snap it onto Jodie's wrist in return.

Finally, I ease the platinum ring off my left ring finger and turn it so it catches the light from my phone, reading the inscription one last time.

Heather & Liam, Prior Park 14-7-07

'I'm sorry, Liam.' I ease the wedding ring onto her finger. 'I'm sorry, Jodie.'

Once I'm a mile from here, away from the Arches, I will put in an anonymous call to the ambulance service. Give them the location and tell them to send someone to take care of my friend, then turn off Jodie's mobile and send it to the bottom of the Avon.

But before that, I have another call to make. I pick up the phone and dial Amy's number.

61

AMY

Amy stood in the centre of the small room, a damp tissue clutched in her hand. Not wanting to go too close; not yet. It was the first time she had done this and she wasn't sure of the protocol.

Steven, the coroner's officer, had met her in the main reception area of RUH and escorted her down here, through two locked doors and down into the basement, a restricted area away from A & E and all the main wards, away from wandering patients to an underground part of the hospital most people never saw.

Before they went in, she'd put a hand lightly on his arm to stop him at the door. Asked a question, even though she didn't really know how to articulate it.

'Is she . . . ?' Amy's voice was unsteady; she couldn't seem to find the right words. 'How does she . . . ?'

But Steven knew what she was trying to say: he had been escorting grief-stricken family members into this basement room for the best part of twenty years. He had turned to her, his fleshy face creasing with sympathy.

'She has a little bit of bruising on her arms,' he said gently, 'and some around the sternum area. But that's all.'

Amy nodded and followed him into the little room. She had thought there might be a glass screen or a curtain or steel tables like you saw on the TV, but it was nothing like that. It was very simple and plain, like a GP's consulting room but with a second door on the opposite side, nothing on the walls, nothing else there at all really. Just a handful of plastic chairs, a box of tissues on a side table and a kind of bed on wheels in the corner.

The body on the bed was mostly covered by a plain white sheet.

Amy didn't want to approach. Not yet. Instead, she stood in the centre of the room with the damp tissue in her hand, arms crossed tightly over her chest.

Steven stood a few respectful paces to the side, clipboard in hand.

'Would you like to sit down for a minute, Ms Vernon? Can I get you a glass of water?'

'No,' she said quietly. 'I'm OK.'

Only Jodie's head, shoulders and left arm were uncovered, her skin waxy and pale, with a yellowish tinge in the harsh strip lights of the mortuary room. Her features were drawn back, somehow, slackened in death in a way they had never been in life.

Amy had only known her for a matter of days but she felt the tears coming easily, naturally. She imagined that people in this situation reacted in many different ways; Steven had probably seen them all.

After a minute, she moved closer to the bed, dabbing at her eyes with the tissue again.

Steven took this as his cue to ask if she was ready to proceed. When she nodded, he read out the legal formalities from a form on his clipboard.

'Can I confirm that you are Amy Alexandra Vernon, the deceased's next of kin?'

'That's right.'

'Are you able to confirm the identity of the deceased?'

'Yes.'

'And you can confirm this is your sister-in-law, Heather Elizabeth Vernon?'

Amy swallowed hard, another tear chasing down her cheek.

'Yes,' she whispered. 'It's Heather.'

She reached out, stopped. Looked over at the coroner's officer, still busily writing on his form.

'Am I allowed to . . .'

Steven gave her a sympathetic nod. 'You can hold her hand if you want to. Some people like to do that.'

Amy slipped her right hand into Jodie's uncovered left, the skin as cool and unyielding as rubber. The palm was coarse from years of hard living, calloused where Heather's was smooth. One of several inconsistencies – along with Jodie's dental records, the precise measurement of her height – that would have become apparent if the body had been subject to a full forensic examination.

But that wasn't going to happen.

Not when there was no foul play. Not when next-of-kin had confirmed identity. Not when it was *just another addict*. Just a tragic statistic of street living, an ex-offender who couldn't hack it back in the real world, who couldn't reintegrate and had chosen the oblivion of an overdose instead. Her sister-in-law and Jodie were the same build, close in height and similar colouring. Heather was slightly older but only by a few years.

For an overstretched police force, there was no incentive or time to delve too deeply. As Amy had quickly discovered when she'd spoken to the polite young police officer who had come to the house to break the news.

'And you've seen her, have you?' the officer had said. *'Since she came out of prison?'*

'Yes. A few times.'

'How did she seem to you?'

Amy had taken a moment to answer. *'She was struggling.'*

'With life on the outside?'

'With everything. I think, maybe . . . it all just got too much for her in the end.'

This was the script; these were the lines they had agreed that Amy would use with her parents, with the police, with anyone who asked. That Heather had fallen into a deep and long-term depression in jail, that she had gone through periods of drug use and withdrawal while serving her sentence and had found herself sharing a room at the probation hostel with a petty criminal, alcoholic and long-term drug user. That she had been distraught at the prospect of never seeing her sons again, after her release from prison.

Steven had finished filling in the paperwork on his clipboard.

'Can I get you something?' he said. 'How about that glass of water?'

'No, thank you,' Amy replied. 'I just want to sit with her for a little bit.'

'I'll give you some private time,' Steven said, opening the door. 'I'll be outside in the corridor when you're ready.'

Amy nodded her thanks and turned back to the body on the bed.

PART III
TWO WEEKS LATER

62

The funeral is almost unbearable. Being so close to Theo and Finn, seeing them upset and not being able to go to them, comfort them, feels as if my heart is being clawed out of my chest. Mixed with the guilt at what I have done to Jodie in taking her identity, my grief at losing her. I sit in the balcony's shadows at the back of the church, anonymous, invisible, saying my own silent goodbye. Slipping down steep curving stairs and out through a side door as the final hymn starts.

It had been a risk, coming here. But only two people in the world knew the real identity of the person in the coffin, and I was one of them. Paying my respects was the least I could do. Even though I had only known Jodie for a week, our friendship had grown deep roots in that time and I felt as if I'd known her for years. I make a silent promise that when this is over, I would put things right. I would put *all* of it right, make sure that Jodie was honoured and recognised in the proper way. I like to think that wherever she is now, she's laughing at the idea of all these people sitting in the pews, at a funeral for someone who was actually sitting among them in the congregation. But mostly I try not to think about it too much.

I walk quickly away from the small church, down side streets and alleys to where my car is parked, my mind returning to Theo and Finn. Amy and her parents would be taking them to Dormers tonight, straight from the ceremony, allowing them to miss a day of school tomorrow and spend the weekend at the Vernons' 'holiday house', as Theo had called it when he was small. Give them a chance to get away from the city, the press, awkward questions and prying eyes.

In theory, the police could have triangulated the location of my phone using the masts it had connected to on the way to the Arches, but they wouldn't go to the trouble if there was no crime to be solved. Unless there was a reason to doubt next-of-kin identification of my corpse. And even if they *did*, tracking would show I ended up there and that's where my phone was found. There was no reason for the police to follow electronic breadcrumbs. Ditto DNA testing: there was no reason for the police to take the time or devote scant resources when identity was not in doubt. In any case, the only way to make a match was with one of my sons, and my in-laws – at Amy's very strong insistence – had denied permission for the police to take DNA samples from the boys on the grounds that they didn't want to put them through it.

I had been the prime suspect in an attack on Trevor Boyle after my phone, the one Jones had taken from me, was discovered at the scene. Jones and his men, it seemed, had attacked Boyle at his office and staged it to look as if I was responsible, prompting the police to knock down Owen's door the following day in their hunt for me. Until news of my 'death' brought that line of enquiry to a close.

In the fortnight since then, I have worked on my adopted identity as Jodie McCarthy, lying low in a B & B and thinking of the ways that might trip me up. My emergency cash would keep me going for a bit and Amy had been helping me with money too, as well as a new phone. I pay no bills online, claim no benefits and have no social media presence. I cut my hair short and wear the clear-lens glasses everywhere, always a hat too. Dress in unisex greys and faded blacks to blend more easily into the background.

I move through the world like a ghost, meeting no one, talking to no one. I was on the far side of the moon, the dark side, where no light could reach. There was no way back. The only way forward was through, to keep going, keep pushing until I found the truth.

I've disciplined myself to wait, to give everyone time to get used to the idea that I'm dead. Let it sink in, let them cross me off their lists, move on to the next thing, the next priority. Let it become *real*. Time for the inquest to be opened and adjourned, for a post-mortem to determine the cause of death as an overdose of painkillers, the body released back to next of kin at that point for the funeral so they can see with their own eyes that I'm gone.

I have to continue, staying hidden in the shadows.

But still, it feels like an ending: our little group was scattered. Broken. Owen had been at the funeral, grey-faced and alone – I've heard second-hand that he's been to the hostel several times, looking for Jodie. I've resisted the urge to contact him because the more people who know my secret, the less secret it becomes. Amy has not told anyone, even her parents. *Especially* not her parents.

I still don't know why he hadn't answered my calls when I tried to reach him that night, as I fled from the police. Why he had not been there. Suddenly absent when we needed him most.

It's not the only question that lingers about Owen.

It was Jodie who had raised doubts about him in the first place, who had asked whether he could be trusted. Her words come back to me from a conversation we'd had just a couple of days before she died.

How did you meet Owen?

You just sent a message to a random email address and this big tattooed guy turns up the next day?

There's something odd about him, but I don't know what it is . . .

Perhaps she had tried to warn me, and I just hadn't wanted to hear it. But I keep hearing her words now, in the silent hours and days and weeks that my solitary life has become. Doubts sprouting like weeds in the freshly turned earth of a new grave.

I had never seen Owen *with* anyone else. Never heard him mention friends, colleagues, a partner, a wife. Never seen evidence of a real life behind what he chose to show us. Perhaps he was just a lone wolf, protective of his privacy.

Or perhaps all of it was just a facade.

Perhaps he was working to an entirely different agenda.

Because it was Owen who had held back from going to the police when we found the smoking gun, the document that proved money had changed hands before Liam was killed. Owen who had persuaded us all to wait.

Twenty-four hours later, Jodie was dead and I was on the run.

Maybe if we'd gone to the police sooner, Jodie would still be alive.

So many maybes; so many questions.

Most of all, it's not lost on me that Owen is the only one of our little group who had not been a victim of Jones's violence. Who hadn't been followed, threatened, or attacked.

Had the reason for that been staring me in the face all this time?

63

I have spent the last two weeks waiting for Owen to make the next move.

Waiting for him to take the evidence we have gathered, to fill in the remaining blanks, make the last connections and uncover the real story of what happened that night in 2013 and why my husband lost his life. To link all the relevant facts and take it to the police.

I am still waiting.

Owen has not moved forward with it, not pushed on with our investigation. I keep waiting to hear in the news that Liam's case has been reopened in the light of new evidence, that a fresh investigation has been launched by the police. Instead, there is a brief flurry of stories about me. My death makes headlines for a couple of days, the obituary writers brief and not particularly kind before I slip off the news pages entirely. It is a weird, dislocating feeling to read about your own passing. To be spoken of in the past tense, a hard black line drawn beneath your life.

Owen is all I have left to rely on now.

I'm in hiding; Amy is still traumatised by what's happened and has barely left the house except to go to the funeral. After a week, I come very close to re-establishing contact with him – intending to keep him at arm's length. With a new burner phone, I compile a message to his number and my thumb hovers over the *send* button for a full minute before I change my mind. Before I slowly and carefully delete every word.

Instead, I start to watch him. My fellow hunter now becomes my quarry.

He spends long hours at home, often going days without leaving the house, the curtains drawn across most of the windows. Sometimes he seems almost nocturnal, working long into the night and sleeping much of the following day. Alone; always alone. I replace the black Corsa with an even older Renault and start to learn his habits, his routines, his routes. At other times I lose him for days at a time as he travels to Bristol, to London, to God knows where else.

The week before the funeral, I pick up his trail in the centre of Bath at a cafe he likes to frequent. He works on his laptop for a couple of hours, goes outside to take a call, then hurriedly packs up his stuff and heads west through the city streets, backpack over his shoulder, black leather jacket on, eyes hidden behind dark sunglasses. I have become good at following, at blending in, at disappearing, and keep him in sight all the way as he walks away from the city centre. He walks with the confidence of a man who does not think he's being followed, and does not turn to look behind once as he strides along the pavement. He moves through the tourists and lunchtime office workers like a shark through shoals of fish, but it's not until he turns left onto New King Street that I feel a pulse of unease.

I know this street; I have been here before, a few weeks ago. Following Philip Boivin from his meeting with Christine Lai. Owen walks to the same anonymous office building now, six storeys of dark reflecting glass with the numerals 125 over the entrance, black cameras covering every angle.

Owen slows and steps confidently into the large revolving door. Through the tinted glass of the ground floor I can just about see him striding across to the reception desk, signing in, being handed a lanyard by the smiling receptionist, strolling casually to the lifts like a man who knows exactly where he is going. Like a man who has been here before.

I feel sick.

A plunging, acidic taste of betrayal churning in my stomach as I watch from the shadows on the other side of the street.

Of all the places he could be, Owen was *here*. Quite openly and without disguise, without any subterfuge that I could see, he had just walked right in as if he had an appointment. As if he knew where he was going, who he was there to see. A man who was familiar with this building.

He spends almost an hour inside.

I remember, while I wait, that he'd claimed he was investigating which companies were based here at 125 New King Street, but then had never mentioned it again. Perhaps he'd never looked into it all, because he'd known all along.

My feet are heavy as I watch him leave, follow him back to his car and back to his tired little house in Larkhall. My heart is heavy as I finally admit the truth: it was no good waiting for Owen to go to the police. It might mean waiting forever – if he'd ever even intended to do so in the first place. Was he on someone else's payroll as well? The harsh reality is that I'm truly on my own in the world, in a way I've never been before. Prison taught me that I had only myself to rely on, but at least I was alive, a flesh-and-blood person with a name and a cell and a place on a list. Now I'm nothing, I'm a ghost, a spirit, and I feel the reality of myself ebbing away with each passing day. Little pieces of me breaking loose and drifting off, the longer I spend beyond the realm of normal life.

I had to act before I lost myself completely.

And something keeps returning to me, three words that are always there when I'm lying awake at night. Three words that I had heard not long ago.

Follow the money.

Whichever way you looked at it, the money led to Christine Lai.

She was at the centre of this. I knew it in my bones; she was the key to unlock it all.

And now I was officially dead and buried, it seemed like the right time to move things up a gear.

I couldn't rely on Owen.

Tonight, *I* would get answers. One way or another.

64

Christine Lai's smart Georgian row house in Weston Park is dark when I arrive.

I have got to know her again the same way I know this street, the way I know the car her cleaner drives and the days she comes in. I know the cleaner's name. I know which of the decorative rocks in the garden the spare key is hidden under for when the cleaner forgets to bring her own. I know which neighbourhood park Christine visits for a run, what time she leaves for work in the morning. I know where she goes on a Thursday evening, the eight o'clock spin class at the expensive gym near the Royal Crescent. I know she'll leave the house just after 7.30 to make sure she gets there in plenty of time.

Most importantly, I know she can give me what I need.

And once I'm inside, I decide I may as well have a look around. Maybe a quick search will turn up something interesting while I wait for her to return.

* * *

Everything inside the house is shades of grey. Light grey, dark grey, slate and stone and charcoal and ash, a monochromatic colour scheme that extends all the way from the front doormat to the pillowcases in the pristine spare room. Even the prints and photographs on the walls and mantelpiece are black and white. Everything is neat and in its place, tidied away so all the surfaces can be kept immaculate.

I don't find anything relating to her financial life, her bank account or dealings with North Star, past or present. My search of the spare room she has turned into a study doesn't turn up a direct link between her and the US multinational although I suspect it's more likely to be on her computer, which resists all my attempts to log in.

What I *do* find is unexpected, to say the least: a copy of John Musgrove's unpublished manuscript. What the hell is it doing *here*?

It's on a shelf in an A4 box file, clearly marked with a label. The title page is just the same as the one I took from the ex-detective's house on Rockcliffe Road. *Death of an MP: the inside story of a murder that shocked Britain.* But this copy has a diagonal watermark that says 'Strictly confidential not for circulation' across every page. It seems to be version three of the document, earlier than the one I had stolen a fortnight ago.

There's a letter in the box file from a firm of solicitors, and someone – presumably Christine herself – has gone through the whole document and stuck in little coloured tabs on every page on which her name is mentioned. On some of the marked pages there are also question marks, exclamation marks or sections crossed out in red pen.

I still can't work out why she has a copy. For some legal reason? Had Musgrove been trying to get Christine onboard? Or perhaps to get her input?

One thing I knew for sure: it was coming home with me. I slot the empty box file back onto the shelf and take the manuscript back down to the kitchen, to read while I wait. I flick to the index page, to find the entry I had looked at more than two weeks ago in Musgrove's empty house but not had a chance to read before the pages were taken from me by Jones and his men.

Artemis Tech, 99

I flip to page ninety-nine, my eyes skating greedily over the page. There are two references to the name, in the top and bottom paragraphs.

I assigned several members of the homicide team to look at potential links between the victim's role within Parliament on various select committees and sensitive information to which he may have had access. In particular, how this might have related to the financial technology firm, Artemis Tech, which had made bids for several UK government contracts in the preceding years and was subsequently purchased by a US firm (North Star) in 2014 for a figure believed to be in excess of £3 billion.

I read it again, trying to absorb the information. North Star had bought this smaller company, Artemis, the year after Liam's death. The year I had been convicted of his murder. But how could there possibly be a link? Liam's connection to this can only have been tangential at best.

I shine my torch lower down the page.

There were even rumours that highly sensitive information may have been leaked from one or more sources in Parliament, in relation to Artemis Tech following due diligence audits carried out on behalf of the government. At one stage, certain 'conspiracy theories' began to circulate suggesting the victim had been preparing to act as a 'whistle-blower' – although these were never substantiated and in fact no evidence whatsoever was found for any such leak.

Just like Owen had said. *Follow the money.* A lot of money had potentially been made in the purchase of Artemis, a multi-billion pound deal brokered behind closed doors. One of those supposed 'triumphs' of capitalism that you sometimes read about, where a small group of people became insanely rich overnight. Perhaps Liam had threatened that? But Musgrove's team had discounted the theory.

I open the browser on my phone and google 'North Star Artemis Tech 2014'.

One of the first results is a nine-year-old story on Bloomberg. com, the business news website.

I read the first paragraphs, a frown drawing tight across my face. I scroll down further, still not really understanding, then go back to the top and start again.

North Star's purchase of Artemis had not been a triumph.

It had been a disaster.

Artemis had been a house of cards, its value massively over-inflated through 'creative' accountancy.

North Star's stock market value had gone through the floor and it had almost destroyed the company.

But that didn't make sense. Did it?

I'm reading the story again when I'm interrupted by the metallic slide of a key into the front door lock. I shove the thick manuscript into my backpack and switch off my torch, plunging the kitchen back into darkness.

Just after 9 p.m.: Christine is right on time.

From the hall I can hear soft sounds of the street outside, the front door opening and closing. Footsteps on the tiles, keys dropped into a bowl. A wash of light from the hall. From my vantage point behind the kitchen door, I watch as she pads past in her bare feet barely a metre away, flipping the lights on in here and filling a tall glass with water from the tap. She has her back to me as she drinks the water down in one. She's wearing hot pink leggings and a purple aerobics top that accentuates her slim, toned figure, her long hair tied up and back in a high ponytail. AirPods still in her ears, phone strapped to a band around her arm.

She puts the glass into the dishwasher and turns to a wine rack built into the wall unit, selecting a bottle of red and filling a large wine glass. Still with her back to me, she takes a sip, then another, staring out of her dark kitchen window into the carefully manicured back garden.

I push the kitchen door shut.

Christine whirls around and drops the wine glass onto the floor where it shatters with a loud *tishhhhh* of breaking glass, red wine exploding across the white tiles like blood spatter at a crime scene. She lets out a high-pitched scream, hands instantly going up into a defensive posture in front of her face, eyes wide and her mouth open in an 'O' of shock.

I put an index finger up to my lips. *Shhh.*

She's blinking fast, but doesn't scream again. I imagine what she sees as I step forward out of the shadows behind the door: a figure all in black, black jacket, black boots, black woollen hat, my face darkened with black boot polish, one of her own kitchen knives in my gloved hand. I must look like some kind of vision from hell.

'Hello, Christine.' I gesture with the knife. 'Put your phone on the table, the AirPods too.'

She does as she's told.

'You're ...' The terror is mixing with shock now and she's unable to complete the sentence. 'You're ...'

'Heather.'

'But I thought you were ... You *died*.'

'Do you know what a revenant is, Christine?' I move towards her and she flinches back against the sink. 'Did you see the movie?'

She shakes her head. 'A ghost, or something?'

'A spirit that returns from beyond the grave, to right a wrong. To find justice.' I tap my chest with the tip of the knife. 'That's me. I died ten years ago and that's what I am now. Do you understand?'

'Please, Heather, there's money upstairs, my credit cards, the car keys are just—'

'I don't want any of that.'

'What *do* you want?'

'Why don't we go into the dining room first? Then I'll tell you.'

Taking her by the arm, I lead her into the sparse white dining room, flicking on the main light as we walk in. It looks as if this room is barely used. I imagine Christine mostly eats alone, at the breakfast bar in the kitchen, unless she's hosting or entertaining. The room has only one door, which makes it much more suitable for my purposes. I push the door shut behind us as she takes it all in: the phone set up on its little collapsible tripod, the closed curtains, the roll of duct tape on the table. The single chair pulled out, a large sheet of thick black plastic laid beneath it.

The sheet of plastic, like the knife and the boot polish, is really just for show. At least, that's what I tell myself.

'What is this?' she says, her voice shaking. 'Why are you in my house?'

I gesture to the chair at the head of the dining table. 'Sit down.'

Again, she does as she's told and I use the duct tape to fasten first one wrist, then the other to the arms of the chair. When they are secure, I do the same with her ankles, wrapping the tape round and round the chair legs to hold them fast.

'Please, Heather,' she whispers. 'Please don't kill me.'

'Tell me, Christine.' I pull up a chair facing hers and sit down. 'Why would I want to kill you?'

'Because of . . . that's why you're here, isn't it?'

'Why did you come to my funeral?'

She opens her mouth. Closes it again.

'I thought . . . I don't know. Honestly? I don't know. I thought it might be like . . . closing a chapter, or something.' She looks up. 'Who *was* buried then?'

'A friend of mine. A good friend.'

'I'm sorry.'

I sit back in my chair and consider her for a moment. Her breath is coming in short gasps, all the colour gone from her face.

'You know what I think? I think you came to pay your respects because you know the truth. You know I didn't kill Liam. Because you've always known, haven't you, on some level? You've gone along with it all these years to protect yourself, to conceal your part in it.'

Her eyes drop to her lap. 'Heather . . .'

'Please understand me.' I tap the point of the knife against her kneecap. 'I'm going to ask you some questions now and if you lie, if I think you're lying, if it *sounds* like you're lying, I'm going to have to hurt you. Nine years in prison taught me quite a lot about pain. And I'm already dead, so I have literally nothing to lose. Do you understand?'

'Yes.'

'You're not due in work until 8.30 tomorrow morning, which gives us about eleven hours to play with. You, me and this very sharp paring knife.'

'I understand.'

I line up my camera in the tripod, framing it tightly so that only Christine's head and shoulders are in the shot, and press to start the video recording.

'Let's begin, shall we?'

65

'Christine,' I say, after identifying her and giving today's date. 'You knew I was set up, didn't you? That I was caught in the middle of something else. Something bigger.'

She shakes her head. 'Not at first. Only later, much later, after the trial. After an anniversary thing for Liam, organised by his family. It brought it all back.'

'Why didn't you speak up?'

'Because I was fighting my own battles by then.'

'The libel case, Owen Tanner's story implicating you, in the *Guardian*?'

'Yes.'

'Not because you'd been taking money from North Star, for access to confidential parliamentary material?'

'No!' Her eyes flash. 'That's what the libel trial was all about, why I had to take Tanner to court. I won. He lost.'

I unfold a printout of the document Owen had sent to our Telegram group, the bank statement showing receipt of £75,000 into her account from Black Dragon Holdings.

'He lost because he didn't have *this*.'

She leans forward to look at it on the table, shaking her head.

'I don't know . . . what that is.'

'It's proof that you took money from a foreign multinational to subvert Parliament. To provide confidential information to a foreign entity. Proof of corruption.'

'No.'

'How many payments did you receive overall? How much was it worth to keep quiet about the people who actually killed my husband?'

She looks me straight in the eyes. 'This bank statement is bogus. Fake. I never took any money, from anyone.'

'We found it in Liam's files. Hidden all this time.' I tell her about the other evidence we had found: the minutes of a meeting between her and two high-level North Star executives shortly before Liam was killed. One of them was Philip Boivin, with whom she still seemed friendly. The blackmail threat that had been sent to him at our home address, warning Liam that he would be framed and vilified if he went public with his suspicions.

I lay the printouts on the table next to the first, showing her the date at the bottom of the blackmail threat with the day and month in reversed order – month-day-year – the standard format in the US.

'He was ready to blow it wide open, he had the evidence, but they got to him first.'

'No, no, no,' she says, her voice rising. 'This is all fake, all of it. I had some ... dealings with North Star but it was all above board, it was all documented and logged, it was approved. There was nothing secret about it. There were discussions about the select committee that Liam chaired, they wanted to talk to him about procedures and technical stuff about presenting to the committee, it was all pretty boring actually. Liam actually asked me to handle it for him because he was so busy with other work.'

'You met them behind Liam's back. He confronted you about it.'

She's shaking her head. 'He knew about it. I swear. It was routine.'

'You met Philip Boivin recently. I followed you to a bistro in town, straight after I came to your house. Are you involved with him, is that it?'

'No.'

'Sleeping with him?'

'No.' She colours slightly. 'There was a time, years ago, when we were close. When Owen Tanner first accused us of involvement in your husband's death. Philip was implicated by association with North Star, he helped me with some of the legal side of things. We had the same problem, found ourselves on the same side.'

'You were lovers.'

'We were . . . involved for a short time. But that was years ago. Now he's a friend, more of a mentor really. When you came to my house, I knew I could talk to Philip, that he would understand because he knew all of the background.'

I tap the bank statement printout with the tip of the knife. 'But you *did* take this money, probably more of it too.'

'I've told you, I didn't.'

'Otherwise how could you afford a place like this?'

'An inheritance. My parents.' Her eyes are pleading. 'Only child of an only child.'

'*Stop* lying!' It's the first time I've raised my voice and she flinches visibly in her seat. 'Are you still on the payroll? Is that why you're still keeping their secrets?'

'I swear to you, Heather, I never took any money.' A bead of sweat trickles down from her hairline. 'I can't help you. I wish I could.'

I stand up, pace the length of the room before coming back to my seat and switching off the video recorder on my phone. From the backpack I pull out a pair of pliers, a lighter, a thick plastic bag and a length of blue nylon rope knotted into a figure of eight, each item laid out carefully on the table in front of her.

'Choose,' I say.

'What?' Her voice cracks into a sob. 'What do you mean?'

'The guys who came after me, the men working for North Star trying to silence me, they used one of those.' I point to the plastic bag. 'Asphyxiated me until I thought I was going to die. I don't think you're being truthful with me, Christine, so we're going to have to push things up a notch. Which one do you want me to start with?'

She's practically vibrating with fear now, with frustration, with protestations of her innocence. Her terror is palpable, almost as if I can hold it in my hands, and I wonder if this will be the night when I lose myself entirely. When the last remaining fragment of my old life is jettisoned, scattered in the wind and replaced by this hard, uncompromising stranger. Or whether I'm doomed to fall somewhere in between, in some grey place that is neither one nor the other.

'Please, Heather. I can't—'

'Which. One?'

Her voice is suddenly loud. 'You think you're the only one who's been warned? The only one who's been threatened?'

This brings me up short. 'When?'

'A few weeks ago.' There's a deep red flush at the base of her neck. 'They came here. To the house.'

66

She describes it to me. Three men. A black Mercedes van. Threats, handcuffs, a violent warning to remain silent. A horribly familiar story, but something was not adding up. I sit back down in my chair, put the knife on the table.

'Hold on,' I say. 'If there's nothing to hide, if no money changed hands ten years ago, why are they threatening you?'

'I don't know! They just told me if I talked to anyone about you or your case, if I did anything, they'd be back. That they could come back any time they wanted and I'd wake up one night to find them standing over my bed. That they would only give me one warning and next time they'd kill me.'

'Did you believe them?'

'Yes.'

I nod. 'Me too.'

I switch on the video recorder on my phone again.

'Let's talk about the trial.'

She nods. 'OK.'

'The prosecution case hinged on the claim that Liam had been having an affair, I had discovered it and attacked him in a drunken, jealous rage.' She nods again, but says nothing. 'You worked closely with him, spent more time with him than I did when his work was busiest. You were best placed to know whether it was true. So, did you ever suspect he was having an affair?'

'I never saw any evidence of it, not really,' she says. 'Not until after he died.'

A niggling question returns to me, one I have always wanted to ask her.

'Perhaps it was you,' I say. 'Perhaps *you* were the one? A high-pressure environment like that, two colleagues working closely together, often late into the evening. It must happen with MPs and staff members all the time.'

She shakes her head. Gives me a sad smile.

'Liam was strictly a one-woman man.'

The same thing Amy had told me. She was biased, of course, she had loved Liam and didn't want any stain on his memory. To hear the same thing again from Christine, though, is another confirmation of what I had always known in my heart was the truth. His sibling and his closest colleague, both saying the same thing.

'What about other women? There were fans, admirers, devotees, right?'

I had sometimes teased him about it. *Heat* magazine had run a double-page spread on the 'Top Ten House Hotties' after the 2010 election. Liam featured at number three and had been ribbed about it for weeks afterwards.

'Plenty,' she says. 'And not just women.'

'Men too?'

'Of course.'

The police had followed up on a few of Liam's most persistent fans. Although not with any great vigour, after they had locked onto me as their prime suspect.

'What about the blonde woman in the photographs, the pictures on the burner phone they found in his study? Did you ever see her before?'

'No,' she says. 'I don't know.'

'Which is it? No, or you don't know?'

She swallows. 'I mean, the police showed me some photos but you couldn't see the face, could you? You couldn't tell who it was.'

'You're certain about that?'

She nods.

But there is a change in her demeanour, a shift in her posture so subtle I almost miss it. A moment ago she was confident, almost defiant when I had confronted her with the evidence about North Star. Now she avoids my eye, slumping back against the chair.

I tap the printed-out news story with the tip of the knife.

'When I found the blackmail threat,' I say, 'I assumed that they were just generic pictures to serve a purpose, posed by a model or something.'

Again, she hesitates before answering, staring at the pale grey carpet beneath our feet.

'He never told me directly,' she says quietly. 'But I did suspect there might have been one admirer who was more persistent than the rest, who had been in touch and wouldn't leave him alone. He wouldn't talk to me about it though, just denied it and said it was no big deal. I assumed he would have flagged it with Andrew if he thought it might turn into a problem.'

'Andrew?'

'Young.'

I shrug. 'Am I supposed to know who that is?'

'The chief whip, back then.'

Liam had not had many dealings with the whips' office, and in any case it was so long ago that most of the names of his colleagues had vanished from my—

The realisation hits me with an almost physical force.

AY.

The notation in Liam's diary.

AY was Andrew Young.

The chief whip, the MP in charge of party discipline, of keeping his colleagues in line, of dealing with any issues of reputation or wrong-doing that might have a wider impact on the parliamentary party.

If Liam had been about to turn whistle-blower, the chief whip was a logical place to start.

Christine looks up at me. 'What is it?'

'Liam had been due to meet the chief whip at eight o'clock on Monday morning, just two days after he was killed.'

'I don't . . . think so,' she says. 'I ran his diary and I would have remembered something like that.'

'He didn't put it in his main diary,' I say. 'It was a private meeting. I don't think he wanted anyone else to know about it.'

'I suppose, he could have arranged it himself and—'

'This person who wouldn't leave him alone,' I say. 'Any idea who it was?'

She shakes her head. 'It was just a few things I overheard at work. A few phone calls, arguments. Thin walls in that office, you know?'

I think back to that last conversation I had had with my husband, on the night he died. The strange phone call I had interrupted when I stormed into his study.

'No I have to do it and you know why, I can't carry on like this, I need to be honest about it and I need to tell her . . .'

'Did you tell the police?'

'Yes,' she says, 'but they didn't seem very interested. They'd already charged you with murder at that point.'

My mobile buzzes with a new message – which is odd, as barely anyone has the number. I stop the video, take the phone from the tripod and click to open it. A picture fills the screen.

The world stops.

It's a photo of Amy, lying flat on her back with a handcuff around her wrist. Her eyes closed, her mouth slightly open and a horribly familiar, waxy pallor to her skin.

Empty pill packets and an empty bottle of gin by her side.

Just the same as Jodie.

No, no, no. Not Amy too.

There is an icy liquid feeling in my stomach and the fear is racing, raging, pulsing through me like a tidal wave.

The text below the message says:

Another tragic overdose on your conscience. You were both warned. You should have listened.

My heart plunges into my shoes as I read the rest of the thread.

Finn is next. Then Theo.
Or you can trade your life for theirs.
Dormers. 1 hour. No police.

'What is it?' Christine says. 'What's happened?'
'North Star,' I say, typing a quick reply to the message.

On my way. Don't hurt them.

Dropping the phone onto the table, I pick up the paring knife again and Christine flinches, pressing herself into the high-backed dining chair. With one upward slice of the razor-sharp blade I cut the duct tape around her left wrist, freeing it from the arm of the chair.

'You're not . . . you're not going to hurt me?'

I shake my head, slicing through the tape on her right ankle too before scooping the rest of my props – the plastic bag, pliers and everything else – into my backpack.

'I was never going to hurt you, Christine. I just need the truth. I'm sorry.' I scribble my number at the bottom of the bank statement. 'If you think of anything else, anything at all, this is how you can reach me.'

She starts to cry then, for the first time since I surprised her in the kitchen, sobs racking her chest with the realisation that her ordeal was nearly over. Tears of relief spill onto her cheeks and she wipes them away with her free hand.

'Where are you going?'

'To my boys.' I swing the backpack up onto my shoulder. 'To finish this.'

67

It was my fault.

They had gone after Amy again, gone after the boys, and it was my fault. I had not stopped looking for answers, not stopped digging, and Amy had paid the price. Jones had carried out his threat and now it looked as if I would have to pay too.

But if that was the only way to save Theo and Finn, so be it.

I fight back tears as I drive out of the city, thoughts tumbling through my head, too many to hold in. I think of the boys, of how frightened they must be at this moment. Of Amy, of her fears that this would happen, of *exactly* this. Of her parents, the horror and devastation of losing another child. Of Jodie. My friend, who had not died of an accidental overdose: she had been murdered, the same way Amy had been murdered. That was what her last message meant. *999*. A final desperate plea for my help.

I'm sorry, I say under my breath, over and over again. For both of them. *I'm sorry.*

Traffic is light as I head north, the Renault's engine protesting as I push it to the limit. An hour is only just enough time to get to Dormers, my in-laws' weekend place in the Cotswolds, and I will have to keep my foot to the floor all the way if I'm to meet Jones's deadline.

And by the time I get there, I need a plan. Going in alone seemed like the worst of all options, but there was only one other person left that I could call. One person who understood the situation, the stakes. A man who believed I was dead.

Whether I could trust him was another question. But it was the only card I had left to play.

Stopped in traffic queuing at a roundabout, I pull up Owen's number on my phone and send him a message.

Need your help. Please come now. Urgent, will explain when you get here. Jodie

I add the postcode and the name of the house.

His reply is quick.

What's going on?

He sends another moments later, then two more, but I can't read and respond to them while I'm driving. After another minute my phone vibrates in its cradle with an incoming call. I touch the screen to answer and cut him off before he can say anything.

'Owen,' I say, 'answer me one question or I'm hanging up right now.'

There is a stunned, empty silence before he replies.

'Heather? What the—'

'What were you doing at Boivin's office building this week? I saw you there, on New King Street. Are you on his payroll too?'

'No.' It comes out firm and fast. 'Of course not.'

'So what were you doing there?'

'I was interviewing him off the record,' he says. 'About North Star.'

I listen for any tremor of deception in his voice, but detect none. There is only surprise at hearing from me again, from beyond the grave.

'Why should I believe you?'

'Because it's the truth,' he says emphatically. 'Listen, Heather, what the hell is going on? I just went to your *funeral*. And I need to tell you—'

'There's no time for that,' I almost shout into the phone. 'The boys are in danger and I'm on my way to that address right now. I can explain everything later but please help us. I need you.'

I hit *end* and reject the calls that follow. There's no time for long explanations now and I need to concentrate on the road.

Pushing the little Renault as hard as I can, I overtake car after car and flash past speed cameras on the A46 as it winds its way north into Gloucestershire. Crossing over the M4 and heading deeper into the Cotswolds, I try to gather my thoughts, to put them in some kind of order. There are still so many questions after what Christine told me, after what she had denied and what she had hinted at: some kind of stalker that Liam had kept secret from everyone. The new information in Musgrove's unpublished book, the revelation about Artemis Tech and my sense that there was a loose thread somewhere there that might unravel the whole case against me.

It is past ten o'clock by the time I turn off the country lane. The gate is open, the long private driveway unlit. My headlights pick out the avenue of trees standing sentry on each side of the curving drive as I approach and park up in front of Dormers' grand north wing. Peter Vernon's Jaguar is here, but there is no sign of Owen.

The house is in total darkness, not a single window lit.

I turn off the engine and get out of the car, slipping the knife into the back pocket of my jeans and grabbing the phone from its cradle on the dash. In among the messages and missed calls from Owen, there is a single message from Christine's number, sent almost forty minutes ago.

You're looking in the wrong place.

I frown at the screen. The wrong place? What did that even mean? I was here, at Dormers, where the message had told me to come. Had I told Christine where I was going? I send back three question marks in reply and shove the phone back into my pocket, hurrying across the drive to the big front door.

The night air is unnervingly still, an intensity to the quiet that I had forgotten after so many years of close living with hundreds of others. There had never been true quiet in prison, not even in the middle of the night. Not like this. There is no man-made noise to disturb the silence here, no one living nearby. The nearest village, Hale's End, is almost a mile away and consists of a half-dozen houses, a tiny church and an old red phone box.

The front door of the house is ajar. I climb the steps and push it open all the way, aware of the dark eye of a camera mounted over the threshold.

Inside the house, the silence feels even more concentrated, more intense than it had outside. There is no life, no sound. The smells of this grand old place are the same as they always were: of polished wood and fresh flowers and high, airy ceilings. Of money.

I leave the lights off. I knew this house once, had spent many happy hours here and I still know it well enough to navigate in the dark as my eyes adjust. The wide staircase curving up to the right, drawing rooms on the left, the broad central gallery directly in front, to take me through the middle of the house to the dining room, kitchen and sun room at the back. We had come here the day after we'd got engaged, to tell Liam's parents face to face. Had our rehearsal dinner here in the exquisite dining room, the weekend before our wedding. Theo's naming day party. Dozens of times before and afterwards too.

In the kitchen, I push through another open door and step out into the courtyard.

The black Mercedes van is here, squatting like a giant beetle in the dark.

I skirt around the front, staying in the shadows to check the van's cab. Empty. I keep going across the courtyard to the old stables where a pale wash of light is just visible through a crack in the heavy wooden doors.

Taking the knife from my pocket, I creep to the doors and peer in. Inside it's the same as it's always been, a row of straw-filled stalls at one end, a workshop-cum-garage at the other. Low light from the far end illuminates something else: two people.

The first is a figure sprawled awkwardly on the ground, an older man with his head down, handcuffed to an iron ring in the cobblestoned floor. A smear of blood visible in the thinning hair at his temple.

Peter Vernon.

Behind him is the balding man, sitting in a folding chair, a double-barrelled shotgun cradled in his arms. At the sight of me, the side of his mouth turns up in a cruel smile. He gestures at me with the gun. *Come in.*

I do as he says, my shoes clicking on the uneven floor as I move closer. Peter doesn't acknowledge my approach and seems dazed, stunned, his movements slow and unsteady.

'Where are the boys?' I say, my voice echoing inside the stable block. 'Where are Theo and Finn?'

The balding man points at my hand. 'Drop the knife.'

His voice is a flat, Thames Valley drawl. It's the first time I've heard him speak since I plunged a different blade into his leg, two weeks ago.

Again, I do as I'm told, letting the weapon fall from my hand and clatter to the cobblestones in a way that might almost be within Peter's reach, if he can just raise his head.

'I'm here,' I say. 'I'll do whatever you want, just let the boys go.'

The balding man stands, takes a couple of limping steps forward. Puts the stock of the shotgun into his shoulder and the muzzle to the back of Peter Vernon's head. For a horrible moment I think I think he's going to execute my father-in-law right here in front of me, but after a few seconds he raises the gun and points it squarely at me, at my chest, finger curling around the trigger.

'Payback time,' he says, his lips curling again in a cruel smile of triumph. 'I'm going to enjoy this.'

'Tell me the boys are safe. That was the deal.'

He shakes his head. Keeps the shotgun levelled at me as he calls out over his shoulder.

'OK,' he says, his voice raised. 'We're good in here.'

The heavy wooden door behind him swings open with a creak.

Two men walk into the low light of the stables.

Rennick and Jones.

More footsteps click on the cobblestones, as a third figure emerges from the darkness and comes to stand between them.

68

Amy.

Very much alive.

'Family,' she says, 'it's the most important thing in the world, isn't it? A child's love for her parents, a parent's love for their children – look how far it's brought you. How far you've come in the last ten years. Family can make us do anything.'

'Amy, I thought you were . . .' I look behind her. 'Where are the boys?'

She ignores my question.

'Ever wonder what you would do,' she says, her eyes blazing, 'if everything you knew and loved was threatened with absolute devastation? *Every* last thing that meant something in your life? If everything you'd worked for, everything your parents had built, everything your grandparents had slaved and sacrificed for, all of it was suddenly balancing on the edge of a blade? One tiny push and it would be gone. What do you think that would do to a person?'

While she talks, Peter gets to his feet. Produces a key from his pocket and unlocks the handcuff around his wrist, his movements quick and assured. With a handkerchief from his other pocket, he wipes the red smears away from his forehead. There is no wound beneath.

He looks grim, determined. Deadly serious.

There is a weird dynamic between them, between this old man and his younger child. I've never seen them like this before: as if she is calling the shots, she is in charge and he is merely playing his part. Jones and his two men are the same. Rennick puts a heavy hand on my shoulder, forcing me to my knees. He takes the handcuffs from Peter and loops them around my wrists, the short chain between them passing through the iron ring in the rough cobblestone floor. He pats me down roughly as well, extracting my car keys and handing them to Peter.

All the while, fragments of my conversation with Christine Lai float, just out of reach. The text she'd sent me on the way here.

You're looking in the wrong place.

'What are you doing?' I say to Amy, indicating Jones and his hulking colleague. 'Why are *they* here? They attacked me, they attacked *you*.'

'Hmm.' She wrinkles her nose. 'Yes and no. With me it was more of a . . . collaboration.'

'This is mad, Amy, what the hell is—'

'The boys are fine, by the way.' She gestures to Rennick to back away from me and he does so instantly, his big hands leaving my shoulders. 'They're in the dairy with Colleen, having a sleepover. You don't need to worry about them.'

The old dairy. On the edge of the estate, the one part of it that the Vernons had allowed to be fully modernised. It had been the boys' favourite, ever since they were small, with its own cinema room and games room, where they had been allowed to make a camp and as much mess as they liked.

'I don't understand,' I say. 'What about North Star? Corruption, pay-offs, Liam blowing the whistle about Artemis Tech? All the evidence we found?'

She reaches into her pocket and pulls out a key on a familiar black-and-orange fob. Total Storage.

The lock box.

'You thought you were the only keyholder, didn't you?' She jingles the key as if taunting me. 'It never occurred to you that someone else would have one too – the person who helped your mum gather all that junk in the first place? Made it easy to prepare a few good forgeries where I knew you'd eventually find them.'

I stare as her words sink in.

'The minutes of that meeting? The North Star connection that tied in Christine Lai?'

She smiles. 'Convincing, weren't they? Although, to be fair, we did have a *long* time to get everything ready. Those years while you were sitting in jail. All I had to do was reread all of Owen Tanner's rambling stories about the case – we've got folders full of them at home – and craft something that fitted his narrative. Give you enough to set you off in the wrong direction. I put the document into that storage box a couple of months before your release date, knew you'd end up digging through it.'

'And the files supposedly in your parents' loft? The bank statement? You manufactured all of it?'

'The statement took a bit more work. His diary was real enough – didn't even realise it was there until you found it. But it didn't seem too much to worry about when you showed me.'

'I know he was due to speak to the chief whip on the Monday after he died.'

'But you don't know *why*, do you?'

'He was going to go public on what he'd found,' I say. 'Corruption in the House. People selling information to the highest bidder. He was going to blow it all up.'

She smiles, shakes her head. 'Poor, poor Heather. Close, but not quite, I'm afraid.'

'So why don't you tell me?'

'You're not listening, are you? I'm trying to tell you, about *family*.' She crosses her arms. 'Family trumps everything, it's more important than anything else. Family is what this is all about.'

I look at the five of them – Jones and Rennick on one side of Amy, Peter Vernon and the balding guy on the other, arrayed around me in a semicircle – before my eyes return to her. There is an intensity to her, a concentration of emotion that I have not seen before. But I have a feeling this is my first glimpse of the reality, the real woman beneath the mask.

'I don't get it, Amy. What do you mean?'

'My stupid, arrogant, holier-than-thou big brother who thought he was more important than this family, thought he was above us. Everyone always thought he could do no wrong, that the sun shone out of his backside. He always felt he was better than everyone else too, smarter than everyone else, more virtuous. Certainly better than his stupid little sister.'

I've never heard her talk about Liam like this. Never heard her say a bad word about him. But now it all seems to be coming out in a flood, as if a lifetime's worth of bitterness and sibling resentment has been unleashed.

'I can't remember him ever saying anything like that—'

'He didn't need to!' A fleck of spittle flies from her mouth. 'It was in everything he did, everything he said. He *never* took me seriously. Always too good for us, up there on his bloody high horse.'

Peter Vernon looks at his watch. 'I'll go and fetch her car, bring it here around the back. Then we need to get on with this, Ames.'

He walks out the way I came in, but Amy's gaze stays locked on me.

'Liam was just trying to do the right thing,' I say quietly. 'He was going to blow the whistle on what he'd found at Westminster, MPs selling secret information to the highest bidder.'

She barks out a short laugh, but there is no humour in it.

'Is that still what you think?'

'Isn't that why he died?'

'In a roundabout way,' she says, 'I suppose it is.'

I pull at the handcuffs, the chain rattling against the iron ring in the floor.

'Please just tell me what's going on, Amy.'

'It's hilarious,' she says, 'that he still has this whiter than white reputation, that everyone still thinks he was so wonderful. Even his poor sap of a wife who did ten years in jail for him.' She makes quote marks with her fingers. 'Saint Liam Vernon. Makes me sick.'

'What are you talking about?'

'He was going to betray us.'

'He was your brother.'

'He was going to betray his family! His parents, the company, everything Dad built over the last fifty years, everything Grandad built in the fifty years before that.'

'This is about your dad's company?'

'It's about loyalty.'

A sob rises in my throat. The realisation finally slamming into me like a wave breaking, crashing over my head, the brutal ice-cold shock of it almost overwhelming.

'You've been lying, all these years. You took Liam away from me.'

'No,' she says, index finger stabbing at me. 'He brought it on himself. You want to know why? You've actually convinced your-self that Liam was some modern-day martyr, that he was perfect, this perfect husband and father, this white knight who was going to expose corruption in the Houses of Parliament.'

'I've never said he was perfect I just—'

'That man never really existed. And do you know why?'

'Tell me,' I say quietly.

'Because he was the leak. Liam was the one who'd been pass-ing secrets on. When he died, he wasn't about to blow the whistle on someone else.' Her face is contorted with anger. 'He was about to confess.'

69

My head spins.

'What are you talking about?'

Amy crouches down to put herself at my level, forearms on her knees.

'Your perfect husband had been leaking information to us, to Dad's company, for *months*. Starting with the multi-billion pound acquisition of an up-and-coming outfit full of Silicon Valley geniuses called Artemis Tech.'

I frown. 'But ... your dad's company wasn't involved in that. Vernon plc didn't *buy* Artemis.'

'We were *about* to. You know why we pulled out?'

The answer is suddenly staring me in the face.

'Liam.'

'*Finally*, the penny drops,' she says, giving me a slow hand clap. 'Civil service had done due diligence work on the company when they were bidding for government contracts. High-level stuff, extremely sensitive. Not made public – all that kind of work is supposed to be kept secret. But the due diligence investigation found out that Artemis was on the brink, a house of cards waiting to collapse. Liam got wind of it through his parliamentary contacts. He knew Dad was about to buy the company, go into massive debt in the process.'

'So Liam tipped you off that Artemis was a poisoned chalice.'

'Saved his dad's company.'

'And broke the law in the process,' I say. 'Broke confidentiality, violated the parliamentary code. It's basically insider trading.'

Her face creases in disgust. 'So what? You think it would have been better if that deal had gone ahead? Dad's company would have gone under. We would have lost everything. A century of hard work, *gone*—' she snaps her fingers '—just like that.'

'So North Star stepped up to buy Artemis instead, and they got burned. Almost bankrupted them.'

Amy shrugs. 'All's fair in love and war.'

I remembered how preoccupied Liam had been in those last few weeks and months. At the time I had put it down to workload and stress but now I finally knew the truth: he had been wrestling with his conscience. And the argument we'd had, the night he died – he'd said he was talking to 'a colleague' about potential law-breaking in Parliament. Sensitive information leaked to a third party. But he wasn't talking about someone else. He was talking about himself. About what he'd done *himself*. It was his way of telling me in so many words, without actually coming out with it. And that was what the email was about too – the message he drafted but never sent.

I've done something I will regret for a very long time.

I've betrayed everything, I've let you down, I've let our sons down and that is something I never wanted to do.

I need to tell the truth.

I'm not excusing what I've done, or asking for you to understand, but I hope one day you will be able to forgive me.

'Liam was in an impossible situation,' I say. 'Stay quiet and watch his dad's company go bankrupt, or break the law to save it.'

'He was weak,' Amy says dismissively. 'By the summer, the guilt had got too much for him to handle. He said he had to come clean, to admit what he'd done, confess before Parliament broke up for the summer recess because he couldn't bear the guilt any longer. He'd set up a meeting with the chief whip, first thing on a Monday morning – he was going to tell Andrew Young everything. My selfish brother was going to fall on his sword for his own ego, his own vanity, his own poor tortured *conscience*.' She spits the word as if it leaves a bad taste in her mouth. 'He said he couldn't face lying to you anymore – he was going to admit it all. The scandal would have dragged Dad's company down with him.'

I remembered the notation from Liam's diary, the night before he was due to see the chief whip: *8 p.m. – call N.*

'He was going to call his best friend the night before,' I say. 'To tell him what he planned to do. To talk it over with him.'

'No doubt.'

'You didn't have to kill him.'

'I never *meant* to kill him!' She's up in my face again. 'It was supposed to be a *warning*. A demonstration of how much he had to lose. Show him how much damage a burner phone full of nudes could do to his marriage, to his happy family set-up. Get him to imagine how heartbroken you'd be.'

'What happened?' I say carefully. 'That night?'

She sighs, running a hand through her hair.

'It had been building for a couple of weeks but it was never supposed to happen that way. I didn't mean for it to . . . end the way it did.'

'It was you on the phone that night, wasn't it? And he was giving you some kind of ultimatum? I stormed into his study to ask him about it and he lied right to my face.' The memory still drives a shaft of grief right through my chest. 'It was the last conversation we ever had.'

'I told him he'd regret it,' Amy says. 'But he couldn't see how much he had to lose.'

'So you came over to our house, after I'd gone to sleep.'

'I had to make him understand,' she says, in a matter-of-fact tone. 'To show him what it would do to our family. I'm sitting with him in your lounge at two o'clock in the morning, and he wasn't *listening* to me. He looked as if he didn't even care, as if he didn't love us at all. And it made me angry, so angry, so *furious*, that I could sit there ánd beg him and he still wouldn't take me seriously. I was still just his stupid younger sister given a job by our dad, given *everything* by Dad, and he looked down on me like I was shit on his shoe. He had *always* looked down on me. That was when I went and got the knife to show him I was serious.' She swallows hard. 'I said it would be easy to wreck his marriage, easy to turn you against him. He'd lose the boys, you, the house, everything. He didn't even take me seriously then, didn't try to defend himself. I was standing over him with a blade at his chest and he wouldn't even get up off the sofa. That made it even worse. I was just so *angry* with him, that he could be so selfish and self-righteous.'

'And?'

'When he eventually did try to snatch it off me, I . . . lost my footing. The knife was between us.' She wipes a tear at the memory. 'I fell on him.'

I'm frozen.

I can't speak.

Or cry.

Or do anything, apart from stare at my sister-in-law. My chest feels as if it's being squashed in a vice.

'Liam,' I whisper finally.

'It's not as if you ever even appreciated him!' She swipes another tear angrily away. 'Always moaning on about how hard he worked, and you never saw him, and you had to do everything with the boys. Never really knew what you had. You never loved him the way his family did, never treated him the way he deserved.'

'So,' I say, a chill creeping over my skin. 'After you'd killed him, then what?'

She stands, a flash of anger pinching her face. 'I couldn't tell the truth, because then all the rest of it would have come out too.

It would have been for nothing. And then I thought, why should Heather be allowed to get away with it? It was because he couldn't stand lying to *you*, being dishonest with *you*, that he was going to confess. That gave me an idea.'

There is a fierce pounding pain in my head.

'This is insane.'

She ignores me. 'It wouldn't be fair if you were allowed to bask in sympathy as the weeping widow, carrying on with your life with everyone giving you an easy ride because of this *terrible* thing that happened, and *Oh aren't we sorry for her*, and all that crap. I could punish you both. It was perfect.'

Outside in the courtyard there is the sound of a car pulling up, the Renault's ragged engine sputtering and cutting out. My mind, on some level, still trying to look for a way out of this. *They're moving the car so it can't be seen from the road. Preparing for what comes next. I don't have much time.*

'You were never even a suspect, were you?'

She shrugs. 'Of course not.'

'Even though they found your prints, your DNA, all over the house. Same as with mine, Liam's, Peter and Colleen's fingerprints too. But they eliminated you as a matter of routine because . . . they never even considered it. Why would they?'

The same reason the dog hadn't barked. He knew her footsteps, her voice, her scent. Even through the kitchen door, Jet knew her because she was a regular visitor to our house. He wasn't worried about her being there, he knew she wasn't an intruder.

'In any case,' she says, 'I had a rock solid alibi from Mum and Dad.'

Peter Vernon walks back into the stables. He says something to the balding man, who nods. All of them playing their part in this grim drama, with Amy pulling the strings.

I point at him with one cuffed hand. 'You helped her that night, didn't you? After she'd killed Liam?'

He looks at me with a level gaze, the way a farmer might assess livestock at auction. The way he has always been: measured, analytical, lawyerly. Gauging and judging a situation and how he and his family can best emerge from it.

'No,' he says evenly. 'I didn't even know until two years afterwards. When your appeal was being heard, Amy finally told us the truth.'

I remember looking at him once in court, at the blazing hatred in his eyes. That was real. There was no faking it.

'Amy told us everything,' he says. 'And I knew there was no point in making this terrible situation, this tragedy, even worse. That was when we started to think about what would happen when you got out.'

I stare at him, trying to take it all in. Peter knew. He had known for *years*.

'That night,' I say. 'What if I'd woken up?'

Amy shakes her head. 'You were out for the count with one of your Friday night sleeping pills, as per usual, because Liam always did Saturday mornings with the boys. And I wanted to be sure he and I wouldn't be disturbed, so I'd crushed up another couple of pills and put it in the half-finished bottle of red wine before you got back from work. Knew you'd dive into it as soon as the boys went to bed, the way you always did. Liam didn't drink red.'

I look from father to daughter, the twin pillars of this crazy family I had married into. The shock of it all is like a series of stunning blows raining down on me, each one coming from a different direction. To discover that the story of that night – the story I had told myself over the last ten years – had been so incomplete as to be almost a fiction.

Because after all, who were the people best placed to set me up? The people who knew me better than anyone else.

'You thought of everything, didn't you?'

'The burner phone under your pillow was a neat idea, I thought,' Amy says. 'A nice touch.'

I shift position, the handcuff digging into my wrist. 'What about the pictures?'

'Bought them on a revenge porn site on the dark web.'

'You sent one to my phone,' I say, 'made it look as if I'd discovered an affair.'

'*Exactly.*' Amy points a finger at me again. 'Give the police something to get their teeth into.'

'You covered the whole thing up. Framed me for it.'

I've never heard my father-in-law raise his voice before. But he does now.

'What *choice* did we have?' He shouts the words, but is back in control almost immediately. 'Lose both Liam and Amy, both children in one go? And both my grandchildren too? You would have blamed us for what she did, for not stopping her, for spoiling and indulging her to the point where she didn't know right from wrong. You would have taken the boys away too and we would have had nothing left. Nothing.' He is breathing hard, his narrow face reddening. 'Not to mention the scandal, the headlines, our family's reputation torn to shreds. One sibling kills another? A family feud? Perhaps on a scummy drug-ridden council estate, or some inbred caravan park. But not *us*. Not the Vernons. At least if it was an *outsider*, a jealous spouse, a wife who had never quite measured up —' he points at me with a bony index finger '— that at least made sense. It could be explained, understood on some level.'

The cover-up is always worse than the crime. It was just like Owen had said.

'I was expendable,' I say softly.

Peter crosses his arms. 'You're not family.'

'I'm Theo's mother. Finn's mother.'

'Not any more,' Amy says, shaking her head. 'I've been a mother to those two boys for the last ten years. A mother to them for far longer than you ever were.'

70

Owen had been half right: there *was* a conspiracy. Just not the one he had been chasing all this time.

'So you fabricated it all?' I say. 'All of the evidence we found after I came out of prison?'

A small smile creeps across Amy's face.

'Most of it. The thing about cons, Heather, is that they don't fool us because we're stupid. Cons fool us because they tell us something that we *want to believe*. Whether it's winning the lottery, or finding true love, or revealing some secret truth that reinforces our own view of the world. Tanner wanted to believe in some grand international conspiracy, this big bad American company, blackmail, corruption, fraud, murder, every ingredient for the scoop of the decade. I just had to nudge him in a certain direction, that was all. And *you* wanted to believe it just as badly, because you thought it was your way home, your way back to the boys. You and Tanner encouraged each other.'

I glance up at Jones, who stares back impassively. Amy and her father had even gone to the trouble of hiring an enforcer whose American accent could slot neatly into the same narrative.

'And you just watched,' I say. 'While we went on your wild goose chase.'

'I was going to get rid of Tanner at the start,' Amy says. 'Steer you away from him. But then when I got closer to your little group, I realised how useful he might be to keep you looking in the wrong direction. My very own useful idiot. All I had to do was throw him a bit of red meat, watch him swallow it. He was the gift that kept on giving.'

'And Musgrove?'

'I wasn't worried about him – he was a believer from the start. Once he had the knife, the fingerprints, the burner phone, the nudes, he was never going to change his mind.'

I think back to that day after I'd walked out of prison, going through everything in the big storage box my mum had left for me.

'So the documents,' I say. 'The paperwork we found in the storage unit, the evidence Owen had been looking for, pointing the finger at Christine Lai. Was that document even real?'

'Partly. But just some dull old meeting minutes I found among his stuff in Mum and Dad's attic, with a few special touches added for Tanner's benefit.'

The blackmail threat, planted in the same place.

'What about the bank statement?'

'That one we created from scratch.'

Christine's reaction is still fresh in my mind from earlier this evening. *It's bogus. Fake. I never took any money, from anyone.* The reason why our weeks-long pursuit of her had never yielded any more solid evidence.

The Vernons' letter, the offer to help me relocate far away from Bath, had been a feint as well. A ruse to draw Amy and me together. To let her draw closer alongside me in those first days and weeks after I was released.

I stare at her, this woman I thought I had known, who had suffered with me, helped me, encouraged me. A woman who I had thought was becoming a friend again. All the while, I had failed to recognise the dark power this longed-for daughter, this beautiful, spoiled, over-indulged youngest child held over her parents.

'You're a parasite,' I said. 'You latch on to people and hold them close, then when eventually they see you for what you are, you dispose of them. Just like you did with Liam. Or if you think they're a threat – just like you did with Jodie. You didn't want her around me because you knew she'd always fight back.'

'That skank was always going to end up dead in an alley, sooner or later.'

The fury is boiling in my stomach, threatening to rise up my throat.

'You planted a bag full of money in her backpack, fifteen hundred pounds to make me suspect she'd been bribed.'

'You've got a suspicious mind, Heather. Doesn't take much to spin you around.'

'Jodie was worth a hundred of you,' I say. 'And you killed her.'

'Not me *personally*.' She shrugs towards Rennick. 'And it wasn't exactly part of the plan. To begin with, we were just going to make sure you breached the terms of your parole, get you sent back inside for the rest of your sentence. But that was still just postponing it for another nine years and I started thinking there might be another way, a better way. A more *permanent* way. When you called me that night and asked me to ID her body as you, it was almost too perfect.'

'She was my friend,' I say. 'A real friend.'

'If you had just behaved yourself when you came out of prison, just got on with your life, none of us would even be here now. Jodie would still be alive. Her death is on *you*, not me. You chose this. And now you're going to go away. For good.' She motions to Rennick and he produces a clear plastic hood from his pocket, a length of nylon rope threaded around the opening to draw it tight. The same as the one he had used on me before.

I raise myself into a crouch and wrench hard on the handcuffs, but the iron ring they're threaded through stays as solid as a rock.

'Promise me you'll take care of the boys.'

Amy smiles again.

'You know I will. But I don't really have to promise you anything, Heather. Do you know why? Because we can do whatever we like – no one is going to come looking for you. No one's going to raise the alarm, or report you missing, or get the police involved.' She leans closer, a triumphant glint in her eye. 'Because you're already dead.'

71

Rennick moves behind me and slips the plastic hood over my head, pulling the ligature tight in one fluid movement.

The world turns instantly opaque, a milky shroud in front of my eyes and the constriction painfully tight around my neck. I jerk my head away, from side to side, trying to shake him loose, but his grip is like iron and it only increases the pressure on my throat. The links between the handcuffs rattle as I try to wrench them free of the rusty ring in the ground, the cuffs are loose but not quite loose enough, the steel biting agonisingly deep into my wrists.

The pain gives me an idea. I haul back on the cuffs again as hard as I can and blood starts to flow, slick and hot, from the torn skin at the top of my palms.

Amy is still talking, her voice muffled to my ears now but still just about audible.

'I'm sorry, Heather, but this is the best way, for everyone. For the boys, most of all. I know it's hard but I'm sure you can see that, and we all want what's best for them, don't we?'

I try to reply but the thick plastic sucks into my mouth when I take a breath, the words lost in a desperate gasping battle for oxygen that is almost gone.

'Legally, formally,' Amy says, 'for all intents and purposes you're already dead.' She studies me for a moment, as a child might examine an ant burning under a magnifying glass. 'We're just going to finish the job that you started.'

The cuts in the fleshy part of my palms deepen as I twist my hands back and forth against the angular steel of the cuffs. The pain in my wrists is intense, a hot, burning agony as the steel slices deeper into skin but more blood means less friction, more chance of sliding a wrist free of the handcuff, and I only have to get one hand free to pull the cuffs free of the iron ring and dodge away from Rennick, run for the door and out into the night air, into the darkness where I will at least have a ghost of a chance.

Amy has stopped talking to me now but is saying something to Jones instead, the American man nodding and checking his watch, giving one-word replies.

I remember his parting message from the last time we had met.

One warning, Heather. Next time, I let him leave the hood on for ten minutes and then we put you in the ground somewhere no one will ever find you.

There is no oxygen left inside the plastic hood, I'm drowning in the hot carbon dioxide of my own exhaled breath as it poisons my system. The edges of my vision are greying, a crushing pain in my head, my chest, as if I'm buried under a ton of earth and there is nothing left in my lungs.

My hands are slick with blood.

But my right hand is almost free, slippery on the cuff, I just need to get it over the knuckle of my thumb, just a few millimetres more, I just have to lean into it, embrace the exquisite sharpness of this pain and then it will come loose and my hand will be out and I can—

Over the roaring in my ears comes another sound.

Mechanical.

Urgent.

Very loud, and very close.

The wooden double doors to the courtyard explode inwards in a shower of splinters and sparks, the little red Renault careering into the stables, engine screaming, smashing into the balding man before he can react. The shotgun booms in his hands as the car strikes him and he goes straight over the bonnet, over the top of the car and landing with a sick *crunch* of flesh on stone. Peter Vernon tries to dive clear but he is too old and too slow, the offside wing cracking his trailing leg and spinning him to the ground.

The Renault brakes, skids, and crashes into the far wall, the engine stalling with an abrupt cough.

For a second, there is a stunned silence as all of us stare at the wrecked car crumpled and smoking a few yards away. At Peter Vernon groaning in agony, the other man face down, inert on the hard floor.

Behind me, behind all of us, there is a huge wet *smack*, like the sound of a watermelon hitting concrete from a great height, and I turn in time to see Rennick falling sideways like a dynamited chimney stack, his face a mass of blood. He goes down hard, hitting the ground with every ounce of his twenty-stone bulk, his unconscious head bouncing off the cobbles. His nose is a pulpy mess and he lies there with arms outstretched, unmoving.

Owen Tanner stands over him gripping a baseball bat, the *Boston Red Sox* lettering smeared and half-obscured with blood.

With Rennick down, the ligature around my neck loosens and a whisper of relief leaks into the plastic hood. Owen drops to one knee to ease it off my head and I fill my lungs, the night air mingling with the stench of burned rubber and exhaust and the acrid stink of the shotgun blast. As I cough and gasp, he finds the key and eases the handcuffs off my bleeding wrists.

Theo and Finn clamber out of the front seats of the mangled Renault, both looking absolutely terrified.

Amy picks herself up from the floor.

'What are you two doing?' she says to the boys. 'Are you mad? You could have been hurt.'

Finn, I realise with a pang of tenderness, is wearing his pyjamas and a dressing gown.

'I saw her,' he says, turning his phone towards me. 'On the doorbell camera. Thought she was a ghost. Theo told me not to be stupid but I showed him and then we both ran up here.'

'Almost knocked them over as I came up the drive,' Owen adds. 'Boys, you were only supposed to cause a *diversion*, not use the car as a battering ram.'

Jones's voice cuts across them both.

'Shut up, all of you,' he shouts. 'It's time to finish this.'

He has the shotgun levelled at my chest.

He advances towards me, the stock of the gun tight into his shoulder and the twin black barrels steady on me. As he passes Rennick, he gives him a little nudge with the toe of his boot, but the big man does not move or flinch in the slightest. He's out for the count.

I struggle to my feet as Owen takes a step forward, the tattooed muscles of his arms rippling as he grips the baseball bat.

'Your mate fired one of the barrels,' he says, his voice low and hard. 'You've only got one shell left.'

'So?'

'So which one of us are you going to shoot?'

'Her,' he says, jabbing the gun towards me. 'That's what we came here to do.'

'OK. As long as you and me are clear on something.'

'What?' Jones looks irritated.

'That a half second after you pull that trigger, this bat is going straight through your stupid skull.'

Jones swings the gun to level it at the reporter's chest.

'So maybe I'll shoot you instead, asshole.'

'In front of five witnesses?' Owen frowns. 'Then what, genius? When the gun's empty?'

Jones considers this for a moment, his brow furrowed with anger.

'I'll take my chances with you, big boy,' he says dismissively. 'When the original job is done.'

He swings the gun back onto me, the barrels horribly large and black up close. But in the same moment, Finn darts over and stands in front of me, his hands up, using his skinny frame to try to shield me from harm.

'Leave her alone!' he shouts. 'Don't hurt her!'

A surge of pure liquid fear pulses through me. The muzzle of the gun is only a few feet from his chest, Jones's finger curling around the trigger.

'Finn,' I plead, trying to move him out of the way. But he plants his feet and grabs hold of me, refusing to move. '*Please* I'm begging you, he's serious, just go to your brother for a minute.'

My youngest son shouts at the gunman, his high voice breaking with fear and defiance.

'I'm not going to let you hurt her!'

Amy starts screaming at the same time, screaming at Finn and Theo to *get out of the way,* both my boys are shouting too, then Owen is shouting at Jones to *put the gun down* and I'm screaming at everyone to *please please just stop*, my voice cracking with terror.

What happens next, happens very fast and all at once.

Amy scrambles to throw herself between Jones and her nephew.

Theo makes a grab for his brother.

Owen makes a grab for the shotgun.

I try to push Finn clear.

And then—

The explosion of the gun going off is deafeningly loud in the enclosed space.

ONE MONTH LATER

72

The city is spread out below me, a graceful arrangement of honey-coloured stone stretching all the way across the valley.

From this vantage point high on a bluff on the south side of Bath, I gaze down at church spires and busy streets, at the curve of the Royal Crescent and the lines of tall Georgian row houses, bright in the morning sunshine. It was here, on our favourite bench in Alexandra Park, where Liam had first told me he wanted to be an MP. To make a difference; to help people. On a day just like today, the sky a perfect cloudless blue from one side to the other.

How much time has passed. How much has been lost in the years since.

The bandages on my wrists have come off for the first time today, the skin beneath healing, stitches gone. The bruises on my neck have faded too. Memories mix and swirl of that night, of those terrible last moments in the stables, of gunshots and screams, of blood and pain and, most of all, a pure, visceral terror in those last moments unlike anything I've ever known before.

I'm speaking at the memorial service for Jodie next month.

Police opened a murder enquiry into her death after picking up Jones as he tried to leave the country on a false passport. From what I hear, he is cooperating with detectives if only to lay the blame for everything on his two colleagues. The balding man – whose name is Hodgman, I have since discovered – also decided to cooperate with police as he lay in a hospital bed after multiple surgeries. Evidence has also connected them to the attack on Trevor Boyle, who is recovering from his own injuries and planning to take an extended leave of absence from the probation service.

Amy lost an eye to the shotgun blast and she too, has had multiple surgeries over the last few weeks. Under police guard, like the rest. My mother-in-law is cooperating with the investigation, the shock of almost losing her beloved daughter finally breaking down the wall of silence they have maintained for the last ten years. Industry experts predict that Vernon plc is unlikely to recover from the scandal.

Rennick and Peter Vernon are the only ones who are still not talking, but it shouldn't matter. Hopefully, the police will have enough. There will be a review of my case in light of new evidence and witness statements, although the wheels of justice turn slowly and I've been warned that it will take many months before that process even gets underway.

It will include a full re-examination of all the original evidence, but John Musgrove will not be around to see his investigation unpicked, piece by piece. The ex-detective's obituary had appeared in the *Bath Chronicle* last week. The police are mulling over a few new charges in connection with events since my release, but I've been told – off the record – that they're highly unlikely to start a fresh prosecution against someone who should never have been jailed in the first place.

I am still officially out on licence but I hope, at the end of everything, that the original verdict will be overturned. I hope that justice will finally be done and Liam's spirit can rest.

Hope. It is a strange word. I had forgotten the meaning of it, over all those years in a cell. But maybe now I can learn how to hope again.

A soft summer breeze is blowing across the hilltop, carrying the joyful shouts of children in the little playground behind us.

Jet lies at my feet, gnawing a stick, his tail wagging a slow rhythm in the thick grass.

The boys sit either side of me on the bench.

Theo on my left, Finn on my right. Each of my hands in one of theirs. Theo is a head taller than me and he has a million questions, about what happens next and how long it will take, about my time in prison and the years we have spent apart. Finn hasn't said much yet, he just grips my hand tightly and keeps looking at me with a shy smile, as if he can't believe I'm real.

The social worker keeps her distance, on the next bench along. It's the first of my supervised visits and she will stay with the boys, with the three of us, for the full hour. But I don't mind. As long as I can keep them within touching distance, it's enough for now.

Owen got his story in the end. Not the one he was expecting, but a pretty incredible story all the same. We've seen each other a few times since then, just for coffee. Maybe in the future, something more. But not yet.

I still remember his urgent words that night, as he had helped me to my feet.

'Heather,' he had said, 'my car's out there on the drive, we can get the hell out of here before the police arrive. All four of us, I'll take you anywhere you want to go.'

'No,' I had replied, reaching for my sons. 'No more running.'

Theo had noticed my wounds first, pulling off his shirt and gently wrapping it around my wrist. Finn had pulled out the cord of his dressing gown and wrapped it around the wounds on my other hand.

I will never forget their words as we sat there, waiting for the police and ambulance and everyone else, Finn hugging me and Theo holding my bandaged hand in both of his, crying quietly. I cling to those words, holding them close to my heart.

'I never believed you did it, Mum,' Finn had said. 'I never believed it was you.'

Mum. The word sounds foreign, strange. It is the first time anyone has called me that in ten years. It will take a while to get used to it. But we have time now.

We have all the time in the world.

Acknowledgments

A number like *two million* is quite hard to picture. It's difficult to visualise what it looks like in book terms. So to find out recently that my novels have sold more than two million copies in the UK – since publication of my debut *Lies* in 2017 – seems almost unbelievable, and I certainly never dreamt I would have passed such a milestone just six books later. First and foremost, I'd like to give my thanks to *you* – for picking up this book (and hopefully some of the others too).

People who know the city of Bath may have noticed that I took a few liberties with local geography to fit the story of *The Mother*. A little bit of writer's licence. I also took a small liberty with library opening times – perhaps just wishful thinking on my part that they were open on a Sunday. Like all authors, I owe a debt of gratitude to our wonderful libraries and the staff who keep them going.

I had the pleasure of many library visits this year, and I want to say a huge thankyou to all the staff who made me so welcome. More importantly, for their work championing books, reading and literacy every single day – for which they don't get nearly enough credit. Also: a shout-out to the wonderful Bromley House Library in Nottingham, where some of this novel was written.

Camilla Bolton has been my agent for more than a decade now and I wouldn't be where I am today without her. Likewise the brilliant team at Darley Anderson, including Jade Kavanagh, Mary Darby, Rosanna Bellingham, Kristina Egan and Georgia Fuller. Special thanks to Sheila David for helping to bring my novels *The Holiday* and *The Catch* to the screen.

My editor at Bonnier Zaffre, Sophie Orme, continues to make every single book better with her insight and judgement. I'm very grateful for the excellent work of the wider team at Bonnier, particularly Blake Brooks, Eleanor Stammeijer, Isabella Boyne, Ellie Pilcher and Ciara Corrigan.

I first read about the concept of 'noble cause corruption' in an article written by US defence attorney David Rudolf (who features in the Netflix documentary *The Staircase*). His book *American Injustice* focuses on wrongful convictions and the many factors that can conspire to send innocent people to prison.

I enjoyed the novel *Prisoner* by Ross Greenwood, which helped to give a flavour of life behind bars from a prison officer's perspective. I also found Elizabeth Greenwood's book, *Playing Dead*, very interesting and informative on the subject of faking your own death (it's a lot harder to get away with than you might think). For help with my financial and legal queries, thanks to Jennie and Jon Hullis. Any errors are, of course, entirely mine.

A big thankyou to my brother Ollie and his family for putting us up when we've come to visit Bath, and for answering my strange questions about the city and its surroundings. Thanks as ever to my own family, my wife Sally and my children Sophie and Tom (currently a student at the University of Bath), for their help and support.

This book is dedicated to my mother, Vera, who has had a tough time of it over the last year but has always been a source of inspiration and encouragement. She takes a keen interest in how the books are doing and every single time I have a launch event for a new one, she always – without fail – buys the most copies. Thank you, Mum, for everything.

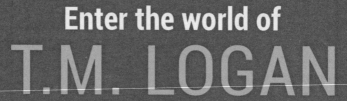

Hello!

Thank you so much for reading this book – I really hope you enjoyed reading it as much as I enjoyed writing it.

The first germ of an idea for *The Mother* came to me at the end of 2021. I was watching a TV documentary about the trial of Louise Woodward, the 18-year-old British nanny convicted of the involuntary manslaughter of the baby in her care. My wife and I had followed the case on TV back in 1997 as it unfolded in a Massachusetts courtroom, one of the first trials screened on UK television.

Watching it all again brought back memories of the case, of the prosecution, the medical evidence, the media coverage – and the fact that the defendant has always maintained her innocence. It got me thinking about other cases in which women have been on trial for the most serious crimes and the way they are sometimes portrayed. What would life be like for someone like that? How could they even start to rebuild their life after years in prison? And what if they were innocent all along?

From there, the story of *The Mother* was born.

My next thriller starts with a cryptic message – the kind that can turn your world upside down.

Fran is the only child of a single mother, working long hours to care for her ailing mum and all the while feeling that life is passing her by. Until the day she receives a message that changes everything – along with an invitation to a beautiful island off the Croatian coast.

The isolation is perfect: no phone signal, no tourists, no other residents. The perfect place to find out the truth about her family. But she soon realises there is more to this reunion than meets the eye. Because the stakes are higher than she could ever have imagined, and not everyone is going to get off the island alive.

Fran is about to discover that family can be murder . . .

It's a story of sibling rivalry, loyalty, inheritance and toxic family relationships taken to the extreme – and it will be out in 2024!

If you'd like to hear more about my books before then, you can go to www.tmlogan.com to become a member of my Readers' Club. Just click on the yellow 'Sign up' button – it's absolutely free to join, it only takes a moment and I promise I won't spam you with lots of emails.

Bonnier Zaffre will keep your information private and confidential, and it will never be passed on to a third party. I'll get in touch now and again with news about my books, cover reveals, competitions and more. When I have news, people in the Readers' Club are always the first to know – so sign up if you'd like to become a member (you can unsubscribe at any time).

If you'd like to get involved in a wider conversation about my books, please do rate and review *The Mother* on Amazon, Goodreads or any other e-store, on your blog or your social media accounts, talk about it with friends, family or reading groups. Sharing your thoughts and views helps other readers, and I always enjoy hearing what people think about my books.

Thank you again for reading *The Mother*, I really appreciate it.

Best wishes,

Tim